Katie Colman Crosses the Water

Elizabeth Shorten

CORONET BOOKS
Hodder and Stoughton

First published in 1998 by Hodder and Stoughton
First published in paperback in 1998 by Hodder and Stoughton
A division of Hodder Headline PLC
A Coronet Paperback

10 9 8 7 6 5 4 3 2 1

A CIP catalogue record for this title
is available from the British Library.

ISBN 0 340 68244 2

Printed and bound in Great Britain by
Clays Ltd, St Ives plc

Hodder and Stoughton
A division of Hodder Headline PLC
338 Euston Road
London NW1 3BH

Date Due

MAR 0 6 1999	JUL 2 4 2004		
SEP 1 5 2003	AUG 1 4 2004		
MAR 1 8 2004	MAR 1 0 2007 67		
SEP 0 2 2004			
SEP 2 3 2004			
SEP 2 4 2009			

Acknowledgements

My thanks to:

In England

My agent Patrick Walsh; my editor Carolyn Mays and her assistant Diana Beaumont; Sir Ranulph Fiennes and Roger Mear for advice about the Antarctic; Mike Johnston of Spider Kites for his expertise on parafoils; Philip Walton of Woldingham for his tour of a girls' boarding school; Robert Powell-Jones for his insights into the life of a barrister at Lincoln's Inn; Lady Potter for her wonderful anecdotes about holidays in Cornwall; the Royal Marsden Hospital for medical advice about cancer patients.

In Key West

Karen Thurman of Uniglobe; Kate Miano of Ambrosia House; John Marburg of Whispers; Dave of Banana Fosters; Tom Holt and Jim Thomas of The Pines; Steve Trouba of The Curry House; Bob Davidson for his anecdotes about Key West politics; Don Kincaid for his insights into treasure hunting; Mel Fisher for dancing with me at the Schooner Wharf Bar; Tom Sawyer and Lori-Anne Cummings for their observations and advice; Darlene for all her stories; and the many other wonderful people I met in Key West.

Chapter One

~

There is a great white light at the bottom of the world. At least, that is how it appears to astronauts as their orbit revolves above the vast glacial land mass that is Antarctica, five and a half million square miles of brilliant desolation where man has hardly dared venture, though he has walked on the moon. Where a handful of hardy scientists eke out a harsh existence on a continent bigger than Europe, larger than the United States and Mexico combined.

It is the ice sheet that makes this great wilderness glow like a lantern in the dark of outer space, a permanent mantle reaching in some places over a mile in depth, and holding captive in its frozen grip some seventy per cent of the world's water. It is the ice, too, that makes this land so implacably hostile to man, and so endlessly fascinating.

Katie Colman raised her head from the book she had been studying with such intense concentration. It would be wonderful, she thought, to see that shining light, if only you didn't have to go up into space to do it. It must be awesome, too, to witness the stark almost lunar landscape of the southernmost continent, but she knew she could never endure the hardships that went with it – the penetrating chill of a polar summer, when even layer upon layer of wind- and waterproof clothing can leave you feeling naked against the elements; the blinding glare of a sun that never set on endless vistas of snow; the weariness of toiling on, ever on, across the interminable stretches of that inhospitable land.

No, Katie would never be able to do what her sister Jemima was planning – a solo and unsupported crossing of the Antarctic, sudden death in a crevasse or slow extinction through hypothermia an ever-present possibility. Katie couldn't even begin to understand what would motivate anyone to make the attempt.

The trouble was, Jemima said, there were so few challenges left. To cross alone and on foot one thousand seven hundred miles of treacherous Antarctic land mass was one of the few that remained, made possible for a woman only recently by the invention of the latest wind assistance devices, which cut to a minimum the enormous effort required to drag all your supplies on a sledge behind you. That feat had, till now, been accomplished only by men, and there were many who doubted that, even with the help of a parafoil, Jemima could do it. That, she often said, was one of the main reasons she intended to try.

But Katie knew there was more to it than that.

'All explorers are really trying to find out what's inside themselves,' Jemima would confess in rarer, more intimate moments. 'You can only know that when you've tested yourself to the limits.'

'But we can't all go rushing off to the ends of the earth in search of our inner selves,' Katie would point out irritably. 'Someone's got to stay behind to keep the home fires burning.'

'Rather you than me,' Jemima would say with a superior smile.

Katie sighed and tried to force her attention back to the book she had instinctively chosen from the mountainous pile by her desk, because its subject matter had hit a nerve. She mustn't think about Jemima now, she must concentrate on the job in hand. Pressed as usual for time, she had only managed to read the publisher's blurb and a tantalising paragraph here and there in order to reach her decision. And then she'd let her concentration wander because of her nagging fears about this latest crazy ambition of her sister's, and there really wasn't the time for that, she reminded herself rather crossly.

When she had first taken the job as cataloguer for the Kensington and Chelsea libraries there had been eight of them doing books. Now there was only her. Budget restraints and computerisation had taken their toll, so that now there was no one to ask when she wanted a second opinion, no one to share the load when Monday's flood of new acquisitions stood piled in ominous ranks by her desk.

There was, however, to Katie's relief, still Marigold, divorced and in her forties, with her pencil-straight black hair and Edna Everidge glasses and endless fund of dreadful jokes. While Katie dealt with books, Marigold handled audiovisuals, recordings and compact discs. If Marigold went the way of the others, Katie's last contact with the outside world would vanish with her.

The support staff, the cataloguers like her and Marigold, were shut away in the back rooms of Kensington Central while the public librarians dealt face to face with readers' enquiries and book suppliers and meetings with other branches. Though classification skills were perhaps the most valuable a librarian could acquire, Katie sometimes wondered if the public even remembered that people like her existed. She would certainly never merit any column inches in a newspaper, like some of the more daring exploits of her sister.

Perhaps, anyway, the days of the cataloguer were numbered. Many libraries these days were choosing the cheaper option of buying in the data for their computers – a trend which Katie worried would lead to lower standards. But doing things right seemed to be a dying creed, as people like her were in danger of becoming a dying breed.

'I don't know why you want to stick it out anyway,' her husband Guy often said. 'It's not as though we need the money any more.'

But Katie would not have been comfortable living a life that was not busy or useful. Since Lucy and Hannah were growing up and so often away at boarding school, she found she needed to channel the energy that had once been absorbed by caring for her children into this job she did for the library and the community. The trouble was, shut away in her basement room, she too often felt completely cut off from the very people she wanted to serve.

There was little doubt in her mind where the Antarctic book belonged. She would be using the Decimal Classification invented in the nineteenth century by Melvil Dewey but still very much in favour with the libraries in her borough. Legend had it that, at the tender age of five, Dewey reorganised his mother's kitchen shelves in a more logical and systematic fashion. The story gave Katie a sense of kinship with the great man. She remembered well the childhood bedroom she had shared with the tomboyish Jemima, where she would tidy away dolls into their own chest, neatly labelled in her precocious copper-script handwriting, and Lego into another, and books in yet another, only to find them all thrown out in a jumble on the floor whenever Jemima wanted to use the containers to create some difficult obstacle course or imaginary mountain to climb.

As soon as she turned eighteen, Jemima had invested in a backpack and a good camera and set off to go where few travellers had been intrepid enough to venture before. Not for Jemima the well-beaten path of the tourist trail. She forced her way through the impenetrable jungles of Papua New Guinea to confront tribes who had seldom seen the people of the neighbouring valley, let alone a white woman. She set off by canoe over the rapids of the wild Kazan River in the Canadian Arctic to hear the traditional 'throat singing' of the indigenous Inuit people. She journeyed to the remote and unexplored Indonesian islands, strung across the equator, where Sinbad the sailor found pearl divers and cannibal kings, and the world's largest bug, *Bellostoma indica*, hunts in the dark and attacks even small children.

But for Katie, the unknown territory that was her own future held potential pitfalls enough, and she could not contemplate them without the security of, at the very least, a university education. So she followed in the family footsteps to Oxford, where she read English and joined the debating society. A further year of postgraduate studies saw her with a solid qualification in librarianship and an engagement ring on her finger, though Guy Colman was only the third man she had ever dated. But her decision had been a sensible one. Guy was now a successful barrister and a solid husband and father, and at thirty-seven Katie had a house and a lifestyle that were the envy of her less fortunate friends.

But not of Jemima. Her elder sister simply couldn't understand how Katie could settle for an existence with so few surprises. But better that, Katie was inclined to tell her rather sharply, than driving your family half mad with worry at your life-threatening antics.

'If I tell you one of my skeleton jokes, will you stop staring out of that window?' Marigold's voice broke into her thoughts.

Guiltily Katie turned away from the uninspiring view of a narrow alley where the bins were put out and she could see a pale slice of what was probably bright July sunshine.

'Is it as bad as all the others?' she asked in tones of resignation.

'What do you expect for no charge? . . . OK, then, why couldn't the skeleton go to the dance?'

'Why?' Katie came in on cue.

'Because he had no body to go with.'

'Oh dear.' Katie rose and stretched her legs. 'I'll make us some tea, shall I?'

'You could at least crack a smile – it wouldn't kill you.'

'Sorry – things on my mind.'

'But not work things,' Marigold said, eyeing the undiminished pile of books beside Katie's computer. Katie's eyes came to rest on them too, and she hastened to the corner where the tea things lived on an ugly table with a yellow Formica top.

She brought back two cardboard cups and put hers down at

a safe distance from her keyboard. Then she tapped in her familiar user ID to gain access to the input screen. She knew exactly where to add this book into the catalogue, the sacred blueprint of every book available in the borough's libraries. The reference to astronauts, she felt, was misleading. The main subject clearly dictated a classification and shelf number of 919.9 for Antarctic Expeditions, not 999 for Extraterrestrial Worlds.

Of course Melvil Dewey could hardly have been expected to anticipate in 1851 – when he published the results of his arduous task of reorganising the entire classification system – the advent of the age of space travel. But those who followed after him had constantly updated his work so that now extraterrestrial exploration had its own shelf number in the 900s, suitably close to man's quest for adventure on land and sea.

What made people do it? Katie wondered – take such risks with life and limb and no idea what they would face along the way. The astronaut John Glenn said it was sheer curiosity, the desire to go where no one has been before.

But Katie still didn't get it. What she understood was organisation and order and things in their proper place. She had catalogued the Glenn book under biographies – a more suitable place for it, she decided, than space travel. Classification, a long-ago lecturer had told her, is an art rather than an exact science. Any decision about the subject of a book is bound to be a personal one. But there were firm rules to guide you, and Katie felt safe when following rules. Without them there could only be descent into chaos.

The same lecturer had also pronounced that the first duty of any librarian is to help other people find what they are looking for. That was what Katie had been doing unquestioningly for the past fifteen years. Only now there were days when she wondered what it was that other people *were* looking for, and whether they ever found it. Or whether, for that matter, she had found it herself.

Had Jemima discovered the answers, on her constant travels

to places Katie had only read about? Katie doubted she would ever know. Jemima was more of a doer than a talker, and she hated being questioned about all the exotic, faraway places she had been. 'You can't describe them,' she would say impatiently, 'you have to see them for yourself.'

But Katie knew she never would. She couldn't just take off on a whim – she had family, responsibilities, commitments – all the things Jemima had deliberately chosen to live without. Jemima's life, she seemed to imply, was far richer than Katie's even though she lacked these everyday things.

Katie's fingers tapped away at the keyboard, working their diligent way down the list of required entries: author, publisher, edition, subject name, shelf number . . . The book was now officially classified and catalogued, safely tucked away into its relevant compartment. But Katie had the uneasy feeling that the experiences it described couldn't be reduced to anything so comfortably understandable.

Head into the wind, Jemima Fraser looked out across the frozen expanse of Alaska's Eklutna Glacier. Though she stared in fixed concentration through her tinted goggles, it was impossible to make out through the flurries of snow the telltale blue shadows of the sheer crevasses that lurked treacherously beneath a sometimes thin veneer of ice. If she slipped inadvertently into one of these fissures on her solo polar crossing, she knew her chances of extricating herself would be minimal. The heat of her body would cause her to slide downwards until she became hopelessly jammed in the narrowing bottleneck, where she would suffer a slow and inevitable death.

'Wind's a bit strong today,' shouted Duncan, her trainer. 'Think you can handle it?'

'Ready when you are,' Jemima hit back immediately. Duncan was army trained, ex-SAS, and Jemima knew just how much it riled him that, under the worst of conditions, she could always hold her own against him.

She wore a captive harness attached to the four-line kites

Duncan was teaching her to use. Both she and the kites were also hooked up to two lorry tyres weighing a hundred pounds each, the total load a simulation of the sledge laden with essential supplies she would have to haul across the Antarctic in just a few short months' time.

'When you're going downwind, there's no problem except in controlling your speed,' Duncan explained. 'But the only way to go upwind is to follow a zigzag course, tacking and jibing, just like a sailing boat.'

It was an image that lifted Jemima's heart. 'I'm going to be the first woman to sail right across the Antarctic,' she thought euphorically. She would let the wind carry her across that vast continent in the short summer season between November and February, after which no boat could make the treacherous journey through the pack ice to extricate her.

'You add more miles to the journey by zigzagging,' Duncan continued, 'but at least you can keep going towards your goal, whatever the wind direction.'

She stamped her skis impatiently, longing for the lecture to be over and the action to begin. Standing there listening to Duncan, the cold seemed to penetrate her bones to the very marrow. But she knew that conditions here were almost a summer picnic compared to what she would encounter in the southernmost latitudes of the world. On a good day in Antarctica temperatures might reach the balmy minus-thirties, and you didn't experience that incessant ache in your nose and fingers that was sometimes a relief because it meant you had not yet lost all feeling in them. On a bad day the wind chill factor might reach minus a hundred, and katabatic winds of eighty knots blew sharp spicules of snow into your eyes, while the smallest intake of breath caused a burning sensation in the lungs.

She would have to sit it out in her tent during the worst of the storms. No kite could function safely in those conditions.

'Ready to give it a try?' Duncan asked.

'I thought you'd never ask.'

She gripped the handles, replaying Duncan's instructions in her mind. The lines running into the top of the handles were the power lines, and the bottom ones the brake lines. By twisting and pulling the handles, she could alter the position of the kites and so the speed and direction of her travel.

It would be easier, Duncan had told her, to take off slightly downwind and then turn back into it. She positioned the kites in front of her, as instructed, and let the wind take them up and bear her away.

She almost flew across the snow, the formidably heavy lorry tyres dragged effortlessly along with her. 'It works,' she cried to herself with exhilaration. She felt as weightless as the kites themselves, borne along freely on the wind.

'You're going too fast,' Duncan yelled. 'Turn back upwind.'

And that was when she realised that she was no longer in control. The kites seemed to have a mind of their own, pulling her where they pleased. Almost at once Duncan sensed her dilemma. 'Let go,' he shouted. 'Let go of the handles.'

There was a built-in safety system called the dead man's release. Once the handles were dropped it applied the brakes, instantly forcing all the air out of the canopy and collapsing the kites.

For a moment, frozen with the realisation of her powerlessness, she couldn't let go, but then her brain sprang back into action and she dropped the handles a fraction of a second too late to prevent herself from plunging face forward into the snow. Within moments the kites deflated and fell to earth like wounded birds, and she stopped hurtling forwards and came to rest in an undignified heap.

Duncan hastened over to check if she was all right. He quickly established that at least she had avoided impact with the lorry tyres and no bones were broken. 'Bloody hell,' he said, looking down at her with no attempt to hide his disgust. 'We've got a lot of work to do.'

She squinted up at him through goggles that had been knocked askew. She knew he didn't believe women were cut out for this sort of caper. He'd almost said it in so many words.

'I'm the one doing the work,' she reminded him sharply. 'You just do the talking – and that won't get your name in the record books, will it, Duncan dear?'

Katie paused in the dark hallway, her key still in the latch, and listened for sounds of movement from within. She had never quite got used to coming home to an empty house, as she too often had to these days, now that Hannah had turned eleven and joined fourteen-year-old Lucy at boarding school in Wiltshire. Guy, of course, was never home from the Inns of Court any earlier than seven – and that was on a good night.

But today was one of Angie's cleaning days, and Katie could hear her whistling tunelessly upstairs as she went about her work. Angie liked to do afternoons, so she could go straight on to her second job as a waitress in a local wine bar.

Katie sprinted lightly up the stairs and laid down her bag and brolly on the newly made-up bed. Then she called up the stairwell, 'Hello, I'm home'.

'Knew you would be,' Angie called back cheerfully. 'Five-thirty on the dot.'

She appeared in pink rubber gloves, her henna-tinted hair tied into a ponytail on top of her head so that it sprouted like a palm tree in a flaming sunset. 'I was late getting to you today,' she said without a hint of apology. 'Mum had to go for one of her check-ups.'

'When's she due this time?' Katie said, making a conscious effort to keep the disapproval out of her voice.

'Oh, not for another two months yet.'

Lizzie Slater, Angie's mother, had six children already by four different fathers, and not a wedding ring from one of them. Now that the seventh was on its way, she showed no more inclination than the previous times to marry the proud father-to-be.

'How on earth can she afford to keep on reproducing like this?' Katie said with some exasperation.

'The more she has, the more the state coughs up,' Angie replied without a trace of irony.

'And doesn't she think it's unfair to burden the taxpayer with the cost of supporting her family?'

Angie looked at Katie rather blankly. 'I don't think she has the time to worry about things like that, not with all the cooking and cleaning and trips to the doctor—'

'But she wouldn't have quite so much on her plate if she would only stop breeding, would she?'

'I s'pose not.' Angie stripped off her gloves and glanced idly at her brightly coloured watch. 'But whenever she's with a new bloke, she says she wants to have 'is child to cement the relationship.'

Katie shook her head in disbelief. 'That didn't work the first four times . . . Why doesn't she just try marrying one of them, making a proper commitment?'

'Dunno,' Angie said, clearly losing interest. 'Maybe none of 'em ever asked.'

As Angie was the eldest, her father had been the first to go. She didn't even remember him, she had told Katie with an air of acceptance that Katie found achingly sad. She had trouble remembering some of the boyfriends too, except the one who'd tried to touch her in funny places when she was only six. Lizzie had thrown him out in an uncharacteristic fit of fury. It was the only relationship she didn't try to 'cement' with a new addition to the family.

'So anyway,' Angie said as she descended to the kitchen, Katie following, 'I had to look after little Josie and Daniel till Tilly got back from school, then I left her to it and came on over, but I still haven't managed to get much done.'

'What about the shopping?' Katie said anxiously.

On week nights Katie's father always ate dinner with her – and Guy, if he was back in time from chambers. Dr Robin Fraser lived in Cumberland Terrace just the other side of Regent's Park, a brisk walk away from his rooms in Harley Street where he practised as a heart specialist. His wife Fiona detested London and preferred to remain at their home in Wiltshire, where Robin would join her at weekends. Two days a week was quite enough time, she stated bluntly, for any husband and wife to spend together. Though Robin maintained a tactful silence on the subject, Katie suspected the arrangement suited him too. Her mother was not the easiest of women to live with. In fact, the only person Fiona seemed truly to get on with was Jemima – possibly because each had a greater than average need for their own space and respected that need in the other.

Tonight Katie had planned a Thai green fish curry for supper. Her father, after all the heart cases he had treated, favoured a low-cholesterol diet of vegetables, chicken and fish. Guy was basically a meat and potatoes man, but then he was so seldom home in time for supper, Katie could usually get away with leaving him his own meal in the warmer drawer.

Jemima had been to Thailand, and bought her fruit and vegetables from the floating market at Damnoen Saduak. Katie had to make do with her local Sainsbury's, where in these days of unlimited choice she knew she would find most of the ingredients she needed on her carefully prepared list, down to the lemon grass and blocks of creamed coconut. But even Sainsbury's didn't stock galangal, a ginger root with a distinctive peppery lemon flavour. So Katie had made a point of asking Angie to pick some up for her from an oriental greengrocer in Camden which she knew Angie would have to pass right by on her way to take the bus to Katie's house.

'Silly me – forgot all about it,' Angie said brightly. 'Can you make do without?'

Katie bit her lip. It wouldn't help to get angry, but sometimes she wondered why she put up with Angie and her never-ending family problems and her chaotic ways. Now the new recipe she was trying out for Robin wouldn't be as perfect as she had planned. Katie liked to spoil her father, perhaps to make up for the fact that her mother never did.

'Have you at least got time to finish the cleaning?' she asked wearily.

'Oh, yes – heaps of time,' Angie said, unfazed by the obvious exaggeration. She would, in fact, have to be leaving quite soon to go to her job at the wine bar. No doubt her timekeeping for them was as erratic as it was for Katie, but they probably put up with it for the same reason – because Angie's unfailing good nature made it impossible to be angry with her for long.

'I'll just do the floor, then,' Angie said, making soapy circles in Katie's direction with a mop.

Katie had been hoping to start the dinner preparations, but there was no point even trying until Angie was out from under her feet. Reluctantly she went to pour herself a weak Scotch and soda in the sitting room.

She sat on the edge of the sofa, covered in a muted eighteenth-century check, and looked up at the portrait of her and Guy, painted when they first moved into this house so that the decorator would have a substantial canvas to hang over the fireplace. Though they had bought the house only five years ago, anyone casting a look around would assume the Colman family had lived here for ever. That had been Guy's quite deliberate brief to the decorator when he gave her the commission. He wanted her to convey the impression that all was not newly bought, that the various artefacts had been in the family for generations.

So the decorator had skilfully thrown worn rugs over brand new wall-to-wall carpets, and inserted threadbare tapestry chairs among the stiffly upholstered chintz sofas. The modern German cooker had been replaced by an Aga, and Edwin Landseer hunting prints adorned the walls, together with trophy horns of animals which could have been shot by earlier generations on the Colmans' non-existent acres. So the appearance of old money was artfully created, the sense that it was not all store bought. Which, in a sense, since much of it came from auction rooms, it wasn't.

The old stuff had been sent off to be sold in junk shops – the bargains Katie had hunted down and lovingly stripped and repainted for their first small flat in Notting Hill, when Guy was still a barrister's pupil and earning next to nothing. There had been no money then for a professional decorator, and Katie had worked tirelessly in her spare time to make their modest surroundings as cheerful as possible, stencilling brightly painted birds and flowers round the doorways, and making up colourful curtains from end cuts of fabrics on an ancient sewing machine her mother had dug out of the attic.

But she had enjoyed the sense of being needed that came from making a home for her and Guy, and later the girls. Of course, when they were born, they had to sell their one-bedroom flat and move to a larger one in Bayswater, which they could just afford once Guy became a tenant and then a junior barrister. As the girls grew and needed more room to play, they moved again to a maisonette with garden in Hampstead, and Katie took a job as a librarian in the local private prep school so that the girls would get a discount on the exorbitant fees that would have been a strain on their still-limited budget.

By the time Guy was in his early thirties his earnings were rising sharply, and there was less and less need for such economies. They had made a tidy profit each time they sold flats during the property boom of the eighties, and then Guy's parents passed away, leaving him their semi-detached in Surbiton on which the mortgage was fully paid. Guy sold it and used the money to put down a deposit on the house in St John's Wood. This, he assured Katie, would be their last move. As far as he was concerned, they were now the proud owners of a sufficiently desirable residence to make further struggles up the property ladder an unnecessary inconvenience.

Katie looked around her at the pale egg-shell blue of the flat emulsion paint on the walls ('low-key and tasteful,' the decorator had assured Guy) and the formal arrangement of the furniture. She had never felt entirely at home in the St John's Wood house, perhaps because all her familiar bits and pieces weren't grand enough for it, or because, after decorating all their other homes herself, she had felt so left out of the decisions on the rather conservative look of this one. But if Guy was aware of her unease he gave no sign of it, seeming to believe that she, like he, must feel that they had finally arrived.

Looking up at his familiar face in the portrait – the sandy hair and fair complexion, the eyes of a pale, indeterminate sort of blue – Katie wondered when he had begun to seem to her like a stranger. Then his face was suddenly blocked out by Angie popping into her line of vision, so that her ponytailed head appeared incongruously above Guy's conservative suit. Lordy, I clean forgot,' she said. 'This came for you in the post.' She dropped a bright yellow envelope into Katie's lap. 'I think it's a letter from your sister Jemima.'

Guy came home earlier than expected – but only, as he lost no time pointing out, so that he could do some work in peace since the phone hadn't stopped ringing in his chambers. He would be heading straight to his study, he said, as soon as he had fetched himself some mineral water from the fridge.

When Guy had chosen the law as a profession, it had been with the deliberate intention of bettering his lot in life. His father, a civil servant in local government, had brought home a modest salary cheque that made tuition for his son at a fee-paying school wholly beyond his means. But Guy was clever enough to win a place at a grammar school, and hardworking enough to gain entry to Oxford, where he studied Russian and French amongst the more privileged classes and courted Katie, slightly awed at first, since she was the daughter of a wealthy surgeon of solid social standing. When Guy moved to London to do his year at the Council of Legal Education, in preparation for what he was determined would be a glittering career, he was quite set upon Katie going with him. She would be, he told her, the perfect wife for a man in the position he aspired to. So he proposed, though he was just twenty-two and she twenty-one, and seemed greatly relieved when she accepted.

It was all such a long time ago, Katie thought, opening the blender to check whether her green paste was the right consistency. Sixteen years – half a lifetime, really.

'What's that awful smell?' Guy said, wrinkling his nose.

'Just some ingredients for the Thai fish curry.' Satisfied, Katie scooped the paste out into a bowl.

'Now look here,' Guy said irritably, 'you know damn well I don't like curry.'

'It's for Daddy—'

'Fond though I am of your father, and much though I don't mind him having dinner here, I don't see why he can't just fit in and eat the kind of food we like.'

'But I like the same things Daddy does,' Katie pointed out.

'Really? I can remember a time when you were perfectly happy with cottage pie and peas.'

But that time was long ago, and since then she had moved on, her tastes had changed and so had her needs – only Guy was always too busy to notice.

'If it's cottage pie you want, then that's what you'll get,' Katie said, pulling a pan out of the cupboard with a loud and angry clatter.

'Thank you,' Guy said with exaggerated politeness, placing his mineral water on a tray with glass and ice, and carrying it stiffly off to his study.

For a moment Katie almost stuck her tongue out at his retreating back. Then she wondered what on earth had come over her to react in such a childish way. Guy worked so hard for all of them, he had a right to expect her support at home. It was the unspoken deal they had made, a partnership in which each played their agreed role. That was why their marriage, though perhaps not a physically passionate one, had succeeded. Guy worked long hours to finance their lifestyle while Katie uncomplainingly provided the back-up, turning up in an unfashionable dress and hat at charity cocktail parties on the lawns of Lincoln's Inn, holding sedate dinner parties in the St John's Wood house for Guy's colleagues and their rather mousy wives, looking after the girls without any assistance, since Guy was never back from chambers early enough to do more than give them a goodnight kiss. While Lucy and Hannah were still young enough to need care in the afternoons, Katie's job at the prep school enabled her to be home at the same time they were. It was she who supervised homework and drove them to extra lessons and sewed costumes for Christmas plays and went to meetings with class teachers. So it was she who missed them most when boarding school beckoned and the girls were suddenly no longer there.

'Do they really have to go away?' she had wailed when Guy had first sent off for all the prospectuses, not sure she could bear to be parted from them.

'I don't see why you're making such a fuss. You and Jemima went to boarding school.'

'Exactly – and I hated it.'

But Guy had been adamant. It was for the girls' own good, he said, and they must all make the best of it. So when the time came for each of them to go, Katie packed their cases and dried their tears and held back hers, and tried not to feel, as she was driving away from the school gates, that she would never again be the centre of their lives, never truly necessary to them.

Katie chopped furiously at the onions for the cottage pie, fighting away the dreadful feeling of emptiness that came over her whenever she thought of the girls. It wasn't that she blamed Guy, really, for their absence. She had been brought up with privilege and took it for granted. But Guy was haunted by the need to provide for his children those advantages in life that he had longed for as a boy and his own parents had never been able to afford. And the girls themselves had settled in much better than she had expected, phoning home a little less often as the months went by, assuring her that yes, of course they missed home, but it was fun, too, being with all their friends, and there were so many things they could do in the country that would never have been possible in London. 'I can ride at least three times a week,' Lucy said excitedly, and Katie tried to suppress a small, selfish feeling of disappointment that this might be more important to her than being at home with her mother.

But Jemima said it was wicked of Guy to send the girls away. It was different when she and Katie were children, they were stuck out in the country with fewer choices. But there were plenty of good day schools in London offering a perfectly good education. 'Face it – all Guy cares about is having them in the "right" school where they can meet the "right" people. He doesn't give a damn whether they're learning anything really valuable about themselves or the world, shut away in their little cocoon of privilege.'

'That's not fair,' Katie argued loyally, 'he just wants to do his best for them.'

'Rubbish,' Jemima snorted. In her eyes Guy was nothing but a stuffed shirt, a boring pillar of an old-fashioned establishment Jemima simply had no time for. No more than Guy could understand Jemima's complete disregard for rules and conventions of any kind. She had no fixed address, no permanent relationship, no career path, no assets to speak of apart from the richness of her experiences – a commodity too intangible for Guy to appreciate. He and Jemima were as far apart from each other as the two poles she was determined to reach in what was for him her incomprehensible desire to risk everything just for the sheer challenge of it.

And Jemima wasn't the only oddball in Katie's family, Guy was fond of pointing out. There was her mother Fiona, who had completely turned her back on London society, preferring the company of her horses and dogs, and pretending she was tied to Wiltshire by the need to look after Katie's great aunt Flora, since no one else in the family had offered. Aunt Flora must be ninety if she was a day, but she still persisted in flirting outrageously with any man who came into her orbit, Guy included, batting at him thinning eyelashes coated in layers of mascara and smiling coyly with vermilion-painted lips.

'Grotesque!' Guy would shudder to Katie afterwards.

But great aunt Flora had been a famous beauty in her day, with a self-confessed weakness for successful men and vintage Bollinger and high stakes bridge and good jewellery. She had a rather substantial collection of the last, garnered in her racy past when her name was connected with some of the richest men in the world. 'Can't understand this women's lib thing,' she would say to Katie and Jemima when they were younger, shaking a head encased in an immaculately curled red wig. 'Why would women want to go to all the effort of competing with men when they can get anything they want just by being nice to them?'

'Because it's more satisfying doing it for yourself,' Jemima would say even then.

'What's satisfying,' great aunt Flora insisted, 'is being given a four-carat square cut emerald just to match the sparkle in your eyes!'

At least Katie took after her father, Guy would say with profound gratitude – a man Guy understood, who had worked hard, risen to prominence in his field, and provided a good life for his family. Katie had always been a daddy's girl, but it was her mother's fine looks she favoured. The red highlights in her strawberry blonde hair were a legacy from both great aunt Flora and Fiona, whose Scottish roots had endowed them with enviable heads of auburn curls. Jemima, too, had a little red mixed with the chestnut she had inherited from Robin. 'But the true red always skips a generation,' Fiona said, and sure enough it had emerged again in all its glory in Lucy, while Hannah had to make do with Guy's sandy blond. Lucy showed all the signs, too, of the independent spirit that was in her grandmother and her aunt, while solid little Hannah seemed to be cast entirely in her father's dependable mould.

'She'll break a few hearts, your Lucy, just like I did,' great aunt Flora would crow, while Jemima smiled secretively to herself, believing in her soul that Lucy was destined to follow in her own adventurous footsteps. And Katie, beset with all a mother's natural anxieties, tried to ignore these prophecies about her wilful daughter and believe that she and Guy had instilled in her enough common sense to counteract the pull of wayward genes. Yes, Lucy might give her some grey hairs, but there would be few headaches from dear sensible Hannah – dismissed by great aunt Flora as irredeemably plain. Almost from the day she could walk Hannah had made it quite clear that she disliked rough games and dangerous sports of any kind (her refusal to ride a horse was anathema to Fiona) and preferred to keep her feet firmly on the ground.

Katie shoved Guy's cottage pie into the oven with unnecessary force. Then she stared at the reflection of her face in the glass door. It was a face not unlike her husband's – the same fair colouring, eyes also blue though of a stronger shade. She was tall too – almost the same height as he was. 'Could be brother and sister,' great aunt Flora had said almost accusingly through a mouthful of champagne at the wedding reception.

What Katie must try to remember was that she and Guy also wanted the same things out of life – to put down roots, to build a solid future, to make whatever sacrifices were necessary for the sake of family and duty and children. Or at least, that was what she had firmly believed when she agreed to marry him all those years ago.

Robin came at seven, when Guy was still shut away in his study and Katie, having finished preparing her husband's meal, could at last concentrate on the fish curry. They put on Radio Three and talked companionably while Robin poured them some red wine (a glass or two a day increased longevity, he claimed), and Katie carefully boiled up coconut milk and chopped coriander leaves into fine, even pieces.

'The damnedest thing happened today,' her father told her. 'I was contacted out of the blue by some American lawyer. Said an old patient of mine had left me something rather substantial in his will.'

'What is it?' Katie asked curiously, cutting the fish into identical, bite-sized chunks.

'Of all things, some guesthouse in the Florida Keys. Can't think what the devil I'm supposed to do with it.'

'Why leave it to *you*? Didn't he have family?'

'Apparently not – not close family anyway. The lawyer said he was grateful to me for saving his life – triple bypass it was, if I remember correctly, very successful too . . . and then the poor old chap goes and buys it anyway three years later in a road accident. Just shows you what could happen to any one of us at any time.'

Katie dipped the fish into the gently simmering sauce. Robin began laying out cutlery and plates on the kitchen table, seeming to know from long experience of eating with his daughter that supper was nearly ready, as though they were an old married couple well used to one another's ways.

'Perhaps,' Katie said, 'you should take Mummy on a trip to Florida and see what this place is like.'

'What – and tear her away from her horses and great aunt Flora? Not a chance, I'm afraid. I expect I'll just ask this lawyer chap if he can find a buyer for it . . . Unless *you* fancy going out there with me, Kitty-kat, and taking a look?'

'I wouldn't be able to get the extra leave. Guy's booked the house in Rock again this summer.'

'Doesn't he ever get tired of the place?'

'I'm afraid not.'

Guy had discovered Rock through a colleague in chambers when Hannah was still in nappies, and after that first visit had insisted they keep taking their holidays there, year after year, with a select group of friends who went as regularly as the Colmans did. 'People like us', Guy liked to say, not foreigners who spoke a different language and tried to overcharge you for the smallest thing and with whom one basically had nothing in common. So they rented the same little house near the beach every year in the summer and even sometimes at Easter, and played Scrabble at dinner parties with the same group of friends, and their children played with the children of those friends, and watched each other grow up a little more each year till they were of an age to start eyeing each other up and disappearing down the beach for passionate clinches. 'At least,' Guy reasoned, 'the girls will have their first romantic adventures with people like us.'

'But don't you sometimes want a change?' Katie would ask in the early days, before she gave up trying, as she lingered longingly over brochures of sun-drenched tropical islands and snow-covered mountain peaks. But no, Guy said, he was not like her sister Jemima. What he wanted was continuity. That was what family life was built on.

Katie spooned out the curry on to pre-warmed plates and garnished it with evenly spaced bay and coriander leaves. 'It won't taste exactly as it should,' she warned her father, 'because Angie forgot to buy the galangal.'

'Darling, you mustn't worry so much when things don't work out exactly as you planned. If you don't want to listen to your daddy then listen to your doctor – it's bad for your health.'

Her face relaxed into a smile. 'To a long and happy life for us both, then,' she said, clinking her wine glass against his. When her father was with her, he seemed to fill all the empty spaces in this too-large house with his infinite love.

'I had a letter from Jemima today,' she told him, wanting to break the news to him in private before Guy joined them for dinner. 'It seems she can get a two-week break in her training programme to come and visit us in the summer.'

'Well, well.' Robin shot her a surprised look. 'Your mother will be over the moon.'

'I thought perhaps we could all go down to Rock. The house is quite big enough.'

'And how will Guy feel, having to entertain the Fraser clan *en masse*?'

'Oh, he won't mind,' Katie said, aware that she couldn't quite meet her father's eye.

Robin gave her a searching look but said nothing.

'Anyway, the girls will want Jemima to come with us.' Especially Lucy, Katie thought. Lucy positively hero-worshipped her adventurous aunt.

'You'd better ask him first,' was all Robin said.

Katie took out Guy's cottage pie from the warmer drawer and went to call him from his study. He greeted Robin cordially enough, but began to eat almost immediately, as though anxious to get the meal over with and return to his briefs.

'How is it?' Katie asked, watching his face.

Guy swallowed a mouthful before answering, 'Go a bit easier on the seasoning, would you?'

'Sorry.'

'This is absolutely delicious, Kitty-kat,' Robin said, rolling the curry round his mouth with relish.

She tasted a mouthful of sauce. She had substituted ground ginger and a little lime juice for the galangal, and it hadn't turned out too badly.

As soon as they had finished eating, Robin looked from his daughter's strained face to Guy's weary one. 'I ought to be going – leave you two in peace.'

'Not on my account, I hope,' Guy demurred. 'I'm heading straight back to my study.'

'Oh dear,' Robin commiserated. 'Another urgent case?'

'It's this Greek chap I've started doing so much work for. Shipping magnate – got himself into a spot of bother for tax evasion. Trouble is, as soon as a Greek is paying your fee, he thinks he owns you body and soul.'

Never a truer word, Katie thought. There were weeks at a time when Mr Kassianides saw far more of her husband than she did, and Sunday mornings when they would just be leaving for church and the phone would ring and Guy would come back with a sheepish expression saying she should go on without him as he had to dash round to Eaton Square. Katie's modest jewellery collection was made up almost entirely of 'sorry' presents for all the times Guy had cancelled at the last minute some dinner party or theatre trip she had been looking forward to, or abandoned her and the girls to their own devices at weekends.

Guy put his knife and fork down and dabbed away a last trace of mashed potato from the corner of his mouth. 'Best get to it,' he said, pushing his chair back abruptly and standing up.

'I'll love you and leave you too, my dear,' Katie's father said.

'Oh, please don't,' Katie cried with a touch of desperation. 'There's a programme I wanted you to watch with me on the Duke and Duchess of Windsor and their Nazi connections.'

She knew her father's weakness for anything to do with the Second World War. 'In that case,' he said at once, 'perhaps a small brandy—'

'And could I have a coffee?' Guy added, already halfway through the door.

It was an hour till the end of the Windsor programme, and by that time Katie felt almost ready to face the climb alone up the stairs to the bedroom she shared for what seemed like only a few hours a night with her husband. When she had given her father a fierce goodnight hug, and switched on the dishwasher, and turned off all the lights, she made her way slowly past Guy's study door which was still firmly closed. The single bright line of light underneath did little to dispel the shadows from the silent hallway.

Chapter Two

~

Katie sat propped up on pillows covered in Victorian lace on the imitation four-poster in her bedroom. The pillows rested against a headboard of heavy royal blue velvet that matched the Gothic-style pelmet. 'English,' Guy had stated baldly to the decorator. 'The style throughout must be traditional English. No trendy foreign rubbish, thank you.' And though the decorator was herself an American, with a certain following in fashionable London circles, she took no obvious offence, assuring Guy instead that she sympathised with his patriotic sentiments entirely, and knew exactly what he required. And so, to judge by the rather staid results, she did.

So Katie sat encased in lace and tried to concentrate on the Antarctic book, which she had checked out of the library on a whim on her own card. She was quite simply horrified by the stories of hardship and impossible hazards faced by the intrepid team of explorers as they battled their way through crevasse fields and white-out conditions on their quest to reach the South Pole. 'No one who wasn't there,' the copy pronounced, recounting the hair-raising descent of a particular glacier, 'could imagine the terror . . .'

But Katie didn't want to imagine it, she didn't want to picture Jemima, disfigured by cold sores and frostbite, risking her neck in their midst.

What made people do it? Katie truly wanted to understand, but her imagination simply couldn't make the leap. Why did children at a funfair head straight for the most stomach-churning, death-defying ride? Why did punters pay good money to be frightened out of their wits by some film-maker's contrived fantasy of violence? Why jump off a bridge and go into freefall with only a bungy cord round your ankle to save you from certain death?

'There's no point not taking risks,' Jemima always said. 'Cowardly people get hit by disasters just as often as brave ones.' But Katie just didn't have the nerve. Even as a child she had been over-cautious, never climbing right to the top thin branches of a tree as Jemima did, waiting till she was absolutely confident of her balance before she asked her father to take the training wheels off her bicycle.

'Kathryn's the sensible one,' her mother would say. 'But Jemima – she'll jump straight off a cliff and only realise halfway down that she's falling.' There was an edge of pride in Fiona's voice, even when seeming to criticise her elder daughter, that was never there when she spoke about Katie's accomplishments.

Fiona, naturally antisocial, had always believed that people had to be at one with nature in order to be truly in touch with themselves. Human beings were really nothing more than animals who had developed their intelligence beyond the point that was good for them, she said. They were never supposed to live packed together in the artificial environment of cities – and that, in Fiona's opinion, was the source of most of their problems. She had taken her stand by insisting on living a simple country life, but how much more admirable were Jemima's pilgrimages to the great unspoilt wildernesses of the world which man had not yet desecrated with his greed and stupidity. In that virginal landscape, how much closer Jemima must come to that true harmony with nature which should have been man's natural condition.

She was daydreaming, Katie realised, her eyes wandering back again and again to the same paragraph and not really taking any of it in. Her mind was elsewhere, with Jemima and her family and the rather thorny problem of the summer holiday.

Guy had never been able to take Jemima in large doses. She made him feel, he would complain to Katie, that she was always looking down her nose at him, trying to make fun of the things he held dear. It was, Katie had to admit, a not inaccurate assessment of Jemima's whole attitude towards Guy and what she considered his crass materialism. So how was Katie going to persuade him to let her sister stay with them for two whole weeks in Rock?

Somehow she would have to talk him round. It was unthinkable that Jemima should have these few precious days off and not be able to see all her family. How would Katie live with herself afterwards if anything . . .

Guy must simply see reason, she told herself firmly, he must understand that Katie needed to spend this important time with her only sister. Since they'd grown up and Jemima had set off on her travels, there had never been the chance for the sort of closeness they had enjoyed as children, despite their different natures, nor for the kind of heart-to-heart talks you could only really have with your own flesh and blood.

But maybe the simple truth was that they had grown apart, chosen paths in life so different that they would never cross again. At thirty-nine Jemima showed no sign of wanting the permanence of married life. There had been men, of course, but most of them as nomadic as she was and equally determined to avoid commitment. In her backpacking days they had frequently been unsavoury types who, when they inevitably moved on, were inclined to take her little hoard of cash with them. In later years they had been explorers, loners like her, always driving themselves on to the ends of the earth in search of the next challenge, the obstacle they hadn't yet conquered. Men like that travelled light, and seldom took women with them.

But Jemima didn't seem to mind. If anything she looked down on Katie's settled domesticity. 'I don't know how you can stand it,' she would say on rare visits home, roaming round the succession of London flats which Katie and Guy had purchased on their climb up the ladder, seeming, in her restlessness, to want to burst through the too-confining walls. And within days she would be gone, and all Katie would know of her life were the enigmatic scrawls which arrived months apart from remote areas where postal services were minimal and other means of communication non-existent.

Jemima loved the children, though, and Lucy in particular was a kindred spirit. 'I wouldn't mind one like that,' she once confided in a rare moment to Katie, 'if I could just put it on my back and head off with it, like the Inuit do. But oh, how they'd frown on that in good old England, wouldn't they? No father, no formal education, no fixed address . . . There'd be telegrams from the social workers wherever I tried to go. So I'm afraid it's up to you, sister dear, to keep the Fraser genes going into the next generation.'

Katie had made that decision for herself in her early twenties, dealing with bottles and nappies when most of her contemporaries were still going to nightclubs, and never once regretting it. Being a mother made her wonder how Jemima could bear not to be. But they'd never really talked about it after that one conversation, never had the chance . . .

She must grab the bull by the horns, Katie decided, leaping off the bed and for once forgetting to smooth the covers back to their customary neatness. She must do what had to be done before her courage deserted her completely.

It was a long time since Katie had made the trip to the isolated haven of Lincoln's Inn, cut off from the city bustle all around it, jealously guarding its atmosphere of a secluded Oxford college. There was something positively Dickensian about the place, she thought as the security guard nodded her in through the main western entrance. It had surely changed very little since the author set the opening chapters of *Bleak House* in the historic Old Hall. And just outside the walls, tourists could still visit The Old Curiosity Shoppe, preserved in all its quaintness.

'Old' was a word that kept cropping up in relation to Lincoln's Inn, and perhaps it was no accident that this was the setting Guy had chosen as the backdrop for his career, starting as a student eating his dinners the traditional twelve times a term in the Great Hall, and learning the ropes of his profession from a more senior sponsor. She remembered his pride when his name was first painted on the bottom of a board in one of the staircase entrances of the handsome eighteenth-century Stone Buildings, where the great prime minister William Pitt once had rooms. So Guy developed his practice surrounded and nurtured by all the weight of the history that had gone before him – or was he, Katie sometimes wondered, simply crushed by it? Without all that hidebound tradition, would Jemima still have been able to accuse him of being a young fogey?

Katie walked on in the shadow of the towering neo-Gothic library towards Guy's rooms. There was a time, she remembered, earlier in their marriage, when his court appearances had been full of eloquence and fire, and she had made a point of going just to hear him speak. She had sat anonymously in the back and listened, wholly caught up in the drama, as her husband played his central part. Then, in the lunch recess, she'd taken his favourite roast beef sandwiches that she'd made fresh that morning to share them with him while they talked over the arguments and tried to guess which way the jury was leaning.

But that was in the days when Guy was still practising criminal law, with all its opportunities for powerful theatre. Katie would thrill to the spectacle of it all as she sat amongst the families of the accused and listened to their comments, passing on the relevant bits to Guy in his lunch break. She was his eyes and ears out there, he said, and Katie felt all the secret pride of being useful to him.

But now he had moved on to commercial law with its lesser

human dramas but steadier flow of case work, and Katie anyway never had the time to watch him in action, having taken on longer work hours herself to fill the empty spaces in her days now that the girls were so often away. It was only at times like this, when the holidays loomed and she would have to drive down to Wiltshire that afternoon to fetch them from their boarding school, that she took time away from her desk at Kensington Central and the piles of newly acquired books awaiting classification.

It was now or never, Katie decided, looking at Guy's neatly painted name which had risen over the years to halfway up the list of those who shared his chambers. She wanted his blessing before she left to fetch the girls, so she could break the good news to her mother when they stopped off there for tea on the way back.

There was a new secretary in reception who looked rather alarmed by Katie's unscheduled appearance. 'There's no one in with Mr Colman,' she said warily, 'but I'll have to see if he can—'

'That's all right – I'd rather surprise him,' Katie said firmly, sweeping past before the girl could object.

She had stopped off on the way over at one of those shops that make sandwiches fresh to order, and in a brown paper bag she carried two roast beef with salad. With luck Guy wouldn't think to ask if they were home-made.

His face when she entered without knocking was a picture of disapproval. 'Oh, it's you,' he said, his expression softening only slightly. 'What's up – nothing the matter, is there?'

'Why should there be? I brought you some lunch, that's all,' she said, smiling sweetly.

He stared suspiciously at the brown paper bag. 'You really didn't have to come all this way—'

'But I wanted to.' She sat down opposite him in the straight-backed chair he kept for clients. 'I haven't been by your rooms in so long.'

He shrugged, gesturing at his paper-strewn desk. 'Nothing much changes.'

But Guy had changed, Katie thought. He was looking tireder, older than his almost thirty-nine years. 'Get him out on a golf course,' her father always said, but there was never the time for that except when they were at Rock.

She unwrapped his sandwich and pushed it carefully over to him on its square of brown paper through the obstacle course of his scattered briefs. 'Guy, I want to talk to you about the summer holiday.'

He gave a thin smile, as though he'd known all along there was a reason for her visit. 'Why? It's all arranged, isn't it – the house and everything?'

'Yes, but I want all my family to come too,' she said in a rush.

He raised a quizzical eyebrow. '*All* of them?'

She knew what he was getting at. 'Jemima too,' she said firmly. 'She has a two-week break in her training programme to come and see us.'

He stopped chewing then, and let a small silence fall between them. Katie shifted nervously in her chair. The rather flat colour of his eyes made it impossible for her to tell what he was thinking.

'You know they might allow me to apply for a silk rather earlier than expected?' he said suddenly.

Katie stared at him, thrown off balance by the change of subject. Because he seemed to be waiting for a response, she said rather woodenly, 'That's wonderful, darling.'

'They turn you down anyway the first couple of times. But I could make QC by, say, forty-one.'

The usual age to start applying, Katie knew, was forty-three or four. The powers that be must feel that Guy had considerable promise if he already fulfilled their criteria: genuine ability, good earnings, a big practice, and above all, no scandals of any sort – no shady financial dealings and preferably no divorce.

31

'Henry's going to have a word for me in all the right ears,' Guy said eagerly. 'He thinks I have a very good chance.'

Justice Henry Blackstone and his art dealer wife Sylvia were personal friends of Guy and Katie. More particularly, the Blackstones always went to Rock at the same time as the Colmans. Katie began to see where this conversation was leading, even before Guy said with emphasis, 'I wouldn't want Jemima showing me up in front of Henry.'

'Oh, Guy, she wouldn't do that—'

'Yes she would, and you know it.'

The chapel bell tolled the lunch hour. Guy resumed eating, as though the subject were closed. Katie almost stood up to leave, as she normally would when Guy had pronounced on a given subject. But she found that an unaccustomed anger was beginning to burn inside her which wouldn't quite allow her to move.

As the bell's deep chimes rang out, she remembered how Guy had told her with pride about the age-old custom that it would toll in the middle of the day whenever news was received of the death of one of the Inn's most senior members, a bencher, and the various judges and barristers would anxiously send their clerks to find out who had passed away, inspiring Dr John Donne, one of the Inn's most famous preachers, to write the immortal lines, 'No man is an island . . . any man's death diminishes me, because I am involved in mankind; and therefore never send to know for whom the bell tolls; it tolls for thee.'

In the silence after the chimes Katie said quietly, 'Have you any idea how dangerous this Antarctic crossing of Jemima's is going to be?'

'I am fully aware of how thoughtlessly your sister is putting her life at risk, yes,' Guy replied pompously.

'Then you must also be able to imagine how badly I want to see her before she goes.'

'The fact of the matter is, she *shouldn't* be going, not if she had the least consideration—'

'But she *is*, and I *have* to see her first. So if you don't want her in Rock – if your only concern is what's good for your career – then I'll just have to stay in London and spend time with her here.'

'Katie,' Guy said patiently, as though speaking to a child, 'that's out of the question and you know it.'

'Why? Because for once *you'd* be stuck with all the cooking and dishwashing? That wouldn't quite fit in with your golfing schedule, would it?'

There was a stunned silence. Almost at once Katie felt a little rush of remorse for the way she had spoken to him. But there was something else inside her, an even stronger impulse, that wouldn't allow her to back down.

It was Guy who eventually broke the silence. 'I hope you realise that my "golfing schedule", as you put it, is the only time I get to relax away from . . . all this.' He gestured vaguely at the clutter of papers around him. 'And my chances of getting that relaxation with your sister around are pretty damn slim.'

He gave her a hard look, but she held his gaze and it was he who dropped his eyes first. 'However, if it means so much to you to have her there,' he conceded wearily, 'I suppose I'll have to try and make the best of it.'

'Thank you,' Katie said. Tentatively she reached out her hand to touch him, but the desk was too large an obstacle between them and she drew it back again.

'Just do me one favour,' Guy said. 'See if you can persuade her not to humiliate me totally in front of the Blackstones.'

Even in victory, Katie felt the old unease stirring inside her. She wanted to say something reassuring, but she couldn't remember a time in their lives when she had ever been able to talk her headstrong sister out of doing anything which took her fancy.

Wolton Abbey School was set in a valley amid gently rising fields with good grazing. The school owned the land, and the policy was to lease it out for farming rather than sell it for development, to preserve the rural setting in which the girls could get a good education in peaceful surroundings and at the same time follow sporting country pursuits, like horseriding and canoeing. 'Such a bonus,' said Guy, who had never done either.

But Lucy loved both, and Wolton Abbey gave her every opportunity to indulge her passions.

Katie's wheels crunched on the gravel in front of the main Victorian building, once a very grand private residence, which now housed the administrative offices and living quarters for the most senior girls. Several of them sat on the steps surrounded by piles of luggage, waiting for their lifts home. Those who had already taken their 'A' levels would never return. They jostled each other, and shared jokes, and looked as though they hadn't a care in the world.

Lucy and Hannah lived during term time in one of the purpose-built modern brick buildings that had mushroomed up around the main Victorian one as the school expanded and the need for them arose. Each age group was on a different floor. Lucy, being older, had only one room-mate, while Hannah shared with three.

Of course there were sometimes fights and feuds as one clique ganged up on the others, and then Katie would get tearful phone calls demanding to know what to do, and she would try to dispense to her children sound and objective advice across the miles while all the time her heart cried out to hold them close and dry away their tears. But the next time they phoned, the entire drama would be forgotten.

As she rounded the corner, Katie's heart leaped at the sight of Hannah sitting on one of her suitcases, waiting patiently, the cage housing her guinea pig placed carefully in the shade beside her. The younger girls were allowed a small pet at school, and Hannah gratefully took Gulliver with her, and her bright blue duvet cover with a pattern of fluffy white clouds.

As Katie stepped out of the car she looked around for Lucy, but she was nowhere to be seen. Hannah ran straight into

Katie's arms. She was still too young to mind if she hugged her mother in front of her friends, but Lucy would have thought that was totally uncool.

'Where's that sister of yours?' Katie demanded, squeezing Hannah tightly.

'I told her to wait, but she said you were taking too long. She said it was hot in the sun and she was just going for a quick dip in the pool—'

'But she's not allowed to do that without asking, is she?'

Hannah maintained a loyal silence. Looking at her deliberately shuttered face, Katie suspected that her elder daughter got up to rather a lot of things she wasn't supposed to.

'Let's go and see if we can find her, shall we?' But as Katie took Hannah's hand, Lucy suddenly burst around the corner, her damp red hair flying out behind her.

'Oh, there you are at last, Miss Tamsin wants to talk to you – here she is, Miss Tamsin.'

A petite brunette in a tracksuit emerged from behind the willowy Lucy and held out a hand.

'Nice to see you again, Mrs Colman. Lucy's coming on so well in gymnastics . . . but she says she wants more of a challenge, so I've suggested she go in for an award scheme we run here, only she'll need your permission.'

'Of course you'll say yes, won't you, Mummy?' Lucy said impatiently.

'What does it involve?' Katie asked.

'It's designed to get young people involved in community and sports and adventure—'

'*Adventure*,' Katie said sharply.

Miss Tamsin looked a little surprised. 'You know – journeys on foot or horseback or by canoe, expeditions to interesting places.'

Katie shot Lucy a dark look. 'I think one explorer in this family is quite enough.'

'I knew it,' Lucy cried angrily. 'I knew you'd try and spoil it for me.'

'Come now, Lucy,' Miss Tamsin intervened. 'Your mother is quite right to want all the information before she gives her permission.' She smiled apologetically at Katie. 'I'll send you some brochures in the post, shall I?'

'I'd be very grateful.'

'Don't worry – we have a lot of students who enter the awards, and no harm has ever come to any of them.'

Maybe not, Katie thought, but I don't want her getting a taste for things that'll bring me nothing but grey hairs.

She helped the girls pile their suitcases and tuck boxes and book bags and duvets into the boot of the car. Lucy refused to meet her eye. Hannah climbed into the back seat and perched the guinea pig's cage carefully on her lap.

'I have news for you,' Katie said as she drove away, uncomfortably aware that she was using it as a bribe to cheer Lucy up. 'Jemima's coming away with us for the holidays.'

Her words had the desired effect. Lucy's face brightened immediately. 'Good,' she cried. 'I bet *she'll* understand why I want to do something *interesting* with my life.'

'Domestics', as Fiona referred to them, were not her strong suit. She simply couldn't see the attraction. Supper was often cheese on toast, though the dogs might get a sirloin steak. Visitors had to make do with whatever was on offer, and today it was some rather stale lemon cream biscuits – which Katie suspected had been mouldering in the tin since her last visit – and a supermarket fruit cake wrapped in cellophane.

The girls, not surprisingly, had opted to give tea a miss, and were at this very moment somewhere outside in the grounds, Lucy no doubt hanging round the horses, and Hannah combing the long grass for daisies to make chains.

'Imagine Jemima taking the time off to see us when she must need every moment for her training,' Fiona said in the tone of one upon whom a great favour is being bestowed.

Katie sipped her overbrewed tea and resisted the urge to remind her mother that Jemima wasn't the only one who was putting herself out. Though it seemed a little churlish, Katie couldn't help noticing how her mother had accepted the offer of the family trip to Rock without so much as a thank-you or the least expression of concern about the possible inconvenience.

Great aunt Flora was a great deal more effusive. 'It's so civilised to travel in the summer,' she had said with a gleam in her painted eye. 'There's bound to be the odd reclusive old millionaire who has retired to the Cornish coast.'

'I think it's just marvellous what Jemima's trying to achieve,' Fiona continued. 'All that money she's going to raise for the children's cancer ward.'

Katie sat on several fundraising committees for Downs Syndrome and spina bifida and other worthy causes, and had stood on many a rainy Saturday morning outside various underground stations shaking her collection box, but she had never turned in anything like the two million pounds Jemima would raise if her crossing were a success. Even if she didn't make it all the way, her sister would still raise unbelievable amounts for every kilometre she covered – more than Katie could hope to in a lifetime of shaking tins.

'If Jemima had any suitable men friends, a little word in their ear would be quite sufficient to secure a substantial donation to the charity of her choice,' great aunt Flora said tartly.

'I'm sure she'll want to do something to keep fit while she's with us in Rock,' Fiona went on with a frown of concern. 'After all, she can't just let everything go, can she, not with her start date only a couple of months away. I do hope Guy will be understanding.'

It was beginning already, Katie thought, this battle between opposing factions, with her placed firmly in the middle trying to defend them all to each other. It was starting before Jemima even put in an appearance.

'Daddy's looking forward to getting in some golf with Guy,' she said to change the subject.

'Oh, your father.' Fiona waved a dismissive hand. 'I expect

you'll spoil him as usual. I don't know why you go to all the trouble of cooking those elaborate meals for him every night, when he can easily fix himself something simple like I do.'

'But then he wouldn't have the company – and nor would I.'

'I just hope he isn't making a nuisance of himself, that's all.'

Great aunt Flora quickly snatched a last lemon cream before Fiona started putting the tea things away. Katie noticed that her mother's fingers were shaking.

'I just wish she wasn't trying Antarctica again,' Fiona said, her mind returning, as it inevitably did, to Jemima. 'I know it's silly, but I can't help feeling superstitious about it, after what happened the last time . . .'

Katie felt a shiver along her spine, as though a cold hand had been placed on the back of her neck. 'You mustn't think like that – it's morbid.'

But though she wouldn't admit it, the same thoughts had been recurring to Katie, the nightmare memories of those terrible four days when they had believed Jemima might finally be beyond rescue.

'The girl has no business gallivanting off to foreign parts with no male protection,' great aunt Flora said.

Fiona sank down on a chair, and suddenly she looked older than her sixty-six years. 'It's just that I have this absurd notion that she isn't meant to go there, that the last time was a warning.'

'Don't,' Katie said sharply. 'If anything, what it proved was that she has the will and the resourcefulness to survive if—'

Too late Katie realised the danger of this train of thought. When she looked across at Fiona, she was aghast to see tears in her mother's eyes.

The kitchen door flew open and Lucy burst in, a crown of daisies in her glorious red hair and two spots of excited colour in her cheeks. Hannah followed placidly behind, a more modest chain in her hands.

'Grandma, I've been riding bareback at school. It's so much more fun – can I try it on Hercules?' Lucy demanded.

Fiona dashed a discreet hand across her eyes. 'Not now, darling. You know it's almost time for his supper.'

Lucy drew her lips into a little pout. Then she turned to great aunt Flora. 'Can we go up and see your jewellery, then?' She liked to hold the gleaming gems up to the light, and drape them round her slim neck and on her long fingers, and drop large hints about which ones she wanted left to her in great aunt Flora's will.

'You're not going to get me up those stairs again, not till bedtime,' aunt Flora grumbled. 'I'm not as young as I used to be, you know.'

'We should be getting home anyway,' Katie said, gathering up her jacket and handbag and ignoring Lucy's rebellious look.

They made their way out to the front of the mellow stone Georgian farmhouse with its symmetrically spaced sash windows. Katie glanced up involuntarily to the room she and Jemima had shared as children, converted now into a haven for her aging great aunt and filled with the bric-a-brac of her colourful life.

'I suppose we won't see you again till we make the trip to Rock,' she said to her mother, giving her an impulsive hug.

Fiona allowed the embrace for a few moments, then disengaged herself. 'Jemima,' she said, 'should travel down with us. We'll have more room in our car.'

'Of course,' Katie said, pretending she hadn't noticed the even more mutinous expression that darkened her elder daughter's face.

As soon as they had burst in through the front door, Lucy and Hannah raced each other up the stairs. Katie stood in the hall and listened to the pounding of feet above her, and the shrieking of laughter, and was filled with a wonderful contentment.

She knew it wouldn't take long before Lucy's room looked

as though it had been hit by a tornado. There would be jodhpurs and school ties spewing out of her suitcase which would remain unpacked for days, and black jeans and lace blouses and skimpy satin slips pulled out of the cupboards and left discarded when she decided she just had to wear something else. Posters of last term's pop idols would be half torn off the walls, the latest heroes partially pasted over them. Soon Angie wouldn't be able to get in there to do any cleaning, and Guy would start muttering darkly about grounding Lucy if she didn't 'do something about' her room.

Katie hadn't made the mistake Fiona had of putting two very different daughters in the same bedroom. Hannah had her own room next door to Lucy's, where she would methodic-ally unpack her bags and put everything away in its place, where she could be found on long summer afternoons drowsily reading a teen horror book on her neatly made-up bed, or cleaning out the guinea pig's cage, or sending e-mails to Cartoon Network for competition prizes, or trying to defeat the computer in some interminable game. Lucy was sometimes invited in to play with her, but couldn't sit still long enough to make much headway.

Katie left them to settle in and went to rustle up a light supper. It was already past seven, and she planned on doing no more than smoked salmon omelettes and the girls' favourite chips and a large mixed salad to satisfy Robin's insistence on a nutritionally well-balanced diet (a necessity he had never been able to impress upon his own wife).

Katie was just whisking up the eggs when Guy appeared. Involuntarily she glanced up at the clock.

'I came home early to see the girls,' he said rather pointedly.

'They're upstairs.'

'Yes, well I'll go on up, then . . . unless you need some help?'

Katie stared at him. She wasn't sure he even knew where the knives and forks were kept. 'It's all right,' she said. 'Daddy will be here soon to give me a hand.'

He wandered off towards the stairs. Watching him go, Katie wondered if he was still feeling wary of her after her outburst earlier in his chambers.

Supper was a raucous affair, the girls still over-excited to be home, but for once Guy didn't try to quell their exuberance with a stern look. Robin was in excellent form, recounting hair-raising tales of the operating theatre in the vain hope of shocking his granddaughters, raised, like most children their age, on a diet of realistic hospital soaps and general television violence.

'So they brought this man into Accident and Emergency,' Robin was saying, 'with a steel girder straight through his heart – still breathing, mind you—'

'He couldn't have been,' Hannah objected sternly.

'That was what I thought, too. But there was a reason for it, see. When I got the girder out, and took a look inside the open wound, I discovered that he didn't *have* a heart.'

'Everyone has a heart,' Hannah insisted stoutly.

'Not everyone – look at the way some people treat their horses,' Lucy countered.

'It was a real mystery,' Robin said, 'because the man had a pulse all right . . . and then it dawned on me that I'd better look on the other side of the chest cavity, and sure enough, there was his heart, on totally the wrong side and beating away as though nothing had happened.'

'But why was it on the wrong side?' Hannah demanded.

'Turns out he was what's called a mirror twin – very rare, but one twin has his heart on the correct side and the other one on the opposite side, so that when they're standing facing each other it's like they're looking into a mirror.'

'Weird,' said Lucy.

'Lucky,' said Robin. 'If his heart had been where it was supposed to be, he would've been dead as a doornail.'

'OK, Daddy, I think you've milked enough drama out of that one,' Katie said, catching sight of Guy's rather pale face.

The girls groaned.

'Don't worry,' Robin said. 'I've saved up a really gruesome one for your bedtime story.'

He winked at Katie and she smiled back, like a contented mother hen with all her chicks for once safely in the nest.

Chapter Three

~

There were two large wet hessian sacks on the back seat of the car, which Katie had carefully covered with a beach towel before making the trip to Port Isaac. From time to time the sacks writhed ominously. Watching them with growing unease, Katie began to regret her rather ambitious plans for dinner tonight.

She had wanted to show her appreciation to Guy, who was making an effort, albeit a grudging one, with Jemima. She had wanted to lay on something special for the Blackstones, upon whose patronage Guy was placing such hopes. She had wanted to spoil her sister, who would soon be facing a daily diet of dried rations rehydrated with melted snow. But she did *not* really want to face the daunting task of boiling alive eight innocent lobsters.

'Here, let me give you a hand,' Jemima said, gliding over and hefting one of the sacks effortlessly over her shoulder. Katie wondered what the locals had made of their rather strange progress from the house in Rock to Port Isaac and back, with Jemima insisting on rollerblading all the way beside the car, toting her specially designed weights, while Katie crawled along, ignoring the odd angry blare of a horn as she tried to keep pace with her sister.

It wasn't quite what she'd had in mind when she'd asked Jemima to go with her to fetch the lobsters. She'd been rather hoping to have a little chat, to ask Jemima to tread softly with Guy in front of the Blackstones.

'Watch out for the sharp, pointy bits,' Katie warned her sister now, trying to get a hold on the other sack that would not result in being poked by an escaping antenna herself. The claws, she knew, wouldn't be a problem – Mr Clayburn at the fishmonger had tied rubber bands securely round them to prevent any nasty nips.

'Come on – I'll take them both.'

'Thanks,' Katie said meekly as her sister grabbed up the other sack and started gliding gracefully towards the back door of the sprawling Cornish stone cottage with its herring-bone walls and slate roof and jumble of interconnected rooms that now housed both the Colman and the Fraser families.

It was hard work running a house for eight people and assorted visitors. Though everyone chipped in to help, they also frequently disappeared all at once for the day's activities. That very morning Guy and Robin had gone off to meet Henry Blackstone for eighteen holes at St Enerdoc Golf Club, where they all had holiday membership, and Jemima had driven off to St Ives Bay with Lucy to practise her parafoil skills in a specially designed beach buggy, and Fiona had taken Hannah for a swim, leaving Katie to clear away the breakfast things and put towels in the washing machine and make the piles of sandwiches for lunch and listen to great aunt Flora's rambling stories about holidays on the Mediterranean in the Roaring Twenties, when she was in her prime.

'Will Lucy be safe on that thing?' Katie had asked Jemima nervously, watching her pack the collapsible kite buggy into the boot of the car.

'Of course she will – she's got me to help her,' Jemima had said dismissively, while Lucy looked silent daggers at Katie.

All teenage girls went through a period of rejecting their mother's authority, Katie reminded herself firmly. She must not feel jealous when she saw Lucy whispering in a corner with Jemima, sharing with her aunt who knew what intimate details that she kept hidden from her own mother. She must not resent their closeness, or despair of ever again having the same bond with Lucy herself.

In the kitchen Jemima laid the heaving lobsters down on the floor as though she'd done her bit and felt no further responsibility for them. She bent down and began unfastening the bindings on her rollerblades. Katie watched with mild fascination the solid muscular bulk of her sister's unfamiliar body. She had exercised relentlessly for the upper torso strength needed to handle the kites in a high wind, and eaten her way to a formidable size in preparation for the deprivations ahead, until she hardly resembled the Jemima Katie knew at all.

Reluctantly she tore her eyes away and approached the sacks, wondering how best to get their strange occupants out on to the floor without sustaining an injury. 'Just keep them cool till dinner time,' Mr Clayburn had said, assuring her that a slate floor was as good a place as any.

Plucking up her courage, Katie unfastened the tie and held open the neck of the first sack. A couple of angry red antennae waved at her through the opening. She backed away and eyed them warily from a distance.

'Heavens, they won't *eat* you,' Jemima said scathingly. She padded over in her socks and tipped up the bag, spilling four startled lobsters, legs churning wildly, out on to the floor. Then she opened the second sack and dumped its contents out with just as little ceremony.

'My, isn't he a big fellah?' she said admiringly as her eye fell on one lobster at least twice the size of the others.

'A three-pounder,' Katie said a little faintly. 'I know you need the extra protein, so he's all yours.'

'Good. I like my men big and hunky.'

Guy had never been hunky, but he was tall and had a certain way of carrying himself that commanded respect. Except from Jemima. It was time, Katie thought, to get in that word of warning about the Blackstones.

'Jemima, you're back at last!' Fiona swooped in and pounced possessively on her daughter. 'Katie's been hogging you for quite long enough. I want you to come and tell me all about your parafoil – and explain the way it works so I know exactly how you use it.'

'It's very technical, really,' Jemima said, following her mother from the kitchen. 'I'm sure you don't want all the boring details.'

'Yes I do – every one . . .'

Their voices faded away and Katie was left staring stupidly at the lobsters, crawling off to all four corners of the kitchen as they investigated their strange new surroundings. Delila the house cat, springing in through her flap, was outraged by the invasion of these alien creatures and, after inspecting one or two with hackles raised, retreated out the way she had come with a howl of protest.

By the time she was ready to put them in the boiling water, Katie had grown quite used to the lobsters crawling around her kitchen, keeping her company as she chopped the salad ingredients and made a savoury saffron rice. They had become familiar fixtures to her, even friends.

'Are you sure they won't suffer?' she asked Robin as she peered into the steaming fish kettle, and her father, looking at her anxious face, replied firmly, 'They won't feel a thing.'

She had to shut her eyes when she put the first one in. A strange, high-pitched sound emanated from the fish kettle, but Robin assured her it was just steam escaping from the shell, not a cry of distress. She looked at him with huge eyes, willing him to be telling the truth.

But all her hard-won faith and self control collapsed when she tried to cook the big three-pounder who had, in the course of their afternoon together, become quite her favourite, exploring with solemn curiosity his new home, so that she had been hard pressed to keep the wet sacking over him, as instructed by Mr Clayburn.

She had left him till last, putting off the moment, so that by the time his turn came the lid of the plate had been open too long, the Aga had lost heat and the water in the fish kettle wouldn't quite come to the boil. When Katie put him in, trying not to feel a complete traitor, she was horrified to see, moments later, the lid rise up and clatter on to the stove as the lobster tried desperately to claw his way out of the pot. Quickly she pushed him back in and slammed on the lid, but immediately it began to tremble once more and then tip over as the lobster made another desperate bid for freedom.

'Daddy,' Katie shouted, close to hysteria, 'come and help me.'

Her father rushed over and rescued the frantic lobster from the pot. 'Poor old chap,' he said. 'I think he's just too big to boil alive. I'll put him out of his misery, shall I?'

Robin took a large kitchen knife and, with a deft and practised hand, plunged it through the back of the lobster's head. The legs jerked and waved for a last time, then were still.

When Katie put the dead lobster into the pot there were tears streaming down her cheeks. Her eyes were still damp half an hour later when she served the fragrant meal to her family and the Blackstones. She herself could not touch even a mouthful of salad.

'Bit of an upset cooking the lobsters,' Guy said by way of explanation to Henry and Sylvia.

'But they're absolutely delicious,' Sylvia cried, devouring a forkful. 'Are you sure you won't have just the tiniest taste?'

Katie went very pale, as though she might be sick.

On the other side of the table, Jemima was eating quite enough for her and Katie put together – a mountain of lobster and pasta and assorted steamed vegetables – and Henry, watching in fascination, said, 'Is it all frightfully scientific, the way your diet's worked out?'

'Not really. I need complex carbohydrates for energy, and starch to increase my glycogen storage levels, and then it's just a matter of putting on enough weight.'

'I'm constantly running out of pasta and rice,' Katie said,

making a determined effort to join in the conversation.

'I dined on lobster with the Aga Khan once,' great aunt Flora told the company, 'beneath an Arabian moon.'

'Aren't you afraid you won't be able to lose all the extra pounds afterwards?' Sylvia asked Jemima with a little *frisson* of sympathy.

Jemima gave her a look of contempt. 'I won't exactly have to join Weight Watchers. It's an unavoidable fact that I'll lose a third of my body weight through slow starvation while crossing the Antarctic.'

'Gosh – how useful,' Sylvia giggled. 'Any chance I can come along with you?'

Guy steered the conversation towards golf. 'I would have had you this time,' he challenged Henry, 'if I hadn't gone into that bunker on the fifteenth.'

'Who on earth cares?' Jemima said, sucking on a claw. 'It's such a juvenile way to spend your time – grown men chasing after little white balls.'

Katie stiffened. Guy said coldly, 'And I suppose crossing a frozen desert just because it's there is a *sensible* way to spend your time?'

'It is if you're the first and you get your name in the record books,' Jemima said smugly.

'Guy nearly got his name in the record books today,' Henry joked, 'for the highest ever number of strokes to get out of the bunker on the fifteenth!'

Guy tried to laugh along with the rest. Katie looked at his white face and her heart sank.

'I think it's just marvellous what Jemima's doing for the image of women,' Sylvia said gushingly when the merriment had died down.

'Women did very much better in my day by staying at home where their men knew where to find them,' aunt Flora declared.

'What about the Mediterranean,' Katie reminded her, 'and Arabia . . . ?'

'I was *always* escorted.'

'I'm not doing it for the "image of women". I don't give a damn about that sort of thing,' Jemima stated baldly.

'You don't give a damn about much, do you?' Guy said. 'Including your family's feelings.'

There was a small embarrassed silence. Katie gave her father a look of mute appeal, but he only lifted his shoulders in a helpless shrug.

'Anyway, haven't women done the Antarctic before?' Henry stepped in.

'Eight women have reached the South Pole,' Jemima said coldly, 'but none of them have crossed the whole continent, as I'm trying to do. The only one to reach the Pole solo and unsupported was the Norwegian Liv Arnesen. That's why *I'm* determined to do the whole crossing first, before the Norwegians run away with all the glory.'

'I didn't know you were so patriotic,' Guy said.

'There's a lot you don't know about me,' Jemima shot back.

'So you're saying you're just doing it for your country?' Sylvia sounded rather disappointed.

'There's no "just" about it. There's always been this rivalry between the British and the Norwegians in polar races, ever since poor Scott reached the South Pole in 1912, only to find that Amundsen had beaten him to it by just over a month. I believe his death on the way back was caused as much by a broken heart as by hunger, cold and exhaustion.'

'How sad!' Sylvia cried. 'But surely this isn't just for the sake of poor old Scott – you must want recognition for yourself as well?'

'Of course. And to "know myself", as the Greeks would say. And because some people don't think a woman can haul her own supplies all the way across, by herself, and I'm going to prove them wrong.'

'I've never even carried my own suitcases,' great aunt Flora barked. 'What else are men for?'

'I say, that's a marvellous ruby.' Sylvia stared transfixed at the enormous pendant round great aunt Flora's neck. 'Can I have a closer look?'

Flora puffed out her scrawny chest like a pouter pigeon. 'Given to me by the Raj of Jaipur . . . or let me see, was it dear Howard Hughes, before he started locking himself away and forgetting how to have any fun?'

'Jemima's also going to raise millions for charity,' Fiona said, turning the conversation back to her remarkable daughter.

'And worry us all half to death!'

'Why, Guy,' Jemima mocked, 'I didn't know you cared!'

'But aren't you secretly terrified?' Henry demanded with morbid fascination.

'Of course I am,' Jemima said. 'All good explorers are, just like experienced sailors are afraid of the sea, because they know exactly what can happen to them. But it isn't a reason for not doing it. You and dear Sylvia are statistically just as likely to get wiped out in a car crash on the motorway from Rock back to London as I am to die in a crevasse in Antarctica.'

'More's the pity,' Guy muttered.

Sylvia went rather pale. 'Now steady on, you two,' Henry said.

Katie thought she should be doing something, anything, to limit the damage, but the episode with the lobsters had drained her energy and nothing came to mind.

'Jemima's just putting a brave face on things,' Fiona interjected, unable to bear this attempt by her daughter to minimalise the risks she was facing. 'Even if she avoids an accident, there's the discomfort of the journey itself. If she so much as cracks a goggle her eyeball could freeze over, not to mention the blisters she'll get on her feet, and the—'

'Now then, Mother,' Robin said soothingly, 'Jemima's trained for this, she knows what to expect, and she'll have the best medical supplies her father can get his hands on.'

'Still sounds damn foolhardy to me,' Henry said. 'I don't know why you're letting her do it.'

'Oh, you can't go laying down the law to your children

once they're old enough to make up their own minds,' Robin laughed.

'Yes you can,' great aunt Flora muttered.

'But what's your advice?' Henry insisted.

'He's just told you,' Jemima said sweetly. 'It's up to me and other people should mind their own business.'

'Jemima,' Katie cried, standing up very quickly, 'please help me clear the table.' And then suddenly everything went black.

Lucy leaned nonchalantly against the wall outside the Mariner pub, the mandatory meeting place for the young and the cool, and let her eyes dart furtively through the familiar faces, seeking out the tall muscular bulk of Tom Blackstone.

She was wearing her newest designer jeans and trainers and a black leather jacket. Once her father had dropped her and Hannah at the Mariner, with his usual warning not to get into any trouble, she had undone her jacket buttons to reveal the skimpy bodice underneath. But though she'd been waiting an hour or more, chatting distractedly to friends she hadn't seen since last summer, Tom still hadn't put in an appearance.

'He's over there,' Hannah said, nodding in the direction of a small group where Lucy suddenly distinguished Tom talking intimately to, of all people, Sophie Jackson. And just then, when she knew her face betrayed her fury, he looked up and caught her staring at him.

He nodded in her direction. She gave a brief wave and turned her back, her cheeks burning. 'Let's go,' she hissed to Hannah.

'But Daddy's coming in the car to fetch us at ten, he said so—'

'I don't care. I want to go *now*. Let's walk.'

'OK, OK,' Hannah said. 'You don't have to get so worked up.'

'What's she getting worked up about?' a familiar voice behind them teased.

Lucy turned very slowly, flicking her red curls back over her shoulder, and gave Tom what she hoped was a nonchalant smile. 'Nothing. It's such a dead bore here tonight, I was thinking of going home.'

He'd grown up so much since last summer. He was sixteen now, and over six feet tall. He towered over her like a Greek god. 'Things might start looking up now that I've arrived,' he said.

Lucy shot Hannah a sideways look that sent a very clear message to get lost fast. Hannah raised her eyes to heaven and went off in search of some of the younger girls, the ones you could still have a normal conversation with because they hadn't been bitten by the boy bug yet.

'Want a drink?' Tom drawled, passing over a clear plastic cup filled with a dark golden liquid. Lucy inhaled the heady fumes of scrumpy, the local cider. 'As long as you're under age, you may not drink anything alcoholic,' her father always told them on the way down to the Mariner. 'Lucy, I'm counting on you to set an example to your sister.'

'I'd love some,' Lucy said, taking the cup from Tom who grinned, egging her on. Hannah wasn't around to see anyway, and Lucy knew all the other girls her age got older boys to go into the pub and buy Alcopops and beers for them. Her father was such a stick-in-the mud about things like that – after all, it wasn't as if she was doing drugs or anything really stupid.

As she took a long mouthful of scrumpy, grimacing a little at the strong taste, Tom slid a hand up the back of her leather jacket and stroked the bare skin above her bodice. 'Great outfit,' he murmured, his lips against her hair.

She gave a little shiver of delight.

'Why don't you come down to the beach with me so we can be alone,' he said.

Lucy had already seen many other couples making their escape to the beach, where giggling and other noises could be heard from among the dunes, and irate parents would later come searching with torches, calling out their daughters' names.

'I can't,' she said.

'Why not? Would Hannah tell on you?'

'No, she'd never do that. But Daddy's coming to fetch us soon.'

He withdrew his hand from under her jacket and took the drink from her. As he knocked some back, she looked at his face in the moonlight, but she couldn't make out if he was angry.

'Some day,' he said, 'you should come down here on your own, without little sister, and tell the old man to stop treating you like a baby.'

'Maybe I will,' she said a little fiercely.

He grinned at her then. 'You like to live dangerously, don't you?'

She did, she wanted to tell him, but her parents didn't understand. The only one who had ever really understood her was aunt Jemima – and now Tom.

He reached down and kissed her lingeringly on the lips. Even Sophie Jackson must have seen him do it. In that moment she would have done anything for him, anything he asked.

The walk from Trebetherick to Polzeath is the finest in England, John Betjeman said – but he no doubt did it at a gentle amble which allowed the time to appreciate his glorious surroundings. Katie, on the other hand, was struggling to keep up with the punishing pace set by Jemima, who was carrying the weights that had almost become extensions of her arms, and was moving at something between a fast walk and a slow jog.

'I've never fainted before,' Katie puffed. 'I think it was just a combination of nerves and too much wine on an empty stomach.'

'Did Guy give you a hard time about letting him down in front of his fancy friends?'

'They're my friends too – and no, as it happens, he was very concerned.'

But he had been angry too. Later, in the privacy of their

bedroom, after the Blackstones had left and Robin had helped Katie to bed and the dizzy spell was over, Guy had made his feelings quite plain on the subject of her sister. 'She humiliated me,' he said, 'just like I knew she would.'

'But why do you take the bait?' Katie had cried in frustration.

'What am I supposed to do – just let her insult me without defending myself?'

It was no use trying to reason with either of them, Katie though wearily. Like adult rodents, they couldn't be put in a confined space together. They would fight to the death.

She said rather crossly to Jemima, 'Why do you always have to take the mickey out of Guy in front of his friends?'

'I don't suffer fools easily.'

'And who are you to call him a fool?' Katie cried, stung to anger.

Jemima had put some distance between them, but she stopped now, jogging on the spot to give Katie time to catch up. 'Hey there, take it easy,' she said.

'I wish *you*'d take it easy. You know perfectly well I'm nowhere near as fit as you are. It's no fun trying to have a conversation with you when I can't even catch my breath.'

Jemima gave her a surprised look, then flung herself down on the grass. 'There, is that better?'

Katie collapsed beside her and took several deep breaths. When she raised her head, she saw the blue-grey sea rolling away from her in a dance of shifting light and shadow from the clifftop to the distant horizon. 'Much better,' she murmured.

They watched for a while the seagulls wheeling above the water. Then Katie said, 'I'm sorry, I didn't mean to snap at you. It's just that I never get to talk to you properly, you always seem to be going somewhere—'

'Maybe it just seems that way because you don't go anywhere interesting at all.'

Katie frowned. She didn't want the conversation to take

this turn. 'Look,' she said, pointing at a child on the beach below who was throwing a stick for his puppy, only to find it being snatched away time and again by one of the many other dogs being walked by their owners at this time of the day.

'They're all labradors,' Jemima said.

'I suppose you think that's boring, but people here don't want to be different.'

'That's not just boring – it's pathetic.'

Katie clenched a fist. When she raised it, she found she had torn up a handful of grass by the roots. 'You don't understand. Not everyone wants an adventurous life.'

'And what about you?' Jemima demanded, taking a hunk of cheese out of her pocket and demolishing half of it in a single bite.

Katie gave a little shrug. 'I think you got more than your share of the risk-taking genes. By the time it came to me there weren't any left.'

For once Jemima said nothing. Gathering courage Katie continued, 'You're the pioneer, the one who braves new frontiers, but I've always been the settler, the one who stays at home.'

Jemima stared out to the distant horizon, as though it were a well-loved friend. 'You're right, I don't understand,' she said. 'I don't know how you can spend your life washing Guy's shirts and kowtowing to shallow social butterflies like the Blackstones.'

Katie followed her sister's gaze and saw the fat cumulus clouds hanging low on the horizon. Though it was midsummer, they hadn't yet had many days of clear sunshine. Jemima must think of her home country as a grey little island under grey skies.

'It's not as bad as you make out – leading an ordinary life. Exploring yourself, or your potential, or whatever it is you think everyone should do – that's just an indulgence. Most of us have to live in the real world, get on with the things that have to be done. Most of us have other people to think about.'

'That's just an excuse not to look inside yourself too deeply,' Jemima said. 'You and Guy are only angry with me because of what you haven't done yourselves.'

'Oh, that's just not true—'

'Isn't it?' Jemima jumped to her feet and brushed the grass from her tracksuit trousers, the irrepressible energy welling up in her again. 'Shall we move on, then?'

By the time Katie had dragged herself up, Jemima was already several paces ahead of her. As she watched the gap between them widening, she felt a stirring of regret not so much at what had been said as what had been left unsaid. She hadn't meant to argue with her sister, or to concentrate on the differences that divided them. She had meant to tell her that she loved her, and wanted her to come home safely.

'There's a game of Knockers on this afternoon,' Lucy announced to her mother at breakfast.

The word had gone out the evening before at the Mariner, just before Lucy slipped down to the beach with Tom. This time she had let him put his hand inside her bra, and had been confused and embarrassed by the sudden quickening of sensation between her legs.

'Oh dear,' her mother groaned. 'I'll have to make a quick trip to the village.'

They would play on Daymer Beach at low tide, a rowdy group of teenagers armed with hockey sticks borrowed from a master at the Dragon School, and then they would come back ravenous to Katie's house afterwards, expecting to munch their way like locusts through a feast of food and drink.

'Ugh, count me out,' Hannah said. She had watched it once, and vowed never to do it herself, as she saw hockey sticks connect with shins and faces and the inevitable casualties result.

'You're such a baby!' Lucy said in disgust.

'Well, count me in,' Jemima said. 'It sounds like fun.'

'Grown-ups aren't allowed,' Katie explained.

'Jemima isn't *really* a grown-up,' Lucy said quickly. 'She'd be wicked at Knockers – everyone would want her on their team.'

'What's all this about Jemima's knockers?' great aunt Flora demanded, staring beadily at Jemima's chest while consuming a croissant with raspberry preserve.

Looking at her mother, Lucy saw she had that expression on her face that meant her feelings were hurt. Lucy had always banned her mother from taking part in their beach games. But she couldn't ask her along, she was bound to make a mess of it, it would be too embarrassing for words. Especially in front of Tom.

'We need you to make the tea, Mummy,' she pleaded.

'I know.'

'Want some help, Kitty-kat?' her father said at once.

'I'll manage.'

'Good,' said Guy. 'I've booked some golf with Henry and a judge he wants me to meet.'

Fiona had gone off early to paint a watercolour on the cliffs. It was getting on top of her, she said, having so many people around, and she didn't expect to be back till much later. Hannah would soon be engrossed in one of the ghoulish novels she had carefully packed for her holiday reading – the kind that had titles like *A Weekend in Camp Nightmare* and *The Stepmother From Hell*. Sooner or later great aunt Flora would start scribbling in a yellowing A4 notebook – 'Writing my memoirs,' she would say to anyone who asked, 'and they're not to be published till after the deaths of all the men involved.'

Katie had been hoping to get in a bit of sunbathing since the weather was for once fine, but there would be no time for that now, not with the shopping that would have to be done for tea, not to mention lunch beforehand . . .

'I hope you realise your mother is a saint,' Robin said sternly to the girls.

'Oh, sure,' Lucy said. 'Let's go, Jemima.'

* * *

Katie had taken out the huge Women's Institute teapot she had bought years ago for holidays in Rock and now couldn't manage without. It had big handles at the front and back for pouring, and could serve twenty-two people. She had also been to the bakery for cakes and pies and bread, and Robin had carried all the packages, and now he was helping her make the mountains of sandwiches that would disappear in no time flat as soon as the hordes descended.

Katie switched the radio on and Marianne Faithfull's husky voice filled the kitchen: 'The morning sun shone sweetly on / The eyes of Lucy Jordan.' At least it was something Katie recognised, something with a tune, not one of those rap bands Lucy was always playing at top volume in her bedroom.

> 'At the age of thirty-seven
> She realised she'd never ride
> Through Paris in a sports car
> With the warm wind in her hair.'

Katie suddenly stopped chopping the tomatoes and stared down at her hands, at the sapphire engagement ring and single slim band of gold on the fourth left finger. Robin said, 'What is it, Kitty-kat?'

'I just realised,' she said slowly. 'I'm thirty-seven years old.'

'That's nothing. I'm about to reach my three score and ten.'

'I feel as though I can't possibly be that old, and then there are other times when I feel much older.'

Robin put down his bread knife and gave her a little squeeze. 'You should branch out a bit – do something completely different.'

'Like what?'

'Oh, I don't know. An evening class, maybe, in Mandarin Chinese.'

Katie giggled. 'And what use would that be?'

Robin looked at her wistfully. 'It might be good for your soul,' he said and then began slicing bread again, as though

58

nothing of consequence had been said.

'At the age of thirty-seven,
She realised she'd never ride . . .'

Katie leaned over and switched the radio off.

The sandwiches were piled on plates, the cakes put out, the kettle boiling, when the rabble arrived.

'First aid kit!' Lucy yelled.

From years of experience, Katie had it ready and waiting.

'OK, line up here,' Robin said, at once exchanging his sous-chef's hat for his surgeon's.

'I'll give you a hand,' Jemima said.

The maimed and the wounded presented themselves for their ministrations while the luckier ones fell on the food. Katie, brewing up the tea, noticed that Jemima handled the butterfly stitches almost as deftly as her father did. Her charges chatted easily with her, recalling the high points of the game. Jemima, it appeared, had impressed them all with her instant grasp of strategy and her uncanny ability to score goals.

'Is there any more of that cake, Mrs Colman?' asked a freckle-faced boy with a butterfly stitch over his left eye.

He had called her 'Mrs Colman', but they all said 'Jemima' to her elder sister as they exchanged laughing banter with her. Katie bent down to take out the secret supply of cake she had kept back so that everyone, even the injured, would get their fair share. 'Thanks, Mrs Colman,' said the boy through a mouthful of fruit sponge.

At some stage in the proceedings Hannah had wandered in, still engrossed in her book, and was now stuffing a sandwich into her mouth with one hand while she held the book up to the light with the other. Lucy was squeezed into a corner with Tom Blackstone. As she giggled coyly at something he said, Katie saw Tom's hand come up and caress her daughter's cheek.

'I think another pot of tea is required,' Jemima said beside her.

Katie didn't move. 'How long has that been going on?' she said in a tight voice, nodding in the direction of Lucy and Tom.

'Oh, I'm not sure anything's actually going on, apart from the usual adolescent crush.'

'But she told you about it?'

'She mentioned that she's been seeing him down at the Mariner,' Jemima said, switching the kettle on since Katie obviously wasn't going to.

Katie rounded on her angrily. 'And don't you think you should have told me?'

'I'm not in the business of betraying confidences,' Jemima said coolly.

'Really? And if she does something silly, if she gets pregnant or catches some disease, where will *you* be? In Antarctica, that's where. *I'm* the one who'll have to pick up the pieces.'

'Don't be so dramatic,' Jemima said evenly. 'Lucy's an intelligent girl. She's not going to get pregnant *or* catch anything antisocial.'

'I'd just like to know what's going on,' Katie said. 'I *am* her mother, after all.'

She looked back towards the corner, but Lucy and Tom were nowhere to be seen. Anxiously she scanned the throng of faces. 'See, now they've gone off on their own,' she said in a quivering voice.

'They're in the garden playing croquet with some of the others,' Robin said, coming up behind Katie and putting an arm round her shoulders. 'It's all right, Kitty-kat, at Lucy's age you were madly in love with Bobby Butler, then we bought you a guitar and you forgot all about him, didn't you?'

'I must have done,' Katie said, smiling tentatively. 'I have no idea who you're talking about.'

On Jemima's last night, Robin took them all to a famous seafood restaurant overlooking the bay. It was to be just as much Katie's treat as Jemima's, he told her privately. It would save her slaving again over a hot stove.

They had all dressed up for once in honour of the occasion. Great aunt Flora's scraggy neck was swathed in ropes of pearls and diamonds that wouldn't have looked out of place in St James's Palace. Katie wore more standard beach holiday finery – white trousers and a good blouse and Gucci shoes and her gold jewellery – and looked very much like most of the other women in the room. Jemima had on a trouser suit from Mongolia in brightly coloured silk.

'It's an amazing place,' she told them. 'The people are so determined to overcome obstacles and build up their country. I saw them pulling carts filled with rocks for incredible distances – women as well as men – so they could make a new dam across one of their rivers. And Westerners seem to consider it impossible that a woman could haul a sledge across Antarctica!'

'Luckily you won't have to do it that way,' Robin said.

'I know, technology has made man-hauling obsolete.'

'I never wore trousers in my life,' great aunt Flora interrupted sharply. 'Don't approve of them – nasty un-feminine things.'

'There's almost nothing women can't do now in Antarctic exploration,' Jemima said. 'With a little bit of help from the wind, anyone can achieve what all those big butch Neanderthals used to think of as their exclusive domain. They're going to wind up on the scrap heap of history – where they belong!'

She threw Guy a challenging look, but with Katie's eye on him he merely smiled at her and said, 'I think your trouser suit is very attractive,' and she slumped a little, deprived of the treat of one of her usual confrontations with him.

Guy wasn't the only one being extra nice to Jemima. Robin now handed her a menu and asked solicitously what she would like to eat, as though she were a condemned woman ordering her last meal. Fiona sat next to her and every so often, when she leaned over to say something, she would touch her hand, as if to reassure herself that Jemima was still there.

They ordered almost everything on the menu, and everyone kept offering Jemima a taste of their grilled sea bass with lemon mayonnaise or their crab salad with dill. Jemima tried it all, and ate every last morsel of her three courses. Great aunt Flora demanded decent champagne in honour of the occasion. Katie tried not to think of the telephone figure total that was bound to appear on Robin's bill.

'Yummy,' Hannah said when the feast was all but demolished, licking chocolate-ice-cream smeared lips. Lucy was picking at a lemon sorbet. She seemed these days to be on an almost permanent diet.

She was sitting on Jemima's other side, as far away from her mother as possible. They had been on particularly poor terms since Katie had tried to slip her a gentle word of warning about letting Tom Blackstone go too far with her.

'Honestly, Mummy,' she'd said, 'I'm not a child any more. I know how to run my own life.'

'Even grown-ups can make those sorts of mistakes,' Katie had tried to reason with her.

'I wish you wouldn't lecture me. Jemima never does.'

'Yes, well she's not your mother,' Katie had retorted rather more sharply than she'd meant to.

'More's the pity,' Lucy had flung back, and Katie had felt the hurt hit her almost like a body blow. But if Lucy was sorry afterwards, she had too much pride to say so.

Robin banged his fork on his champagne glass and called for silence. He rose to make the toast. 'To our brave and beautiful daughter,' he said. 'May she achieve her dream, and come back home to share her triumph with the people who love her!'

There were tears in Fiona's eyes as she raised her glass. Katie, glancing quickly round the table, saw that she wasn't the only one.

It had always been like this for as long as Katie could remember. The prodigal daughter went out into the world, and her family feared she would never return to them, and when she did they killed the fatted calf and forgot all about the other daughter, the reliable one who had been there for them all along, quietly waiting for them to notice her.

Chapter Four

~

'You have to stop, Mummy, I can't hold it in any more.'

Katie glanced quickly into the rearview mirror at the traffic in the left-hand lane. There was an exit up ahead to one of those small towns that dotted the English landscape, with the same shops up and down its high street that you could find the length and breadth of Britain. There was nowhere you could go in Old Blighty these days, Jemima often said, and find something different.

'Why didn't you go before we left home?' Katie grumbled as she performed a rather tricky last minute lane change, and the car behind her indignantly flashed its lights.

'I did too,' said Hannah, who had been drinking cans of fizzy cold drink throughout the tedious journey.

The Wiltshire landscape wasn't what one could call inspiring to look at. In childhood days, roaming around the countryside, Jemima had been dismayed by the flatness of it, the way it rolled evenly away as far as the eye could see with no surprises. She and Katie had poured over stories in the local papers about sightings of UFOs above the Salisbury Plains, and mysterious crop circles on some neighbouring farmer's land, and determinedly set out to make a supernatural discovery of their own – anything, in fact, that was the least bit out of the ordinary – but nothing ever came of their efforts. Even Stonehenge, which Jemima had demanded Fiona take them to see, was a disappointment, set as it was now beside an unsightly main road. The old Celtic magic had long since passed away from Wiltshire, Jemima decided, and must be sought elsewhere.

It seemed a long time since the summer holidays when they had last seen her. Half-term had come and gone, and now Katie was driving the girls back to school again, and Jemima, after a final spurt of training, had left for Chile, gateway to the Antarctic, and her November start date. There would be no time now for second thoughts, no possibility of turning back.

As the exit took them into the centre of town, Katie scanned the restaurants along the High Street, looking for a likely stopping place. She pulled up in front of a pizzeria, a known quantity, part of a nationwide chain. 'We might as well get something to drink once we're stopping. Will this do?' she said.

'Do they have cappuccino?' Lucy demanded in a sulky voice that suggested her mother's choice might not be up to her sophisticated new tastes.

'I should think so. It's Italian, after all.'

Lucy climbed languidly out of the car. Hannah rushed into the restaurant with indecent haste and headed for the Ladies.

When she returned, skipping with relief, Katie scanned the plastic menu and asked the girls if they wanted anything to eat. There was plenty of time before they had to be back at Wolton Abbey, and they had weeks of boarding school food ahead of them.

'Pepperoni pizza for me,' Hannah said, but Lucy only shook her head and sipped her cappuccino with an air of not wanting to be here in the first place. Katie didn't dare push the point in case it sounded like nagging.

At the beginning of term Lucy had, with the permission of both parents, signed up for the award scheme that promised her the action and adventure she seemed to crave. It was the only way Katie had been able to patch up their quarrel after the Tom Blackstone incident.

'Are you sure you don't want to send me off for a pregnancy test?' Lucy had enquired sarcastically when they returned to London from Rock, and Katie had said of course not, she hadn't meant to imply anything like that, and she'd been thinking again about what Miss Tamsin had suggested and how it was perhaps not such a bad thing after all. And for weeks she had been holding her breath and praying that, by putting a toe in the water, Lucy would not develop her aunt's obsession for pushing herself to the limit of danger and beyond.

Scanning the menu, with its rather unappetising photographs of dishes Katie had no wish to sample, she ordered a simple mixed salad to keep Hannah company. It came with some tired-looking lettuce leaves and a few chunky slices of tomato and cucumber. On Hannah's pizza the pepperoni slices swam in little pools of oil, but she ate it quite happily.

Lucy, not bothering to disguise her boredom, looked across at the next table. A couple in their late teens sat with heads almost touching. The girl, in short skirt and sandals, had her bare legs entwined around her boyfriend's blue jeans. They were smoking furiously, American cigarettes, and Katie wondered if that would be Lucy and Tom in a few years' time.

'Would you like anything else?' she asked her daughters, imagining they must want to put off for as long as possible the moment of going back to school.

'No thanks,' Hannah said cheerfully, and Lucy began to wriggle in her chair, as though impatient to be off.

Katie paid the modest bill and headed back on to the motorway towards Wolton Abbey. Her life, she thought, seemed to circle endlessly between London and Wiltshire and Rock, round and round, never really getting anywhere.

Punta Arenas, the southernmost city in the world, lies at the very end of the Chilean mainland, looking out across the Straits of Magellan to the island of Tierra del Fuego, 'land of fire', the last land mass before the continent of Antarctica.

'*Hotel de Trovador, por favor,*' Jemima told the taxi driver, and immediately he broke into rapid Chilean Spanish in which the consonants seemed to be lost and with them all possibility of understanding for Jemima.

'*No comprendo*,' she said, and her radio operator Vivian Jennings, sitting until then quietly beside her, gave her a questioning look and said, 'I thought at least one of us did.'

'I've never been to Chile before,' Jemima said by way of apology.

'Really – you said you'd been everywhere.' Vivian ran a finger through light brown hair that she kept cropped conveniently short so it wouldn't get in the way of her radio equipment.

'I've visited what I suppose you'd call one of the Chilean territories – Easter Island, or Rapa Nui, as the Polynesians call it – but it's a long way from here, or from anywhere, come to that.'

'Isn't that the place with all those extraordinary giant stone statues?'

'The *moai*,' Jemima said dreamily, remembering the rows of massive figures carved from volcanic basalt that lined the shores of the island and defied all explanation by the experts.

The taxi took a corner on two wheels, and Jemima began to fear that the Chileans drove almost as fast as they spoke. In the absence of a rear seatbelt, she found herself grabbing Vivian's arm for support.

'This could be more dangerous than crossing the Antarctic,' Vivian said wryly, clutching in turn a rather rusty door handle.

They had flown from London to Santiago and on to Punta Arenas with one thousand two hundred pounds of luggage – mostly Vivian's radio equipment – and the tab fortunately picked up by their sponsors, hoping to gain worldwide exposure from this first attempt by two women to conquer a solo crossing of the whole Antarctic continent. The bulk of their baggage had been stowed at the airport to await the seven-hour flight to Patriot Hills in Antarctica, where Vivian would make her base camp and Jemima would be flown on in a Twin Otter ski-plane to the starting point of her epic journey.

'I'm glad it's you doing the dangerous bits,' Vivian often said, but Jemima wasn't fooled. Vivian's part in this drama would involve its own tests of endurance, and win her none of the glory. And Jemima knew she would go positively mad from being enclosed in a tiny space for weeks on end, as Vivian would be, with a constant noise in her ears. 'Each to his – or in this case her – own,' as Vivian was also in the habit of saying.

They were passing now through streets lined with impressive old buildings, monuments to the golden age of Punta Arenas when sailing ships and steamboats carrying goods from the Orient to the West were obliged to stop here and it became one of the busiest ports in the world. But then had come the cutting of the Panama Canal, and the town fell into decline until it was rescued from obscurity by the discovery of petroleum and natural gas in the region, and the establishment of an important naval base, so that now it was thriving once again.

But Jemima had little interest in this or any other city. She knew that, just beyond its limits, would be an icy land of unspoilt mountains and forests and lakes unlike any other apart perhaps from Norway, a savage coastline of bleak fjords with great glaciers tumbling down mountainsides to meet the storm-tossed sea.

'*Mira, mira,*' the taxi driver shouted as they passed through a large square lined with trees and neat gardens and impressive buildings. He was waving at a huge bronze figure that dominated the centre of the square. '*Magellan,*' he said in tones of reverence.

Jemima and Vivian craned their necks to see the statue of the great Portuguese navigator who had assured his place in the history books by discovering the route around the Horn and establishing an alternative gateway to the lucrative trade with the East. It must have been wonderful, Jemima thought, to be an explorer in those days of vast uncharted territories, with a new surprise around every corner.

'Are you secretly hoping to have a monstrosity like that erected in your honour?' Vivian teased, eyeing the bronze effigy quizzically.

It was the question people always asked, straight after, 'How do you pee in temperatures of minus-fifty?' And then, invariably, 'But *why* do you want to do it?' Jemima had never been able to untangle the complex web of desire for fame and fortune and adventure, even perhaps martyrdom, the incoherent mixture of patriotism and sheer curiosity, and come up with anything like an honest answer.

'I prefer the statues on Easter Island any day,' she said evasively.

The Old Rectory stood as it always had, serene in the symmetry of its classical proportions, giving no clue as to the revolutionary changes taking place within. Katie parked her car beside an unfamiliar white van with a bright slogan painted on the side, and walked round to the terrace door, which she knew was nearly always open. Passing the TV room which doubled as her mother's office, she saw Fiona fluttering round a very young man in a shiny suit, the sleeves and trousers of which were distinctly too short for his gangly limbs.

'Mr Bicknell has just installed my Internet and explained to me very patiently how it all works,' Fiona declared when her daughter appeared, hovering politely in the doorway.

'Ralph,' the young man said, waving a chiding finger. 'I told you to call me Ralph.'

Katie looked from one to the other with astonishment. 'Why on earth do you want—?'

'I do believe I now know how to find a page on the Web,' Fiona said proudly.

'And if you don't, you just call me any time, night or day,' Ralph insisted, beginning to pack up his bits and pieces.

'Thank you – you've been just marvellous,' Fiona said, following him out to his van like a devoted dog.

She returned after what seemed like quite a long time, and

sat down in front of her computer with a little self-satisfied smile. 'Great aunt Flora is very interested in the possibilities of e-mail. She says it would have come in mighty handy in her day for making romantic assignations.'

'But why do *you* want all this?'

'Because now I will know where Jemima is on an almost daily basis,' Fiona said with satisfaction.

Katie removed a pile of her mother's gardening magazines from a chair, and brushed the dog hairs off the cushion covers, and sat down beside her. 'How?'

'Jemima explained it all to me. She said I wouldn't have to worry so much, with modern technology making communications so much easier. I'll be able to keep my own tabs on her, she said.'

It would work as follows. Jemima would be carrying with her a tiny instrument – no more than half a pound in weight – a satellite position locator, which would tell her where she was within a hundred metres merely by pressing a few buttons. She would then relay this information to Vivian at her radio base in Patriot Hills in her nightly attempts to establish contact, and Vivian would log Jemima's latest position on the Internet, and Fiona would then be able to 'surf the Information Superhighway' and find out for herself about Jemima's progress.

Katie stared at her mother, wondering how she had managed to pick up the jargon so quickly. Ralph must have hidden talents despite the appalling suit.

'So much easier than relying on the beastly press – who are only the least bit interested when there's a disaster to report,' Fiona said with distaste.

Katie could sympathise only too well with this sentiment. It was through the television that Fiona, and then the rest of the family, had learned eight years ago that Jemima's first attempt on the South Pole had come to a premature and terrifying end. Jemima's party had set out in an ice-breaking vessel from New Zealand, bound for the Scott Base from which the famous British explorer and his four companions had made their last tragic journey. This would be Jemima's starting point too, from which she and three team-mates would set out on skidoos and sledges laden with sufficient supplies to get to the American base at the South Pole.

It is not for nothing that even the most experienced sailors fear the notorious storms of the Southern Ocean. In the gale-swept Roaring Forties and Furious Fifties, where there are no land masses to stop them, massive waves roll around the world unchecked, gaining in size and momentum until they form great perpendicular walls of green water forty or fifty feet in height, which come crashing down on the superstructure of a boat with a force that can scarcely be imagined.

They were still some distance from the Antarctic coast when Jemima's boat ran into one of these legendary storms, and by the time the winds had risen to force fourteen, after which point their speeds could no longer be measured, a freak wave of colossal proportions crashed into their ship, causing it to list over permanently on to the port side. Drifting helplessly in the treacherous seas, their world turned over, their control of the ship completely lost, the crew established that one of the portholes was leaking and the inexorable flow of water would soon fill the vessel. The captain activated the distress beacon, but everyone knew the distance they had covered from New Zealand, and that they were at best four days from any rescue attempt. This was what Fiona had learned from the BBC that night, when she innocently turned on the news little suspecting that one of its main items would be her daughter's almost hopeless plight.

Jemima said afterwards that right from the start she refused to believe it was the end. Before she headed for a lifeboat, as instructed by the crew, she made a determined raid on her Antarctic rations, grabbing her waterproof outer clothing and bottles of water and emergency stashes of Mars Bars.

There were four of them to a life raft, and the little boats were soon separated by the massive swells, so that none knew the fate of the others until it was all over. Jemima was with one of her team-mates and two of the crew, all men, but they said afterwards that it was Jemima's sheer determination to survive that kept them all from giving up. She knew that, in an open boat lashed with freezing water, the greatest risk was from hypothermia. They must not sleep for too long, she warned them, they must keep moving, keep the blood flowing. She organised shifts, so that they woke each other after only half an hour's rest, and then she made them bail water from the boat and jump around and even sing, whatever it took to keep them active and alive. She rationed out the water and the chocolate and the other meagre supplies they had managed to grab on their way to the life rafts, giving less to herself because of her lesser body weight.

And even so they were barely alive when the New Zealand rescue services reached them four and a half days later. By then Fiona and Robin and Katie, all staying together for comfort in the house in Wiltshire, their nerves stretched to breaking point by the endless hours of waiting, scarcely dared to hope that Jemima had survived. But the good news reached them via radio from the rescue vessel and its headquarters back on the New Zealand mainland that alive she was, and suffering from nothing more severe than dehydration and some frost nip to the fingers.

But the news for many other families was far bleaker. Jemima's was the only boat in which survivors were found. Only one other life raft was recovered, its occupants dead from exposure. All the others were lost without trace.

Jemima could so easily have been one of the tragic statistics. Her family knew it, and so did she. Her boyfriend at the time, a strong and burly veteran of many polar expeditions, was one of those whose body was never recovered.

For a while Jemima remained in England, in Wiltshire with Fiona, recovering from her ordeal and her loss. As the months went by, her family even began to hope that she may at last, through bitter experience, have got the adventure bug out of her system. But then one day, quite out of the blue, she

73

announced to her mother matter-of-factly that she was joining a diving expedition to the Yucatan caves, and they knew that they would have to start learning to live with the worry all over again.

And so they had, to the best of their ability. They knew they couldn't stop Jemima, any more than you could halt the rolling waves of the Southern Ocean. But it was hard for Fiona to know that her daughter was going to the South Pole again, almost too hard for her to bear . . .

'She's going to make it this time,' Katie said to her mother, squeezing her hand firmly.

'I know she is,' Fiona said, staring at the screen-saver pattern of little fishes blowing geometrically increasing strings of bubbles, and avoiding Katie's eye.

By the time the DC6 came in to land over Patriot Hills Jemima was four days behind schedule, delayed from take-off by weather that would have made landing an aeroplane on a blue ice runway – hazardous at the best of times – well nigh impossible.

The pilot came in for a practice run, testing the fifty-knot winds. Beside Jemima, Vivian tensed and glared at the 'no smoking' sign. As the pilot lurched back up to try another circle and descent, Jemima began to regret that last portion of king crab and rice she had gorged just before leaving Punta Arenas, to fuel up for the lean days ahead. She had heard all the hair-raising tales about Patriot Hills landings, and though she wasn't afraid, she was beginning to feel distinctly queasy.

She looked across at little knots of Norwegians in anoraks and woolly caps, the press corps who had accompanied Kristin Notaker to photograph for an eager public the start of their heroine's voyage across the Antarctic. The Norwegians lionised polar explorers much in the way that other countries idolised their football stars.

The announcement by Notaker that she would attempt to be the first woman to cross the Antarctic solo and unsupported had been made, rather theatrically, at the last possible moment. Now, as well as fighting the elements and the limits of her own endurance, Jemima would be up against a formidable competitor. The old rivalry between the British and the Norwegians was alive and well in the polar regions.

If anything Jemima welcomed the challenge. It gave her a little extra rush of adrenalin for the task ahead. She knew her specially designed kites, which could make use of wind from almost any direction, were more flexible than the para-wings favoured by the Norwegians. She was in with more than a fighting chance.

'Cripes – here we go again!' Vivian said as the plane swooped down towards the glittering makeshift runway. She crammed an unlit cigarette into her mouth and shut her eyes tightly.

Jemima glanced across at the Norwegians. From beneath a thick blonde fringe, Kristin Notaker gave her a level stare. Her eyes were as hard and cold as the blue ice rushing up to meet them. All around her, Jemima was pleased to note, her syco-phantic followers were disintegrating into various states ranging from mild panic to sheer terror.

The plane hit the runway with shattering force and bounced back up into the air. Stomachs lurched, and a bearded Norwegian reached for a sick bag. The plane came down again and slithered alarmingly across the uneven surface. There were long moments when it seemed to Jemima that the brakes would never take, then gradually the speed seemed to diminish until the view out of the cabin windows was no longer a blur of rushing white. The Norwegian made some unpleasant noises into the sick bag, the plane shuddered to a halt, and suddenly all was silent. Vivian opened her eyes.

'Either this is the afterlife, or we've arrived in Antarctica,' she said, 'and at this point I'm not sure I care which.'

The base camp at Patriot Hills housed pilots, doctors, cooks, radio operators and various client relations personnel. One of the latter (it was impossible to tell of which sex, since all that was visible were a pair of concerned eyes peering through a balaclava) guided the white-faced bearded Norwegian to the medical quarters. The rest of his countrymen went in search of shelter from the wind and a stiff drink.

Vivian stayed by the DC6 to supervise the unloading of her radio equipment. She had brought her own in preference to using what was available through the base because, as she said, 'If I'm going to spend all day breathing into something, I don't like knowing that someone else has been breathing into it before me.' She had similar feelings about public telephones, which she would only use if she covered the mouthpiece first with a handkerchief, thereby muffling her voice and giving the unfortunate impression, to those who were not used to her foibles, that she was an obscene caller.

Patriot Hills was the end of the line for Vivian, but only the beginning for Jemima and Kristin. The Norwegian girl made a beeline for the base camp leader, while one of her underlings barked instructions at Chilean skidoo drivers who began ferrying her gear to a Twin Otter ski-plane parked nearby. Locked in conversation with the base camp leader, gesticulating at the ski-plane, Kristin appeared to be instructing him that she wanted to be flown immediately to her chosen starting point.

Jemima wondered where that would be. She knew that, at the outset, Kristin would keep it a closely guarded secret. It was part of the psychology of the game not to reveal plans that would soon become common knowledge, when both Kristin's and Jemima's exact positions would be radioed to base camp and logged into the Internet, and the information would automatically become available to anyone round the world who cared to look it up. It would also be passed on to each of the two girls, so they would know exactly how far their competitor had progressed.

But for now mum was the word, and Jemima would not disclose either her intended drop-off point on the Filchner ice shelf, where she knew she could pick up a good wind to propel her the two hundred or so miles to the true edge of the continent, the real beginning of her journey. The floating ice shelf was pitted with crevasse fields, and treacherous to camp on in a storm, but it was, Jemima reckoned, as good a place to start as any.

After four days of waiting for the weather to improve, Jemima could almost hear the clock ticking. She glanced over at the second Twin Otter sitting silently on the runway. It was time she made her own arrangements to head out into the white wilderness that had been beckoning to her for so long in her dreams.

Crammed in amongst her supplies which filled the interior of the Twin Otter, Jemima stared down at the featureless white expanse below her, and tried to distinguish some mark from the map she had memorised that would help her recognise where she was. There seemed to be nothing out there but the endless white glare, and inside the constant drone of the plane's engines which made conversation – and even coherent thought – almost impossible.

But the pilot must have seen something she couldn't, because the whining pitch of the engines changed as the plane began to lose altitude, heading down towards some stretch of ice the pilot obviously considered both suitable for putting his plane down and close enough to the point Jemima had requested.

This second ice landing was less nerve-racking, now that she knew what to expect. When the noise of the engines finally died out, the pilot – a melancholy-looking Chilean of Spanish descent – turned to give her an almost pitying look, as though she were a mad woman with no idea of what was out there waiting for her.

He helped her unload her supplies on to the ice. That, they both knew, was where his responsibility for her ended. He climbed back into the plane with a little half-shake of his head, and she watched him take off into the blinding light and heard the noise of his engines fading and found herself left at last to the great engulfing silence of Antarctica.

She wondered what she had looked like to him as he left her far below him, a tiny matchstick figure surrounded by her matchbox supplies, marooned on the vast frozen wastes of the Filchner and Ronne ice shelves with a combined area as big as France, hundreds of miles from the nearest human being. Perhaps she truly was as mad as he thought her.

But she couldn't allow those thoughts to take hold. Determinedly, Jemima began to pack her supplies, one item at a time, on to her sledge. Methodically she arranged tent and sleeping bag and fuel bottles and cooker and food bags and radio equipment, and remembered Fiona gamely helping her to pack these same items into their crates for the flight to Santiago, though she had to keep stopping to dab at her eyes with a handkerchief.

Jemima could afford to take only the absolute essentials. Her toothbrush had been stripped down to a few bristles, and she remembered the look of dismay on Katie's face when she had told her she would carry just one change of underwear and socks for a sixty-day journey. In that time she would have to cover one thousand seven hundred miles, a distance that took Sir Ranulph Fiennes a hundred and ten days in 1993 when he man-hauled his sledge across Antarctica in the longest self-supporting expedition in history. With the aid of her kites, Jemima planned almost to halve his travelling time. Theoretically, with the new technology, she knew it was possible. The Norwegian Borge Ousland, using his less flexible parawing, had made the crossing in 1997 in just sixty-four days.

But there would be little margin for error. Jemima knew she lacked the sheer physical strength needed to drag her two-hundred-and-fifty-pound sledge on the days when the wind failed her. That meant she would have to cover far more ground than previous expeditions on the days when she could travel, if she were to reach the other side of the Antarctic without running out of essential food and fuel. The kite manufacturers said it could be done, but then they, she thought rather sourly, were not the ones trying to do it.

One day at a time, Jemima told herself firmly. She must not think of the awesomeness of the whole task ahead of her. She must face the necessities of each day only as and when they arose.

She strapped on the chest-mounted gimbal-compass which would ensure that, no matter how poor the visibility, she would always be travelling in the right direction. She unrolled her kites, great rectangles of vivid red and purple and green that would soon provide a jaunty splash of colour as they flew above the unbroken whiteness of the snow-bound southern-most continent. She climbed into the all-purpose harness that would attach her to kites and sledge and the essential dead man's release system that would collapse the kites if danger loomed. Then she looked down at the fluttering wrist strap of her ski pole, trying to assess the strength and direction of the wind. It was a moderate easterly breeze, she decided, possibly as strong as fifteen miles an hour at a hundred and fifty feet where the kites would be flying. With a crosswind like that she should get a good beam reach and make steady progress.

Jemima let out the lines directly in front of her at the point of maximum wind strength and felt the tug against the handles. She thought briefly of the scepticism of her trainer Duncan and the long hours they had spent preparing for this moment. Then she pictured Kristin Notaker somewhere out there in the vast whiteness, poised too for take-off, and felt the quiver run through her like a greyhound at a starting gate.

The race was on. It was time to find out if she really could do it. It was time to discover what she had inside her.

Katie wandered from the kitchen to the dining room to the sitting room and back again, round and round in circles, looking at drooping cushions and the thin film of dust Angie hadn't quite removed from some of the surfaces, and wondering whether she had the energy or inclination to do anything about it.

What was it Lucy Jordan said in her ballad?

> 'She could clean the house for hours,
> or rearrange the flowers,
> or run naked down the shady street
> screamin' all the way.'

Stop that, Katie told herself fiercely.

She grabbed the television guide from the pile of glossy magazines on the coffee table but a glance at the day's listings gave little hope of relief. There was really nothing on she wanted to watch, and she felt far too restless for the concentration required to read a decent book.

She sat, defeated, on the sofa, and stared up absently at the portrait of her and Guy. He was working this weekend for Mr Kassianides, and had warned her she could expect to see very little of him. He would probably, he said, have his meals in the office or with his client.

'You should put your foot down now and then,' Sylvia had trilled when she phoned to say she and Henry were going for the weekend on the Eurostar to Paris. Sylvia simply insisted on Henry taking her off now and then for a little romantic interlude, and Katie should do the same with Guy. After all, every marriage needed spicing up from time to time . . . Katie tried to picture Guy on the Champs Elysée, wrinkling his nose at all the foreign sights and sounds. At the age of thirty-seven, Lucy Jordan knew she'd never ride through Paris with the warm wind in her hair . . .

If only she had her father for company, but Robin had gone faithfully down to Wiltshire. There had been a moment when Katie had been tempted to join him, but she couldn't quite face the prospect of Fiona hunched over her Internet, waiting tensely for news that would be a long time coming.

All they knew of Jemima's progress so far was that she had been dropped off at her starting point. There would probably be no update for another twenty-four hours. That was too long a period to be confronted by the sight of her mother, eyes glued to her screen, unable to focus on anything but the appearance of two simple coordinates that would prove her daughter was alive and well.

Lucy had phoned to say that she was off this weekend on a camping and canoeing expedition that had her in a state of barely suppressed excitement. Hannah would be involved in the usual round of weekend activities available at Wolton Abbey. It was only she, Katie thought irritably, who seemed to be at a complete loose end.

The trouble was, after so many years of family life and motherhood, she wasn't used to having time on her hands and the choice of how to fill it in ways that suited only her. She had forgotten what she used to do before Guy and Lucy and Hannah absorbed all her attention, how she amused herself when the choice was hers alone. Did she go to art galleries and foreign films with subtitles? Did she sit in coffee bars and have intense conversations with friends about how to save the planet? She supposed she must have done, like most under-graduates, but it was all such a distant memory it seemed quite unconnected with the person she was now, something that might as well have happened to someone else.

Katie fiddled repetitively with her watch strap and wondered how on earth she was going to fill the long and empty hours till Monday morning and the welcome need to be at her desk in the library. The very fact that she was at a loss to think of anything made a mockery of her claim to Jemima, when they had spoken on the cliffs of Trebetherick, that her life was busy and full of seeing to the needs of others, that she had no time for her own adventures or the luxury of inner contemplation.

She was glad Jemima was so far away, that she couldn't see how alone Katie was, or how incapable of making good use of what Jemima would have considered this valuable time to herself. Instead all Katie could think was that she had never felt so little needed by those she loved, so completely abandoned, in all her life.

* * *

Jemima thought that she had never felt so utterly and completely exhausted in all her life.

Her arms ached from gripping the kite handles and battling the wind over miles of snow. Her legs throbbed from the hours spent upright on her skis. Her hips hurt where the harness had rubbed against skin. Her feet were blistered and painful to the touch. The strain of constant physical exertion was taking its toll on her thirty-nine-year-old body, and every joint and muscle screamed at her to give it rest.

She hadn't yet got used to the incredible cold, almost like a physical presence, and the constant gnawing hunger. She wasn't sure how many calories she was burning each day, but she did know it was a great deal more than she was replacing with her dehydrated rations. Soon her problems would be compounded by the progressive physical deterioration of a body that was being subjected to slow and inexorable starvation.

This is too hard, a little voice inside her kept saying, you should give up, give up . . .

She stopped for a moment to wipe the rime from her goggles and give herself a mental shake. She mustn't allow these negative thoughts to take over, she must focus her mind on practical problems like the crevasse field looming up ahead. She must think only of survival.

The problem was, apart from the faint blue shadows of the crevasses, there was nothing to look at, no feature of the landscape to fasten on. She was disoriented by the utter whiteness, the constant sameness, like a subject in a sensory deprivation chamber. It had the effect of making her feel that she was moving forward and yet going nowhere, that time itself was standing still. It was like the landscape of a waking dream, a surrealistic nightmare.

The less there was to see around her, the more she found that she was turning in on herself, living in her own thoughts, so that there were long stretches of time when she was not in Antarctica at all but back in England, with the people she knew best and so seldom spent time with. Like a dying woman she saw her life flash in front of her, against the white backdrop of the endless snow, and it was often the childhood memories that were the most vivid.

The one that kept recurring was of Katie's first day at school. She arrived looking even smaller than her five years in her too-large uniform, with her hair tied neatly in two fair pigtails framing a frightened white face. Jemima, who had been there two years already and quite forgotten her first-week nerves, was faintly repulsed by Katie's obvious fear at the strangeness of it all, and longing for her sister to put on a brave face. She refused to mother her, to hold her hand through the ordeal, believing her younger sister had better learn quickly to stand on her own two feet. So she left her alone at playtime, though Katie had as yet no friends, and hardened her heart against the sight of her younger sister sitting lost and bewildered beneath a cherry tree in the playground, the tears forming dirty streaks down her face.

'I'm sorry,' Jemima said out loud to the great white open spaces. She had felt no remorse then, but now she was learning something about what it felt like to be afraid, to find yourself totally alone . . .

'I'm so sorry,' she said again, and just then, when all she saw before her was her sister's childish tear-streaked face framed by the ridiculous pigtails, she felt the sickening lurch of ground giving way beneath her feet and in a single terrifying instant found herself up to her armpits in snow, her feet flailing helplessly in nothingness.

Crevasses have always been the greatest danger to polar travellers. Jemima knew that, and cursed herself now for her lapse in concentration. Instinctively she had dropped the handles of her kites, and the dead man's release brought them fluttering to the ground. Now she carefully tried to crane her neck around to look back at the position of her sledge. At any moment its weight could break suddenly through the rotten snowbridge and drag her down to her death in the cavernous depths below.

Heart pounding against her layers of thermal clothing, Jemima began to inch herself with painful slowness up the lip of the crevasse. Any sudden movement could mean instant oblivion. She tried not to remember the fate of Ninnis on his last tragic polar journey with Mawson and Mertz in 1912. When he jumped from the edge of his sledge to guide it through a crevasse field, his foot plunged through collapsing snow and both he and his sledge plummeted down into the abyss of an unsuspected crevasse, his dogs howling in terror. His companions circled helplessly round the gaping hole, listening to the faint death cries of the dogs, knowing there was nothing they could do to rescue either the animals or their friend from this icy grave.

There was no one to help extricate Jemima if she made one false move. Sweating with that knowledge, she wriggled up the last few inches and found her hips at last out of the hole. At once she unclipped the harness attaching her to the sledge, and lay there shivering with the knowledge of her narrow escape.

After she had hauled the sledge to safety, Jemima crawled back to the rim of the crevasse and peered over the edge. Its sheer vertical walls plunged down from pale glacial blue to indigo to black nothingness. It was impossible to gauge the depth, but she knew it was sufficient to ensure that, had she fallen, she would never have got out of there alive.

She crawled away and sat very still, looking out across this hostile continent that she had decided, in her arrogance and innocence, to try to subdue. What she felt deep within her was the quiet satisfaction of knowing that Antarctica had thrown its worst against her and she had come through, she had conquered fear, she had survived.

But another small, insistent voice inside her kept reminding her that there was a long, long way to go yet.

Chapter Five

On the eleventh day of her journey, Jemima crossed from the ice shelf on to the true Antarctic continent and began the strenuous eleven-thousand-foot climb to the summit of the polar plateau. It was rough terrain, pitted with crevasses and strewn with ice debris. As the slope grew steeper and more difficult to scale, she found she had to tack at a forty-five-degree angle, adding many unwanted miles to her journey.

In her nightly talks with Vivian back in the base camp at Patriot Hills, Jemima had kept close tabs on the progress of Kristin Notaker. The Norwegian had chosen to start from Berkner Island, and on the days when she picked up more favourable winds she seemed to streak ahead, creating a gap between them that Jemima feared would never be closed. But then Jemima had been blessed by a rare north wind and for an entire day sailed straight towards the pole, covering a staggering hundred and twelve miles and putting herself in the lead. Now, on the difficult terrain of the plateau, the two competitors seemed to be neck and neck.

Using the kites in these conditions was hazardous. Jemima had to keep all her wits about her to avoid being driven on to weak crevasse bridges or thrown with shattering force against sastrugi, the ridge-like formations cut into the snow by the winter winds. Some of these ice-sculpted shapes were the most weird and wonderful she had ever seen.

Up on the plateau, away from the coast, Jemima could no

longer hear the familiar cry of the snow petrels. Here there were no birds, no animals of any kind – not even any germs, according to her father. Of the many difficulties she faced, at least infection would not be top of the list.

Her heart lifted one morning when she unzipped her tent to brilliant sunshine. It would be a glorious day's travelling, stripped down to only one layer of protective clothing against the dangerous ultraviolet rays pouring down through the hole in the ozone layer. Jemima knew that the hole, first discovered by the British Antarctic Survey, grew larger every year and was at its worst now in November, when she would be travelling directly beneath its centre. She had heard the tales of increased cancer-related deaths amongst people in Australasia, and whole flocks of sheep going blind in Patagonia. She would take no chances.

She lathered every potentially exposed area of skin with protective cream, and ventured out into the blinding sunlight with only her lips and nose uncovered so that she would not fog up the goggles she would have to wear at all times to prevent damage to her eyes from the glare of sun off snow.

There was a gentle easterly breeze, ideal for kiting. As Jemima let the wind take her and the sun warm her, she experienced a sense of physical well-being that was almost euphoria. Today it felt good – good to be in the Antarctic and making such wonderful progress, good just to be alive.

She sailed for fifty-five miles with the sun shining its blessing on her, reminding her of the hot summer afternoons of her Wiltshire childhood, when she and Katie would take turns to push each other on the rope swing Robin had made for them and attached to a sturdy branch of the big old oak. Katie was always begging not to be pushed too high, and Jemima impatiently demanding to go higher. Afterwards Fiona would bring them out a picnic tea, and they would lie drowsily in the shade of the oak with the sunlight dappling their faces, and try to recognise shapes in the leaves. Katie always saw practical things – a boat, a horse, a spoon – while Jemima discovered the fantastical creatures of her imagination. But even these were as nothing to the phantasmagorical shapes she had seen hewn from the ice on this, her strangest journey.

When she pitched her tent that night she was filled with contentment. She thought that out there on the sun-drenched white plains, despite the salt sweat dripping into her eyes and the stench of her unwashed body, it had been the most exhilarating day of her life.

But as soon as she tried to eat her rehydrated spaghetti bolognese, she realised that the ultra-violet rays had burned deep cracks and blisters into her lips, and the blood from them dripped down into the cooking pot to mingle with the melted snow and form a nasty red mush that she could only face eating because she was so hungry. It was no worse, she told herself wryly, than some of her mother's less inspired attempts, particularly now that Fiona was getting older and couldn't be bothered. Jemima thought of how Katie had patiently taught herself to cook from recipe books, how she had made a real effort to be a proper home-maker and how Jemima had despised her for it. She would have given anything, now, to have her father ministering a soothing balm to her lips and one of Katie's home-cooked meals.

In the morning scabs had formed over the sores, but as soon as Jemima tried to force her lips apart to eat her porridge oats, they cracked open and the blood seeped out again. Looking down into the now familiar red mush, Jemima sighed and decided it might be better if she ate with her eyes shut.

Outside the sun was still beating down mercilessly. It was going to be another perfect Antarctic summer day.

It was one of those bleak end of November days when almost no light from the grey skies overhead reached the narrow alley outside the basement window of Katie's office.

The overhead neon strip-lights glinted off Marigold's glasses as she turned them Katie's way. 'Heard any good jokes lately?' she said.

'I never remember jokes,' Katie confessed.

'Well, I've got one for you. What do you call a boatload of lawyers at the bottom of the ocean?'

'A good start,' Katie said. It was one of the few jokes she did remember. Guy had been less than amused when she'd repeated it to him after the last time Marigold told it to her.

She turned back to her pile of books. There was nothing very challenging that needed classifying today: another royal kiss-and-tell, some bodice rippers for the fiction shelves, a rather dry book on modern architecture. Katie skimmed down the pile and decided she would try a new book on the Romantics that looked marginally more interesting than the others. She opened it randomly on a middle page.

'Romantic philosophers made no distinction between the self and the outside world,' she read. 'All nature, both mind and matter, was seen as a reflection of one world spirit . . .'

She flicked on a few pages further, and dipped into the wisdom of Novalis, one of the leading lights of the day. 'The path of mystery leads inwards,' he apparently said.

'Do you think you can learn all about the world just by looking inside yourself?' she asked Marigold.

'Personally I'd rather not. You never know what you might find there that you'll wish afterwards you hadn't.'

Katie was inclined to agree. These days her own mind was a turmoil, subject sometimes to dark flights of fancy. Even her father seemed to have lost his customary good humour, and on his last few visits had exchanged none of his usual light-hearted banter with her. There were shadows under his eyes that suggested he wasn't sleeping well. Damn Jemima, Katie thought.

'Philosophy,' Marigold said suddenly, 'subsection Romantic . . . No need to take so long over it – even I know where to put a book like that.'

Katie did too, but she was reluctant to relinquish it just yet. She skipped a few more pages and stopped at some fanciful lines by the English poet Coleridge: 'What if you slept? And what if, in your sleep, you dreamed? And what if, in your dream, you went to heaven and there plucked a strange and beautiful flower? And what if, when you awoke, you had the flower in your hand? Ah, what then?'

Katie closed her eyes, and tried to dream herself into the unchanging white world of Antarctica, where there was nothing to see for miles and no visible distinction to be made between earth and heaven. She bent, in her dream, to pick up a handful of the whiteness, the powdery snow, in her gloves. She opened her eyes and looked . . . but her hand was empty.

'I've got one you definitely don't know,' Marigold said. 'Why did the chicken cross Antarctica?'

Katie gave her a stricken look, but Marigold didn't seem to notice. ' 'Cause the weather's so fowl,' she said, chuckling heartily at her own wit.

Almost exactly halfway to the pole, Jemima found herself confined to her tent while katabatic winds of seventy knots wreaked havoc with the world outside. The storm had whipped up the snow into forty-foot spirals that sometimes joined together to form huge moving white walls. Visibility was zero, and travel in such conditions impossible. The winds were far too strong to allow the use of her kites, and the terrain too hazardous. She could not risk falling into an unseen crevasse, like the one whose gaping mouth she had spotted up ahead just the evening before when she had pitched her tent under calm and sunny skies.

But the delay was making her champ at the bit. Her previous night's radio contact with Vivian at base camp had revealed that Kristin Notaker had somehow managed to pull ahead of her by some thirty miles. She must have caught more favourable winds, and now she might be clear of the storm and able to keep going while Jemima fumed impotently inside her tent.

For a moment the winds outside seemed to subside, and Jemima eagerly tried to open the zip a crack to see out. But at once a flurry of snow blew in through the gap, coating her sleeping bag and cooker and food rations in a layer of white powder. Jemima quickly closed the zip again. There was nothing for it – she would have to sit this out.

In the days of man-hauling, some polar travellers had tried to keep going in white-out conditions and suffered the consequences. They described the experience as like trying to move blindly in a landscape without shadow, earth and sky indivisible as though enveloped in a blanket of white night. The sensation could be physically sickening. Eyes couldn't focus, depth perception was nil, goggles misted up but couldn't be removed because of the threat of snow blindness, like a million hot needles in the eyeball.

Jemima wriggled impatiently in the confining tent. Though it was of an aerodynamic tunnel shape designed to withstand high winds, it seemed an impossibly frail shelter against the storm raging outside. She remembered the British Antarctic Survey group who had died from exposure when their tent was ripped away by katabatic winds. She pictured those who had strayed too far from shelter and found themselves half choked with snow that forced its way into ears and nose and throat. She shivered involuntarily.

As long as she couldn't make any progress, she didn't dare eat any more than the little bits of leftover rations from the week before – a cup or two of beef soup and porridge. She couldn't risk running out of food if delays from bad weather prevented her from making it across to safety in the sixty days of her planned schedule.

To take her mind off the hunger and the boredom, Jemima searched for the miniature pack of cards that was her only frivolous addition to the weight on her sledge. She began to lay them out for a game of Patience, taught to her by Fiona (who knew just how little of that virtue there was in her elder daughter's make-up) on the quiet afternoons Jemima had spent recuperating in Wiltshire from her ordeal in the Southern Ocean.

Thoughts of her mother brought a vague pang of guilt. She

knew Fiona was finding it more difficult than ever to cope with the knowledge of the risks Jemima was facing. Her parents weren't getting any younger, and perhaps it wasn't fair to put them through all the worry at their time of life.

But she had to think of her own ambitions too, Jemima reminded herself sharply. If she let her life be run by other people's feelings, she would never do anything at all.

Having settled the matter in her mind to her own satisfaction, she turned her attention to the tiny cards and the less than thrilling challenge of how to keep herself occupied with them through the long hours until the storm abated and she could get moving again.

In the upstairs room that had once been quite big enough to double as both bedroom and playroom for her two young daughters, Fiona bent over the small, almost shrunken form of great aunt Flora, who seemed dwarfed by the vast old double bed with heavy wooden headboard that she had insisted on bringing with her when her house had to be sold, because it wasn't safe for her to live on her own any more. What secrets, Fiona wondered, could that bed tell, if only it could talk?

'Hold still, now,' she said as she dabbed arnica on to the nasty bump on aunt Flora's shin. She had given herself a rather spectacular bruise when she slipped getting out of the bath.

'Used to be the finest pair of legs in London,' aunt Flora mourned as she looked down at the wasted flesh, the fine tracing of varicose veins. 'I'll have you know, my girl, that these legs have danced with the Prince of Wales at the Café de Paris.'

'There's life in them yet,' Fiona said soothingly. But it was a very frail life. When had she started noticing that all of life was so fragile?

She supposed she would have to put special handles on the bathroom wall for aunt Flora to hold on to at bath times. Or would it be safer to take the bath out altogether and install a shower? But danger lurked in every possibility. What if aunt Flora dropped the soap on the wet shower-room floor, and fell over trying to retrieve it?

Fiona wrapped a bandage round the wound to prevent the arnica getting on to aunt Flora's fine cotton sheets. They presented a nightmare on laundry day, when Mrs Beasley from the village would have to make sure not to let them go through the spin cycle, and to hang them out very straight on the line, and then iron them afterwards to get out all the creases. Mrs Beasley had been working longer hours since aunt Flora's arrival, but old people, in Fiona's experience, never gave any thought to the practicalities. They seemed to assume that staff were as easy to come by as in their carefree youth.

'There, all done,' Fiona said, tucking aunt Flora's legs beneath the offending sheets. 'Shall I bring you a nice cup of tea?'

'A stiff brandy would be more to the point,' aunt Flora said darkly, 'when you consider the shock—'

Fiona went off in search of the brandy bottle, glad of the excuse to fuss over someone who wasn't thousands of miles away and beyond her help. She brought the glass back and placed it carefully on a little cork mat that protected the gleaming rosewood surface of the antique table by great aunt Flora's bed.

'That's more like it,' Flora said, taking a large gulp. 'Cover me up, there's a dear, I'm so cold.'

Fiona took a beautiful shawl of heavy black lace and placed it over her aunt's bony shoulders. She looked down at the exquisite workmanship and wondered which of her long-ago lovers had given it as a gift to the crotchety old lady whose famed beauty now lay in ruins. The odds were she wouldn't remember herself.

'You ought to have a lie-down too,' aunt Flora said, peering at her sharply. 'You look a bit peaky yourself.'

'I'm just afraid,' Fiona said almost before she was aware the words were out. 'I have this feeling that something terrible is about to happen.'

Beneath the bedclothes aunt Flora made an awkward attempt to shift her painful leg. 'I thought it already had,' she said sourly.

'You're right,' Fiona placated her. 'Don't pay any attention to me – I'm just being silly.'

She didn't remind her aunt of the old superstition that accidents always happened in threes.

Sticking her nose cautiously out of the tent, Jemima established that the worst of the storm appeared to be over. The wind, lifting up swirls of snow, was still strong but no longer quite so terrifying. Visibility had improved from nil to a few feet. It wasn't wise to proceed in such conditions, but neither was it out of the question.

The storm had made communications with Vivian impossible, and Jemima had no way of knowing how far Kristin Notaker had progressed while she was holed up in her tent, willing away the bad weather while pretending to concentrate on her cards. She wasn't very good at Patience, she had decided. Like needlepoint and knitting, it was an old lady's pastime.

She had to get going again, the waiting was driving her crazy. She couldn't risk allowing the gap between her and Kristin to widen any further. She couldn't allow the very real possibility that the delay would cause her to run out of food.

Using the kites in the still high winds without being able to see far enough in front of her would be risky, she knew that. But she could compensate for the wind strength by choosing a smaller kite surface, and anyway, she was far more experienced now at manouevring herself away from danger. If she got into real trouble, there was always the safety mechanism of the dead man's release to save her.

Having made up her mind, Jemima began to pack away tent and supplies on to her sledge. A strong gust tore an empty ration bag from her grasp and it blew away before she could retrieve it. She felt a pang of guilt at her unintentional polluting of this beautiful, empty land.

As she let out the ropes of her parafoil, she braced herself to do battle with the wind. As well as the usual crevasse hazards, there were a lot of moraines in the area. Though the kites tugged at her arms with unaccustomed force, she found the strong winds a help rather than a hindrance in surmounting these icy obstacles.

But it wasn't quite so easy to control her speed, to prevent the winds from pulling her too fast towards some yawning fissure. Using the brake lines to steady her, she reassured herself that there was really nothing to worry about, she had mastered the techniques of parafoiling and should be able to use the wind strength to her advantage.

From out of nowhere a sudden gust of unexpected force filled the sails of her parafoil so that they swelled like huge over-ripe melons. At the same time both she and her sledge were jerked forward with such impetus that the heavier sledge smashed into the back of Jemima's legs, tripping her over in a great muddle of skis and poles and tangled ropes. She slammed down on top of the sledge, her head making sickening impact with a metal alloy fuel bottle, before somersaulting over the back and falling on to the hard ice. The ropes of the kite became hopelessly entangled round the sledge so that, although her hold on the handles had slackened, it did not have the usual effect of activating the dead man's release.

The winds were rising again as a new storm front descended. The kite continued to drag the sledge with Jemima's inert body behind it across the bumpy, ice-strewn terrain. Because she had lost consciousness, Jemima was unaware that they were heading at high speed straight for the tell-tale blue shadows of a crevasse field.

The alarm went off at six-thirty, as it always did on weekday mornings. Katie stirred a little, burrowing instinctively into the warmth of her duvet. She would doze for half an hour while Guy showered and shaved and listened to the 'Today' programme. Then, at seven, she would go downstairs and make breakfast for them both, as she always did, before coming back up to soak in a hot tub and dress for her day at the library. She didn't have to be at her desk till nine, by which time Guy's working day would already be well underway.

She listened for the usual morning sound of Guy swinging his legs over the side of the bed and searching with his feet for his discarded slippers. But instead she heard the groaning of the bedsprings as he shifted his weight towards her, and felt his hand come up to stroke her hair.

She froze. This was Guy's unspoken signal that he wanted sex. Katie lay very still, wondering what on earth had made Guy deviate from a routine that was usually written in stone. They mostly had sex on weekends and the odd night when he made it out of his study before she was already long asleep. It seldom happened more than twice a week – and never, never in the mornings.

Katie wasn't at her best first thing in the morning. She never felt quite human till the clock struck nine and she had put away at least two cups of good strong coffee. She always had to make a conscious effort to respond with the good humour that came quite naturally to people with a different constitution. Katie didn't even feel up to having a demanding conversation first thing in the morning – let alone sex!

But Guy was still stroking insistently at her hair, making it difficult to pretend, as she was tempted to, that she wasn't yet awake. Finally her sense of wifely duty overcame her reluctance, and she rolled over towards him on to her back. Guy began to remove his pyjama bottoms as Katie hitched up her nightie, trying to suppress the disloyal thought that she hoped he wouldn't take too long about it.

Just as Guy manouevred himself on top of her, the telephone began to ring. He jerked his head in the direction of the sound, and she could see that he was torn between his gut instinct to answer it and his desire to continue what he and Katie had started. But she had little doubt which impulse would win out. Guy would never have the willpower to ignore a ringing telephone, not when it could be Mr Kassianides trying to reach him, or Henry Blackstone, or any one of a dozen other people he considered far too important to offend.

He rolled off her and grabbed the receiver. 'Hello.' He looked momentarily thrown by the voice at the other end, then he passed the phone over to Katie. 'It's for you.'

She frowned, wondering who could be calling her at such a time. But it was her father's voice that greeted her. 'I wanted to ask you,' he said, 'if you could possibly come and see me this morning before you go to work?'

Fear clutched at her heart. 'Why?'

'I'd rather not talk about it on the phone, if you don't mind.'

The fear tightened its grip. 'Shall I come to your rooms then?'

'No, I'm not going in today.'

Her father never took a day off work, except on the rare occasions when he had picked up some bug that might be infectious to his patients – and that time when Jemima had been lost in the southern seas. The fear became a heavy stone in the pit of Katie's stomach.

'I'll come to your flat, then, and call the library from there.'

She put the phone down and stared stupidly at it, for long seconds unable to move. From the bathroom came the every-day sounds of Guy splashing in the shower and the steady drone of the radio commentary. But Katie knew this wouldn't be just another normal day. She knew something had happened that would change their lives for ever.

The flat in Cumberland Terrace had French windows leading out on to a balcony, and a magnificent view over Regent's Park. Robin liked to have a feeling of space around him even though, unlike Fiona, he was rather fond of cityscapes.

Katie stood at one of these windows and looked out over the park. She had heard quite clearly the words her father had said to her, she had even grasped their meaning, but to take it in was completely beyond her. Her mind was quite simply blank with shock.

She gazed unseeingly at the park where she and Jemima had made so many childhood visits, Robin taking them to the zoo when they were little, and later to the Open Air Theatre to see *A Midsummer Night's Dream* and even a bit of light opera. They had felt so grown-up and sophisticated amidst all the adults, with Robin sitting proudly between them. Fiona wouldn't come up from Wiltshire even in those days. London excursions were always a treat from their father.

'Are you all right?' he said now, rather shakily, from his seat by the fireplace. But she couldn't trust herself to speak. You could try to prepare yourself for bad news, to protect yourself from the suffering, but in the end, when it came, you were never prepared, and there was nothing you could have done to prevent the pain.

He came to her then, and stood behind her with his strong arms round her waist. She had become so used, over the years, to those arms protecting her, keeping her warm and safe. But it was beyond even Robin's powers to defend her against this.

'Kitty-kat,' he said into her hair, 'can I ask you something? It's just, I don't know how I'm going to find the right words to explain this to your mother—'

'Don't worry,' she said automatically, because she had always done what was needed, even when she had no idea how she would find the strength herself. 'I'll tell Mummy. But there's something else I think we should do first.'

The pilot of the Twin Otter flew on a course due south towards the pole from the last recorded position of Jemima Fraser. There had been no contact with her for forty-eight hours, the lady radio operator had said, which was not, after all, such a very long time – he must be able to find her within a certain fixed radius.

As soon as he reached the coordinates given to him by the radio operator – the place where Jemima Fraser had been when she made her last transmission – he began to scan the ground below him very carefully, looking for any signs of life in the vast, unchanging whiteness below. She should not be very difficult to spot from the air, not if she was in her tent or travelling with those kites that would make little splashes of colour against the snow. The only way he would not spot her was if she had fallen – God forbid – down one of those terrible crevasses that lay hidden beneath the snow, waiting for the unwary.

But there was no reason to fear the worst, just because for two days there had been no message from her. Communications in the Antarctic could be a hit and miss affair, often interrupted by the conditions peculiar to the region – disturbances in the earth's magnetic field caused by strong solar flares or ionospheric storms. The Met Office said there had been a bad storm in the region. If she were sensible, Jemima Fraser would have sat safely in her tent, waiting it out.

The problem was, she didn't strike him as the sensible type. The pilot wasn't sure he approved of women setting off on their own on a dangerous exercise like crossing the Antarctic. It would never be encouraged in Chile – only in crazy countries like England and America and Norway, where they took this women's lib thing too far. Women were not suited to an undertaking that required such physical strength and rational planning. They were emotional, unpredictable – you never knew quite what they were going to do next.

Then he saw it, far below him – a break in the whiteness, the outline of what could be a sledge and a figure beside it. He couldn't tell from this height whether it was moving, but at least it was there.

Quickly he scanned the terrain and settled on the most suitable stretch of ice for a landing. There were many crevasses in the region, but he saw a good patch to the west with none of the warning blue shadows lurking beneath the surface.

When the pilot climbed out of his plane and approached what he could now see was definitely a human figure, he realised that it was indeed moving – in fact, it seemed to be waving frantically at him in a way that was quite the opposite of welcoming.

'Go away,' Jemima screamed. 'Go away!'

She had never been so angry in her life. She couldn't believe that, after her heroic battle for her life, after clawing her way out of certain disaster and surviving to fight on, her entire mission had been compromised by this stupid man coming to check whether she was all right when she deliberately hadn't asked for any assistance, because it would nullify all claim to have crossed the Antarctic solo and unsupported.

She just couldn't believe it. At least, if she had died in that crevasse, it would have been good reason for the end of all her hopes. Not that she would really have wanted such a death. When she came to and found herself bumping along on the icy ground, dragged relentlessly by the wind and the weight of the sledge, she had thought that this was it, finally the end, and there were so many things she hadn't said to her family back home, things she had learned about herself and them and wanted to share with them and now never would. And then, gradually, her old fighting spirit had struggled to the surface and she told herself there had to be a way out, she must try to see ahead so that she could assess the extent of her predicament. Her vision blurred, her head pounding, she dragged herself with the ropes of the kite towards the sledge and saw how they were snagged around it. Scrabbling with her hand in the back of the sledge, she pulled her ice axe loose and began hacking wildly at the ropes until, after what seemed like an eternity, she finally severed them and saw the parafoil plunge to earth. The speed at which they had been hurtling forward kept them moving for a while until the weight of the sledge finally slowed their momentum and they ground to a slow halt almost on the lip of a vast, gaping crevasse.

Jemima couldn't believe the narrowness of her escape. Taking no more chances, she dragged the sledge as far from the yawning hole as possible, and sat down to assess the damage to the kite lines. By hacking through them she had lost about twenty feet, but she could re-attach the shorter ropes to the handles and still be back in business – or she would have been, if this infuriating man hadn't arrived, sent, no doubt, by an over-anxious Vivian.

'I don't need help,' she shouted at him again. 'Go away.'

The pilot looked at the angry girl with her blazing eyes and wild curly hair. She had suffered some physical deterioration since he last saw her, but she had spirit, this one, and passion and fire. She would probably have made it, even though she was a woman. He felt a great sadness for her in his heart.

'Not you,' he said. 'London. Very bad news from London. You must go home straight away.'

'It's Jemima, isn't it?' Fiona said, her hand flying up to her mouth. 'I knew it, when there was no word—'

'It's not Jemima,' Katie said flatly. 'It's Daddy.'

She should have known that life had a nasty habit of springing its own cruel surprises, that disaster always struck from the quarter you least expected.

Fiona peered at her, confusion furrowing her brow. 'I don't understand—'

'He has cancer. He's dying, Mummy.'

'Your *father*.' Amidst the turmoil of emotions Katie saw crossing her mother's face, she could have sworn that one of them was relief.

'He says there's nothing to be done,' she said stiffly.

'How long?'

'At best – three weeks.'

'*Three weeks*,' Fiona cried. 'That can't be right.'

It was just what Katie had said, shouting to her father and the heavens themselves her non-acceptance of this horrible, insidious thing that had invaded their lives, caught them off-guard while their attention was focused elsewhere.

'I won't see Christmas, Kitty-kat, I'm sorry,' he had said, as though it were all his own fault. 'I'm so sorry.'

'But *why* is there nothing to be done?' Fiona demanded.

Katie supposed she would have to go through all the terrible practical details of it with her mother, as her father had done with her.

'It's disseminated lung cancer,' he had told her.

'*Lung* cancer. But you've never smoked,' Katie had cried in objection.

'Ironic, isn't it? I didn't know for a long time because the symptoms only manifest at a very late stage.'

He had described to her, then, how he found his hands shaking during routine surgery, and had to ask his assistant to take over. The headaches came soon afterwards.

'I had my suspicions so I went for a CT scan. It showed that the cancer had spread to the brain and it was the metastases – or secondary tumours – causing the headaches.'

'But surely in this day and age, with all the advances in cancer treatment, there's something they can do?' Katie had insisted, begging for a straw to clutch at.

The smile he gave her, full of the irony of his predicament, tore at her heart. 'I may be the patient now, but I'm also a doctor, my darling, and if there was any hope of a cure, I would know. I'm afraid it's a case of, "He helped others but he cannot help himself".'

He went to put his arms round her as though to shield her from the blow, and she leaned against him with a sort of horrified fascination, knowing that within him was a silent enemy that was busily turning his own body against itself. She put her head on his chest that had always seemed so strong and now would waste away till the ribs showed through the skin, and she was overcome with anger at the unfairness of it, at how little he deserved this hand he had been dealt, he who was the kindest of men, and the most cautious. It was Jemima who took all the risks, knowing the price she might be called upon to pay, and ready and willing to pay it if necessary. Why, then, was it not Jemima who would forfeit her life but Robin, who had never done anything foolhardy, never smoked or drunk to excess or even eaten the wrong foods?

There's no point being careful, Jemima always said, because disaster strikes anyway. But Katie had never really believed her, she had clung to her faith that if you made safe choices you could keep danger at bay. She had arranged around her, like reinforcements in battle, husband and children and father, never once imagining they could be felled by enemy fire. She had relied most of all on Robin because he had always been there for her, for as long as she could remember, so that it had seemed inconceivable to her that when disaster did strike, it would choose him as its victim.

Chapter Six

~

There was little that was different about Robin's bedroom, Katie thought, apart from the trim black nurse in a starched white uniform sitting by his bed. Yet somehow, after only a week, it had already acquired the smell of a hospital.

Robin had refused to go to a proper hospital, or to submit himself to treatment of any kind, apart from morphine for pain relief and steroids to take the pressure off his brain. He knew that the radiotherapy he had been offered would do nothing to halt the progress of his disease. He preferred, he said, to die with what dignity he had left, and in his own bed.

His deterioration had been as rapid as he had warned. The weight was dropping off him, his skin was sallow, and there were times when his mind was no longer lucid. Fiona blamed the morphine, having a natural suspicion of drugs of any kind, but perhaps she didn't want to face the potency of the enemy that was wreaking its own havoc inside her husband's brain.

Fiona had left her beloved Wiltshire to come and stay with Robin in Cumberland Terrace. It was ironic, Katie thought, that it had taken death to bring her here at last. Great aunt Flora was forced to accompany her because she couldn't be left alone, and now she occupied the third bedroom where she could be heard muttering about the lack of menfolk in the family – 'All women, too many women, and now this!'

Katie listened to the little flick-flick of the nurse's fingernail against the syringe as she prepared to administer Robin's morphine injection, and thought wearily that somewhere out there, outside this room where she had been sitting for days on end, people were going about their everyday lives, heading for work on the tube, and pushing round supermarket trolleys filled with the weekly grocery shop, and scouring the department stores for nick-nacks to fill Christmas stockings. It was impossible for Katie to imagine that such a normal world still existed.

Robin was sleeping now, after the efficient administration of his injection, his lashes resting against his hollow cheeks. Katie was glad he was so heavily medicated, relieved he had fewer waking hours to agonise about his fate. Silently she blessed the morphine and the peace it brought her father, longing sometimes for its oblivion herself.

There was a stirring outside the door, and then it opened and Jemima's face appeared around it, eyes wild in a strangely sunburned and blistered face. She looked almost as gaunt as Robin, and every bit as devastated as the permanent look Katie knew now haunted her own face.

Jemima's eyes moved to her father's still form beneath the bedclothes. 'Am I too late?' she whispered with a sort of suppressed desperation.

Katie made tea for everyone in the kitchen – just teabags in mugs, she had no energy for the niceties now – and noticed how they all ladled large spoons of sugar into it, as though the shock were still fresh.

When she had taken a cup in for the nurse, she returned to the kitchen to sit with her mother and sister and great aunt. They all looked dazed and lost, like refugees in a foreign land who don't yet know the language or the rules.

'What are we going to do,' great aunt Flora said, 'without a man at the helm?'

'That's not the point,' Jemima cried, but with none of the usual fight in her voice. 'It's losing a father . . . and a husband.' She gave Fiona's hand a squeeze of solidarity.

'There's never a good time to go,' aunt Flora said. 'Even at my age, there's never a good time.'

'It's watching him slide downhill like this,' Fiona said. 'I don't know how we're to bear it.'

'We must,' Katie said firmly, 'for his sake. We can't burden him with our own pain. We mustn't make him worry about how we'll manage when he's gone.'

Jemima hunched over her mug of tea. She had faced hardships over the past few weeks that the rest of them could scarcely imagine, yet she looked as though it was this illness of her father's that would be the undoing of her.

'I was never here,' she said in a hollow voice. 'Since I was a child, I've spent so little time with him.'

'You mustn't blame yourself for that,' Fiona protested at once. 'He wanted you to do what made you happy. He was so proud of you.'

She was talking about Robin in the past tense, Katie noticed, as though he had already ceased to exist.

Katie put an arm around her sister's shoulders. 'He didn't want us to send for you, you know. He said there was nothing you could do for him anyway, and he so much wanted you to achieve your dream.'

'There'll never be another chance for Jemima,' Robin had said. 'If she's made to pull out now, the Norwegian girl will be the one to set the record. There'll be no going back again next year.'

Jemima ran her fingers through her wild curly hair. 'There was a moment when I thought that too,' she confessed, 'but it didn't last. All that stuff about the record books seems so unimportant now. When I was alone in the Antarctic, struggling to stay alive, all I thought about was the family, all I really cared about was making it out of there so I could see you all again. Of course you were right to tell me, of course I had to see Daddy before—'

She turned away from Katie and buried her face in her mother's neck. 'I should have come home more often,' she sobbed, 'I should have made the time to be with him before this horrible thing—'

Fiona held her daughter tightly against her and stroked her hair, as though she were still a child. 'There, there,' she soothed, 'no one could have known.'

They were too absorbed in comforting one another to notice Katie quietly leaving and returning to the sick room.

There was no space in the flat in Cumberland Terrace for Katie to stay the night. Robin, of course, had a room to himself apart from the succession of bright-eyed, vigilant nurses sent by the agency, with the authority to administer the morphine. Fiona was sharing with Jemima, and she had put great aunt Flora in the only remaining single bedroom.

So Katie returned every night to the house in St John's Wood and supper with Guy. She supposed it wouldn't be fair, anyway, to leave him to fend entirely for himself. Robin's illness did not mean any less of a workload for Guy, who still needed his meals cooked and his suits sent to the dry cleaner if he was to function properly in court.

As she prepared the lamb chops with mint jelly, the new potatoes, the green beans, Katie sipped at her accustomed glass of red wine ('Doctor's orders,' Robin had said, 'if you want a long life' – oh Robin!) and tried to ignore the great void inside her that could be filled only by her father's presence. The house seemed so empty without his chatter to fill the silences. The knives and forks and spoons seemed to stare at her accusingly as though wondering why it was she laying them out in their accustomed places, instead of Robin. 'You'll have to get used to it,' she told them rather fiercely, 'and so will I.'

The front door slammed and Guy's footsteps echoed across the hallway. He was trying to get home earlier these days – at least in time for supper – and to bring less work back with him. Katie knew he was doing his best to give her support, but it was so long since he had spent his evenings in small talk or watching television, he seemed to have forgotten how. Soon he would be pacing anxiously, his brow furrowed in thought, and Katie would find herself wishing he would just go back to his study desk and whatever urgent case was on his mind and be done with it.

'How was your father today?' Guy asked as he did every evening.

'Not so good. He slept, mostly – hardly spoke at all.'

'Important for him to get his rest, I expect,' Guy said, sitting down with relish to his lamb chops. Katie picked at hers, not only because she had so little appetite. She had never really cared for plain English cooking. Still, she would have to develop a taste for it, she supposed, now that it was only her and Guy. She couldn't see herself going to all the bother of making a Thai curry for one.

'Jemima arrived today,' she told Guy.

'How did she feel about giving up Antarctica?'

'She says it's not at all important. She's feeling terribly guilty about not seeing enough of Daddy before this happened.'

'She wouldn't have listened, though, if anyone had told her that before. She'd have bitten their heads off.'

'I suppose so—' Katie took a deep breath. 'Guy, I want us to take the girls out of school early.'

They had been told, of course, about their grandfather's illness, but not how serious it was. Katie had agreed with Guy's suggestion that they should put off the moment of truth, wait until it became absolutely necessary. They would know soon enough, she had told herself, with the Christmas holidays looming.

'It's just that the way things are going, I'm just not sure he'll make it till school's officially over,' Katie whispered.

'I thought we'd made up our minds on this,' Guy said with a trace of impatience. 'I thought we'd decided not to alarm them.'

'It was seeing Jemima's reaction today that made me realise we may have been wrong. She said she would've been devastated if nobody'd told her, she wouldn't have been able to live with it if she hadn't seen Daddy before he gets too bad to know the difference.'

Guy chewed thoughtfully. 'I'm still not convinced,' he said. 'Isn't it a bit morbid for them to be at a deathbed – aren't they better off at school?'

'No!' Katie almost shouted. 'They're better off knowing the truth because they'll have to face it sooner or later. They're better off being surrounded by family who can help them through their grief.'

'Katie, I know you're upset, but there's no need to take it out on me. I'm only trying to do what's best for the girls.'

It was Guy's way of backing down gracefully. Now all Katie had to do was make him see that he must take the time off work to drive down to Wolton Abbey. Katie didn't want to leave her father, not even for an afternoon, just in case.

'He's having a good day – jabbering away like a jackdaw,' the trim black nurse told Katie. Her name was Harmony and the smile that came so readily to her face showed neat little evenly spaced white teeth. She was Robin's decided favourite.

Katie entered the sick room to find Robin propped up on his pillows, gossiping away with great aunt Flora.

His face lit up when he saw Katie. 'Have a seat, darling. Aunt Flora was just telling me all about "that dreadful woman" Wallis Simpson.'

'They say she learned her tricks in an eastern brothel,' aunt Flora said darkly. 'But if I know the Prince – and I did – it was more of a psychological hold she had over him, like some dominatrix.'

Robin's eyes widened in mock horror. 'You mean whips and thigh-length boots?'

'I wouldn't know about all that,' aunt Flora replied with exaggerated primness. 'I only know he let her call all the shots – most undignified for a man in his position!'

'Ah, but once she was through with him, he had no position,' Robin pointed out wryly.

Flora shook her head sadly, and indicated to Nurse Harmony that she was rather tired now and would like to be helped back to her room. Robin told the nurse that she could take her tea break after that, as there were things he wanted to discuss in private with his daughter.

'I've been a lucky man, haven't I?' he said when the door had closed behind them. 'Surrounded by all my women.'

Katie smiled at him. 'Guy's fetching the girls from school today.'

The trembling of his hands had grown worse over the days and, as though embarrassed by it, he gripped the bedclothes in an effort to stop them.

'You mustn't worry so much about Lucy,' he said. 'She'll be all right in the end, you know. It's a rocky path, adolescence, but she's got your example, and Guy's, to show her the way.'

'I know, she also tells me I should trust her more, and she's right.'

'If anything, the one to keep an eye on is little Hannah. She keeps everything bottled up inside – just like you do. But Lucy may have more of you in her than you think. She's not just a carbon copy of Jemima.'

Robin smiled, a distant smile that seemed to be focusing already on another world. 'I've had such wonderful talks with Jemima – and your mother. Sad that it's taken this to make us really open up to each other.'

He turned to look at her, and he seemed to be making an effort to come back, for the time being at least, from that faraway place. 'Now it's *our* turn to have a chat.'

'We've always done that,' Katie said simply.

'I know. But for all that I've left too many things unsaid, and there isn't much time left to say them.'

Katie took his hand. The skin was almost translucent, the blue veins clearly visible beneath.

'I feel I haven't always given my girls the guidance they needed,' he said.

'Oh Daddy, that's just not true—'

He held up a hand to quiet her. 'Let me have my say, Kitty-kat . . . I still believe you have to give your children the space to do what they choose with their lives, but perhaps what they choose isn't always what they really want. That's where I could have been more help.'

He paused, and squeezed her hand with his, but there was little strength left in it.

'Did Jemima really want to keep on risking her life, trying to prove something over and over again to herself or the world or us, worrying your mother half to death? Sometimes, now, I wonder.'

He looked quizzically at Katie.

'And you, my Kitty-kat, you've devoted your life to your family and that's a good thing, an admirable thing, but what about your own dreams? You've let us all rely on you, take advantage of your good nature – even your mother does that. Oh, I know she treats Jemima like the favourite, and I also know how much it sometimes hurts you – but at the end of the day, she depends on you more than she knows herself.'

He let a little silence fall, as though to give time for his words to sink in, then he went on, 'You've always been the elder, the sensible one, because Jemima didn't want the job. But it doesn't mean you have to take on all the things she rejected. It doesn't mean you can't be irresponsible too, just once in a while. Now I want you to promise me something.'

She nodded, not trusting herself to speak.

'Promise me you'll live for yourself too, just a little, when I'm gone.'

Katie gave him a wan smile of reassurance, but she couldn't really imagine a life when he was no longer there. He had a serenity about him now that was not of this world, and she knew he was almost ready to take his leave – but she wasn't ready yet to let him go.

There was a discreet knock at the door. As it opened, Robin wagged a finger, preparing to scold Nurse Harmony for the interruption. But it was Fiona's face that appeared, her greying auburn hair pinned into its neat bun even in the midst of this crisis.

'Your solicitor's here to see you, dear.'

Robin smiled as though at some private joke. 'You'll have to leave us, darling,' he said to Katie, 'while Mr Harkness pays his last respects.'

Five days before Christmas Robin slipped into a coma. He had explained gently but firmly to his family what the various stages of his deterioration would be, leading to the coma from which he would never awake. It wasn't the worst way to go, he had said, just a slow, quiet draining of the life from his body. By then he would be beyond knowing or caring.

Until this moment Katie and the girls had been practically living in Cumberland Terrace, going home only to eat and sleep. Guy had made several dutiful visits armed with *pâté de foie gras* and Belgian chocolates which Robin was too tactful to point out he could no longer stomach. Lucy, incapable of hiding her emotions, had been weeping buckets, even in Robin's presence, but he assured her he didn't mind in the least and it was healthy to have a good cry. Hannah was quiet and stoical but alarmingly pale.

Looking at Robin lying heavy against freshly laundered pillows in the deep slumber from which he would never awake, Katie tried to remind herself that they were lucky to have had so many chances already to say their goodbyes to him. She had always thought it must be so much more difficult if someone you loved died suddenly, like in a road accident. When Jemima's boyfriend was lost in the Southern Ocean, his family didn't even have a body to bury.

But now that the moment was upon them, Katie realised that death was no more welcome just because it was expected. You still tried to hold off the moment of its coming because you didn't want to face the terrible fact of for ever.

She needed to get away from the waiting, just for a little while. She stood unsteadily and went out to the sitting room to check on the girls. Guy, whose rooms were closed for Christmas, was playing Chinese checkers with them, to keep them from the deathbed vigil. Lucy looked up at her mother, eyes widening in alarm, and Katie quickly said, 'No change yet.'

Dr Butler had been round earlier, summoned by Nurse Harmony who, realising Robin's fondness for her, had worked as many days as she could manage. Katie was eternally grateful to her for lighting up her father's last days, and taking away so much of his pain. The doctor fussed over Robin for a while, monitoring his vital signs, but there was nothing much he could do. The coma could last quite a while – twenty-four or even forty-eight hours, he said. He had other patients to see to, but they should call him at once if there was any change.

In the event, it was over by the afternoon. Robin, surrounded by all his women, gave a sudden gasp, fighting for the last breath he would ever take, and then the struggle was over. His eyes never opened, so Nurse Harmony didn't have to close them again. She bound up his slackened jaw with a bit of white surgical tape.

It was too soon to let go. They took it in turns to sit on either side of him, holding his limp hands. Fiona and Jemima bowed their heads and wept over him like two old women. Great aunt Flora keened in a corner, her head covered by the black lace shawl. Katie stood behind her daughters, hands placed comfortingly on their heaving shoulders as each of them sobbed their final goodbyes to their grandfather, Guy hovering awkwardly in the background. By the time Katie bent to kiss Robin's forehead, it was already starting to go cold.

She left him, the others still crowding round him, and went to phone the doctor so that he could come and pronounce officially what they already knew, that Robin was dead, and write out the certificate. It would all be practicalities now. She dialled the funeral parlour her father had specified, having some experience of these matters. They expressed their condolences – strangers the first to do it – and said they would be there as soon as traffic and other obligations permitted.

Fiona made only one phone call – to the vicar – though she and Robin had never been regular church-goers. When Dr Butler had finished his business, the vicar asked the family to join hands in prayer, and he read to them a passage about Lazarus rising from the dead as all who believe in Christ will rise, and Hannah looked up with a dazed expression, as though expecting to see her grandfather hovering somewhere above the bed, while Katie, who *was* a regular church-goer, tried to rid herself of the horrible notion that Robin was simply gone, extinguished like a light, and the rest was nothing more than wishful thinking.

He would belong to them for only a few minutes more, until the undertakers came. Jemima didn't seem to want to let go of his hand. Fiona held Jemima's, and patted it ineffectually from time to time. When the doorbell rang Katie told them they should all leave the room now, they shouldn't stay to watch the body being taken, it would be too distressing. Guy gently prised Jemima's fingers from her father's hand, and herded them all out, except for Nurse Harmony who was capably straightening Robin's limbs before the rigor mortis set in.

When Katie had shown the men from the funeral parlour where to go, she went to join her family in the sitting room. They had the look of shell-shock victims, sipping the brandies Guy had poured for them (aunt Flora had requested a double), trying to ignore the noises across the hall. But it was impossible to block out the creaking of the trolley wheels as they crossed the wooden floor to the front door.

'I never knew it would be this painful,' Jemima cried. 'He was so sweet to me at the end, he forgave me completely for never being there.'

'I told him I was so sorry I never stayed with him in London, but he wouldn't hear of me feeling guilty about it,' Fiona said brokenly.

There had been words of absolution from Robin for both

wife and daughter, expressed with the generosity brought on by approaching death. But they seemed to feel their suffering was greater because of their regrets. And Katie, who had nothing to reproach herself with as far as her father was concerned, was tempted to tell them, in a sudden burst of anger she had to force herself to conceal, that it didn't make her any less stricken than they were by his loss.

The funeral had to take place on Christmas Eve because, as Mr Pringle at the undertakers tactfully put it, 'the deceased should not be left until after Christmas'.

For three days Katie sat at her father's desk in Cumberland Terrace and wrote notices for the papers and telephoned Robin's friends and colleagues and arranged organist and soloist and order of service. She tried to consult her mother about the choice of hymns but Fiona had given in to her grief in a way Katie couldn't afford to, not yet, and she seemed content to surrender all responsibility for Robin's funeral to Katie, as she had so often left him to the company of his daughter in his lifetime.

Jemima was even less to be relied upon for assistance. She was swallowing a succession of little pills to prop her up during the day and others to make her sleep at night, and alternated between a trance-like state and total oblivion. Dr Butler said it was partly the effects of her journey, the exhaustion and total solitude and lack of food followed so abruptly by the forced return to London, the need to face people and tragic events, and no halfway house in between to accustom her to the change. Dr Butler suggested they place as few demands on Jemima as possible, and Fiona was fiercely determined to implement his instructions. She guarded her bedroom door when Jemima was sleeping, or sat on the sofa with arms entwined around her and Lucy and Hannah, while they drew from each other the comfort Katie didn't have time to share.

Great aunt Flora refused to have any truck with funerals, saying she didn't want to be reminded that her own was too close for comfort. No one asked Katie how she was holding up. They seemed to assume she would cope with the Herculean task of organising the church service, without assistance, to everyone's satisfaction. Guy was sporadically helpful but often tied up with the girls, taking them to the cinema or friends' houses to keep their spirits up. Katie was grateful to be relieved of that task at least.

Hannah had said to her one morning, 'If Adam and Eve hadn't eaten the apple, would grandpa still have had to die?' And Katie, who had never been comfortable with the concept, had answered lamely, 'Perhaps we should ask the vicar,' and felt guilty afterwards for not providing the proper consolation when the opportunity presented itself.

But she was so tired, so completely worn out by the need to keep going until everything was done as her father would have wished it. Her mind kept leaping crazily back to the months of elaborate planning that had gone into her formal church wedding to Guy, when her father had led her proudly up the aisle to 'give her away' ('nasty expression', he had said, 'I shall do no such thing'), and now she was having to arrange this other equally important ceremony in only three days of frantic and inadequate phone calls.

But in the end it was all accomplished somehow and the church in Regent's Park was almost full – despite being the day before Christmas – of well-known surgeons and their well-dressed wives, who must have postponed setting out for their country houses, or perhaps come back up especially for the service. Either way it was very gratifying, Guy said, and a suitable mark of respect for his father-in-law's position.

But Katie, sitting amidst her family in the front pew, was conscious of little besides the coffin just a few feet away from them, draped in black velvet with a huge spray of white lilies on top. Katie had decided to cover it because the coffin itself was simple pine, Robin having requested a cremation. He preferred his remains to be scattered freely, he had said, not imprisoned beneath hard earth.

'I don't like it, Mummy, it's scarier than in books,' Hannah had said when she had seen the bare coffin, holding tightly on to her mother's hand. Both the girls were wearing their navy blue school coats, since Lucy possessed so few respectable items of clothing apart from her uniform. People didn't really stick to black any more for funerals, Katie had noticed on her way in, though Guy had insisted that it was still the proper thing. She herself was wearing a black and white hound's-tooth check suit that Robin had bought her the Christmas before. There would be no gift from him tomorrow beneath the tree, nor in the long years to come . . .

Jemima, rejecting her exotic silks, had borrowed a plain brown dress from Fiona that made her look almost unrecognisable, like a distant relative whose face no one could quite place. Great aunt Flora was huddled in her black lace shawl, like some ancient Italian crone.

They made their way through the Order of Service that Katie knew by heart, but she felt oddly outside it all, as though the whole thing were happening to someone else, and Robin might walk in at any moment and ask why they were all looking so glum. Only when the soloist burst into 'Amazing Grace', her pure soprano filling the hushed spaces and bringing out the goosebumps on the back of Katie's neck, did the tears begin to flow, washing away her sense of unreality and with it her self-control.

'You must try and bear up,' Guy whispered, 'for the reception line.'

Everyone shook their hands on the way out of the church. Everyone murmured something kind. Katie, who had collected herself again, stood with a straight back and a word of thanks for each, while Guy nodded his approval.

There had been an announcement in church that the guests were expected for tea at Cumberland Terrace. A caterer had been hired, at Guy's insistence – the one he required Katie to use when they were holding a dinner party for 'people who mattered'. Katie was often tempted to say that if you invited people to dinner in the first place then they must, of course, matter to you, or why bother to ask them at all?

But she knew he was right not to entrust the food arrangements to Fiona, and Katie hadn't had the time to make anything herself, so it was a relief when cheerful Edwina from the home counties arrived with perfectly sliced sandwiches and heavy fruitcakes and fluffy scones with strawberry jam and Devon clotted cream, all beautifully laid out on platters and covered in clingfilm. And now she was helping to hand them out while Lucy, in a sudden uncharacteristic fit of co-operativeness, offered side plates with little folded paper napkins. Katie poured the tea.

'It's Kathryn, isn't it?' a smoothly tanned, silver-haired man said as he accepted a cup from her hand.

'That's right.'

'I'm Dr Brett-Jones. Played tennis with your father. You were quite a favourite topic of conversation with him, you know.'

She tried to smile. 'Did he show you the family snapshots?'

'Nothing so dull. He told us all about Jemima's adventures, but the one he spoke most highly of was you.'

'I haven't done anything very interesting to deserve it,' Katie protested, passing him the sugar.

Dr Brett-Jones touched her fingers lightly. 'I think he loved you more for what you are than for what you've done.' He waved the sugar away. 'But he also believed you have hidden depths. Whenever I asked after you, he used to give me a wink and say, "Watch this space".'

'I don't know about that,' Katie said, at once touched and embarrassed. 'He always gave me more credit than I was due.'

'He also said you have too little faith in yourself.'

Dr Brett-Jones moved on, making way for the other guests in the tea queue. Katie's hands, as she poured, were trembling.

'Watch what you're doing, my girl,' great aunt Flora grumbled when it came to her turn. 'I prefer my tea in the cup, not the saucer, thank you all the same.'

Fiona was seated in a corner, accepting the tributes due to

her position as grieving widow. Guy was circulating, playing the host. The odd phrase floated across to Katie: ' . . . a fitting tribute . . .', ' . . . grateful for your attendance . . .' She glanced over to see Jemima by the fireplace, surrounded by an admiring group of older men pressing her for details of her exploits in the Antarctic. Lucy had given up handing out plates and was hovering nearby, hanging on her every word.

The one your father spoke most highly of was you, Dr Brett-Jones had told her. But perhaps it was only her father who had seen her in that light.

Katie poured yet another cup of tea, smiled another perfunctory smile, and wished they would all just go home. She was afraid the intrusion of so many people might drive away the last lingering traces of Robin that still clung about the place where he had lived and laughed and suffered and breathed his last.

Christmas was just something to be got through, between the funeral and the scattering of the ashes. No one could face church again because of its associations with the day before. No one was in the mood for carols or tidings of comfort and joy.

The family had arranged to meet for a quiet lunch at Katie's house, without champagne or crackers or silly hats. Even opening gifts would have seemed in poor taste, and the adults had agreed to give presents only to Lucy and Hannah, who unwrapped them in their bedrooms because there was no tree with electric candles and ribbons and fat Santas to put them beneath. Katie wondered if Christmas without Robin would ever feel quite like Christmas again.

Though lunch would be a muted affair, the preparations were still hard work, but Katie was glad to have something to keep her mind occupied. Guy was trying to play his part in the kitchen, doing his best to fill her father's shoes. Katie tried not to notice how he pushed the chairs around to disguise the empty place where Robin should have sat, or how clumsily he laid out the knives and forks, not in neat, even rows as Robin would have done.

'Do you think your mother would like some assistance in sorting out the practicalities of the will?' Guy enquired, breaking the heavy silence.

Katie remembered how Fiona had burst into tears when Robin's bank manager had instructed her to cut up his credit cards. 'I know he won't be needing them any more but it seems so brutal, so . . . final,' she had wept.

'I'm sure she'd appreciate whatever you can do,' Katie said to Guy.

'Well, then, if you get the go-ahead from her, I'll pay a visit to your father's solicitor.'

She knew she wasn't showing enough appreciation for the way he was trying to help, but somehow she just couldn't make the effort. 'Thank you, Guy,' she said flatly.

When Katie finally called everyone to the table, no one seemed tempted by the turkey or disposed for conversation. Jemima was anxious only for some water to take her pills. Lucy fidgeted, saying she wanted to eat quickly so she could phone some of her schoolfriends. The urgency on her face made Katie wonder if she really wanted to escape to her room to hear whispered words of comfort down the line from Tom Blackstone. Great aunt Flora refused to leave her armchair by the fire, pronouncing that her arthritis was playing up. In the end Katie suggested the unthinkable for a Christmas lunch – that they should all just help themselves to however much or little they wanted and eat on trays in front of the television.

They watched *The Sound of Music* for the 'trillionth time', as Lucy said with disgust, disappearing as soon as she could. Those who remained were relieved not to have to make any small talk. Afterwards, when Katie was clearing up, she thought that unless she found some hungry stray cats, they would be eating turkey sandwiches until next Christmas.

At last darkness fell and the awkward day was over. Fiona and Jemima and great aunt Flora returned to Cumberland

Terrace with visible relief. Katie saw them off, feeling much the same way, and fell into bed to sleep for a solid, forgetful twelve hours.

It was the day after the ashes had been scattered in the Garden of Remembrance beside the old stone church in Fiona's Wiltshire village, the day after Katie's final farewell to the earthly remains of her father, that Guy came back from his meeting with Mr Harkness looking rather disconcerted.

'What is it?' Katie said. 'Surely there aren't any problems with the will?'

'Not exactly. That is, everything's quite in order, technically speaking.'

'Then why do you look so . . . disapproving?'

Guy sat down heavily on the sofa beside her. 'Katie,' he said, 'there are some aspects of your father's will that may come as something of a surprise to you. In fact, to put it bluntly, Robin has made some bequests that I consider downright peculiar.'

Chapter Seven

Though it was called a 'Garden' of Remembrance, the area in which Robin's ashes now lay was no more than a large paved courtyard adjacent to the church and reached through one of its side doors. But it was pretty, in a quiet way, Katie thought as she sat on the single wrought-iron bench provided for the bereaved and looked around at the potted blooms left by families of the deceased, the trellises with orderly climbing plants, the sparkle of pale sunlight off the water of the stone fountain.

She had driven down to Wiltshire in search of answers, as though by sitting here alone with Robin she might receive some sign from him, some clue as to what he had meant by the last will he had written, in the weeks of his illness, drawn up 'with indecent haste', Guy had said, by Mr Harkness, and witnessed by nurse Harmony and great aunt Flora.

The lilies that had covered his coffin now lay wilting in a corner beneath the simple bronze plaque that sometimes seemed to be all that remained of her wise and witty and warm-hearted father. 'Dr Robin Michael Fraser, heart surgeon, husband and father, In Loving Memory...'

'Your father has made some bequests that I consider downright peculiar,' Guy had said to her the day before in London.

'What do you mean?'

'Well, he's left some cash to all of you – that's as it should be

121

– but I can't see why you're the only one who hasn't inherited any property in England.'

'Didn't he leave all that to Mummy?'

'No. She gets the house in Wiltshire, of course. But she never showed any interest in the flat in Cumberland Terrace, did she?' Guy paused, as though he could hardly bear to utter the words out loud. 'Now your father has left it to Jemima.'

'Oh, I see . . .'

'Well, *I* don't. Where was Jemima when you were cooking his meals and keeping him company? As a daughter you could hardly have done more for him, and she could hardly have done less. I would have thought *you* were the one who deserved Cumberland Terrace.'

Katie looked around her at the drawing room the decorator had worked so hard to turn into a showcase for Guy's success. 'Perhaps Daddy thought I didn't need it and Jemima did.'

'It's hardly your fault if you and I have worked harder than Jemima to make a success of our lives. Why should you be punished for that?'

'Guy,' Katie said wearily, 'I really don't mind if Jemima gets the flat. Daddy must have had his reasons and I think we should respect them.'

Guy threw her a sceptical look. 'It's the injustice of it,' he said, 'and the waste. What's Jemima going to do with a flat in London? She's never stayed in one place long enough to have her name put on a doorbell.'

'Then maybe it's time she did,' Katie said firmly.

Guy got up to mix himself a whisky and soda. Without asking, he poured a second, weaker one for his wife. 'I don't know,' he said. 'Maybe your father was too ill when he wrote that last will, maybe he wasn't in his right mind—'

'I'm sure he knew exactly what he was doing,' Katie said, a warning note creeping into her voice, 'and I wouldn't dream of challenging it anyway.'

'Well, no, I suppose not . . . but you can hardly blame me

for wondering. You know what he left you? Some rundown guesthouse in the Florida Keys.'

Katie gripped her glass and stared at Guy.

'Don't know what he expected you to do with a place halfway across the world – or what he was doing with it himself, for that matter.'

'He inherited it from a grateful patient.'

'Ah, so you knew about it,' Guy said almost accusingly.

'He only mentioned it once. I thought he was going to sell it.'

'And so he should have. I've had a look at the books. The place hardly breaks even – it's a white elephant. You should get rid of it as soon as possible.'

'But Daddy wanted me to have it.'

'For heaven's sake, Katie, I'm sure he expected you to sell it off, just like he intended to.'

But then why hadn't he? Katie asked herself now, trying to hear Robin's voice in the whisper of wind through the foliage in the garden. Why had Robin held on to this foreign guesthouse which he had never set eyes on and which had meant nothing to him, and then made a gift of it to her? While Jemima would have the home he had lived in, where the memories still lingered.

She stared at the bronze plaque, willing it to give her the answers. But it remained as silent as this garden of the dead, keeping its buried secrets.

They should clear out Robin's things as soon after the funeral as possible, Fiona had said, so they could all get on with the business of facing the future. The future for Fiona would be back to the house in Wiltshire with great aunt Flora, back to her dogs and horses and fields and the life she had always known. The future for Fiona would be more of the past, the only changes the inevitable ones wrought by time and age and failing health. But for Jemima it might be something else entirely.

'It seems so completely strange that this flat belongs to me now,' she said as she helped Fiona pack Robin's suits into the cardboard boxes that would be taken down later to the charity shop in the High Street.

Katie ran her hand over a dark green cashmere sweater that had been Robin's favourite. She hated to think of it being fingered and bargained over by strangers.

'If there's anything Guy might like, help yourself,' Fiona said.

Katie shook her head. She didn't think she could bear to see Guy wearing her father's intensely familiar things.

'You're not upset, are you – about Daddy leaving all this to me?' Jemima demanded.

'No,' Katie assured her, 'I'm not.'

'If there are any pieces of his furniture you want, just say so.'

The will had stipulated that Jemima should have the flat in Cumberland Terrace with all its contents. Guy had catalogued in his mind the antique mahogany dining table with twelve matching chairs and the Baedecker sofa in the sitting room and the eighteenth-century gaming table Robin had used as a desk, and had been in a silent fury for days.

'Thanks, but Guy and I don't need any more furniture,' Katie said firmly.

'I'm not sure I need it either,' Jemima confessed in a rather bewildered voice. 'I mean, I've never owned more than a sleeping bag before.'

'Have you decided whether you're going to live here?'

'Oh, no . . . I'm not ready to make any major decisions yet.'

'Quite right,' Fiona agreed. 'There's no rush.'

Dr Butler had counselled them all to take things one step at a time. You shouldn't make any big changes straight after a bereavement, he had said, not for at least the first six months.

Fiona was starting now on Robin's rows of polished leather shoes. Katie's eyes swept down the line to his green Wellingtons at the end, still caked in country mud, and she had to blink away a sudden rush of tears.

'I mean, I'm not sure I'd be any good at actually *living* somewhere like this – all bricks and mortar and solid citizenship,' Jemima was saying. 'Next thing I'd be on the voters' roll and joining the local residents' association – and before I knew it, I wouldn't even recognise myself in the mirror.'

'But life is about change, isn't it?' Katie said gently. 'So is death.'

'What are you going to do about that ridiculous place in Florida?' Fiona said.

'I'm not in a rush to decide anything either.'

'I suppose it's some ghastly tourist trap.'

Katie rather suspected it was too. Florida for her conjured up only two images: the high-rise hotels of Miami Beach, and the plastic playground of Disney World.

'The Keys aren't exactly Florida,' Jemima explained, 'though they're part of the state. They're actually a string of islands, connected to the mainland by this incredibly long road with dozens of bridges.'

'Is it rather exotic, then?' Katie asked, a little hope creeping into her voice.

'I doubt it. It's probably marginally better than the rest of Florida, but I suspect far too over-developed for my tastes. Still, more up my alley than yours, I would have thought. I'm amazed Daddy didn't leave that one to me and give you and Guy the desirable residence in London. Think we should swap?'

'I think we should stick with what Daddy wanted.'

'OK, but don't say I didn't offer.'

Guy would be furious if he knew what she had just turned down, Katie thought, but she had no intention of telling him.

Fiona packed in the last of the shoes and neatly labelled the cardboard box – 'so we don't put those poor voluntary workers to too much trouble,' she said.

'Are there any personal mementos you want, dear?' she asked Katie.

Katie let her eyes wander round the room, and heard in her mind her father's voice reading the stories of Oscar Wilde to her and Jemima as they lay tucked in bed beneath goose down duvets in their chilly Wiltshire bedroom. How she had wept for the Happy Prince and his little friend the Swallow.

'Perhaps just a few of his books,' she said.

'Oh good, go and take whatever you want,' Jemima said as though eager to be relieved of the guilt of too many blessings.

'Do you need me to carry on helping you here?'

'Not at all,' Fiona said briskly. 'We've got it all under control.'

Katie wandered through to Robin's study and trailed her fingers along the bookshelves. She found the Oscar Wilde, and the tattered copy of *Corpus Hippocraticum* that was, her father said, the physician's Bible. The rest she left undisturbed.

She let herself quietly out of the front door. She doubted her mother and sister would even notice she had gone.

Katie sat in the solemn hush of the reference library with an illustrated guide to Key West open on the table in front of her. Opposite her was a boy about Lucy's age, surrounded by books and scribbling frantically in a lined notepad.

Legend had it, she read, that two warring tribes of Native American Indians had waged a final battle on the southern-most island of the Keys. Spanish conquistadors found the island littered with human bones, and named it Cayo Hueso (pronounced KY-o WAY-so) or Island of the Bones, which later Bahamian settlers anglicised to Key West.

'Heavens,' Katie thought, 'how fierce!'

The island's later history was a racy one of piracy and wrecking. So successful were the inhabitants at salvaging the cargo of distressed Spanish treasure galleons that met their doom on the barrier coral reefs hugging their shores (some say they lured these ships on to the rocks themselves by changing or removing navigational lights) that Key West became the richest city per capita in the United States. But with the construction of more lighthouses along the shores, the wrecking industry faded, to be replaced by sponging and cigar-making introduced by Cuban immigrants.

Then, Katie read, one man changed the history of the Keys forever. Henry Flagler, a wealthy New York businessman, dreamed of a railroad that would extend beyond Miami and connect the mainland to the deep water port of Key West. Though many people perceived it as an old man's folly, construction was begun on this mammoth railway line that would have to span one hundred and twenty eight miles of rock island and open water, the longest bridge stretching for seven miles. The dream became reality at a cost of over fifty million dollars and seven hundred lives, and in 1912 Henry Flagler, then eighty-two, rode his private luxury railcar all the way to Key West and entered a hero. Trade with the Caribbean increased and Key West flourished. Henry Flagler died the following year, never to know that his engineering triumph would be swept away by a devastating hurricane that hit the Upper and Middle Keys in 1935.

She was enjoying this, Katie thought. It read rather like the plot of a swashbuckling historical saga.

But there was little to come that compared with the island's colourful past. The railroad was replaced by a modern concrete highway, and Key West was gradually tamed, developed and turned into a naval base and popular tourist destination.

Katie snapped the book shut with a sense of anti-climax. The island had probably become exactly what everyone had warned her – an over-developed tourist trap.

The boy opposite her had put his head down on his notepad and his regular breathing was interspersed with the odd snore. Smiling, Katie rose to return the guidebook to its shelf. It was probably one she had classified herself, though it would have meant nothing to her at the time.

'Sweet dreams,' she murmured as she edged carefully past the sleeping boy.

* * *

Kevin Sweeney, Katie's immediate superior, tried to arrange his features into an expression that conveyed his sympathy and understanding, but she had the feeling this wasn't a situation he had encountered before and he hadn't had sufficient practice to get it right.

They were sitting, for privacy, in his private office, although Katie wasn't sure it merited the name, being separated from the general areas only by partition walls. What's more, having no window, it lacked any view at all, not even of Katie's basement alley.

'This leave of absence you want,' Kevin said, twiddling a pencil between his fingers, 'would that be holiday?'

Katie shook her head. If she took her holiday time now, she wouldn't be left with enough to spend the summer break with the girls. 'Compassionate leave,' she said firmly.

'Of course, we're all very sorry about your father,' Kevin said uneasily. She knew he was mentally flipping through the employment manual, trying to remember the library's statutory obligations towards an employee who had suffered a death in the family.

'I have some things to sort out regarding the will,' she said, hoping to prod him to a decision. He was probably weighing up whether bending the rules for her might open the floodgates.

'Bartholomew on the public desk has some cataloguing experience,' Kevin said tentatively. 'I suppose we could shuffle everyone round a bit and hold the fort.'

'I'd be incredibly grateful.' Katie tried to suppress the little twinge of guilt she felt at placing this extra burden on her colleagues. But this was something she had to do, whatever the consequences. 'Promise me you'll live for yourself too, just a little, when I'm gone,' her father had said, and she was going to keep her word to him.

Kevin studied her anxiously. 'You *will* let us know if you decide not to come back?'

She gave him a wry smile. 'I'm only asking for two weeks.'

'Two weeks it is, then.'

As Katie emerged from his office, Marigold hissed, 'Well, did you get it?'

Katie gave her a thumbs up.

Marigold shook her head. 'Why is the chicken going to Key West?'

'I don't know the answer to that one.'

'That's a pity. Nor do I.'

Katie gave her a lighthearted wave and headed upstairs to the lending library. There would be more tempting reading matter for her to mull over at her leisure, at home, in section 919 for travel guides.

'I'm going to Key West,' Katie announced to Guy over plates of grilled chicken and mashed potato.

'Don't be ridiculous. There's no need.'

'But I *want* to. Besides, I'd like to see this guesthouse I own before I decide what to do with it.'

'There's no decision to be made,' Guy said tartly. 'You should sell it.'

'You're probably right, but there's no harm in looking.'

Guy eyed her with something like exasperation. 'What difference will that make? There's no point hanging on to something that doesn't even make a profit.'

'Maybe there's a reason for that. Perhaps I could do something about it—'

'Really? And what do you know about the hotel business?'

Katie put her knife and fork together over the half-eaten pile of mashed potato and pushed her plate aside. 'I feel guilty about not going before. Daddy asked me to once, with him, and I said I couldn't . . . I didn't know there'd never be another chance.'

Guy gave her hand a brief pat. 'Nobody could have known.'

'But maybe it's a lesson, Guy. You should take whatever opportunities you're offered in life, because you never know what's going to happen.'

'I wouldn't go reading too much into the situation,' Guy said dourly.

'I'd like to get away, anyway. I need the break.'

'Then why not go back with your mother to Wiltshire for a while?'

'A *break*, Guy – away from family and . . . everything.'

Guy peered at her closely, as though seeing for the first time something he hadn't noticed before and didn't much like. 'Well, I can understand that, I suppose – but *Key West*. Where the hell is it, anyway?'

'It's a small island at the tip of the Florida boot, near Cuba. It's actually closer to Havana than Miami.'

'Aren't you worried about going somewhere like that on your own? You don't know anyone there . . . you've never been that far away before.'

'Exactly,' Katie said.

Katie decided to drive down to Wolton Abbey to tell the girls in person, in case they didn't react well to the news that she was going away, on her own, for the first time since they were born.

'It's not as though you'll be on the moon,' Lucy said across a cup of tea in the little sitting room the house mistress had allocated for their chat.

'Your father's behaving as though I will be,' Katie said wryly.

'Daddy's so square. He hasn't even joined the jet age, let alone the space age. America *is* the first world, after all – they *do* have telephones.'

'Will you see Mickey Mouse?' Hannah said.

'It's not in the same part of Florida as Disneyworld.'

'Oh.' Hannah seemed to lose interest.

'I know you won't be able to use your phone cards to reach me there, but I'll call you – every day, if you like.'

'Don't be so dramatic, Mummy,' Lucy said. 'It's not like you call us every day from home.'

Katie looked from Lucy's scornful face to Hannah's placid

one. 'OK, I'll phone every few days, but if something happens you want to tell me about, just let Daddy know and he'll pass the message on to me.'

Hannah turned her concentration to the shortbread biscuits. 'Will it be hot in Key West?' she enquired before stuffing one into her mouth.

'I think it's nearly always hot. It's the southernmost point in the United States.'

'Do try and get a tan, Mummy,' Lucy said. 'You always look so pale – even in Rock.'

Katie resisted the temptation to point out that she was always too busy slaving away over a stove or a washing machine to have time for sunbathing in Rock. But now she was going to live for herself, just for two weeks . . .

'I've been chosen for the netball team,' Hannah said proudly.

'Well done, darling.'

'We'll be playing matches most weekends from now on – some of them away to other schools.'

Her children would be busy all week with lessons and homework, Katie realised, and tied up at weekends with riding and netball and hanging out with their friends. They probably wouldn't even have time to notice she was gone.

'A fine thing to be doing,' great aunt Flora said with a shake of her red wig. 'Gallivanting off to foreign parts where you don't know a soul!'

'Isn't that exactly what Jemima's always done?' Katie pointed out reasonably.

'I thought *you* had more sense.'

'I don't see why some local estate agent couldn't have handled the sale without you,' Fiona said plaintively.

'My argument exactly,' Guy agreed with a scowl.

It was only Jemima who seemed to have no opinion to add to the general disapproval. Jemima, in fact, seemed remarkably subdued.

'Well, I think I've packed everything on my check list – and if I haven't it's too late now,' Katie said brightly, trying to lift the general gloom.

They had all come to say their goodbyes to her before Guy drove her to the airport. The last few days had been a flurry of activity with the end only now in sight, her newly purchased suitcases standing ready and gleaming in the hallway. Inside them, neatly folded, were the pretty flowing floral dresses and strappy sandals that Katie had bought in a reckless splurge after deciding she didn't want to make do with the things she had been taking to Rock year after year. 'Don't they make you look younger!' the canny sales assistant had said.

Katie had also discovered that her little used passport had expired and had taken it down to Petty France in person to have it renewed, which entailed an entire morning spent reading her Key West guidebook while she waited in queues. Then it was off to the travel agent for her air ticket. She would have to fly to Miami, the agent had told her, and then she'd probably be better off driving the rest of the way down US Highway 1 if she wanted the use of a car when she reached the end point. 'Oh, I do,' Katie said, 'and please – make it a sports car.'

'This hotel of yours sounds a little seedy,' Fiona said, 'despite the fancy name.'

'The Tropical Hideout . . .' It was the first time Katie had tried saying it out loud. It sounded deliciously exotic.

'I hope you won't be too uncomfortable there till you arrange the sale,' Fiona sighed. 'And don't let the locals take advantage of you and offer you an unfair price.'

'Bound to – a woman on her own,' great aunt Flora said gloomily.

'You'd better phone and check with me before you sign any contracts,' Guy warned.

'Don't *you* have any advice for me before I go?' Katie said, turning to her unusually silent sister.

'I don't know . . . This is all so strange.'

'What is?'

'I've never been the one to stay behind,' Jemima burst out. 'It's always been *you* saying goodbye and *me* going off into the world. It just doesn't feel right this way round – not right at all.'

On the plane, Katie sat next to a compact little woman with a greying perm who drank rather a lot of the complimentary sparkling wine the flight attendant brought around before take-off. She was delighted to discover that Katie had never been to America before, whereas she herself, as she said proudly, was a 'veteran of many trips', having quite the dearest little grandchildren to visit. Her daughter was married to a time-share salesman in Fort Lauderdale.

'You wouldn't believe how much money there is in it,' the woman confided as the plane banked steeply over Heathrow. 'They have ever such a nice house by the water. And of course, it's a wonderful climate for bringing up children.'

Katie showed the required interest in the grandchildren and learned that there were two, a boy and a girl, and it was no use taking any toys for them – 'like bringing coals to Newcastle,' the woman said 'you should see how many they have,' but she always packed their favourite chocolates, and 'some quality items of clothing, so they're not forever in jeans'.

The flight attendant came round to ask if they'd chosen from the menu yet. Katie, who hadn't had time what with the constant chatter of her companion, opened it with some relief. There was a choice of fish or chicken or steak, all in some microwave-friendly sauce.

'So much nicer in business class, isn't it?' the woman said. 'Of course, I couldn't afford it myself, but my son-in-law being so generous—'

'It's just lovely to be waited on,' Katie said, 'for a change.'

She settled for the chicken, while her neighbour ordered steak. The flight attendant brought round the drinks trolley, and the woman said she'd stick with the sparkling wine, if it was all the same, she didn't want to mix her alcohol.

Outside the sky was darkening, the Atlantic hardly visible below. Katie leaned back for a moment and closed her eyes. Now that she was actually on her way, embarked upon this adventure she had been so determined to allow herself, she felt a little clutch of nervousness in her stomach. What if she hated it all and wanted to go straight home? What if she couldn't cope alone with the complications of getting rid of her 'white elephant', as Guy persisted in calling it.

Their goodbyes at the airport had been a little awkward. They had run out of small talk long before they arrived at Heathrow, Guy preferring to avoid any mention of her trip. 'This crazy escapade of yours,' was how he had more than once referred to it.

At passport control he'd made a quick stab with his mouth in the direction of her cheek, and said he'd better be off, then, before he ran up too high a bill in the underground car park. She was relieved to see him go, taking his aura of disapproval with him.

'Tell me,' Katie said to her companion, 'have you ever been to Key West?'

'Oh no,' her new friend replied, slurring her words just a little, 'but I hear it's quite charming. In fact, before you know it, I think you will find you have quite fallen in love with America – just as I have.'

In her racy red sports car, Katie had somehow managed to negotiate her way out of the rather anonymous urban surroundings of Miami International Airport (what she had seen of the city wasn't much different from her expectations) and had journeyed with anxious concentration down various numbered routes until she finally joined US Highway 1 at its junction with Florida City. 'That's at mile marker 126,' the rental agent had explained, flashing good American teeth, 'and all you have to do from there is follow the road south all the way to Mile Zero.'

'Mile Zero,' Katie repeated to herself with a mixture of awe and trepidation. It was the farthest she could go, the rental agent seemed to imply, without falling off the edge of the civilised world. Katie had only just touched down on transatlantic soil, and now she had to find her way to the end of the American road.

She watched the little green markers with white lettering flash by, and at MM106 she hit the first of the islands, Key Largo, immortalised by the Bogart film. The land now dwindled in places to only a narrow strip, so that all she could see were great shimmering stretches of water – Florida Bay and the Gulf of Mexico on one side, and the vast Atlantic Ocean on the other. Dotted along the coastline were dozens of mangrove islands, wild and uninhabited except by the many birds – herons and spoonbills and pelicans and osprey. In little inlets along the shores of blue lagoons were sprawling houses with wooden docks. The people who owned them, she speculated, would be the kind who enjoyed messing about in boats, as Toad would have said.

Before setting out, she had put the top down on her sports car, and smoothed protective cream into the skin of her face and arms. Now the sun poured down its warmth from a cloudless sky and sparkled off the waves, so that she was glad of the sunglasses she had bought in the New Year sales at Peter Jones. The warm wind lifted her hair and she sang out loud, 'At the age of thirty-seven, She realised she'd never ride, Through Paris in a sports car . . .' She wished she had a tape of the Marianne Faithfull song to play through the speakers. This wasn't Paris but it would do, Katie decided. It would do very nicely indeed.

On exiting Marathon, she found herself at last on the spectacular Seven-Mile Bridge she had read about in the guidebooks, spanning the watery stretch to Bahia Honda. She felt suspended on a mere thread above the all-surrounding ocean. In places she could see the ruined remains of Flagler's Folly, the railroad swept away by the great hurricane of 1935. It would be terrifying, Katie thought, to be caught on this impossibly narrow fragment of dry land during one of the monster storms that plagued this part of the world.

On the other side she entered an area of wildlife refuges for the Key deer and the great white heron. It was beautiful country, and briefly she toyed with the idea of stopping for a look. But her curiosity to see the reason for her journey kept driving her on till she finally crossed the last of the forty-two bridges and her wheels touched down on Key West soil.

The island was only four miles by two, she had read, with a mixed population of twenty-five thousand, swelled to far greater numbers by the constant influx of tourists. She followed Roosevelt Boulevard past what appeared to be a harbour filled with pleasure boats and fishing vessels, the day's catch chalked up on large boards. On she drove down Truman Avenue – the last section of US Highway 1 – heading for the old town. On impulse she carried on past the turn-off she was looking for, heading instead for the final marker that would confirm she had actually reached Mile Zero.

Katie got out of the car and stood beside the symbolic sign. It was frequently stolen by high-spirited or drunken tourists, and just as frequently replaced. 'I've gone as far as I can go,' she thought. 'Now what?'

She doubled back and turned into the bustle of activity that was Duval Street – sometimes called the longest road in the world, the guidebooks said tongue-in-cheek, since it stretched from the Gulf of Mexico to the Atlantic Ocean. It was also where the Key West action was. Even in the daytime its restaurants and bars were humming, its shops filled with brightly coloured wares drawing in the tourists like a magnet. A constant tide of people flowed down the pavements. Music blared from open doors with cool, beckoning interiors. Jemima would no doubt have turned up her nose, but Katie found that all the energy invigorated her after the long drive, so that she felt ready for almost anything.

She turned right into Fleming, and at once entered a different and more dignified world. Elegant wooden-frame houses lined the street, their gardens a riot of lush vegetation. Cats lay luxuriously on porches, soaking up the sun. Tourists rode bicycles with shopping trailing from baskets, and locals strolled their dogs along the sidewalks as though they had all the time in the world.

In the midst of all this quiet splendour Katie came upon a painted board with an elaborate snake entwined around the lettering. 'The Tropical Hideout', it boasted, and on a smaller plank hanging below it: 'Vacancies – Enquire Within.'

Katie pulled up by the kerb and climbed from the car. She could feel the heat from the sidewalk rising up through her thin sandals. She steadied herself against the bonnet. Only then did she raise her eyes and allow them to travel slowly up the façade of the property of which she was now the proud owner, the papers to prove it folded neatly in her handbag.

There was paint peeling from the cypress boards, and here and there a shutter hung crookedly from broken hinges. A riot of vegetation hinted at an overgrown garden at the back. But there was no mistaking the pedigree of the place, just as shabby clothes cannot disguise a beauty of form beneath. The neglected house had an elegance and dignity that came from simple lines and solid construction. An aura of history clung to it, the past of its colourful inhabitants who had lived and laughed in it, their secrets preserved behind an impenetrable screen of luscious foliage and flowers.

Katie took it all in through a shimmer of tears. 'Oh, Daddy,' she whispered, 'I wish you could have been here to see this.'

Chapter Eight

~

As she stepped over the threshold into the dim, twilit world within, Katie's first impression was of worn carpets, fading wallpaper and a general air of neglect.

She found herself in what must once have been an impressive entrance hall with a high ceiling and some heavy pieces of Victorian furniture that only added to the feeling of Dickensian gloom. In the corner was a desk that obviously served as the sole reception area. Placed on it in a prominent position was a sign: '10% discount for cash.' As she stared at it, a voice behind her said clearly, 'Like it says – cash always welcome.'

Katie spun round and found herself facing a small, wiry Indian woman with hair falling in a thick black curtain to her waist. She wore a sleeveless cut-off T-shirt that showed off the muscles swelling in her forearms, and a pair of Harley Davidson blue-jean biker shorts.

'I'd like to see the manager, please,' Katie said in a loud voice that seemed to echo round the room.

The woman gave her a sassy stare. 'Mr Grenville wouldn't tell you any different.'

'It's not about a discount on the room—'

The woman's face hardened. 'If it's money you're after, I told you – he ain't in.'

Katie made a determined attempt to take control of the situation. 'Look, you don't understand, I'm Mrs Colman.'

'Is that a fact?'

'The new owner,' Katie said rather desperately.

A guarded look came into the woman's eyes. In an instinctive gesture she pulled at her cut-off T-shirt, as though trying unsuccessfully to cover her bare midriff.

'I didn't get your meaning . . . You should've said.'

'And who are you?'

The woman seemed to collect herself, and thrust out a powerful hand. 'Nadine – housekeeper and general handyman. It's an honour to meet you, ma'am.'

Gingerly Katie took the hand and winced at its firm grip. 'Which room have you put aside for me, Nadine?'

'It ain't no room, ma'am – it's a suite,' Nadine said proudly.

'That won't be necessary—'

'We don't let that one out as a rule. The last owner used it as his living quarters. Then about five years ago he upped and left – health problems he said it was – and Mr Grenville's been running the place ever since.'

'Could you please show me the way, then,' Katie said, beginning to lift her suitcases.

Nadine sprang to her side. 'Wait up, ma'am, I'll get those. I double as the porter round here too.'

Katie followed her up a flight of stairs, past peeling wallpaper and aging yellow prints. Nadine's powerful arms didn't seem to flinch at the strain of their load. Her shorts were riding up at the back, and Katie could just make out the bottom half of a tattoo on her left buttock.

At the end of the hallway, Nadine put the cases down in front of a door that looked very like all the rest and took a bunch of keys from her pocket. 'This is it – home sweet home.' She stood aside to let Katie enter.

The 'suite' consisted of two bedrooms and a sitting room, filled with the same good-quality Victorian furniture marred by shabby upholstery. Neither was it very clean, Katie noted with disapproval, vowing to have a word about staff standards with the absent manager. But at least she had her own little separate kitchenette and bathroom, and a view over the tangled garden.

'Thank you,' she said to Nadine. 'This will do very nicely. And please be sure to tell Mr Grenville I want to see him as soon as he gets back.'

Nadine made a curious little bob like a lady's maid – an incongruous gesture in her biker shorts – and escaped while the going was good.

Feeling a little like an Amazon explorer, Katie pushed her way through the thick vegetation of the garden out back. It must have been weeks since anyone had tried to cut back its hectic growth, but though Katie was annoyed by the neglect, she was also stunned by the wild beauty. She recognised the bright blooms of hibiscus and the fragrant scent of gardenia, but much of the tropical foliage and flora was deliciously unfamiliar to her. 'I must learn all their names,' she decided as she trailed her fingers over the cool surfaces of leaves.

She came into a clearing with a small swimming pool. The water had a greenish tinge, and a few dead leaves floated on the surface. She dipped her fingers in and found it surprisingly cold. The sun, when not directly overhead, would have little chance of reaching it through the impenetrable foliage. Across some uneven paving stones was a tikki bar, deserted at this mid-afternoon hour, its straw roof drooping dejectedly.

The sounds of male laughter drifted over the dilapidated wooden fence. Katie wondered what sort of revelry was going on next door that was so sadly absent from her own garden. She headed over to the fence and peeped curiously through one of the gaps.

Sunlight sparkled off the brilliant turquoise water of another pool. It took a moment for Katie's eyes to adjust to the unexpected sight of six naked men stretched out on the wooden deck beside it. One was sipping a cocktail, another rubbed oil into his friend's bronzed and muscled body. A third looked up and caught sight of Katie. He grinned broadly and blew her a kiss, so that the others all turned to look.

Katie jumped back from the gap, her cheeks flushed with

embarrassment. More male laughter wafted over the fence. Hastily she turned and fought her way back through the dense growth to the house.

The entrance hall was deserted as before, but now the sign offering the cash discount had been removed. Katie began to try the doors along the passage, looking for the main office where the records must be kept.

A middle-aged couple came into the entrance hall, loaded down with bags from the liquor store. The man had a large beer belly protruding over grubby shorts. The woman's hair hung uncombed to her shoulders, and with her free hand she stabbed a cigarette at him as they argued in sullen, subdued voices. Along with the fag she held a keyring with a large number six on it.

Katie reached a door marked 'Private' and tried the handle. It wouldn't open. Determinedly she marched back to the desk and rang the small brass bell.

After a short wait Nadine appeared, a menacing figure sporting a power drill. Katie hesitated, then gestured to the locked door and said in her firmest employer's voice, 'I'd like you to open that for me with your keys.'

Nadine gave a deep sigh, as though caught on the horn's of an impossible dilemma. 'Mr Grenville won't like it.'

'If you don't open it, *I* won't like it.'

Nadine fumbled grudgingly in the pocket of her biker jeans. 'Long as he knows it was you made me do it.'

'Have you found out where he is yet?'

'I sent word you want to see him,' Nadine said obliquely as she sorted through keys.

Katie pushed open the unlocked door. The office was minimally furnished, with desk and filing cabinets and telephone. The filing cabinets, she noted at once, had no locks.

She would start with the current state of affairs, and work backwards. Flipping through folders, she found what appeared to be an up-to-date rate card, proclaiming that the double occupancy rate for a room in high season was a hundred and fifty dollars per night. The registration book revealed that only five of the twelve units were currently occupied. Moreover the slovenly couple in number six were paying just three hundred dollars for the week, instead of the required one thousand and fifty.

'The tip of the iceberg, I suspect,' Katie muttered to herself as she began working back through weeks of dismal history.

The door opened and a man sidled in with a smile that didn't quite reach his eyes. His dark brown hair was greased back from a face beaded with sweat, and his khaki shirt had damp rings under the arms.

'Wade Grenville,' he announced. 'It sure is a pleasure to meet you at last.'

Katie rather doubted it. As Wade approached the desk she remained deliberately in his seat, so that he was forced to take the visitor's chair opposite.

'Anything I can do to help you with all this?' He gestured at the open files.

'I certainly hope so,' Katie said.

Wade smiled uneasily, showing crooked bottom teeth. "I expect you're wondering why the place isn't full,' he said, trying to head off the inevitable showdown.

'That's one of the things I was going to ask.'

'Competition,' Wade said, spreading his hands in a gesture that abdicated all responsibility. 'There's more rooms to rent in this town than flees on a monkey's ass. We gotta have something to give the punters that they can't find in the very next block.'

'Is that why you offer a discount for cash?'

'Exactly!' Wade grinned, pleased at how quickly the new boss was catching on.

'And tell me,' Katie said, 'are the couple in number six paying cash?'

'Not as I'm aware of.'

'Then why are they getting a discount of over seventy per cent?'

He glanced at the upside-down registration book in a show

of trying to jog his memory. 'As I recall, they said that's what the Green Parrot were offering them, and seeing as how we weren't full—'

'If you attract that type of guest with bargain basement discounts, then how do you expect to bring in the people you really want – the ones who are able to pay full rates?'

'Beggars can't be choosers.'

'But why have we been reduced to the position of beggars?'

'Now look here,' Wade said defensively, 'I've had to run things round here the way I see fit. Mr Maloney didn't take any interest after his heart went funny on him, and your father said just to keep things ticking over till he decided what to do with the place, and that's what I've done, see.'

Katie took a deep breath. 'Was that any reason to let things get so run down? Did you tell Mr Maloney or my father about the state of neglect of their property?'

'Didn't seem much point. If you're just breaking even, where's the money gonna come from to fix the place up?'

'That would have been for them to decide, wouldn't it?'

Wade looked sullen and said nothing.

'And even if you couldn't do any renovating, you could still have made sure the house was kept clean and the garden properly tended, couldn't you?'

'With all due respect, you don't know how things run down here. Good staff are hard to come by.'

Katie thought of the sparkling pool next door, and tried not to think of the men grouped around it. 'Why don't you ask our neighbours how they manage to find good staff?'

'Are you kidding? It's nothing but a bunch of faggots over there.'

Katie was beginning to like this man less with every moment that passed. 'By the way, Nadine says you never rent out the unit I'm staying in, even though it seems perfectly suitable to me. Why is that?'

'We're never full enough to need Mr Maloney's old apartment,' Wade said smoothly.

'Really? Don't you ever get families who ask for interconnecting rooms?'

Wade shrugged. She would get no more out of him than he had revealed already. It was time to wrap up this unpleasant meeting.

'Mr Grenville,' Katie said, 'since you complain of a lack of interest on the part of previous owners, I have good news for you. I'm going to take a very strong interest indeed in the affairs of The Tropical Hideout. In fact, there are going to be a lot of changes round here.'

She hoped it sounded like a threat.

The next morning she woke late but still tired, the beginnings of a headache hovering at her temples and making her quite certain she wouldn't be able to face a morning with Wade Grenville and the books. She had slept fitfully, her body disconcerted by the time change, and then been startled out of a dream about her father, at two in the morning, by the couple in number six screaming abuse at each other and the sickening crash of something breaking. She sincerely hoped it was an empty liquor bottle rather than one of her chairs or mirrors. She had little faith in their ability to pay for the damage.

The water from the bath taps yielded only a slow trickle, so that it took a while before the tub was full and she could soak some of the weariness away. It was mid-morning before she emerged in a neat summer skirt and blouse to ask Nadine if she could get her hands on a cup of coffee and a roll, since she had certainly missed the continental breakfast by the pool which she suspected wasn't quite such a glamorous affair as the brochure made it sound.

'Mr Grenville will be available at eleven,' Nadine said as she served Katie her coffee in the kitchen.

How gracious of him, Katie thought. I, on the other hand, will not. She had decided, in the bathtub, to do some exploring of the Old Town, since yesterday she had seen no more than a tantalising glimpse.

Nadine brought her a plain white bread roll and a knob of butter with a congealed-looking blob of strawberry jam on a plate. Its appearance was distinctly unappetising.

'Was this bought fresh today?' Katie demanded.

'Mr Grenville does the breakfast shop every second day, he says stuff keeps fine overnight.'

'That doesn't apply to bread rolls,' Katie said, staring down with distaste at the hard lump on her plate.

'Wouldn't touch it if I were you,' a voice said from the doorway. 'I got something real special waiting for you next door.'

A smiling man with a deep tan, brown hair and moustache and a gold stud in his left ear was lounging in the doorway. His shorts rode up even higher than Nadine's, and his T-shirt plunged at the neckline. Katie's eyes were drawn to the huge gold medallion nestling against the wiry hairs of his chest.

'Got this from Mel Fisher, our famous treasure hunter,' the man said, fingering the coin. 'Quite a legend in these parts – you must meet him some time. This is a real piece-of-eight from a sunken Spanish galleon.'

'And you are . . . ?'

'Harvey Grossman, your next-door neighbour.'

'Katie Colman.' She offered her hand, and he shook it with an amused glint in his eye.

'Heard you were showing an interest in my place, so I thought I'd invite you over to take a closer look.'

Katie lowered her gaze. She knew the colour had flushed into her cheeks.

'Don't worry,' Harvey said, 'my guests have all gone out for the day. No more unexpected surprises.'

'I wasn't the least bit worried,' Katie lied.

'Good, 'cause I got Chico to make you his Key Lime pie – finest on the island.' He made it sound like a bribe.

Nadine squared up to him, hands on Harley Davidson-clad hips. 'Mr Grenville's on his way to see Mrs Colman. Mr Grenville won't like it if you drag her off to your place.'

That clinched the matter for Katie. 'Mr Grenville,' she said firmly, 'can take a long walk off a short plank.' She snatched up her handbag and marched determinedly from the kitchen, followed by a broadly grinning Harvey.

'Welcome to Paradise Lodge,' Harvey said with a flourish as she crossed his threshold.

The contrast with The Tropical Hideout could hardly have been more startling. Here there was light and colour everywhere – pastel-painted walls and bright scatter cushions and airy spaces and rich rugs on wooden floors.

'All in the best possible taste, isn't it?' Harvey said mockingly. 'We gays put the style back into Key West, made it what it is today, and some of the folks round here appreciate us for it. But there's a group of locals who think we bought up their decaying houses in Old Town too cheap, and forget what a fortune we had to spend doing them up.'

Katie wondered rather forlornly what it would cost to get The Tropical Hideout looking anything like so splendid. She suspected rather more than she could afford.

'Generally, it's a gay-friendly town,' Harvey went on. 'Not much in the way of racial tension either. People live and let live . . . We got boys who come here from Iowa and Kentucky and aren't used to letting it all hang out, but they soon catch on. There's an optional dress policy here 'cause it's gay men only, and most of our guests opt for *au naturel* – don't they, Chico?'

Harvey smiled warmly at an extraordinary creature emerging from the kitchen carrying an enormous pie dish and wearing only the briefest of bikini thongs. Apart from the absence of breasts, his figure would have been the envy of any girl, especially the long shapely legs shaved to smooth perfection.

As Chico passed by, Harvey patted him familiarly on his bare rump. 'This is Katie Colman,' he said. 'And seeing as how she's visiting with us today, why don't you go put on something a little more substantial.'

'I haven't got time to hang round for your tea party – there's work to do,' Chico said sulkily, heading back to the kitchen with a defiant shake of his naked rear end.

'He's Cuban,' Harvey said almost by way of apology. 'Such a proud people – you can't tell them what to do or how to do it.' His voice was filled with a suppressed adoration.

Katie darted a hungry look at the pie dish Chico had left on the coffee table. The paper plates beside it seemed curiously out of place in these chic surroundings. Her stomach was rudely reminding her that she hadn't yet eaten breakfast. Fortunately Harvey seemed to remember his manners, and cut her a huge wedge.

'This stuff is one of the local experiences you just can't miss,' he said.

Katie sunk her teeth into crumbly pie crust and sweet lemon filling and thought she had never tasted anything quite so heavenly. 'A slice of paradise,' she said when she could bear to swallow and let the delicious flavours fade from her mouth.

'Watch out – you can have too much of a good thing, you know.'

Katie supposed you could, but at this moment she couldn't imagine how. She had certainly not reached such a point in her life before.

'Is everything Chico makes this good?' she said through a mouthful of pie.

'He's a superb cook, but a little on the temperamental side. Whenever he gets mad at me, the dishes start flying.'

Hence the paper plates, Katie realised with amusement. 'How on earth do you keep this place so spotless?' she asked, looking round enviously. 'Wade Grenville tells me good staff are almost impossible to find.'

'I doubt he's looking for them in the same places,' Harvey said wryly. 'Anyway, without speaking out of turn here, I wouldn't believe a word that guy says. He's no better than a two-bit crook.'

'That's rather what I suspected.'

'I can tell you all about the scams he's running at The Tropical Hideout. It's common knowledge.'

'I'd be very grateful,' Katie said, trying not to be distracted by the sight of Chico stabbing a bright green feather duster at the framed prints, wearing a frilly apron tied at the back in a bow that in no way covered his naked buttocks. She wondered what Guy would make of such an apparition.

'Well, for starters,' Harvey said, 'every guest who walks in is offered a discount if they pay cash. That way Wade doesn't have to put anything through the books – he just sticks the money in his own back pocket.'

Katie sighed. 'Yes, I've already worked that one out.'

'But the cheating doesn't stop there. He's been living on the premises in that unit he had to vacate in such a hurry when you turned up – and I bet you he hasn't been paying a dime for it.'

That explained the khaki trousers Katie had found stuffed in the back of one of her cupboards and which she had thought might have been left behind by some absent-minded guest.

'He charges all his personal expenses to your business, like the meals in fancy restaurants he buys for all his pals. I don't think he's put his hand in his own pocket since that poor Maloney guy left town. I know for sure he hasn't paid a tradesman for months—'

'Oh dear,' Katie groaned, imagining the backlog of debts that she would have to settle herself, as a point of principle.

'None of the profits get ploughed back into the business,' Harvey continued, warming to his theme. 'He's just milking the place for cash and running it into the ground in the process.'

'In other words, he has to go,' Katie said, dabbing away the last of the pie crumbs from her mouth with a pink linen napkin provided by the plate-smashing Chico.

'You got it. Trouble is, where do you find a manager honest enough to run things properly when you're thousands of miles away and can't do any spot checks?'

'I don't know. I was hoping you could tell me.'

'You won't,' Harvey pronounced grimly. 'But there is another way.'

Katie thought she might be open to any suggestion that would rid her of the odious Wade Grenville.

'You could sell to me,' Harvey said. 'I've always been itching to get my hands on The Tropical Hideout and fix it up the way it should be, the way my clientele like it.'

Katie looked round at the tasteful David Hockney fantasy of her surroundings, and thought it might be quite a shame to mould The Tropical Hideout to the same preconceived perfection. 'I don't know. It's a bit soon to make up my mind . . . I'm not sure I've had a chance to appreciate yet exactly what it means to be the owner of a Key West guesthouse.'

'In that case,' Harvey said with relish, 'it will be my pleasure to give you the Harvey Grossman guided tour.'

He drove a surprisingly conservative black BMW, but the Key West light pouring in through the sunroof transformed it from a city banker's car into a vehicle quite suited to the colourful tropics.

'Our historic district is one of the most charming in the country,' he said proudly, as though he himself were personally responsible. 'Most of the houses are nineteenth century, built after the great fire of 1886 destroyed half the city. But we still have a few staunch old survivors from the days of the Bahamian settlers. I think we should start off with one of those, don't you?'

'You're the boss,' Katie said cheerfully.

'I wish Chico had your attitude!' Harvey headed a block up into Eaton Street. 'Now, first and foremost, you have to understand what a "Conch" is, and then you'll know why they built their houses the way they did.'

He pulled up in front of a white, two-storey house with deep verandahs on two sides, a steep grey shingle roof and wonderful old palm trees rising up all around it. 'This is called the Bahama House because it was originally built there, then taken apart and brought to Key West on a schooner by Captain John Bartlum. That wasn't uncommon in those days. You see, after the Native Americans left the Keys, the first inhabitants were your lot – people of British descent whose ancestors settled in New England and the South, then left for the Bahamas out of loyalty to King George III when the Revolutionary War broke out. But when this same king began to tax his Caribbean territories, they wisely had another change of heart and moved to Key West as good American citizens. Some even brought their marvellous homes with them. They became known as "Conchs" – Harvey pronounced the word 'konks' – 'because they used that tough old shellfish in a dozen different inventive ways, for food and musical instruments. So Conch originally meant native Bahamian, but now it pretty much covers anything unique to Key West.'

Katie gazed appreciatively at the classic lines of the unpretentious yet beautiful house. 'I'm glad it doesn't look like some grand rich man's folly.'

'That's because it wasn't designed by an architect, but a simple ship's carpenter working for his captain. His inspiration would've been the ships he'd sailed in and the homes he'd seen in distant seaports. His chief concern was to make sure the house could withstand high winds and hurricanes. So he built it using the joinery techniques of carpentry, holding it together with wooden pegs, so the house would actually bend in a strong wind and not blow down.'

'Has it been put to the test?' Katie said.

'Sure has. We have our share of hurricanes in paradise, but this old lady's still here to tell the tale.'

'And in such wonderful condition, too.'

'There are very tough regulations in place to make sure the old houses are restored as faithfully as possible. They're considered prime real estate now – you don't see many of them falling to pieces like they were in the bad old days.'

'Except for mine,' Katie said gloomily.

'Don't say I haven't offered to buy it off you . . . Shall we move on?'

Harvey's next stop was the John Lowe Jr House in Southard Street. 'Another fine old Bahamian mansion,' he said, 'but this one was influenced by the Classical Revival style – see those lovely white wooden pillars spaced along the length of the porch?'

Katie was beginning to recognise the distinctive features of these beautiful old homes. They seemed to be no more than two or two-and-a-half storeys high, with porches running the entire length of the front façade. The outside walls were covered with horizontal clapboard, in the Lowe house painted a pretty pale rose. Originally it would have been white, Harvey explained, with green or black shutters. All windows seemed to have louvred blinds which allowed cooling breezes to pass through the house. Roofs were sharply pitched and covered with shingles or sheets of galvanised steel to help in the collecting of rain, the sole source of water before it was piped down from Miami.

'Look at that structure built on the roof,' Harvey pointed. 'A lot of the old houses had them, in the days when wrecking was the chief source of livelihood. They were used as lookout stations by bold men waiting for some unfortunate Spanish galleon to be driven on to the reefs, then it would be an all-out race to see who could reach the ship first, 'cause whoever did would be in charge of the operation. Meanwhile their pale-faced wives would watch from the same vantage point to see if the sea would claim their men too in the salvage effort. Enough of them never returned for the lookout towers to be renamed widows' walks.'

'That's quite a story,' Katie shivered.

'So you can imagine our old houses also have their share of ghosts.'

He started up the engine again. 'Now I'll show you something a little more extravagant. You'll love it, though. It's called the Gingerbread House.'

'Like Hansel and Gretel,' Katie laughed.

This time they stopped in Elizabeth Street, in front of a delightful fantasy in pink and white. 'Oh, it's charming,' Katie cried.

'Deliciously camp, isn't it? But like everything else in old Key West, never over the top . . . Look at the unique way Key Westers began to decorate the façades of their houses. Those lace-like patterns carved into the wood of the porches are called millwork. There are about fifty different patterns on the island, and any house that has them is called a gingerbread house – though this is the best example.'

'My daughters would love it,' Katie exclaimed.

'You have kids?'

'Yes – two.'

'I had two as well,' Harvey said in a voice trembling with pain.

'Oh, dear, I'm so sorry, what . . . ?'

'Cut me out of their lives, when I told them I'd realised I was gay. Or rather I told their mother, and she was so shocked she never spoke to me again. I don't know what she said to the kids, but they don't take my calls, they refuse to see me—'

'How awful for you,' Katie said rather lamely. It was quite extraordinary, she thought, how Americans just came out and said the most intimate things, even if they'd only met you a matter of hours before. She was quite relieved when Harvey stopped in front of a smaller grey and white house in William Street, and the his mind seemed to revert to the safer subject of architecture.

'Now this is something you won't see anywhere in America besides Key West,' he said proudly. 'It's called an eyebrow house. See how the roof extends downwards in front to rest on the columns of the porch? It makes a sort of awning over the second-floor windows, which restricts the view but keeps the sunlight out and makes the place a whole lot cooler. Neat, huh?'

Katie agreed that yes, it was unusual and very quaint.

Harvey promised her a 'shotgun' house next, for which he would have to take her to a district where the Cuban cigar factory owners built housing for their workers. 'That is, if you aren't getting bored?'

'Oh, no,' Katie said hastily. 'It's so very kind of you to show me round like this – I'm having a wonderful time, really.'

'Good. Now look at that.' He stopped in front of a row of what were really nothing more than cottages. 'Even these have their own peculiar sort of grace, don't they?'

Katie looked at the one-storey frame houses with the same painted clapboard sides and porches and pillars and shuttered windows that she was becoming so accustomed to, and nodded her agreement.

'They're being done up now, just like the bigger places, often by out-of-towners – you'd be amazed how much in demand they are as second homes.'

'But why are they called shotgun houses?'

'It's the way the floor plan's laid out, with two or more rooms one behind the other and the doorways all lined up, so if you shot a gun through the front door the bullet would pass straight through out the back without hitting anything.'

'Heavens, why would anyone want to do that?'

'You never know in Key West,' Harvey said with a wink. 'And now for something rather different.'

They were on the Atlantic Ocean side, and he slowed the BMW as they headed into a crowd of cars and people congregated around a giant red and white marker buoy bearing the legend 'The Southernmost Point'. A nearby billboard boasted that from here it was just ninety miles to Cuba.

'This is like a sort of shrine for Chico's family,' Harvey said. 'They sometimes come at night, when it's too dark for the tourists to be here taking photographs.'

'Do they want to go home?' Katie asked curiously.

'I think all our Cubans dream of that. Whether they'd like it when they got there – even once Castro's gone – well, I guess only time will tell.'

He turned into the bottom end of Duval Street, and waved at an extraordinary edifice in cream and turquoise and brick-red. 'This is called the Southernmost House, even though technically it doesn't occupy that position any more. Built by Judge Harris when the Victorian style was in vogue.'

Katie let her eye wander over the different colours and shapes and textures and the extraordinary tower rising up on one side. 'It's rather wonderful, but I don't think I like it as much as the simpler, more classic houses.'

'Ah, but variety is the spice of life,' Harvey said. 'And I assure you, this is a very restrained example of Queen Anne meets the Victorian style, compared with the monstrosities that were erected in other parts of our great country.'

'You're so knowledgeable about these things,' Katie said enviously. 'I could listen to you for ever . . . But I'm afraid I've taken up enough of your time already. I'm sure you have a dozen things you should be doing.'

'Chico might start throwing things if I play truant for much longer,' Harvey agreed, accelerating up Duval Street past the T-shirt shops and the Conch Tour Train on one of its endless rounds, rows of camera-laden tourists peering out from the canopied cars.

'Now if you'd taken their tour, they'd have shown you Hemingway House where the great writer lived with his second wife and his six-toed cats, and Sloppy Joe's bar where he liked to drink, and Truman's Little White House, and Mel Fisher's treasure museum, and Mallory Square where folks celebrate the sunset every evening . . . You'll have to see all those things while you're here, you know.'

'I'm sure I will. But I'm very glad I did *your* tour first.'

'At least now you appreciate the pedigree of that grand old lady you own, and why you have to do right by her . . . Or preferably sell her to me so *I* can restore her to her former glory.'

'I still haven't made up my mind—'

'Not another word,' Harvey cried. 'You mustn't let me bully

you into anything. Take all the time you need . . . And if the answer's no, I'll still be available to offer you neighbourly advice and a slice of Key Lime pie.'

'Thank you so much,' Katie said sincerely. She had the feeling she might need a great deal of both in the days to come.

Late that evening, when she couldn't sleep from the jetlag again, Katie phoned the girls. She sat by her open windows with a warm night breeze blowing in. It was difficult to imagine that in Wiltshire it would be a cold and probably wet winter evening.

'What's it like there?' Hannah asked.

'Just beautiful, darling. I hope you and Lucy will see it one day.'

'What have you been doing?'

'Mostly finding out about my hotel. But I've already met some very . . . interesting people.'

'What kind of people?' Hannah demanded.

Katie hesitated. Not the sort of people Guy liked them to mix with in London and Cornwall, she thought. Not 'people like us' . . .

'They're very nice,' she said firmly. 'I think we're going to be friends.'

'But what's there to see?'

'The most wonderful old buildings.'

'Is that all?'

'No, there are also beaches and palm trees and boats and swimming pools.'

'Oh, that's all right, then,' Hannah said.

'And what about you? How's the netball team?'

'We won our last game. Lucy never watches, she says it's too boring—'

'I'd better talk to her next.'

'You can't – she's at drama club,' Hannah said smugly.

'I'll phone again another time, then. Be sure to give her my love.'

Hannah made a vague grunting noise which Katie hoped was an indication of assent. Her next call was to Guy. She tried home before the office, and was surprised when he picked up almost immediately.

'Are you working in your study?'

'Of course.'

A vivid picture came to her of the house in St John's Wood, all in darkness save for the thin strip of light under Guy's study door where he would be closeted with his briefs. She felt a surge of emotion that had nothing to do with home-sickness.

'And you – are you enjoying yourself?' he enquired, a shade of martyrdom in his voice.

'Oh Guy, it's so wonderful here. The guesthouse isn't at all like we thought. It's a real gem, with so much history to it. Of course it's also in a terrible state of neglect, but if it were just done up—'

'What sort of money would that take?' Guy said without enthusiasm.

'I haven't looked into it yet. But I'm sure the man next door could tell me. He has a guesthouse too, and he's been so kind . . . But he'd really like to buy The Tropical Hideout and do it up himself.'

'That's the perfect solution, then, isn't it?'

Katie twiddled the phone cord. 'I'm not sure.'

'Why? Isn't he offering a fair price?'

'We haven't talked figures yet,' Katie admitted.

'Why on earth not? I thought that was the whole purpose of your trip.'

'I just don't want to rush into anything,' Katie said for what seemed like the hundredth time in the weeks since her father had died. 'Anyway, how are things at home? Are you managing to get your own meals?'

'I'm not completely helpless,' Guy said. 'If all else fails, I'm quite capable of ordering a takeaway.'

Katie had a curious urge to ask whether he was missing her

at all, then, but thought better of it long before the words had left her lips.

'Good,' she said instead. 'I'll let you know how I'm getting on here.'

'Righto, then.' He seemed impatient to get back to his work, and Katie found herself suddenly just as willing to let him go.

With a full moon lighting up the world outside her window, Katie sat sipping a glass of the Californian wine she had bought at the Lost Weekend liquor store, looking out over the wild little patch of garden she owned and wondering what was to become of it all.

Harvey had given her a glimpse of what The Tropical Hideout could be, but she wasn't at all sure she was capable of undertaking a renovation of that magnitude, especially when she would have so little time to see it through. Harvey's offer to buy it from her and restore it himself was almost certainly the most sensible option, as Guy had lost no time in pointing out.

But what she couldn't confess to a relative stranger or even to her husband was the strange possessiveness she felt towards her inheritance that she hadn't quite bargained on. From the moment she'd entered its quiet inner spaces, she'd had a sense of being somehow inextricably bound up with its destiny, as though this unexpected gift from Robin should be more to her than just an old frame house on foreign soil. It seemed that Robin was trying to speak to her in the breezes singing through the shutters and rustling the tropical foliage of the garden, and if only she listened closely enough, she would hear what he was trying to tell her. But if she gave it all up, if she sold out and returned to her life in England with nothing gained except money in the bank, then all that was left of her father's voice would be silenced for ever.

Chapter Nine

~

Spread out in front of Katie on her sitting room table were the audited accounts of The Tropical Hideout for the past five years of Wade Grenville's management, together with the more recent books which hadn't yet been submitted to the local accounting firm he used. Katie wondered whether they were in on his various scams and had doctored the figures to cover up for him, in return for a little brown envelope stuffed with cash. She decided this was a far from fanciful scenario.

Wade had offered to go through the books with her, but she suspected his real purpose was to blind her with dubious science, so she had declined firmly and escaped to her own room to muddle through as best she could. Not that she had any great hopes of getting to the bottom of things. Wade's years of practice at concealing what he didn't want others to see had no doubt rendered him perfectly capable of fooling even the experts, which she, decidedly, was not.

Nevertheless, she told herself, she would have to make the effort to build up some sort of picture of the potential profitability of The Tropical Hideout, as well as its current losses. Without this basic information, it would be impossible to work out whether she could actually afford to keep it on, and what it would cost her to do so. Guy would expect her to back up any argument with firm facts and figures. Guy, she knew, would not be swayed by emotional beliefs in messages from other worlds.

Katie stared at the endless columns of figures and passed a hand wearily over her eyes. Perhaps it would be best to ask the advice of the accountants after all. No doubt she had allowed her imagination to run riot and they were innocent of any wrongdoing on Wade's behalf.

She was pondering her next course when a huge commotion erupted in the street outside. A man's voice was raised to a pitch that carried in clearly through her back windows, making Katie rather concerned for the peaceful ambience The Tropical Hideout was supposed to offer its guests. Grabbing her keys, she hurried downstairs to investigate.

An old man in worn cotton pyjamas stood in the middle of the street hollering and shaking his fist at a retreating three-wheel cycle disappearing down the road, its rear basket filled with six or seven mewling cats.

'Come back afore I makes yer,' the man shouted at the distant figure on the cycle, which paid him no attention whatsoever.

'What's the problem?' Katie said, concerned that the frail old boy might keel over at any moment from the force of his wrath.

'It's that damn crazy woman from across the street,' the man spluttered, still trembling with rage. 'Steals my cats the minute my back's turned. And she needn't think I don't know what she does with them.'

'What?' Katie said, visions of witches and demonic midnight rituals flashing disconcertingly through her mind.

'Cuts off their manhood, that's what. Thinks it's her job to stop 'em multiplying. Come, I'll show yer.'

He clasped her arm with a bony hand and led her down an alley between her property and what she assumed must be his. Rounding the corner at the back of the house, she saw an overgrown garden much like hers, only this one was trampled quite flat by what looked like a veritable army of cats – cats as far as the eye could see.

'Now ain't that a pretty sight,' he said.

Looking with dismay at what appeared to be a field of writhing fur, Katie was inclined to sympathise with this 'mad' woman, whoever she was, who had taken matters into her own hands. 'There *are* rather a lot of them,' she suggested tentatively.

'Cats have as much right to this island as humans do,' the man said defiantly. 'More, mebbe . . . There's seven of 'em to every one of us, you know.'

'Then perhaps you should limit yourself to seven.'

'They've done their share of reproducing over the years, I grant you that. But that's no reason to deprive 'em of all their fun.'

It seemed to Katie that they couldn't be having too much fun, cramped together in this inadequate space, but she could hardly say so to a complete stranger. 'I'm Katie Colman,' she said, offering her hand. 'I own the guesthouse next door.'

'Nice place,' he said. 'Not done up all nancy-fancy like that Paradise Lodge over the other side.'

Katie cast a quick glance at the old man's house, and saw it was in an even more advanced state of disrepair than her own. She suspected that for him, this was a matter of pride. 'Sorry,' she said, 'I didn't catch your name—'

'Willie Vance. Glad to meet yer.'

'Can I help you back to bed, Mr Vance?'

'Wasn't in bed. Always wear these things,' he said, glancing down at his faded pyjamas. 'Can't see the point of getting all dressed up – not when it's just me and the pussies.'

'Oh,' said Katie. 'Well, in that case, I'll leave you to get on with . . . whatever you were doing.'

'I'll be waiting for that hussy to come back with my cats. And when I catch her, I'll make her sorry she was born.' He shook a skinny arm at the heavens. If the display was supposed to look threatening, Katie thought, it was rather less than convincing.

After a few more hours with the books – the more recent ones confirming quite blatantly what Harvey had warned, that few of the current creditors had been paid – Katie decided it was time for a little fist-shaking of her own.

'Why have so few our bills been met?' she demanded of Wade as she sat in her now accustomed place behind his desk in the downstairs office.

He shrugged. 'You've seen the books. Money's a little tight right now.'

'If that's the case, it's a pretty poor reflection on your management capabilities, isn't it?'

'Hey, if you don't like the way I run things—'

'I don't,' Katie insisted before he could intimidate her. 'And I won't be requiring your services any longer.'

Wade looked incredulous. 'You can't just fire me.'

'Why not?'

'Who'll you get to run this place?'

'That really isn't your concern.'

He leaned towards her over the desk. His eyes had lost their look of phoney innocence and become quite menacing. 'You think you're a regular little ball-breaker, don't you?'

Fearful of what his next move might be, Katie held herself still and said nothing.

'Well, I'm not an easy man to break, lady. You're gonna regret this.'

The scent of his stale breath was in Katie's nostrils. She opened her mouth and barely managed to say, 'Are you threatening me?'

'Let's just call it a warning.'

'Then I also have a warning for you. I suspect you've been cheating me and my father blind, but I won't take any action against you – provided you clear out of here without making any trouble.'

'I don't scare easy,' Wade said with an expression of contempt. 'I have connections in this town – I'm one of the main bubbas. You outsiders think you can come to our island and push us around . . . Well, you'll find out, when you try an' get your licences renewed.'

'What licences?' Katie said with the beginnings of alarm.

'The ones I accidentally let expire. The ones you need to run your business.'

'If we need them, then how could you– ?'

'Just slipped my mind, what with all those other responsibilities I've had to shoulder.' Wade moved towards the door, an unpleasant smirk on his lips. 'Nadine knows where to find me, just in case you change your mind.'

And then he was gone, and Katie was staring at the spot where he had stood with a sinking feeling of dread in the pit of her stomach.

Katie found Nadine up a ladder trying to mend a rusting drainpipe. From directly underneath, the giant shrimp tattoo clasping her left buttock was plainly visible.

'May I see you in my office, please.'

Nadine stuck her hammer in the tool belt round her naked midriff, and slid down the ladder with the ease of a cat.

As soon as the office door was closed behind them, Katie said without preamble, 'Wade Grenville's gone. I fired him.'

Nadine paled. 'Oh Lord, there's gonna be trouble now.'

'That's what he said too.'

'He'll bring you to your knees if he thinks you've done him a bad turn.'

'*He's* the one who's done *me* a bad turn,' Katie said indignantly. 'I know he's been milking the place dry, sticking all the cash in his back pocket. What I don't know is how far *you* were in on it.'

Instantly Nadine's face became a picture of fear. She clasped Katie's arm, and for a horrible moment Katie thought she was going to throw herself at her feet. 'You don't know what you're dealing with when it comes to Wade Grenville. He's a powerful man round these parts. I only did what he told me 'cause I didn't want no trouble.'

Katie tried to disengage her arm. 'It isn't really a good enough excuse for participating in his dishonest schemes, is it?'

'Just give me one more chance,' Nadine howled, keeping a firm grip on her. 'Don't throw me out on the street – I need this job. I'm a poor widow-woman with kids to feed. I can't go back to the shrimp boats and haul those nets. These old bones are too tired. You gotta give me one more chance and I'll make it up to you, I swear.'

Katie briefly closed her eyes. She knew Nadine was putting on a performance just for her benefit, but it was a curiously moving performance all the same. She opened her eyes again and looked down at the head of black hair bent over her hand, like a supplicant's before the altar. She noticed now that there were a few grey strands interwoven with the black.

'How old are you?' she said more gently.

'Forty-eight.'

'And your children?'

'The girl's fifteen, the boy's twelve.'

Katie smiled. 'My girls are fourteen and eleven.'

'I knew a woman would understand,' Nadine said, the sparkle back in her eye. 'I knew you wouldn't harden your heart against a mother that's gotta earn a living for her little ones.'

'One more chance,' Katie said firmly. 'If I catch you cheating me again, you're out.'

'I'll play by the rules, I swear. There ain't a soul on this island more loyal than me when I give my word.'

'Good. Now, do you know anything about licences – the ones I'm supposed to have for the guesthouse?'

Nadine shook her head so that her black hair swung out in a wide arc. 'That's paperwork, ma'am – ain't my department. Wouldn't even know where to look.'

Katie had feared as much. 'Then there's just one more thing.'

Nadine eyed her warily, uncertain whether another axe was about to fall.

Katie said, 'Tell the couple in number six that the previous manager, who has now been replaced, made a mistake and allocated them a room that has already been reserved. Ask them to find alternative accommodation as from today.'

Nadine gave her a broad grin. 'You're somethin' else, ma'am. Perhaps you're gonna be a match for Mr Grenville after all.'

Katie was going through the filing cabinets in a so far fruitless search for the elusive expired licences when there was a timid knock at the door.

'Come in,' she said warily, prepared for almost anything.

The door opened a crack and a pale-skinned woman in her early thirties with fine blond hair and a scattering of freckles took a tentative step inside. She seemed dismayed by the whirlwind of papers that surrounded Katie, and hung back on the threshold.

'You look real busy. I'll come by another time when it's more convenient.'

'No, it's all right,' Katie said. 'Come on in.' She removed a pile of papers from the visitor's chair.

'I'm Polly Lowrey,' the girl said, perching on the very edge of the seat. 'The one Mr Vance next door was making all the fuss about.'

Katie eyed her visitor with bemusement. She wore a smock that fell below her knees, with a pretty printed design of fishes and corals, and her fine hair was tied back demurely with a matching bow. She was hardly the brazen hussy of Willie Vance's description. She looked as though she wouldn't say 'boo' to a goose.

'I thought I'd better come explain about the cats,' she continued. 'I heard Mr Vance was bending your ear about it.'

Katie's face must have betrayed her amazement because Polly said, 'I know, you can't even paint your toenails on this island without everyone knowing about it.'

'Thanks for the warning,' Katie said wryly.

'Anyway, about the cats – I know Mr Vance tells everyone I take them off to be . . . fixed . . . But that's not the way it is. I'm just trying to take care of them because he's too old to do it. He's got no business keeping so many at his age.'

'No one has any business keeping that many,' Katie agreed.

'So I take them to be dewormed and have their injections, even though I don't really have the money—'

'What work do you do?'

'I'm an artist. One of the struggling kind.'

'How wonderful to be so creative. I'd love to see some of your work.'

Polly blushed. 'Really?'

'Yes, really.'

'Well, I'm only across the road. You just come on by any time you want. But don't expect anything grand like this place.'

'This place is falling to pieces,' Katie said grimly.

'Oh, it's not that bad – not like Mr Vance's house. I worry he's going to do himself an injury one of these days on those stairs.'

Katie thought that if Polly ever wanted to give up being an artist, she would easily find a vocation in the caring professions. 'It must cost a fortune to keep all those cats in food,' she said.

'I buy the odd tin, but it doesn't go far. Mr Vance doesn't feed them properly – leaves them half wild to fend for themselves. Says that's the way nature intended. But some of the kittens are skin and bone.'

'Surely something can be done about it,' Katie said indignantly.

'Perhaps if *you* had a word with him . . .'

It was very disconcerting, Katie thought, how people here involved you almost at once in their business, even expected you to take sides, though you knew almost nothing, really, of the history. 'Mr Vance doesn't strike me as the kind of man who listens to reason,' she said.

'No – he was real mean today when I brought his cats back. Sometimes he scares me half to death with that temper of his.'

'Well, I'm not sure what I can do, but I'll give it some thought.'

Polly's whole face lit up. 'Oh, would you?'

Before Katie could reassure her again, the door flew open to reveal a flustered Nadine. 'Sorry to butt in, ma'am, but we got ourselves a real problem. Ella and Nadia and the other one just upped and walked out, not a word to anyone. The guests' rooms haven't been touched and now there isn't a soul to clean them.'

'Oh my,' Polly cried, as distressed as if it were her own problem. 'Oh my, oh my.'

Katie told herself to stay calm. This was the first move in the battle Wade Grenville had vowed to wage against her, and she mustn't surrender to panic at the first sign of attack. 'In that case, Nadine,' she said firmly, 'for today you and I will just have to clean the rooms ourselves.'

Nadine scowled. Polly's eyes were huge in her pale face. 'Oh my,' she said. 'I'd better give you a hand.'

'Thank you, Polly. I'll pay you, of course . . . ten dollars an hour?'

'You don't have to—'

'Nonsense, I insist.'

From the way Nadine raised her eyes to heaven, Katie realised the rate she had offered Polly was over the odds – but in the circumstances it was the least of her worries.

There was only one employment agency for domestic staff in town, Nadine had told her, and that was where Katie headed in the late afternoon, after almost a solid day of physical labour that had left her with pains in muscles she didn't even know she had. But by the end all twelve units in The Tropical Hideout were spotless – 'not like when those lazy Polish good-for-nothings were doing the job,' Nadine muttered – and Katie almost hugged her and Polly with gratitude.

She found the name Nadine had given her on the outside of a building in Duval Street, and climbed the stairs to a one-room office where a man sat flicking through a file of what appeared to be employees' details, and barking into a phone that he held cradled against his shoulder. He was large-boned and bearded, and a pair of huge bare feet stuck out beneath his desk. He would have looked more at home on a boat than in an office, Katie decided as he waved at her to take a seat.

'Name's Bob Nichols,' he almost shouted when he replaced the receiver.

'Katie Colman,' she said, 'from The Tropical Hideout.'

Bob Nichols looked her up and down. 'That's Wade Grenville's place, right?'

'No,' Katie said, 'it's my place. And Mr Grenville no longer works there.'

He expelled his breath in a sort of whistling sound through a gap where his front tooth should have been. 'Is that a fact?'

'I'm having a clean sweep,' Katie said. 'I'm looking for new domestic staff as well, to do cleaning and other duties.'

'Is that a fact?' Bob said again, causing Katie to drum her fingers irritably against the metal clasp of her handbag.

'These are all facts, Mr Nichols. So I was wondering if you have anyone suitable on your books?'

'Nope,' Bob said calmly, not even glancing down at the pile of employees' details on his desk.

'I beg your pardon—'

'I said I ain't got no one suitable.'

'But you must have. What are those?' She gestured at the pile.

'These people have all been placed,' Bob said in a tone intended to cut all argument short.

But Katie refused to be so easily deflected. 'Are you seriously trying to tell me that there isn't a single person seeking domestic employment in the whole of Key West?'

'This is high season. Staff are in demand.'

'But surely they don't all stay put in their jobs, it's a transient population, isn't it?'

'All I know is, I got nobody for you.'

Katie cast a desperate glance around. 'Look, what is the going rate?'

'Eight dollars an hour.'

'I'll pay ten,' she entreated.

He hesitated, but only for a moment. 'Like I told you, lady, I can't help you.'

'Then who can?'

Bob Nichols shrugged. 'There's no one does this line of work 'cept me.'

'I see.' Katie rose and said in her most frozen tone, 'I'm sorry to have wasted your time, Mr Nichols.'

As she left his cramped office, she saw him reach out a powerful muscled forearm for the telephone.

'I just know he was lying to me,' Katie said indignantly to Harvey.

'That's the bubba system for you. Wade Grenville is one of the town's good old boys. When it comes to a punch-up with the interlopers – which all of us are, as far as they're concerned – those guys stick together.'

'But what am I going to do?' Katie wailed.

'Have another slice of Key Lime pie – and we'll think of something.'

'I don't like Wade Grenville,' Chico said, coiled on the arm of Harvey's chair in a slinky beaded evening gown and full make-up, two manicured hands rubbing the tension from Harvey's shoulders. 'Wade Grenville is no friend of gay people. I'll clean for you afternoons, after I finish up here, till you find somebody else.'

'You're an angel,' Katie said, tempted, had it not been for her fear of smudging his make-up, to throw her arms round his neck and kiss him.

Two tall and well-muscled men wandered in from the swimming pool area with not a stitch of clothing on. Katie tried to keep her eyes firmly on Harvey's face, and saw him sneak a sideways glance at them as they passed through. Chico's eyes darkened with fury.

'Why do you always have to stare?' he demanded.

'Lighten up, sweetie-pie, it isn't a crime to look.'

Katie, anxious to avoid a plate-throwing session, said quickly, 'Polly from across the road is prepared to carry on cleaning for me too, at least till I find permanent staff. I think she needs the money—'

'Polly has the softest heart on the island,' Harvey said. 'She can't walk away from a friend in need.'

'I hardly qualify as a friend – I only met her this morning.'

'Time doesn't have the same meaning in Key West,' Harvey laughed. 'You'll learn – won't she, Chico?'

'Talking of time—' Chico tapped his diamante evening watch.

'We're going down to see the drag show at the La-te-da,' Harvey explained. 'It's great fun – you must come along one night when you're more in the mood . . . But before we run off, I think I might have a solution for your little problem.'

'What?' Katie said desperately.

'Forget going through Bubba Bob – Grenville obviously got to him first. Rather place an ad in our local paper. I hope you read it – it's a laugh a minute, especially the crime page.'

Katie remembered seeing an item that very morning about an irate wife knocking her husband over with his own Harley Davidson and driving three times over his most sensitive area because she said he 'paid more attention to that damned machine than he ever did to me'.

'I can quite see why everyone here is addicted to it,' she said. 'It's the obvious solution to put an ad in there – I should have thought of it myself.'

'Happy to be of service,' Harvey said, half rising to leave.

'Wait – I have another problem that mightn't be quite so easy to solve,' Katie said quickly, causing him to sink straight back into his seat, while Chico made an impatient pout with his scarlet-painted lips.

'How else can Uncle Harvey help?'

'Wade Grenville announced on his way out the door that he'd let my licences expire.'

Harvey let out a low whistle. 'Boy, are you ever in de-ee-eep shit!'

Katie had been rather afraid of provoking that sort of reaction. 'How deep?'

'Without those licences, you're dead in the water,' Harvey said bluntly. 'You won't be allowed to operate The Tropical Hideout as a guesthouse, and it'll be a whole lot harder to find a buyer. Much though I'm dying to get my hands on the place, even I'd have to withdraw my offer. If I was going to sink that much capital into a property, my bank manager and I would have to know I stood a chance of recouping it from paying guests.'

'You're so insensitive, *querido*,' Chico complained, looking at Katie's white face. 'Why don't you break it gently to the poor girl?'

'It's all right, I want the truth,' Katie insisted.

'To run a guesthouse you need three licences,' Harvey explained. 'First city, then county, then state. They don't cost all that much, but they're worth their weight in gold. Only a limited number of city licences have been issued in Key West because tourist numbers have to be kept under control so they can be evacuated if a hurricane hits. Residents have the option of staying or not, but I think most would choose to take their chances in these solid old houses rather than exposed out on the Seven Mile Bridge.'

'Yes, I can quite see why,' Katie said, remembering how vulnerable she had felt on the long thin strand of road suspended above the endless stretch of ocean.

'So anyone who wants to buy a guesthouse must get one with existing licences. In theory no new ones are being issued, and it's even a problem renewing old ones that have lapsed. Basically, you have to apply to the commission and pray like hell.'

'What do you think my chances are?' Katie said bleakly.

'Frankly, not good. The trouble is, Wade Grenville is from an old Conch family and so are most of the commissioners.

171

They feel the world is invading their domain, and they'd rather not give licences to anyone who isn't one of them. If Grenville's already got to them – which you can be pretty sure he has – then you'll have double the trouble.'

'But I can't just roll over and allow him to put me out of business, Katie said stubbornly.

'That would be giving in to the pig,' Chico almost spat.

'I'll put you in touch with the commission,' Harvey said, 'but I don't have any pull with them, being from the north and a fag on top of it. Chico, on the other hand, comes from an old Cuban Conch family, but they tend to stay out of local politics – basically 'cause they're all just waiting for Havana to open up. Anyway, I'm not sure they'd do Chico any favours. They're not exactly wild about our lifestyle, are they sweetie-pie?'

Chico looked fiercely embarrassed by the revelation. Harvey patted his hand soothingly. 'They're no worse than my lot, who've cut me off completely. But what do we care, huh baby? You're my family, and the islanders, and the people who come to stay with us here. You'll see,' he said to Katie, 'when you've been with us a while, Key West will adopt you and take you to its heart.'

Katie smiled wanly. 'If I can't get those licences renewed, I won't be here long enough to find out.'

City Hall was the sort of monotonous warren of drab corridors typical of government buildings everywhere, and seemed to have little in common with the warm, exotic town Katie left behind as she stepped over the threshold. Her heels clicked on stone floors as she scanned the names on office doors. She was wearing the new sandals that had pushed her credit card bill close to the limit, and a sundress with wispy straps and a handkerchief skirt that revealed a good expanse of calf. Her strawberry blonde hair was newly washed, her make-up applied by Chico in a far more dramatic fashion than she would have done it herself. 'You look ravishing,' Chico had said. 'I just love the fuchsia-pink lipstick.' Whereupon she had felt obliged to give it to him as a token of her thanks.

The whole elaborate preparation had reminded Katie of the tactics she and her teenage girlfriends used to employ to stack the odds in their favour when they took their driving tests. 'Show as much leg as possible,' had been the conventional wisdom. But Katie wasn't so sure that what had worked for her at eighteen was quite as appropriate at thirty-seven.

Nonsense, Harvey told her, she wasn't over the hill yet, and she was a long way from strutting all her stuff by Key West standards. Anyway, she couldn't afford to leave anything to chance in her battle over the all-important licences. Wade Grenville would have used every weapon in his arsenal, and Katie would just have to employ a few of her own. So she floated in her perfumed finery down corridors where, according to Harvey, the wheels of justice were oiled by mutual favours for the home town boys. 'Conchs don't see it as corruption,' Harvey explained. 'Often they don't even profit financially from the strings they pull. It's just that they grew up together, they've known each other all their lives, and they take care of their own.' Wade Grenville, unfortunately, fell squarely into that category.

When she finally stopped in front of the right door, the thudding of her heart was almost as loud as the rap of her knuckles on wood. 'Come on in,' a voice called.

Claude Wyler was going bald with bad grace, the few strands of hair that remained to him combed carefully over his shining pate. He looked Katie up and down with an appreciative gleam in his small, rather piggy eyes.

'If you see him after lunch,' Harvey had calculated, 'he'll have downed a couple of bourbons at the Moose Club – and who knows what you might talk him into then.'

As she sat opposite Wyler now, she crossed one leg over the other, allowing her skirt to ride just a little way up her thighs. Wyler's eyes were drawn to them like a magnet.

'I have a small problem, and I've been told you're the only

man who can help,' Katie said with what she hoped was just the right amount of guilelessness.

'Anything I can do, the pleasure's all mine,' Wyler beamed.

Katie slid across his desk the expired licences she had finally unearthed at the back of the last filing cabinet she had ransacked. Wyler put on a pair of half-moon reading glasses. Slowly the smile faded from his face.

'So you're the new owner of The Tropical Hideout?'

'That's right,' Katie said, keeping her fuchsia-tinted lips arched in a coquettish smile.

'This isn't a "small" problem, lady. These licences should've been renewed six months ago.'

Katie had learned a thing or two in the short time she had been in Key West. She knew better now than to bad-mouth Wade Grenville to one of his buddies. 'It's all been a terrible mistake,' she said breathlessly. 'My father inherited the guest-house quite unexpectedly when he was terminally ill with cancer. What with living so far away in London, and being so sick, there was a breakdown of communication with the manager here . . . and the licences just sort of got forgotten. I'm sure you understand how it was, Mr Wyler.'

The piggy eyes came to rest on her beseeching face. 'I don't mean to sound heartless, ma'am. I'm sorry about your father and all. But the policy round here is once a licence expires, we don't renew it. End of story.'

Katie let her skirt ride up a tiny bit higher. 'I know, Mr Wyler. But I thought just this once, because of the exceptional circumstances . . .' She let her words hang in the air.

Wyler thoughtfully stroked the strands of hair plastered over his scalp. 'Wade Grenville's a good man,' he said at last.

'I know – I'm not saying it was his fault – '

'I hear you and he have parted company.'

'I expect he's used to running his own show . . . doesn't want the boss looking over his shoulder.'

'You planning on staying long, then?'

'At least till I can sort out all the . . . not so small problems.'

Wyler sighed heavily. 'I wouldn't get your hopes up. The commission doesn't look kindly on out-of-town folks who don't keep things paid up to date. As a matter of fact, I'd say the commission will take a very dim view of this indeed. Good day to you, ma'am.'

As she turned to leave, her skirt twirling up in a little arc, Katie noticed that Wyler's eyes, instead of shifting to the flash of bare leg, remained grimly glued to the offending licences, as though he were a judge who had already been handed a guilty verdict and was now trying to decide on the severity of the sentence.

'I don't think I stand a chance,' Katie said almost tearfully to Guy on the telephone afterwards. 'Wade Grenville obviously got to that Wyler man first. He'd made up his mind to turn me down before I even walked through the door.'

'It all sounds an even worse mess than I feared,' Guy said grimly.

'I'm afraid I won't be able to find a buyer so easily now,' Katie continued, kicking off the expensive sandals that had failed to make any real impression on Claude Wyler. 'People only want guesthouses with existing licences. Even Harvey Grossman from next door would have to withdraw his offer.'

'That *is* bad news,' Guy said morosely.

'There's nothing I can do about any of it except wait for the commission's decision.'

'Let's face it, Katie, you're out of your depth. You've never run a business before and you're just not experienced enough to deal with the problems involved.'

Katie gave an weary dab at her fuchsia lipstick with a tissue. Perhaps Guy was right, perhaps she just wasn't up to the job.

'Look, why don't you just enjoy your holiday – do a bit of sightseeing, have a rest,' Guy suggested. 'Then, if you get your licences, you can hammer out a deal with the chap next door. If not, instruct some real estate agent to find a rich New York buyer who wants to do up a second home. There may not be quite so many offers, but someone's bound to take it off your hands.'

I know, Katie wanted to say, but that wasn't what I dreamed of. She had pictured her family spending winter holidays here, year after year, under perfect blue skies, sunning themselves amidst the trimmed-back tropical foliage by the pool, curling on cane rocking chairs in the cool shade of the porch. She had seen it all in her mind's eye as clearly as if it had already happened, and now the dream was slipping from her grasp.

'I suppose you're right,' she said to Guy. 'I might as well make the most of the waiting to have a holiday of sorts.'

'That's my girl.'

When she had hung up the phone, she wandered down into the garden, passing under the whispering trees whose names Polly was teaching her – the spreading *ficus elastica* or rubber tree, planted no doubt by some sturdy sea captain from a cutting brought over from the Caribbean on a long-ago sailing ship, and the jacaranda with its exotic purple blooms. She tried again to listen for her father's voice in the breezes through the leaves.

'I love this gift you gave me, Daddy,' she said. 'I don't want to lose it, but I may not be able to hold on to it if it's down to my efforts alone. Maybe the only one who can help me now is you.'

Chapter Ten

~

Perched on a stool at the bar of the Hog's Breath Saloon, Katie downed her second Key Lime Slammer of the evening. This was another island essential, Harvey had told her, though he himself almost never ventured down town where the locals and straight visitors hung out. But Katie felt she must have the experience, though it was perhaps not quite what Guy had had in mind when he'd suggested she switch her focus to more tourist-like pursuits. Still, she would be able to tell him there were uses for the local key lime which he hadn't even dreamed of.

She toyed with the idea of ordering a third Slammer. It might take her mind off the gloomy fact that there had been no responses to the advertisement she had placed for cleaning staff in the *Key West Citizen*. Harvey was at a loss to understand it. 'We can't lay this at Wade Grenville's door,' he'd said, thoughtfully stroking his moustache. 'He may have a few pals on the commission, but he doesn't control the whole town.'

His words made Katie feel that she and The Tropical Hideout must be under some sort of jinx. And despite the help of Nadine and Polly, and Chico in the afternoons, she was still having to muck in to clean the rooms. Some holiday, she thought wearily, draining her glass.

Beside her a group of locals were bantering with each other in loud, slightly drunken voices. 'Hey, Frank,' said one, 'meet my friend Ferdinand.'

'I don't see no one,' Frank said, ostentatiously looking over the head of a diminutive Cuban.

'He's right there in front of you.'

Frank peered down. 'That's a guy? I got wallet photos bigger than that guy.'

'At least he's not stupid – like that dog of yours.'

'My dog ain't stupid.'

'What about that time you put his supper dish in front of a tree, and he ran at it so fast he knocked himself out on the trunk?'

'He was hungry.'

'Stupid, more like.'

Frank turned away in disgust, and caught Katie's eye. 'Can I buy you another one of those?' he asked, indicating her empty glass.

Katie cast a wary eye over him. He was so large his feet were the size of boats. 'No thank you,' she said with an apologetic smile. 'I was just on my way out of here.'

He shrugged and turned back to his friends. Katie slipped off her bar stool and left them to it. She emerged to a reddening sky, and wondered if she should pay a visit to Mallory Square for the daily sunset celebration everyone kept telling her she had to see at least once. Not that she was truly in the mood for the tourist trail. She'd had trouble concentrating at Audubon House on the naturalist's detailed paintings of the Birds of America. Even while gazing at the bars of Spanish gold in Mel Fisher's treasure museum, she'd found her mind wandering back to her problems at The Tropical Hideout.

But the sun was sinking fast and Mallory Square was only a stone's throw away. Katie decided she had nothing to lose.

There were rows of people sitting along the pier, their legs dangling over the edge, their eyes fixed firmly on the sun slipping down over the Gulf of Mexico towards the distant horizon. Other less serious onlookers stood in knots around various street performers, occasionally clapping or laughing. Katie found herself watching a man who was holding up a flaming hoop so that a cat could leap through it in a perfect arc. The crowd applauded, and the cat sat on a raised stool accepting the adulation like a seasoned film star. Then she repeated her fiery flight in the opposite direction, and a hat was passed round. Katie dropped in some loose change and wandered on.

The next group was watching an aspiring Houdini wrapped in padlocked chains, writhing on the ground in elaborate contortions designed, presumably, to release him from his bonds. His bulging muscles rippled with undulating tattoos, his skintight costume looked none too clean. Katie decided not to linger till he made good his escape.

'What's the most important number in the world?' shouted a man dressed like Uncle Sam in a particularly tall top hat.

'Twenty-two,' chorused his audience.

'You got it,' he cried, passing out twenty-two dollar bills with his photograph on them. 'That's why they call me Love 22. Who won the Nobel Peace Prize in '84?'

The crowd looked blank at that one.

'Desmond Tu-Tu,' came the triumphant reply.

There was a burst of applause from the people sitting along the pier. The sun had slipped below the horizon, marking the end of another day in paradise.

Katie ambled disconsolately past the rows of vendors selling baubles to the tourists. Another day without news of her licences, another day with no replacement staff . . .

'Looks like you be carrying the weight of the world on your shoulders, child,' a voice behind her said.

Its owner was an extraordinary vision in bright purple with a crown like a blazing star on her head. She had squeezed her huge bulk into a tiny stall emblazoned with the legend, 'Know Your Own Future, Have your Fortune Told by the Amazing Lady Lavender.'

'Reckon you needs a little help with them dark clouds be

hanging over yo' head,' Lady Lavender declared.

'Thanks, but I don't really believe in clairvoyants,' Katie said, feeling rather foolish.

'I ain't no clairvoyant, child.' Lavender held up an unfamiliar chain, broken at intervals by tortoiseshell disks. 'I be asking the spirits 'bout your destiny, 'bout how to solve them problems be praying on yo' mind.'

'I don't really believe in spirits either,' Katie objected weakly.

'You be doing the talking, I be doing the believing.'

Katie looked closer at the face beneath the crown. It wasn't young – perhaps the woman was in her fifties or sixties, though it was difficult to tell because the fat beneath the ebony skin kept it smooth and free of wrinkles. But it was the eyes that drew Katie towards the outrageous apparition. They seemed to look right into her, as though they saw into places in her soul that she hadn't even visited herself.

'I honestly don't think you can help,' Katie said awkwardly, but nonetheless feeling quite unable to walk away.

Lavender reached forward and grasped Katie's hands in a movement so lightning quick that she had no time to back off. She closed her eyes and began to chant, 'You be under the hex, somebody be putting the evil eye on you. But you got yo'self protecshun from the other side. Trouble is, it doan reach you 'less you gets yo'self out from under that curse.' Her eyes flew open again. 'You goan tell the Lady Lavender who be wishing you harm?'

Katie felt as though the confession was being sucked from her. 'There's this man I fired from my hotel – Wade Grenville – and ever since then I've had the most terrible trouble.' And the words came tumbling out, one after the other, about her father's death and the guesthouse he had left her and the long journey to see it and the trouble when she arrived – dirty dealings, expired licences, staff who walked out.

'This be worse than I thought,' Lavender said grimly. 'That Wade Grenville, he be one ba-a-ad muthuh . . . But he be no match for the saints, when we be bringing them on to our side. No, sirree, that man goan find out 'bout the power of the rightuss!'

'Excuse me, are y'all gonna be long?' said a young woman with a Southern drawl and baby-doll blonde curls. 'I'd just love to have my fortune told—'

'Honey, we all done here,' Lavender said, heaving herself out of the stall. 'This lady and I got business needs seeing to – yes sirree – we goan rattle some bones tonight.' And she took Katie firmly by the arm and set off with her at a rapid march away from the revellers on the pier.

At the bottom of Duval Street Lavender paused, her mighty bosom heaving in its purple swathing as she fought for breath.

'Where are we going?' Katie said.

'Other enda Duval, behind the lighthouse. Bahama Village, that's where my people stay.'

'Let me get us a taxi, then.'

'You right – no time to lose.' Lavender bore down on a pedicycle driven by a skinny youth with a deep tan and a long ponytail. 'You be taking us ochunside on Emma Street.'

The youth turned on his cycle seat and eyed Lavender's huge bulk with dismay. A row of little corks on strings hung from the visor of his baseball cap. No doubt he was a student seeing a bit of the world before returning to settle down in his native Australia. Katie was afraid that, if he tried to tote Lavender's bulk, he would never make it back.

'Surely a car would be a lot quicker,' she intervened hastily.

'I 'spect you be right.' Lavender glared at the youth as though indignant at having to let him off the hook. 'You git yo skinny ass out of here.'

Not needing to be told twice, the boy pedalled furiously away in search of less cumbersome quarry. Katie spotted a cab with its light on and did a little jig on the sidewalk in an effort to flag it down.

They headed for the area of shotgun houses which Katie had first seen on Harvey's tour. The driver swore as he swerved around chickens scratching in the middle of the road. 'You be minding yo' language,' Lavender warned him.

Her little shack, built close up to the road, was well cared for though the outside was unpainted and the decoration minimal. Inside were the standard two rooms, the first dominated by a near life-size plaster statue of the Virgin Mary with fishermen languishing at her feet. Around her were the garish painted faces of a dozen saints, and also a number of strange objects Katie didn't recognise – huge cauldrons full of stones, and primitive emblems that seemed African in origin. Before them were stacked what appeared to be offerings – piles of melons, coconuts, cakes, bottles of soda and beer. Everything flickered strangely in the light of rows of votive candles.

Lavender marched her down the short corridor into the kitchen. 'Got me everything I needs right here,' she said. 'Juss have to find it. You set yo'self down.'

She began to riffle through clusters of packed and dried herbs hanging from the low beam of the ceiling, her fingers swiftly lighting on their choices. Then she turned to a small stack of the African-looking objects Katie had seen in the sitting room, selecting crude iron tools and a small grey cone with cowrie shells forming eyes and a jagged open mouth that sent a ripple of superstitious fear through Katie's soul. Lavender nodded approvingly as she piled her weird and wonderful booty into a fraying straw basket with a knot of chicken feathers tied to the handle.

'Thas right,' she muttered, 'thas good,' and she pushed open the door to the little back yard where honeysuckle vines wrapped themselves around mango and papaya trees and chickens rooted in the fertile earth. Katie watched through the dusty window as Lavender's purple figure bent to pluck the healing secrets from herb bushes planted in geometric formations.

'This is crazy,' she said to herself. 'What on earth am I doing here?'

They set off to find another taxi on Duval Street, the

contents of Lavender's brimming basket filling its interior with a strange and musky scent. She hugged it to her as though it contained a consignment of gold bars or secret government papers.

'You be setting the world to rights tonight, Lavender?' the cab driver said.

'I be doing my bit, I reckon, Turtlegrass. The res' be up to the spirits, Lord bless 'em.'

Katie wondered whether her guests were out, or safely in their rooms, and if not, what they would make of the Lady Lavender. She had removed the starburst crown while collecting up her herbs, but her vast purple satin bulk was still an awesome sight.

As soon as she crossed the threshold of The Tropical Hideout, Lavender closed her eyes and began swaying back and forth, muttering incomprehensible incantations under her breath. Then she marched purposefully through the downstairs rooms, checking each in turn, rummaging in her basket.

'First we lights some fire,' she said. 'Put them evil forces to flight.'

In each room she lit a pair of candles in half-coconut shells. Soon the scent of jasmine filled the air. It smelled to Katie like some exotic eastern shrine.

'That be better already,' Lavender said with satisfaction. 'Now I got emblems, I got poshuns, goan chase they evil butts right out of here.'

Katie watched with a mixture of fascination and dismay as Lavender took the small grey concrete cone from her basket. She saw now that the 'face' had strange markings on its cheeks, like tribal scars.

'This be Eleggua, opener of the ways,' Lavender said, placing the cone by the jamb of the front door. 'He be keeping out evil that try to come in from the outside.'

Katie looked at the gaping cowrie mouth. He was more likely, she thought, to frighten the wits out of some unsuspecting guest.

'Do you really think it's necessary . . . ?'

'You want them licences or not?'

Katie watched helplessly as Lavender circled round sprinkling scented herbs and withdrawing shadowy objects from her basket which she secreted in dark corners. Katie felt she was a lot better off not knowing what they were.

She went through to the kitchen and sat with her head in her hands, waiting for the bizarre ritual to be over and wondering how on earth she had got herself into all this. That was how Nadine found her.

'In heaven's name, ma'am, what's the Lady Lavender doing here?'

'I was just asking myself the same question.'

'You didn't invite her to do all those rituals, did you?'

'I'm afraid I let her talk me into it. But I don't suppose it'll do much harm – she's just some fortune teller from Mallory Square.'

'Begging your pardon, ma'am, but the folks down in Bahama Village don't think so. That stuff she does for the tourists is just so she can afford to take care of her own if they can't afford the fee.'

'Take care of them how?'

'The Lady Lavender's a priestess of *santeria*,' Nadine said, and Katie couldn't help noticing the tone of awe in her voice. 'It's the way of the saints.'

'And what way is that, exactly?'

'It's the old African religion all mixed up with Catholic beliefs. When the Africans were sent as slaves to Cuba, Spanish law said they had to be baptised Catholic, so they ended up worshipping their old African gods under the names of Catholic saints.'

Katie gave a little shiver. 'You're not trying to tell me she's performing voodoo or something out there?'

'Not exactly. It's more white magic than witchcraft. But there's talk of strange rituals in the cemetery at night, and animal sacrifices—'

'*Sacrifices*,' Katie cried.

'They say it gives the spirits strength to protect the living from harm. It's supposed to be mighty powerful stuff.'

Katie gave Nadine a searching look. 'But surely you don't believe – ?'

'It's not believing causes half the troubles of this world,' Lavender boomed from the doorway. Nadine gave a guilty start, like a schoolgirl caught smoking in the lavatories.

'You can burn them candles right down to they ends, but you doan have respect for the spirits, they doan give you no protecshun. The ancestors neither. It's our belief they be guiding us from the world beyond and from inside our heads, like the voice of the conscience. You remember yo' daddy, child – you show some respect.'

Katie opened her mouth to object, but Nadine jumped in first. 'Can I make you some coffee, Lady Lavender?'

'The only thing we goan drink here tonight be this.' Lavender drew a glass bottle filled with a greenish liquid out of the bottom of her now empty basket. One fierce look at Nadine was enough to send her scurrying for three glasses.

'Now wait a minute, I'm not swallowing anything if I don't know what's in it,' Katie objected half-heartedly as Lavender poured out her cocktail.

'Juss a few of the Lady Lavender's herbs, mixed with some verbena oil – but it be giving you powerful protecshun, yes sirree.'

Nadine's fingers plucked nervously at her shrimp tattoo. But she lifted her glass and downed its contents in one. Lavender nodded approvingly, then fixed her eye on Katie.

'All right, all right,' Katie grumbled. 'It doesn't smell too bad.' The taste wasn't unpleasant either, like a faintly perfumed oil on the tongue. At least it couldn't possibly contain eye of newt and toe of frog . . . or could it? It was hard to tell, since Katie had never, to her knowledge, tasted either.

'That be doing the trick,' Lavender said, 'long as you wears this round yo' neck.'

She took from the bottom of her basket a necklace strung almost entirely with gold beads, with here and there a clear and a red one interspersed. She handed it reverently to Katie. 'This be the necklace of Oshun, spirit of the river, same as the blessed Virgin of Caridad. She be the owner of sweet things, of love and money and things of the heart. She be bringing you health, luck, tranquillity and the good things in life.'

Lavender waited, tapping her fingers on the table, till Katie placed the necklace reluctantly round her neck. 'Thass good,' she said. 'But you keep it hid – don't be showing it to nobody.

That suited Katie just fine.

'Things be different round this place now,' Lavender said, gathering herself and her basket up with a satisfied air. 'But I be keeping an eye on you, juss the same.'

'Thank you,' Katie said, not knowing quite what else was required. 'If you'll just wait while I get my car keys, I'll give you a lift home.'

Lavender spoke little on the drive back, as though all the energy had been drained from her by the work she had done at The Tropical Hideout. When Katie returned, she went round extinguishing candles, telling herself she couldn't leave them burning all night, not with the fire regulations. But she didn't remove the strange beaded necklace even when she got into bed.

That night she dreamed of her father again, as she had on the first day she arrived. Only this time she woke without the feeling of loss, filled instead with an inexplicable sense that he was somehow very near.

Katie had just come back from doing the shopping run for breakfast, the bagels from the bakery down the road still warm in their brown paper bag, when a fearsome scream rent the air. She dumped the bagels unceremoniously on a bookshelf and charged down the passage, almost colliding with Nadine at the other end.

'What's going on?' she cried.

'I think it's Mrs Parish from Number Two.'

She was a soft-spoken old lady from Pennsylvania who walked with a limp from the arthritis in her hip and liked to escape the cold northern winters. Katie and Nadine hastened to her door and found her standing frozen to the spot outside it.

'What's the matter, Mrs Parish?' Katie asked solicitously.

The old lady's gaze was fixed on an object lying some distance away on the carpet. 'I picked it up . . . touched it . . . It was lying right in my doorway and I didn't know what it was, so I just bent down and picked it up.'

Katie and Nadine approached this thing that had so upset Mrs Parish, and knelt down to take a closer look. It seemed small and harmless enough, but Katie's heart sank when she saw what it was.

'Oh Lord,' Nadine breathed. 'A chicken's foot.'

'Who could have put it in my doorway?' the old lady cried in a thin, frightened voice.

Katie's eyes met Nadine's in a look of warning. 'Must've been one of those cats from next door,' she said airily. 'They treat my place like their own home.'

Mrs Parish took a step forward, her expression lightening immediately. 'I have a kitty back in Pennsylvania – Tabitha, she's called. Such a naughty creature. When I first got her, why, she was always trying to make me presents of dead mice and birds. Had to give her many a little smack to teach her not to do it.'

'There you are, then,' Katie said.

'But where would a cat get hold of a chicken's foot?'

'I'll just get rid of it,' Nadine said, picking it up gingerly by one claw.

When the offending object was safely disposed of in the outside garbage can, Katie looked around the entrance hall and said to Nadine firmly, 'We'll have to look in all the nooks and crannies and get rid of whatever other little surprises

Lavender's left round the place – including that thing.' She pointed at the strange little concrete face by the door.

At that moment the doorbell rang. Katie briskly opened it. A young girl with a light olive skin and dark hair stood on the threshold smiling nervously at her. 'I've come about the cleaning job. You still need somebody, yes?'

'Oh, yes,' Katie confirmed.

The girl stepped forward and held out her hand. 'I'm Alvira, I have plenty good references.'

'And I'm Mrs Colman. Please, come this way.'

They had barely crossed the entrance hall when the bell rang again. This time Nadine opened the door. There were two girls framed in the entrance, with the same amber skins and shining dark hair.

'Is this the right address for the cleaning job?'

Katie and Nadine exchanged a long look. Then both their eyes travelled down to the concrete cone by the door.

'Please show the applicants in one at a time,' Katie requested. 'And Nadine, don't touch anything else till I say so.'

For her second and critical meeting with Claude Wyler, Katie wore a businesslike suit and Lavender's necklace nestling beneath her blouse. Gone were the girlish clothes and feminine wiles that hadn't been of the slightest use in drawing Wyler on to her side. In their place were a mood of defiance and an iron grip on her emotions. If Wyler delivered the expected blow, she would take it without flinching. She wasn't going to give him the satisfaction of seeing how upset she was.

From the moment she entered the room, Katie's new demeanour seemed to have the desired effect. Claude Wyler too behaved like a changed man. There was no sign of the libertine, the eyes wandering to her hemline. Instead he respectfully held out her chair. 'Can I offer you some refreshment, Mrs Colman? A coffee, maybe, or a soda?'

'No thank you,' Katie said, wishing he would simply come to the point.

'Well, then.' He sat facing her officially across his desk. 'The commission has considered your case.'

Katie waited, hoping he couldn't hear the thudding of her heart against her ribcage.

'The committee doesn't normally make exceptions in these matters. In your case, however, we have decided that in the circumstances, we will allow you the opportunity to make good the payment and renew your city licence.'

Katie had opened her mouth to object before his words began to sink in. Now she heard herself saying faintly, 'I'm terribly grateful, really I am.'

Claude Wyler beamed graciously. 'You are one lucky little lady, Mrs Colman.'

Katie put up a hand to finger the necklace beneath the fabric of her blouse. A vision of the Lady Lavender floated up before her eyes, the chastising voice boomed in her ears, 'You doan have respect in yo' heart for the spirits, they doan give you no protecshun.' Silently she offered up a prayer of thanks to she knew not what mysterious forces for the unexpected victory she had won in this room today.

The case Guy was working on was the kind he would normally relish getting his teeth into. It was a restraint of trade, his client having discovered that one of the senior directors of his company had secretly set up a rival operation, capitalising on his insider knowledge of the firm he had left only days before. It would be Guy's job to stop the new company from trading.

He scribbled a half-hearted note in the margin of his brief. What with Katie being away, he should have been able to focus almost entirely on his work. The problem was, he was finding his evenings without her a little *too* peaceful, too quiet. Though Katie never disturbed him even when she was around, just the knowledge of her absence created a void in the house that he hadn't quite counted on.

Still, he was managing pretty well in the catering department, he thought with some pride, now that he had discovered the shelf with pre-prepared meals for one in the supermarket. Only there were times when, watching the small cardboard container circling in the microwave, he couldn't help feeling it looked rather pathetic and forlorn.

At least he didn't have to bother with the housework, which was dealt with in the usual haphazard fashion by Angie, whom Guy had never actually met. But that was just the way he liked it. All he had to do was leave the money out on the kitchen table, and purchase the cleaning items on the misspelled list she left him in the same place.

So there was little, really, to interrupt the solitary flow of his days except for this absurd inability to concentrate. Exasperated, Guy went to pour himself a Scotch – something he seldom did while working. He was spared from returning straight to his brief by the ringing of the telephone.

'Oh, Guy,' cried Katie's voice, 'you'll never guess what's happened. It's nothing short of a miracle.'

Guy was uncomfortable with miracles, as was the vicar at the church he attended. The vicar held to the view that the so-called miracles of Christ were intended only as symbols of something rather easier to swallow.

'What do you mean?' he said testily.

'All my staff problems have been solved in one go. I've taken on three new girls with glowing references – some from the big hotels.'

'Jolly good.'

'But the real surprise was my licences. They've been renewed without the slightest hitch.'

Guy couldn't help noticing the way Katie emphasised the word 'my', like a proud mother boasting of her precocious offspring. 'How did you accomplish that?' he asked rather sourly.

'I didn't. I think it's all the work of the Lady Lavender – this amazing fortune teller I met—'

'*Fortune teller?*'

'Well, not exactly. She practices a form of white magic called *santeria* – I don't know much about it, really, but she gave me some potions and lucky charms and now everything's just fallen into place.'

'Katie,' Guy said with horror, 'have you taken leave of your senses?'

'Look, it's not just superstition. Lady Lavender says I'm lucky because my father is watching over me.'

Now Guy was beginning to feel real concern. 'I want you to stop all this talk. It's nonsense, you must know it is. And I don't think you should see this Lady Lavender person any more, if she's filling your head with such dangerous rubbish.'

'Oh, Guy – I can't explain. It's this place – it's so different. You'd understand if you came here. It's . . . it's not at all like England.'

'More's the pity,' Guy muttered.

'Anyway, I don't have time to talk any more because Harvey's taking me off to some party to celebrate, so I'll phone again tomorrow.'

'*Katie*,' Guy exploded, but the line had already gone dead.

He sat down heavily, nursing his Scotch, his brief quite forgotten. Whatever strange events his wife was involved in on the other side of the Atlantic, he had the maddening sensation that they were totally beyond his control.

Alcohol was flowing around the floodlit pool of a house in New Town where the annual party of the Innkeepers' Association was being held. In the car on the way over, Harvey had explained how the smaller guesthouses had banded together to share booking facilities, exchange advice and generally expand their influence. She must come and meet some of her fellow sufferers in the bed-and-breakfast business, he had insisted, in case their horror stories finally persuaded her to sell The Tropical Hideout to him.

'Don't count on it,' Katie warned.

'I never count on anything unless it's green and has George Washington's head on it!'

Entering the hosts' box-like house with all the modern gadgets, Katie felt she could have been in almost any American suburb where convenience was what the average citizen aspired to. When the Conchs had sold their gracious old properties to the developers, this was where they had moved.

'*Enchanté*,' said Brad, an attractive silver-haired man in his fifties, when Harvey introduced her as the new kid on the block. His wife Donna kissed Harvey and Chico on both cheeks. Tonight Chico was wearing tight lycra trousers with a loose pink silk blouse, a gold chain belt and bright pink hoop earrings.

'Brad and Donna run the Banyan Tree,' Harvey said when they all had a glass filled with some wicked alcoholic cocktail in their hands. 'They can tell you stories that will send you running straight back to London with your tail between your legs.'

'You have to be crazy to go into this business,' Donna said. 'Do you qualify?'

'I'm only considering being an absentee owner,' Katie protested. 'I'm not planning on running The Tropical Hideout myself.'

'That's what we all said,' Brad laughed, 'till we got hooked.'

'And it's not like we had shitty lives we wanted to escape from,' Donna went on. 'Brad was a big-time corporate lawyer, I was a banker, we had great salaries and expense accounts and a palatial home up north.'

'You can't buy anything like the same square footage for the money down here,' Brad said. 'God only made so much of paradise . . . Anyway, we sank most of our capital into the guesthouse, and what was left was only enough to buy this.' He gestured around at the modest proportions of his home.

'It's very comfortable,' Katie said politely. 'And the garden looks lovely.'

Donna laughed. 'It's difficult to have a lousy garden in Key West. But at least this is home sweet home, away from the Banyan Tree. If we lived on the premises we wouldn't have a moment to ourselves.'

They led Katie out to join the other guests crowded in noisy chatter around the pool. 'A gathering of your peers,' Harvey said wryly. 'They call Key West the Last Bastion of the Over-Qualified. Most of the people who wind up here gave up pretty impressive jobs to have a piece of the good life.'

'What good life?' Brad objected. 'We still get up at six.'

'Sure, but you put on swimming trunks instead of a suit.'

'I don't put on anything except my make-up,' Chico said.

'We'd all die of boredom if we did nothing. We'd succumb to the drink in no time.' Donna put a friendly arm round Katie's shoulders. 'The word is you just won a big victory to renew your licences.'

'I guess you think your troubles are over, but they're only just beginning,' Brad warned.

'I assume you're planning to renovate?'

'Of course,' Katie said. 'I must do something about the awful condition—'

'Then you'll have to deal with the Historical Society. We call them the Hysterical Society.'

'If you're going to start on them, we'll have to leave you,' Harvey declared, heading off into the crowd followed closely by Chico. Katie couldn't help noticing how intensely Chico observed him as he stopped to kiss a fellow guest here and there.

'The Society's done a great job preserving Old Town,' Brad said, 'but they can carry the authenticity thing a bit too far. Sometimes I wonder if they're going to start banning us from using paint pigment that isn't at least a hundred years old.'

'You need their permission to do the tiniest thing,' Donna said. 'Not to mention the fuss if you want to cut down a single tree.'

'The trick is to hire a Conch contractor with connections on all the committees, so he can pull the right strings to get your permits through.'

Katie took a gulp of her drink and almost had to fight for breath. 'If it's all so much hassle, why did you stick it out?'

193

'We just love it here,' Brad said. 'We were bitten by the bug on our very first visit. How about you?'

'I think the bug has got to me as well,' Katie admitted.

Her eye was drawn to Chico in fierce conversation with Harvey, who seemed to be trying to placate him without much success. Chico suddenly threw the entire contents of his glass into Harvey's face. Harvey flinched as ice cubes struck his forehead, then sheepishly wiped the dripping moisture from his eyebrows and moustache. Katie moved as if to go to him.

'Don't pay any attention to those two,' Donna said, putting a restraining hand on her arm. 'They're always having punch-ups in public.'

'You could say Chico is the jealous type,' Brad grinned.

'But they adore each other – just like we do, right honey-bunch?' Donna offered her husband a pouting mouth and he obliged by giving it a resounding kiss.

'It's great to be at an age in life when we can please ourselves,' Donna said to Katie. 'Our kids are finally off at college so we don't have to worry about staying near good schools. Now that we can live for ourselves, this is where we want to be.'

Harvey and Chico seemed to have made up. They were dancing cheek to cheek beneath the scattering of fine white lights threaded like stars through the trees. The other revellers were in various states of inebriation. In their midst stood a man Katie hadn't noticed till now. Perhaps he was standing on something, but he seemed quite incredibly tall – head and shoulders above the rest – with a thick mane of sun-streaked hair falling to his shoulders. He was watching the drunken revelry around him in an amused, detached way so that he seemed like a rock in the midst of a swirling sea. What was it about truly good-looking American men, Katie wondered, that was so much more ... physical, somehow ... than their English counterparts? She lowered her eyes to her drink before he could catch her staring at him.

'Who's that man over there?' she hissed at Donna, but her words were drowned out by a loud splash as a large-breasted woman discarded her T-shirt and leaped into the pool.

'Welcome to the Land of the Free,' Brad laughed.

Katie sneaked another look through the crowds, but the face she was seeking had disappeared.

Someone turned the music up. Donna wandered off, saying it was time for her to mingle. 'Want to dance?' Brad said.

Katie plucked a loose hibiscus blossom from the drinks table and stuck it behind her ear, then let him twirl her about beneath the tropical stars until she felt quite dizzy with joy.

'Something's wrong with Katie,' Guy said to Jemima, sipping a glass of wine in what he still regarded as Robin's flat.

'What, precisely?' Jemima demanded.

'I don't know. She's behaving very peculiarly.'

He cast a jaundiced eye around the familiar sitting room. Jemima had begun to rearrange bits of furniture – her furniture now, he reminded himself with the usual irritation – moving a lamp here, a chair there. It seemed to Guy to show a lack of respect for Robin's memory.

'She's come under the influence of some very undesirable people,' he said. 'There's this chap next door who's obviously the eccentric kind of homosexual – his housekeeper friend seems to dress in women's clothes and generally behave in a very volatile fashion. And then there's a sort of fortune teller with an outrageous name.'

'*Katie* – consulting a *fortune teller*?' Jemima cried in disbelief.

'The woman's gone and persuaded her that all her problems are being solved through spiritual guidance from your father, or some such nonsense.'

Jemima furrowed her brow in thought. 'When you travel, you do encounter all sorts of different cultures and beliefs, and you shouldn't close your mind against them. But neither should you abandon your critical faculties.'

'I'm afraid,' Guy said gloomily, 'that's precisely what Katie's done.'

'I see. Poor Guy.'

Guy wasn't at all sure he liked being an object of Jemima's pity. 'It's Katie I'm worried about,' he reminded her tartly.

'Well, I shouldn't worry too much. She'll be home in a couple of days.'

Guy drained his glass and set it down with a bang. 'That's what she led us all to expect. But now she's phoned saying she wants to extend her stay. She's dead against selling this wretched guesthouse of hers, as I thought we agreed, even though she's had a very respectable offer from the chap next door.'

'What does she want to do with it, then?' Jemima asked with blatant curiosity as she refilled Guy's glass from a rather good bottle out of Robin's cellar.

'Pour all the cash your father left her into renovating the place. I know it's her money to do with as she pleases, but I've told her in the strongest terms I don't think she's making a sound business decision.'

Jemima was listening with what Guy could only describe as fascination. He wondered suddenly why he was confiding all this to her. After all, they had never exactly been close.

'She wants to bring in another manager to run things for her – even after her dreadful experience with that Grenville fellow,' Guy continued, seeming unable to stop himself. 'She's got this idea into her head that we should all go there for holidays.'

'That might be rather fun,' Jemima said.

'It's not *my* idea of fun. The town seems to be crawling with the oddest sort of people.'

Jemima frowned as a sudden thought occurred to her. 'If Katie's staying on longer, what's she doing about getting more leave from the library?'

'That's another bombshell she's just dropped on me. She's decided to give it up – says what she's doing now has made her realise she hasn't enjoyed it in years. She likes working with people, she says.'

'Come on, Guy, you should be pleased. You've been on at her for years that she doesn't need that job.'

'But I don't like her doing things on a whim. It's not like her.'

Guy wandered gloomily to the French windows, where he had stood so often with Robin admiring the view over Regent's Park. 'She doesn't seem to listen to a word I say any more. I just wish your father were here to give her some sound advice.'

'According to this fortune teller,' Jemima reminded him wryly, 'that's exactly what he's doing.'

Chapter Eleven

~

Harvey paced up and down dingy corridors painted a dull beige and poked his head into the doorways of empty bedrooms to mutter gloomily over faded maroon upholstery. 'This place is in dire need of a colour transfusion,' he pronounced to Katie.

'I know. I have some ideas, but they haven't quite come together yet.'

'I'll put through an immediate call to my decorator if you like.'

'If you know a good gardener, that's where I'd like to start,' Katie said evasively. Though she admired everything about Paradise Lodge, she wasn't sure she wanted to create a mere replica next door. She did know she would go to any lengths to avoid the elegant emptiness of her St John's Wood house. What she wanted was something bright, cosy, intimate, but stamped with her own personality. Until now, the overall vision had eluded her.

'Let's treat ourselves to a couple of cold beers in my "suite",' she tempted Harvey. Living in this heat had made her appreciate the merits of chilled American bottled beer, so different from the warm pints of lager served in an English country pub on a rainy winter afternoon.

Harvey gloomily stroked his moustache at the sight of her cheerless apartment. 'You'll have to do something drastic about this as well – like start again.'

'All in good time.' She led him to the open windows where she had pushed her table and chairs so she could always look out over the riotous garden and inhale the scent of gardenia. 'I've been meaning to ask you,' she said as casually as she could, 'did you talk to that rather tall man with the long blond hair at Brad and Donna's party?'

'Don't tell me you also caught me at it. Chico was furious.'

'I noticed,' Katie said wryly. 'Who is he?'

'The captain of one of those catamarans that takes tourists on sunset cruises or snorkelling at the reef. All I was trying to do was get a discount for my guests.'

'That's a good idea – I should speak to him too.'

Harvey gave her a knowing look. 'I won't tell your husband if you don't.'

'Don't be ridiculous,' Katie said crossly. 'It's only business.'

'That's what I said to Chico, but he didn't swallow it for a moment . . . The guy's name is Lance, runs a boat called *Indigo Jane* from the dock by the Schooner Wharf Bar. You can bet everyone knows him down there – it shouldn't be too tough to find him.'

'Thanks,' Katie said. 'I'll look into it . . . for my guests . . . Now, about that neighbourly advice you once offered – I have to start getting my books to balance.'

Harvey wiped the foam from his moustache. 'I'll put you on to my accountant, he's a genius – even manages to swing it so I can deduct all Chico's frocks off my taxes.'

'Do you think he can also tell me how to make The Tropical Hideout more profitable?'

'Oh, *I* can tell you that,' Harvey said airily, waving his beer bottle at her. 'What you really need is a couple more units. Trouble is, you won't get the licences for them – same old problem with the hurricane regulations and the limit on tourist numbers. So what we all do – though no one tells – is build a couple of phantom units and lock the interleading doors. Then when the inspector comes, you open up again to make it look like just the one suite.'

'But isn't that irresponsible?' Katie objected. 'What if a hurricane does hit Key West?'

'Darling, we guesthouse owners are only a fraction of the problem. The big hotels pay for two hundred licences when they really have double the number of rooms. Round here it's just regarded as good business practice.'

Katie thought how little Guy would approve of such an arrangement, and decided it might be wiser not to mention it to him. 'I've still got to do something to attract the right clientele,' she pointed out to Harvey.

'Once you've done the place up, word will get out. You'll soon find yourself turning folks away at the door. Rooms in the best guesthouses are nearly always full. People can't get enough of paradise, the weather's always good – and then there's the events we run all year round to keep the visitors flocking in.'

'What kind of events?'

'They're all just an excuse for a party, really. There's the Conch Shell Blowing Contest, the Hemingway Festival when all the Papa look-alikes come out of the woodwork, the invasion of the sisterhood for the WomanFest . . . But the biggest celebration of all is Fantasy Fest in October. That's our version of Mardi Gras, and people either dress up in the most outrageous costumes they can find, or take it all off and wear only body paint. You'll have the time of your life if you come for Fantasy Fest, and all the rooms in town are booked out months in advance, which is good news for business too.'

'Sounds wonderful,' Katie sighed, 'but I can't see how I can be here in October.'

There was a discreet knock on the door, and Nadine appeared looking as though she had seen one of the ghosts that were supposed to haunt old Key West houses.

'Excuse me, ma'am, there's a message come for you from Mrs Jessie Wilhelmina Grenville on Caroline Street. She's asking for your company at cocktail hour this evening.'

Katie blanched. 'Who is she – Wade Grenville's wife?'

'Dear me, no,' Harvey laughed. 'I think she may be his great aunt or something, but she's one of the grand old dames of Key West – wife of our late senator, a very formidable woman from what I hear.'

'You've never met her?'

'Very few people do these days. She's rather advanced in years for the social circuit. You're unusually privileged.'

'It's probably just more of Wade's mischief-making.'

'What shall I tell her maid?' Nadine interrupted nervously.

Katie looked enquiringly at Harvey. He gave a firm nod of his head. 'Tell her I'd be delighted to visit Mrs Grenville,' Katie said, fingering Lavender's necklace beneath her shirt.

Because of Harvey's tour, Katie could recognise most of the features of the Bahamian-style mansion that reared up in front of her on Caroline Street. It was a particularly fine example, with bevelled glass and fan windows and ornate millwork. What's more it was still used as a private home, despite being somewhat larger than The Tropical Hideout.

The door was opened by a uniformed Spanish maid, who led her through rooms that wouldn't have been out of place in a museum, filled with exquisite antiques and paintings and Tiffany lamps. In the soft light reflected through coloured glass sat a tiny bird-like woman with a knot of white hair piled on her head. The fine bone structure of her face was still evident beneath the mosaic of wrinkles, suggesting great beauty in her youth.

'Come forward, girl, I don't bite,' the small figure commanded in a surprisingly strong voice.

Katie extended her hand and gently took the one that was offered in return, with its alabaster skin and fine tracing of blue veins.

'Not a lot of substance left to me, is there?' said Mrs Jessie Wilhelmina Grenville. 'But I'm ready. You'll find my headstone standing in the Key West cemetery, next to my late husband, Senator John Grenville. Chose the epitaph myself, so the family wouldn't go making a sentimental mess of it. Only thing still has to be filled in is the date of death.'

Katie found herself at a loss for a suitable reply.

'I know what's on your mind, only you're too English to say it,' the old lady chuckled. 'You think I'm morbid, but the way I see it, it's just facing the inevitable. No point fighting death when you're time's up, 'cause he'll have you anyway. Know what your Welsh poet Dylan Thomas said about death?'

'Yes, actually, I'm a librarian—'

'He's a damn fool. Telling us to rage against the dying of the light, when it's the worst thing we can do. You been through the death of a close family member?'

A look of pain flashed across Katie's face. Mrs Grenville nodded. 'Then you know what I mean . . . Now what sort of cocktail can I offer you? I do keep sherry but that's an old lady's drink. I prefer my gin and tonic.'

'That would be fine for me too,' Katie said.

Mrs Grenville turned to the hovering maid. 'Two of the usual, Dolores, if you please.' The girl withdrew to a drinks trolley in the corner. Katie glanced around and her eye fell on an antique lady's sewing table in beautifully turned wood.

'Fine piece, isn't it?' Mrs Grenville said, her sight obviously still sharp enough to follow the direction of Katie's gaze. 'Acquired from the cargo of a sunken galleon by one of my less scrupulous ancestors. All the old families round here come from wrecking stock, I'm afraid. We're supposed to be more respectable now, but every few generations some bad apple bobs to the surface.'

Dolores handed out the drinks, and Mrs Grenville nodded for her to leave. 'I'm referring, of course, to my great nephew Wade.'

Katie wasn't quite sure whether it would be polite to agree. She chose the more prudent course of keeping silent.

'I'm not so old I can't still keep tabs on what's going on in this town. I know exactly what Wade's been up to in your guesthouse, and I can only offer you my sincerest apologies.'

'It's hardly your fault,' Katie pointed out reasonably.

'I must take responsibility for the wrongs done by my own blood. But don't worry – when I'm through, Wade will answer to me for this.'

The old lady's nostrils flared in anger. Katie speculated that Wade Grenville would probably rather face a firing squad than the wrath of his great aunt.

'Anyway,' Mrs Grenville said, collecting herself, 'I hope I've gone some way towards making amends.'

'Oh yes, it's very kind of you to invite me for this drink—'

'I'm talking about the licences. Are they sorted out to your satisfaction?'

Katie stared at her, comprehension slowly dawning. Mutely she nodded her head.

'And the new staff – are they up to scratch?'

Still Katie found herself quite unable to speak.

'If they give you any problems I'll put Dolores on to them, she'll get their mothers to sort them out in no time flat.'

'No, no,' Katie said faintly. 'They're wonderful workers, I have no complaints. I'm very grateful, truly.'

'Good.' Mrs Grenville took a hefty gulp of gin, and fixed her beady eyes on Katie once again. 'I hear you'll be needing a building contractor next. I'll send you the right man.'

Katie expressed her thanks again for what she suspected was more a *fait accompli* than anything over which she had any say, and marvelled at the iron grip on life of this woman who already had her headstone waiting in the cemetery.

Mrs Grenville nodded, looking weary now, and summoned Dolores to signal that the interview was over. As Katie followed the maid out of the room filled with the jewel-like glow of the Tiffany lamps, Mrs Grenville called after her, 'Do give my regards to the Lady Lavender.'

Thinking about Lavender seemed to have the effect of making her materialise almost instantly on Katie's doorstep. Today she was wearing a sort of lilac wraparound skirt and matching blouse, with a spray of jacaranda blossoms in her hair.

Katie had just been putting out some food for Willie Vance's cats. It had started with the leftovers from breakfast, but lately she had found herself actually piling tins of catfood into her supermarket trolley, after carefully checking the labels to assess the relative merits of the rival brands. If the bowls were not licked clean, she didn't buy that make again.

So far she had made a point of never feeding the cats on her own premises, going to absurd lengths to push the bowls through a gap in the fence. The last thing she wanted was the menagerie moving over *en masse* to her side and becoming a continual nuisance to her guests. Inevitably some sneaked through to search for further delicacies and take annoying liberties in her garden, which necessitated the further purchase of a good pooper-scooper.

'You keep on feeding them pussies, they keep on multiplying,' Lavender said sternly.

'I can't leave them to starve.'

Katie had planned on attacking the garden next with some over-sized shears she had bought in Duval Street along with a jaunty straw hat to keep the sun off her face. She abandoned both now and led Lavender inside.

Lavender's eyes went straight to the door jamb and took in the conspicuous absence of the emblem of Eleggua.

'The spirits be doing you one good turn, you think you don't need they protecshun no more?'

'But it wasn't the spirits, was it?'

Lavender placed hands on fulsome lilac hips. 'You mind yo' mouth, child.'

Katie sighed. 'Why didn't you tell me about Mrs Grenville?'

'What's to tell?'

They were in the kitchen now, and automatically Katie plugged in the kettle.

'You be saying what's on yo' mind,' Lavender demanded, 'or you be standing there all day with that black look on yo' face?'

'All right,' Katie said, sitting down with an angry little thump on the chair opposite. 'It turns out my guardian angel isn't a spirit at all but Mrs Jessie Wilhelmina Grenville, disapproving great aunt of the awful Wade. She got me the staff and the new licences, out of guilt over his behaviour. You let me believe it was your magic, when all along you must have asked her to do it.'

'I didn't ask nobody nothing,' Lavender declared emphatically. 'I heard tell of Mrs Grenville, like most folks, but I doan be taking my Sunday dinner with no rich white folks in no manshun, no sirree!'

'She asked me to give you her regards.'

'Most folks heard tell of me too.'

'But how did she know about the connection between us?'

'You know yo' trouble?' Lavender wagged a purple-tipped finger at her. 'You be all questions and no faith. When the saints do they work, they be choosing whatever instrument takes they fancy, and maybe that instrument be a rightuss old lady with friends in high places. You want to be questioning the how and the why of it?'

Katie smiled tentatively. 'I suppose, when you put it that way—'

'I be taking that coffee now,' Lavender said, 'with three sugars fo' sweetness, like the goddess Oshun.'

While Katie made the coffee, Lavender twitched her nose this way and that. 'They be something else in the air . . . they be more mischief brewing or I ain't the Lady Lavender.'

'Please,' Katie said weakly, 'no more of that.'

'Happen it's them jasmine candles. Can't burn too much jasmine 'less you want to be releasing them spirits of passion. Yes sirree, there's love in the air.'

'It's just the coffee,' Katie said, placing her mug in front of her. 'Or is this the part when you tell me I'm going to meet a tall dark stranger?'

'I doan be telling you nothing, you take that tone with me!'

'I'm sorry,' Katie said, dropping in Lavender's three cubes of sugar with a little silver pincher. 'But it can't have anything to do with me – I'm a married woman.'

'Then you be on yo' guard, 'less you've a mind to git yo'self a barrel-load a trouble.'

Katie laughed. 'Perhaps it's something to do with the guests. I don't think we have any honeymoon couples, but this would be the perfect place for them – especially after it's done up. The rooms are so private . . . and the garden . . .'

Lavender took a gulp of her coffee. 'This be juss the way I like it,' she said, smacking her lips. 'Now you want to be making a love nest here, you go right ahead and do it, child, 'cause what's in the air gonna draw them in like bees to a honeypot.'

'You really think so?'

'I knows so. And don't go inviting no gentleman callers neither, 'less you want to be binding them to you with ties of love, 'cause that where it all be ending and no mistake.'

'Heavens,' Katie objected, 'I don't think I've ever inspired that sort of passion in anyone – not even my husband.'

'That so?' Lavender heaved her bulk from the chair. 'When the waters be all still at the surface, they be trouble a-plenty deep down under . . . Now I best be going about my other business.'

Katie didn't dare ask what that was, much though she was longing to know. Unbidden, a vision came to her of Lavender in the graveyard, muttering incantations over Mrs Grenville's headstone.

When she had shown her self-appointed spiritual adviser to the door, she went upstairs to her room and stood looking at her face in the mirror for a very long time, as though trying to see something there that others might but she could not.

Katie walked slowly along the dock of the old Key West Bight, scanning the boats that bobbed jauntily in the water, their sails folded away, their engines quiet. Pelicans floated on the swells between them, waiting with beady-eyed patience for some snack to be hurled overboard. A dog sat to attention on a foredeck like a skipper on his watch.

There weren't many catamarans, and only one with the bright blue hulls that would most likely belong to the *Indigo Jane*. Katie headed towards it and found that the name in bold white lettering on the side was indeed the one she was looking for.

The only person on board was a girl with stocky thighs and a year-round tan. She was wholly absorbed in the task of restocking the bar, which must have been depleted after the daily snorkelling trip and now needed replenishing before the sunset cruise.

'Excuse me,' Katie called.

The girl looked up with a frown of annoyance. 'Cruise doesn't start till five-thirty,' she said shortly.

'I'm looking for Lance, the captain. Do you know where I can find him?'

The girl seemed even more put out, as though she had far more important things to worry about. 'Try the Schooner Wharf Bar – that's his usual hangout.'

'Thank you,' Katie said, beating a retreat.

She could see, only a couple of hundred yards away, the open-air bar with its tables beneath thatched umbrellas – the sort of place that could only exist where the weather was always kind. As she approached she heard scattered applause from a mixed crowd of locals and tourists, and a lone guitarist told them in a nonchalant drawl that the song they had just heard was the official anthem of the Conch Republic.

Katie scanned the crowd, looking for someone who stood taller than the rest, with a mane of sun-streaked hair. Her eyes searched faces but his was not among them. She headed purposefully for the bar.

'What can I get you?' said a barefoot man with a ponytail.

A woman in designer sunglasses called over, 'Hey Tom, gimme a break, I been waiting for ever here.'

'Few more minutes shouldn't make any difference, then.'

'I swear, if you didn't have such cute buns—'

Katie caught herself glancing down at the barman's tight shorts. He grinned. 'Made up your mind?'

At once she adopted a businesslike tone. 'I'm looking for Lance from the *Indigo Jane*.'

'Hope you like standing in line then, honey,' the woman said wryly.

'Hey, you're giving me a bad name here.'

Katie turned quickly at the sound of the voice and raised her eyes to the owner's face. He was quite as good-looking, in broad daylight, as she remembered him. Up close she could also see that he was no older than twenty-six or -seven – a good decade younger than her, at any rate.

'I'm Katie Colman from The Tropical Hideout,' she said, holding out her hand.

He took it and then seemed somehow to forget to let it go. 'Can I buy you a drink, Katie Colman?'

'Make up your mind any time this century,' said the woman in the sunglasses. 'I'm parched, I'm dying here, but I can wait.'

'Hold on to your pants, Lola,' the barman told her. 'I'll serve you first if you cut the dialogue.'

'We don't have to have a drink if you don't have time,' Katie said, the skin of his palm warm against hers. 'There's some business I'd like to discuss with you, but I know you're doing the sunset cruise and you must be in a hurry—'

'This is Key West,' Lance said, a teasing twinkle in his eye. 'It's uncool to be in a hurry.'

Katie's chin went up. 'In that case, I'll have a margarita.'

'Hey, Tom, we have a decision here,' Lola shouted over.

'I got it.' Tom turned to Lance. 'Another coke for you, cap'n?'

'Sure – and a little privacy.'

'Dream on, sailor,' Lola scoffed. 'Everyone in this town knows everyone else's business.'

Lance paid Tom for the drinks, waving away the dollars Katie tried to press on him, and steered her over to an empty table beneath a thatch umbrella.

'I can see you're not from round here,' he said. 'You have such great skin.'

'My daughter says I'm too pale.' At once Katie felt unaccountably annoyed with herself for mentioning that she had a daughter.

'You got kids?'

'Yes, two.'

'How old?'

'I'm sure you don't want to hear my whole life story.'

'What would you rather discuss, then – business?'

Katie shrugged. 'If you really have the time—'

'I told you – forget about time.' Lance ran a finger along her watch strap, bringing out goosebumps on her wrist. 'You should take that thing off and only put it back on when you leave the island.'

Katie glanced at his forearm with its covering of hairs bronzed by the sun. There was no watch and no tan mark. 'Me – I never wear one,' he said, following the direction of her gaze.

She looked up and caught Lola unashamedly staring at them. She said awkwardly, 'I've got quite a few things I should be getting on with myself.'

Lance threw his hands in the air. 'OK, I give up, let's cut to the chase. What can I do for you, Katie Colman?'

She was annoyed with herself, now, for being so stiff, but it was too late to do anything except come straight to the point. 'I was hoping I could arrange a group discount if I send my guests regularly to do cruises on the *Indigo Jane*.'

Lance gave a little shrug. 'I'm not the boss, just the captain. I don't own the *Indigo Jane* – don't own much, come to think of it, besides my surfmobile and surfboard.'

Katie felt a perfect fool. 'I'm sorry, I didn't think . . . Perhaps if you could give me your boss's name?'

'I can do better than that – I'll talk to him for you. I'm sure I can fix something.'

'Thank you – that's very kind.'

'My pleasure – absolutely,' Lance said, imitating her plummy vowels and making Katie suddenly hate the way she sounded, so formal and so . . . English.

'Hey, Lance, we're ready for you,' a female voice bellowed across from the dock.

Lance gave Katie a rueful grin. 'My first mate does wear a watch. Maybe I should throw it overboard – and her along with it.' He stood reluctantly and stretched his legs. 'I'll swing by The Tropical Hideout and let you know what the boss says.'

Katie could almost feel Lavender breathing down her neck. 'You can phone if it's more convenient,' she called half-heartedly after his broad retreating back.

Almost the last person Guy had expected to see on his doorstep at eight in the evening was Jemima, bearing gifts in the form of two large brown paper bags from which emanated a rather pungent, spicy smell.

'Have you eaten?' she said.

'Not yet. I was just going to warm up one of my meals for one.'

'Heavens, Guy,' Jemima said, pushing in through the door, 'there'll be violins starting up any minute. Now stop feeling sorry for yourself – I've brought us a wonderful Chicken Korma.'

Guy followed her into the kitchen where she at once began making herself at home, banging open cabinet doors in search of plates and cutlery.

'I don't want to sound ungrateful,' he said, 'but I'm not very partial to curry.'

'You'll have to start living dangerously, then. Besides, it's the mildest kind they make.'

As she busied herself emptying containers on to plates, Guy noticed how well she was looking – her figure neither as bulky as before she left for the Antarctic, nor as gaunt as when she returned, but back to its usual trim and athletic shape. With her bright silk blouse she wore some conservatively cut black linen trousers, ironed into creases, and plain black court shoes. She was dressed, for once, at least half like an Englishwoman.

Jemima placed the poppadums between their piled plates. 'Dinner is served,' she announced.

Guy took a hesitant mouthful. It had a pleasantly creamy texture, and the spices, as promised, weren't overpowering. 'Not bad,' he admitted. 'Perhaps it's just the smell that puts one off.'

'In the East they think it's we Europeans who smell awful. They consider us barbarians, really. What they must think of our food is probably unprintable!'

Guy looked pained. 'Must we talk of foreign travel? It's rather a sore point right now.'

'Nevertheless, we must,' Jemima insisted, 'because it's exactly the subject on which I have come to ask your advice.'

'Really?' Guy couldn't help feeling rather flattered. Jemima had never sought his opinions before, had on the contrary always seemed to despise them. It was Katie who had always deferred to him, whereas now . . .

'I'd be glad to help in any way I can,' he said.

'Well, you know I've been trying to figure out what to do with my life, where to go from here. When Daddy left me the flat I never thought I'd be comfortable staying in London, but as time goes on I find to my surprise that I quite like being a settled woman of property.'

'Really?' Guy said. 'I must say, I didn't think you'd stick it out either.'

'I may do more than that.' She eyed Guy warily. 'Now, promise you won't laugh if I tell you—'

'Wouldn't dream of it,' he assured her solemnly.

'The thing is, I thought I might use Daddy's money to start my own little business.'

Guy tried to keep all expression from his face as he attempted to imagine Jemima in a pinstripe suit behind a desk – and failed. 'What sort of business?' he said carefully.

'An adventure travel agency. There can't be many people who know as much about that subject as I do. And this chap I used to bump into in far-flung corners of the world – he thinks he might put up some money and go in with me. We're both getting a bit long in the tooth for what we did before.'

Guy refrained from saying he had felt this to be the case for a good decade. Instead he cautioned, 'Are you sure you won't be tempted to go off yourself if one of your packages sounds too irresistible?'

'I'll always want to travel, but not as a way of life any more,' Jemima said emphatically, breaking a poppadum with a little crack like gunfire. 'I'll be forty soon, Guy, just like you will. Perhaps this is my midlife crisis, but I'm serious about it.'

Guy didn't want to believe, at this moment, in midlife crises. If they really did exist, Katie was hitting hers rather earlier than could reasonably have been expected.

'Antarctica was so punishing,' Jemima said, crunching her poppadum between her teeth. 'My body kept screaming at me to give it all up. It was terrible being pulled out because of poor Daddy, but I was almost relieved to have an excuse not to have to go on.'

'Did the Norwegian girl make it?' Guy asked curiously.

'Yes, I'm afraid she did.'

'And do you mind?'

'Not nearly as much as I thought I would. I'm ready for a different kind of challenge now – like this business venture.'

Guy gave her hand a pat. 'I think it's a marvellous idea.'

'Truly?'

'Yes, truly. Much more sensible way of investing your father's capital than all these crazy notions of Katie's.'

'Oh dear.' Jemima pulled a sympathetic face. 'Are you still worried about her?'

'More than ever,' Guy said grimly.

Katie hadn't found the time before to visit Polly's small, two-room apartment across the street. But now she had climbed the stairs to the top floor – where the light was better, Polly said – and been let by Polly into the room she used as her living space, with sofa bed and dining table and kitchenette all crammed into the tiny area. 'I use the other room only for painting,' Polly explained, leading her through.

The surfaces of the walls were almost entirely covered with canvasses hanging in rows or stacked up in corners. Katie felt as though she had entered a bright underwater world populated by exotic brain corals and spiny lobsters and brilliant spotfin butterflyfish and great green turtles floating over beds of seagrass. The colours had the vibrancy of jewels, the style was at once meticulously real and almost surreal, as though she were looking at some closely observed but magical other world.

'They're wonderful, Polly,' she cried. 'I had no idea.'

Polly blushed. 'I know they're not going to wind up in a museum, but they're what I like doing.'

'They'd be wasted in a museum. Just looking at them lightens my mood immediately. I think they belong on the walls of people's homes. In fact, I want them for The Tropical Hideout.'

Polly looked pleased and pained at the same time. 'I only invited you up to look, you mustn't think you have to go buying anything—'

'But they're perfect for the feeling I want to create – as though when you enter The Tropical Hideout you're marooned in your own little fantasy world, and you can forget the rest of the planet exists.'

'What kind of clientele are you hoping for?' Polly asked, a flush of excitement in her pale cheeks.

Katie glanced down at a copy of the *Key West Citizen* spread out on the floor and dotted with daubs of paint. A photograph showed a couple in scuba gear taking their marriage vows on the seabed. 'I thought the honeymoon market,' she said. 'Or couples of any kind and age . . . Lavender seems to think the place has the right atmosphere.'

'A lot of people come to Key West to get married,' Polly agreed. 'There's a company that specialises in organising the setting of your choice, however crazy it is.'

Katie wandered along the walls, looking at the exquisite colours of the corals reproduced by Polly's palette. 'Have you ever done any decorating work?'

'Not professionally.'

'You have such an eye for colour, I think you'd be wonderful at it.'

'It sure would be fun to try.'

Katie turned to face her. 'What if I hired you to do the colour schemes at The Tropical Hideout, as a backdrop to your paintings?'

Polly's hands flew to her mouth. 'Oh dear, I couldn't possibly—'

'But why ever not?'

'It's such a big place . . . so much responsibility.'

'I've never managed a guesthouse before either. If I can get by, I'm sure you could too – not to mention the money I'd be forced to pay you.'

She could see the battle Polly was waging with herself. 'It *would* be nice to have more space to paint in . . . and to take care of Mr Vance's cats.'

'I've started feeding them too,' Katie confessed.

'I suppose I could make some suggestions, and then if you didn't like them—'

Katie took Polly's hands and smiled. 'I want you to start straight away.'

The grand old Casa Marina Resort had been built by the all-powerful Henry Flagler for the wealthy visitors he envisioned his railroad would bring to the southernmost point of the United States. It had expanded since his day, offering a grand total of over three hundred rooms and suites, two outdoor swimming pools and a hot tub, four clay tennis courts, and numerous other possibilities for the paying guest, Lance had told Katie when he'd called just a few days after their meeting and suggested she should go down and check out the competition.

Katie and Nadine sat beneath an umbrella in the outdoor restaurant by the private beach. Katie tried to shoo away an over-tame seagull that was becoming a little too interested in her club sandwich. Nadine had ordered something Mexican, and was nibbling it warily, one eye on preventing the red salsa from dripping on to her white sundress. From the looks of amazement on the faces of the people they had passed in her street, Katie was sure they'd never seen Nadine in anything other than her biker shorts or jeans before.

She had asked her to lunch as a thank-you for stepping into the breach and helping to keep The Tropical Hideout going in the aftermath of Wade Grenville's disruptive departure. She also wanted company on her reconnaissance mission, though when she had been about to say so to Lance, her courage had suddenly deserted her.

'Lance says I should try to make a deal for our guests to use the beach and leisure facilities here,' she told Nadine.

'That a fact? The kid telling you how to run things now?'

Katie gave her a sharp look. 'I always appreciate advice. I'm new to this game, you know.'

'An' you're doing one helluva job, if I may say so, ma'am.'

'Thank you,' Katie said, a little mollified. 'And isn't it time you stopped calling me ma'am?'

'What should I call you, then?'

'Just Katie.'

'That wouldn't feel right, ma'am.'

She would have to give up on it, Katie decided, gazing into the blue distance where a bright pink parasail floated above the tranquil sea with its matchstick figure strapped into the harness.

'Tell me,' she said to Nadine, 'how did you end up in Key West?'

'They say most folks who wind up here are running away from something.'

'That can't always be true.'

'You got a husband, don't you?'

'What's that got to do with it?' Katie said defensively.

'Me, I was following the hippie trail. I guess I just stopped when I hit the ocean.'

'*You* were a hippie?' Katie said with amusement. 'One of the peace and love kind?'

'In my first incarnation. After a while I settled to working in the bars, in the days when this was a naval base. Dressed real pretty in my skirts and high heels, and dated a sailor boy when he had shore leave. Then they closed the base here and a lot of sailors left the navy. The minute they did, I'd say about a quarter of them came straight out the closet – kissing each other in the streets, they were – my man included.'

'That must've been quite a shock,' Katie said inadequately.

Nadine flicked back her long black hair. 'He said he'd had this thing going all along with a guy on his boat. So I threw away the skirts and the high heels and went to work on the shrimp boats.'

Katie eyed Nadine's forearms emerging from the slender white straps of her sundress. They weren't quite as muscular as Lance's, but they weren't that far off either. 'How did you meet your husband?' she said.

'We hung out in the same bars. He was a trucker, spent most of his time on the road, hardly saw me and the kids. But he sent the pay checks home regular as clockwork. Then one night these bastards hijacked his truck – stabbed him clean through the heart.'

'Oh, Nadine, I'm so sorry.'

'I didn't want to go back to the shrimp boats. There was a lot of renovation going on then in Old Town, so I started working in the construction industry.'

A middle-aged man spread himself out on a massage table beneath the palm trees, submitting his flabby flesh to the attentions of a slim young masseuse.

'Talking of construction,' Katie said, nibbling a crisp from her basket while her old friend the seagull watched for any lack of vigilance on her part, 'Mrs Grenville sent me this man called Joe Roth to do the restoration on The Tropical Hideout. Do you know him?'

'He's a stand-up guy, has the right connections but won't charge you through the nose for them. I'll keep an eye on him though, ma'am, don't you worry yourself 'bout that.'

Katie tilted her face to the sun and closed her eyes. She felt the warmth flow through her, the comfort of being surrounded by the unusual but wonderful team who had chosen her as much as she had chosen them – Harvey, Lavender, Nadine, Polly, Mrs Grenville – and somehow, presiding over them all, the almost tangible presence of her father.

Chapter Twelve

~

The cypress boarding of the façade had been stripped and sanded down by Joe Roth's men, under the tyrannical eye of Nadine, and was now in the process of receiving two coats of the palest apricot paint. Katie had been afraid the Historical Committee might insist on white, but Joe Roth had steered the request through the relevant authorities and obtained the required permits, and now Katie stood assessing the effect of the apricot against the dark green of the shutters and the white of the pillars and porches. The result was very pleasing, she decided, conveying exactly the right tropical flavour.

'It's looking great!' Katie felt a warm hand clasp her shoulder, and her knees went a little wobbly.

'Thank you,' she said, turning to look up at Lance towering above her even in his bare feet. His scooter was parked by the kerb, a loaf of French bread sticking out of the grocery bag. Surreptitiously she tried to peep inside it, wondering if it contained supplies for one or two.

'I had a word with the boss about the *Indigo Jane*,' he drawled. 'Says he'll think it over and get back to me next week. No rush, is there?'

'Oh no, there's never a rush in Key West,' Katie laughed.

'You catch on quick.'

Even standing with him out on the street, Katie caught herself looking over her shoulder, wondering if Lavender knew of his presence here. But her warning could hardly apply now that the inside of The Tropical Hideout looked like a building site, the scent of jasmine candles long since faded away.

'So when do you reopen for business?' Lance said lazily.

'There's still a way to go. Even when the construction work's finished, there's the decorating to be done. My friend Polly who's handling all that – she says there isn't much of a selection on the island and the prices are simply horrible. I really should send her to Miami, but she doesn't have a car and we haven't worked out how she'd bring the stuff back.'

'Easy,' Lance grinned. 'I'll take her in the surfmobile.'

'I couldn't possibly expect you—'

'I have a couple days off this week – thought I'd go someplace and let off steam. You gotta get off the island every so often or the rock fever hits you.'

Katie tried to imagine Lance and the timid Polly letting off steam, Polly kicking up her heels in one of those long skirts she liked to wear on some strobe-lit dance floor. It seemed the unlikeliest of scenarios. But then again, Polly must be about the same age as Lance. At least they probably liked the same kind of music.

'Thanks for the offer, but I can't take advantage of your good nature,' she said firmly.

'You make such a big deal out of things. It's no sweat, I swear. In fact you should come along too, let your hair down a bit. I know my way round Miami – I can show you the time of your life.'

Katie was struggling to remember that she hadn't really liked Miami. 'I can't go off and just leave . . . all this.' She nodded her head towards the banging of hammers and the shouts of the workmen.

Lance shrugged. 'You worry too much. I guess it's just another of those bad habits I'm gonna have to knock out of you.' He pointedly eyed the watch which she had never had the courage to remove.

'Mrs Colman, we need a decision on the floor plan here,' a voice yelled from within.

Lance remounted his scooter. 'The offer's still good. I could head up to Miami Wednesday till Sunday. Let me know what you and your friend decide.'

The engine kicked over and he took off down the sun-dappled street, weaving skilfully between bicycles and cars until his figure was lost to Katie's view.

Breakfast at The Banyan Tree was a rather complicated affair. Brad did the cooking, piling plates with toasted croissants filled with cheese and crispy bacon rashers and a selection of exotic fruits – pomegranates and mangoes and kiwis. Donna circulated amongst the guests sitting out in the little tree-shaded courtyard, encouraging them to mingle and answering queries about the day's proposed activities. This would soon be her role, Katie reminded herself, once The Tropical Hideout opened its doors again for business. Or at least until she found a new manager.

Donna had insisted Katie come to breakfast to meet Annie Foster, whose agency handled bookings for the smaller guesthouses. Annie was small and energetic, with an abundance of curly brown hair and a way of making you like her almost immediately. 'Let's exchange horror stories about our kids before Brad and Donna join us,' she said mischievously. 'I have a thirteen-year-old who's a real nightmare.'

'My fourteen-year-old can be a bit difficult, but they're both wonderful children really—'

'I guess that means they don't live with you full time?'

'No – they go away to school.'

'I can't afford to send Jodie, not on my salary. No daddy to cough up the fees either. So she has to put up with poor old Key West High – but hey, she'll survive, and she's got me, right?'

Katie felt a sudden pang for Lucy and Hannah in their expensive English boarding school. She had a feeling Jodie might be the lucky one after all.

'Is Annie moaning about that daughter of hers again?'

221

Donna demanded as she and Brad joined them with their coffees. 'They fight like Harvey and Chico – but they couldn't live without each other.'

'You're right, hush my mouth,' Annie laughed. 'It's time we heard about the glorious new Tropical Hideout.'

'It's coming along famously,' Katie said. 'I'm expecting a medal from the "Hysterical Society" for all the painstaking restoration we're doing on the façade. And I'm knocking the inside around a bit—'

'Building phantom units,' Brad said with a knowing wink.

'I hope you're not going to tear out any of those wonderful trees and plants,' Annie cried.

'Oh no – just cut them back a little,' Katie assured her. 'And fix the pool . . . and install a hot tub—'

'Essential for all those honeymoon couples,' Donna grinned.

'It's good to go for a particular niche in the market,' Annie said approvingly. 'I'll help you all I can with the bookings . . . but you must be sure to get yourself on the Internet too.'

It was all happening so quickly, Katie thought. Before she knew it she would be handing over to a new manager and heading back home.

'All this building work must be costing you a small fortune,' Donna said.

'It *is* leaving rather a dent in my capital,' Katie admitted. 'My husband thinks I've taken leave of my senses.'

'Oh, husbands!' Annie waved a hand dismissively. 'You're much better off without them. Sure, I can only afford a small place out on Stock Island, but at least there's no one to argue with about what channel we should watch or who should pick up the dirty socks.'

'Except Jodie,' Donna teased.

'Don't let's get on to that subject again.'

'We're almost ready for Polly to start on the decorating,' Katie said. 'She's gone up to Miami to choose the fabrics.'

'Polly? Alone in Miami?' Brad said disbelievingly.

'No, she went with a friend.'

'A boyfriend?' Donna demanded curiously.

For all Katie knew, that could be the way things were by now, two single and attractive people, dancing the nights away . . .

'I don't know,' she said irritably. Perhaps she should have gone along with them, to approve Polly's choices. It was, after all, *her* guesthouse that was being decorated, and *her* money that was paying for it.

'Good for Polly,' Donna said. 'I hope she's found herself a man. You must bully it all out of her, Katie, when she comes back.'

Katie looked down at the sapphire engagement ring winking on her finger, and wondered how many women were bound by the conventions they had always lived by, and the fear of striking out into the unknown.

In Wade Grenville's old office, safe from the chaos of the stripping of walls and sanding of floors that was taking place in her own apartment, Katie sat in front of her computer and dialled her mother's number in Wiltshire.

'Mummy, good news. I've just acquired a page on the Web – or rather The Tropical Hideout has. So if you want to contact me at antisocial hours, you can always send me an e-mail.'

'What *I* would term good news,' Fiona said sniffily, 'is a firm date for your return.'

'Come on, Mummy, I thought you liked playing around on your Internet.'

'I have never "played around" on it, I have always used it for a purpose.'

A memory came to Katie of her mother tensed over her screen, watching for news of Jemima from Antarctica. Her own absence obviously didn't cause the same anxiety, but nonetheless she felt a childish surge of resentment.

'Fine,' she said, 'I won't bother to give you the number.'

'Don't take that tone with me, Kathryn. I'm entitled to show concern at the way this trip of yours is stretching on indefinitely. I certainly hope you're intending to make it back for the girls' half-term.'

'Half-term,' Katie shrieked, running a hand through hair that was daily burned blonder by the sun. 'I'd clean forgotten – when is it?'

'The week after next,' Fiona said stiffly. 'And I cannot imagine what is going on in your life, Kathryn, that would make you forget your own daughters' half-term.'

Katie cast a wild look through the window at workmen laying paving around the hot tub. There were so many things to be done that would never be finished in a week.

'Look, Mummy,' she pleaded, 'you know I've always put the girls first, but just this once it's going to be really difficult for me. I can't leave all the work here half finished.'

There was a disapproving pause on the other end of the line. Then Fiona said, 'Well, this is a fine kettle of fish, I must say.'

Katie stared down at the list she had made before she phoned her mother, of the things she would have to see to that day. It was already lunchtime, and she hadn't even got through half of them.

'Please, Mummy,' she said, 'couldn't you have the girls to stay for the week – assuming Guy can't take the time off work, which is a pretty safe bet. But he could always go down to see them at the weekend.'

Fiona sniffed. 'And how do you think the girls will feel?'

'I'm sure they'll be fine, you know how they love you and aunt Flora and the horses.'

'And Guy? What does he have to say about his wife being away so long? How is he supposed to cope on his own?'

The same way Daddy did, Katie wanted to point out coldly, when he was in town every week and you refused to join him. But she couldn't afford to antagonise her mother at this point.

'Please, Mummy, help me out here,' she pleaded instead.

'You're even beginning to sound like an American,' Fiona said with distaste. 'Well, I suppose I'll have to step into the breach, but that doesn't mean I approve of you gadding off abroad like this. It wasn't the same for Jemima, you know – she had none of your family obligations.'

'I know,' Katie said, and didn't add that everyone should be allowed a little time to themselves, those with family commitments most of all. Sometimes it was the only way to keep sane . . . And she was doing this for all of them, really. She had told Polly that the two-bedroom unit was for her and Guy and the children when they took their holidays in Key West. She had kept her favourite painting aside for it – the one of the green turtle with fins spread almost in flight through the sky-like turquoise of the water above the bed of waving seagrass.

'I will tell Guy and the girls that they're welcome,' Fiona said, 'but please don't take it as a sign that I condone your behaviour.'

Katie thought there was little danger of that. Even as a child, she couldn't remember ever basking in her mother's whole-hearted approval.

Lance and Polly drew up in the surfmobile with a loud blare of the horn and emerged swathed in rolls of fabric and laden with pottery urns and ceramic ornaments, giggling and sharing jokes like co-conspirators.

Katie greeted them a touch coolly and sent the workmen out to help carry their booty inside. It took a couple of trips, with Polly chattering non-stop.

'You should see South Beach, it's so stylish, not at all like the tackier parts of town. I didn't even know about it till Lance showed me round – there are all these great art deco hotels.'

'How about the nightclubs, huh?' Lance said.

'Oh, they're so glamorous—'

'I'm surprised you found the time to do any work,' Katie snapped.

Polly's shining eyes were suddenly round with hurt. 'Oh my, I hope you don't really think that, oh my.'

Katie looked at her quivering lip and relented. 'I'm sorry,

it's just been a nightmare round here with all the building going on. I'm feeling a bit out of sorts, that's all.'

'Told you you should've come away with us,' Lance said.

She rather wished he wouldn't keep reminding her of that. She turned to watch the workmen stacking away the last of the fabric rolls, and tried to remember if Polly had found someone yet to make up the curtains.

'I'm dying to show you everything we bought,' Polly said. 'There's the cutest family of ceramic tortoises—'

'No time for that now, I'm afraid. Joe's men want to get started on the painting, we have to tell them which colours we want for which rooms.'

'Whew, it's all action round here – I'll get out from under your feet.' Lance backed away towards the door. He had that glint in his eye which Katie had come to read as laughter at her expense.

'Thank you so much for driving Polly,' she said, refusing to rise to the bait. 'I really do appreciate it.'

'I told you – no sweat. I had a great time.'

Polly smiled at him shyly. 'So did I.'

'See ya around.'

Katie wondered if the courtyards of South Beach had been filled with the scent of jasmine which had worked its magic spell. She turned her back and began inspecting the names on the lids of paint pots. 'I thought we were supposed to be doing only underwater colours – the greens and blues and corals. There seems to be a batch of lemon yellow here.'

'Oh my,' said Polly, all nerves again. 'Now how can that have happened? Oh my, oh my.'

'I don't think we must make a mountain out of a molehill, Guy,' Fiona said firmly down the telephone. 'The situation is somewhat unexpected, but there it is.'

'I just can't understand what would keep Katie away for half-term,' Guy grumbled.

'I expect workmen are the same the world over, and she

can't turn her back on them for a moment.'

'Not even to look after her own children?'

'Now, Guy,' Fiona admonished, 'you know Kathryn has always been a devoted mother. Just this once she's asked me to take her place.'

Fiona had no intention of divulging any more of her conversation with her daughter, particularly not the disapproval she had felt herself obliged to express. That was family business and at the end of the day, despite the connection by marriage, Guy wasn't actually blood.

'I'm sorry to land the girls on you,' Guy was saying, 'but you know how it is with my work—'

'It's no trouble at all. Aunt Flora and I are looking forward to having them. And you'll come down at the weekend, of course.'

'Of course. And thank you, too, for telling them about their mother. I wasn't quite sure how to put it.'

'I had a perfectly sensible conversation with Lucy, who wasn't at all put out. And little Hannah always takes things in her stride, so there's really nothing to worry about. I have sent Kathryn an e-mail to that effect.'

Guy was heartily relieved that Fiona seemed to be dealing with the problem so calmly and efficiently. It was, in fact, not unlike having Katie to rely on.

'Well, half-term seems settled,' he said. 'And then Katie will be back and we can all return to normal.'

It was almost chilly inside the gracious old house on Caroline Street, despite the warmth of the day. Mrs Grenville wore a long-sleeved dark blue dress buttoned to the neck, with a wonderful glowing turquoise on a gold chain round her neck. Katie wondered if she always looked so immaculate, or only when receiving visitors.

Dolores poured their glasses of gin and tonic from the drinks trolley. As before, Mrs Grenville waited till she had melted away before getting to the point of the visit.

'How are things working out with Joe Roth?' she demanded.

'He's been marvellous,' Katie said. 'I can't thank you enough for sending him to me. His workmanship is excellent, and he gets it all done so efficiently and quickly.'

Almost too quickly, she thought to herself. Soon she would have no more excuse to stay on this island that was almost beginning to feel like home, where she had made such unexpected and wonderful friends.

The ice cubes rattled in Mrs Grenville's glass as she lifted it with jewel-encrusted fingers. 'I think you'd have found a way to work things out with or without my help. You strike me as a very determined woman, Mrs Colman.'

Katie laughed. 'Nobody's ever called me that before.'

'Then they should open their eyes and look more closely.'

She lifted a little silver handbell and rang it. Dolores came in on silent feet, and Mrs Grenville requested a cardigan to put around her shoulders. She eyed Katie's sleeveless dress. 'Didn't feel the cold either when I was your age,' she said. 'Won't feel it any more where I'm heading . . . Youth is a wonderful thing – don't waste it.'

Youth! Katie thought. Had she ever really felt young? Hadn't she always worried and worked and planned for the future? But when did the future finally arrive?

'You'll be glad to know,' Mrs Grenville said, 'that I've had a word with my great nephew Wade. I don't think you'll be having any more trouble from that quarter.'

Katie smiled. How she would have loved to be a fly on a Tiffany lamp during that conversation.

'Now the word is you're looking for a new manager to run things for you when you leave. Is that right?' Mrs Grenville demanded with the sudden, intense concentration she always gave to a problem.

'That's right,' Katie said reluctantly. It would be, she felt, like handing over her newborn baby to a total stranger who'd had nothing to do with the pains of labour.

'I'll send you some applicants,' Mrs Grenville said. 'And I

can guarantee they will all be a great deal more honest than my great nephew.'

Katie tried to muster the correct degree of enthusiasm to express her thanks.

Ray Hawkins emerged into the corridor to see an alarming woman swathed in bright purple heading purposefully towards the office where he had just been interviewed by Mrs Colman for the position of manager of The Tropical Hideout. Surely she couldn't be a rival applicant, he speculated, although you never could tell what people were looking for. Still, he felt he could pride himself on having made a reasonable impression on Mrs Colman, all things considered. And to give the little lady her due, the guesthouse was looking pretty good – hardly recognisable from the bad old days of Wade Grenville. Yes, he could see himself fitting in here very nicely indeed.

Katie looked up despondently as Lavender marched into her office. She was a welcome and colourful sight after the small procession of perfectly suitable but dull men who had presented themselves for the position of manager on the instructions of Mrs Grenville. Every one of them had mentioned the connection, as though it were bound to give them the advantage.

'He ain't the one,' Lavender pronounced, gesturing with her thumb back into the corridor.

'But he had very good qualifications,' Katie said, wondering if she weren't being deliberately picky. The only fault she had been able to find with Ray Hawkins was that he had a rather annoying habit of clearing his throat every time he spoke – hardly a disqualification for the job.

'The Lady Lavender can part them curtains, see what tomorrow be bringing, an' I'm telling you, it ain't him.'

Katie sighed. 'I've got to be sensible about this. I can't keep rejecting people without good reason.'

'You be listening to them voices in yo' head, that be reason enough.'

Katie didn't feel up to pointing out that where she came from, people who listened to voices in their head were liable to find themselves surrounded by professionals in white coats.

'It's getting to be an embarrassment,' she said. 'I don't know what I'll say to Mrs Grenville, after all her kindness, if I don't like anyone she sends.'

The telephone rang and she eyed it with resignation before picking it up.

'I got good news and bad news.'

At the sound of the teasing male voice, Katie cast a nervous look at Lavender, who calmly returned her gaze with the air of one who wasn't going anywhere.

'Tell me the good news first,' Katie said awkwardly.

'The boss is gonna give you your group discount for the *Indigo Jane* – thanks to my good work on your behalf,' Lance drawled.

'That's wonderful, thank you . . . And the bad news?'

'We decided you'd better try it out yourself – free of charge, of course – just so you know what you're getting your people into.'

With one eye on Lavender, whose brows were beginning to draw together, Katie said, 'Are you offering to take me yourself?'

'That's about right.'

Before she could stop herself she said almost huffily, 'Are you sure you wouldn't rather take Polly?'

Although she couldn't see his face, she just knew it had a grin all over it. 'The offer's only good for you.'

'That's very kind, but I wasn't expecting—'

'You gonna make a big deal out of this too?'

'No, yes . . . why not? Of course I'd love to go.'

'Good. Meet me on the dock tomorrow at a quarter after ten.'

Katie replaced the receiver, avoiding Lavender's penetrating stare.

'Where you be goin' thas making you blush redder than a beetroot?'

'Honestly, Lavender, you don't have to worry about everything I do – I'm hardly a child, after all.' Katie jumped up. Despite her denial, she felt like skipping. 'Now get that scowl off your face and help me celebrate the coming reopening of The Tropical Hideout. I have a little party in mind – for girls only.'

The branches of the jacaranda had been trimmed back from the pool so that, looking up, Katie could see the evening stars begin to glow against a deepening indigo sky. She had draped strings of tiny white artificial lights like beads through the trees.

Opposite her Lavender's large head seemed to bob on the bubbly surface of the hot tub like a giant buoy marking the bulk beneath. 'You sho them workmen be headed off home like you told 'em?' she said, rolling her eyes round suspiciously.

'Oh my, do you think they saw us?' Polly said nervously. Even without the danger of being observed, it had taken some persuading to get her to try out the hot tub minus swimsuit.

Nadine reached for her glass of champagne. 'Don't you worry, I sent 'em all packing.'

'I sho hope so. Otherwise they be gittin' the fright o' they lives.'

Katie stretched out languorously in the foaming hot water, allowing one of the jets to massage the small of her back. 'I think this is rather a success, don't you?'

Polly smiled tentatively. 'It just seems so . . . daring . . . to do it with no clothes on.'

Nadine snorted. 'You kids today are such prudes. Woodstock time, none of us wore clothes. Nor for a long time after, as I recall. My firstborn didn't even own a pair of underpants till he was gone three. We lived on a boat then – no need for it. Trouble only came when we tried to send him to school. Teacher used to call saying, "Do you know that child of yours is butt naked again?" Used to take his things off in the playground and hang 'em on the shrubs.'

Lavender gave a rumbling laugh. 'We black folks never been uptight 'bout the body. That's a white thing.'

'It's certainly a very English thing,' Katie said, conscious that she had felt only slightly less awkward than Polly when the time came for them all to strip off. But it was silly to worry about the few extra pounds she was used to covering up beneath a well-cut overcoat, when Lavender seemed so utterly unselfconscious about her own bulk.

'That sho tickles,' Lavender said, squirming so that she made little waves on the surface of the water. 'Them honeymoon couples be liking this an' no mistake.'

'It's a real shame all those guests are coming to crowd us out,' Nadine said, taking another swig of champagne.

'You don't think they'll actually . . . do it . . . in here, do you?' Polly asked, her eyes wide.

Nadine eyed her with exasperation. 'What else you s'pose folks get up to when no one's looking?'

'As long as it *is* when no one else is looking,' Katie said pointedly.

'The boys next door don't mind who's watching,' Nadine laughed.

There was a rustling in the bushes, then the sound of twigs snapping on the pathway. All eyes turned in that direction, Polly's widening in alarm as a figure stepped out of the undergrowth and let out a loud cackle. The figure was wearing striped pyjamas.

'Knew I'd catch yer all here up to no good,' Willie Vance gloated.

'Oh, my,' Polly cried, crossing her arms over generous breasts which weren't quite concealed by the bubbling water.

'Mr Vance, this is private property,' Katie began to object.

'Don't go talking to me about property,' Willie yelled. 'I know what yer been up to – stealing my cats, just like that other hussy.'

Katie felt at some considerable disadvantage, trying to conduct this argument from her current vantage point.

'Nonsense,' she said, looking up sternly at the striped pyjama legs. 'I've merely been giving them some extra food—'

'So ye're a meddling baggage, just like she is.' He glared at Polly shrinking back into her corner.

'Now you mind what you call Mrs Colman,' Nadine objected.

Willie advanced on the hot tub, leering with disgust. 'Look at her, consorting with that crazy woman.' He pointed at the furiously blushing Polly. 'And that witch.'

'Who you be calling a witch?' Lavender heaved with indignation.

'I know yer kind and those dark arts yer practise down in the cemetery—'

'You don't know from nothing. Those grey hairs be making a fool outta you less you gits yo'self the wisdom supposed to go with 'em.'

Willie advanced menacingly, his skinny ankles protruding from his pyjama bottoms. 'I ain't afraid of you witches.' He glared at Katie. 'So keep yer hands off of my cats, yer interfering she-dog.'

'That does it!' Nadine emerged from the bubbles like Venus rising from the sea – only a rather more muscular and tattooed version. 'You get off this property right this minute, you looney old man, less you want me to throw you off.'

Butt naked as her child had been at school all those years ago, Nadine advanced on skinny Willie Vance, who backed away in alarm.

'Now see here, yer can't walk around like that, it ain't decent—'

'Scram!' Nadine hollered. She made a sudden dart at Willie, who turned and fled back through the shrubbery with a speed remarkable for his years.

'Now if only it was that easy to get rid of his damned cats!' Nadine said, climbing back into the hot tub with a satisfied grin.

* * *

Katie stepped jauntily along the dock, her bare legs browned by the sun, the pretty straw hat from Duval Street perched on her strawberry blonde hair. She carried a basket full of boating necessities – suncream and towel and paperback novel and dry underwear. Beneath her shorts and T-shirt was a brand new bikini with a polka-dot pattern which she hoped flattered rather than emphasised her curves.

She had taken off the sapphire engagement ring and wedding band – for safety, of course, so there would be no question of losing them in the water – and locked them in the office safe. She swung her left arm as she walked down the pier, and her hand felt light and free.

She glanced ahead to where the *Indigo Jane* would be moored – and suddenly felt a clutch of panic in her stomach. The mooring space was quite empty. Anxiously she swept the harbour with her eyes and saw the blue hulls of the catamaran disappearing towards the horizon. She stood there helplessly, feeling she could almost weep with disappointment. She had, quite literally, missed the boat.

But she wasn't late, she thought angrily, so why had Lance left without her? She looked down at her watch, which confirmed that it was still two minutes till a quarter past ten – the arranged time of their meeting.

'I keep telling you to throw that thing away,' said a teasing voice behind her.

She was almost too cross to look at him. 'You said we were going out on the *Indigo Jane*—'

'So I stretched the truth a little,' he said unrepentantly.

'And why do you find that so amusing?'

'Hey, lighten up. I'm taking you out on the water, just like I promised, only it'll be just the two of us in my Boston whaler.' He pointed down to a small craft tied up beside the *Indigo Jane*'s empty mooring place.

'So you got me down here under false pretences? Katie said indignantly.

'But at least I got you down here . . . Shall we go?'

Katie toyed with the idea of refusing, but she knew she didn't really want to.

'All right, then,' she conceded, allowing Lance to help her down into the Boston whaler bobbing expectantly on the water, packed with cooler boxes and diving equipment and fishing gear. A dark suspicion came to her that he intended to spend the day doing what he liked best.

'You *are* going to show me what my guests would see, aren't you?' she demanded.

'And a whole lot more.' He delved into his pocket and passed her over a pair of sunglasses. 'Take yours off and use these. They're polarised to help you see things better under the water.'

Katie sat back while he cast off lines and nosed the Boston whaler out into the harbour. As soon as the smell of salt was in her nostrils and the sea breezes in her hair, a sense of delicious enjoyment began to steal over her. The *Indigo Jane* was now no more than a distant dot on the horizon.

'I'm going to avoid the tourist traps, take you Gulf-side instead, out into the backcountry,' Lance said. 'You can only get there in a small boat – and believe me, it's worth it.'

The sun was beating down on Lance's bronzed back as he steered his course, watching with a sort of relaxed concentration for the stakes put in the water by locals to guide their way, looking ahead to avoid the tell-tale brown and white patches which meant shallow beds of sand or rock or seagrass. He explained it all to her in a casual, matter-of-fact way which implied that his navigational skills were no big deal.

They were moving now amidst a scattering of tiny uninhabited mangrove islands. Lance suddenly cut the engine. 'Let's see what we got,' he said, coming to kneel beside her and peering into the shallow water.

Katie found herself looking at a miniature underwater world not unlike the fantasies of Polly's paintings. Among the soft feathery corals and tentacled anemones, she spotted the pointed arms of orangey-brown starfish, the wavy outlines of conch and tulip snails and spindle-shaped molluscs, the distinctive spiky tail and curved shell of the horseshoe crab foraging for algae, the flash of brilliantly coloured fish. She let her arm rest against Lance's as she watched it all with a quiet fascination.

'I've only ever got this close to aquatic life in a dentist's waiting room,' she laughed

'You wouldn't get this close on a catamaran,' Lance said smugly.

They drifted a while, watching the parade of sea-life pass beneath them. Then Lance suddenly pointed to her left. 'Over there – nurse shark.'

Katie snatched her hands from the water's surface and looked round nervously for a circling dorsal fin. Lance watched her with huge amusement. 'They're not exactly "Jaws", you know. I don't think you're on the menu.'

Katie spied the dark torpedo shape snaking along beneath the surface. It was, as Lance had said, reassuringly small. 'How was I supposed to know?' she said sheepishly.

'There's barracuda in these waters too,' Lance said, 'and bonefish and tarpon and snook . . . Great place to come spearfishing, then cook the fresh catch on your barbie that night.'

'I sometimes think,' Katie said softly, 'that everyone I know has led an adventurous life except me.'

Lance flashed her a curious look. 'You never been scuba diving . . . or snorkelling?'

'I've never even visited places where that was possible – till now.'

'What took you so long?'

She gazed out at the twisted roots of mangroves rising from the water. 'I don't know. They say youth is wasted on the young, but looking back I'm not sure I ever had a youth.'

'You mean you were too scared to try things?'

'I'm not sure. Too scared . . . or too sensible. Perhaps I just never realised before how much I was missing.'

'I get the feeling you're gonna make up for lost time.' Lance rose to his feet and stretched his limbs. Bathed in the bright light of near noon, he looked like some Viking sun god, Katie thought, with his mane of hair and broad, muscular shoulders. He reached for a long push-pole and began to heave the boat silently and tranquilly through the shallow waters.

As they wove through mangrove islets he pointed out the bird life – comical brown pelicans with beaks bigger than their stomachs, snowy egrets with magnificent white plumage, tall white herons stalking their prey on long yellow legs, ibises – the sacred birds of Egypt – with their black-tipped wings and curved scarlet bills.

It was a long time since they had passed another boat. It felt to Katie as though time were standing still, as though she, Lance, the birds and the sea creatures had the whole world entirely to themselves.

'Bet you're starving,' Lance said, turning the boat towards an island with the tiniest strip of sand she had ever seen. 'Lucky I pinched some of the tourists' food off the *Indigo Jane* before she put out to sea.'

He dropped anchor just off the island and helped Katie through the water to the thread of sand that would have to serve as a beach. He edged closer to her, trying to make room for the cooler box. 'Two's company and three's a crowd,' Katie laughed as he squeezed up against her.

Lance popped the lids off two ice-cold beers and began to unwrap the rather uninspiring cheese and ham and chicken sandwiches that would have been wasted on the catamaran passengers anyway, he said, with their gross habit of losing their lunch if the boat passed over even the smallest swell. He hoped Katie was made of sterner stuff.

'My sister's the tough one,' Katie said. 'She survived for four days in an open lifeboat in the Southern Ocean.'

Lance gave a low whistle. 'What the hell was she doing in a god-awful place like that?'

'Trying to break some world record or other,' she said,

deciding it was time to risk the new bikini and sliding her shorts down casually over her legs. 'Going for the challenge.'

In a quick, nonchalant movement she removed her T-shirt. Lance stared at her with frank appreciation. 'You look great.'

'I could do with losing a pound or two,' she said self-consciously, folding her hands across her stomach.

Gently he removed one hand and held it in his. 'So what is it with your sister and this pain she puts herself through?'

'I think perhaps the English go looking for hardship,' Katie said, trying not to notice her hand enfolded warmly in his. 'They believe it builds character.'

'Weird,' Lance said, shaking his head. 'Me, I go searching for the good life – and the next wave.'

He released her hand to pass over the cooler box lid, laden like a tray with sandwiches. Katie picked up a rather wilted chicken one and decided she was quite hungry enough to do it justice.

'What do you mean?' she said through a mouthful.

'Surfing, that's my life. I travel the world looking for the next wave, the big one, the one I haven't ridden before.'

'But I thought you drove cruise boats?'

'That's just in high season, so as I can make enough money from the tourists to hit the next surf spot.'

Katie watched him sprawled easily on the sand with his feet trailing in the water, intrigued at the idea of living such an immediate life with no cares for the future beyond where the next unconquered wave might be found. Such a freedom was almost beyond her imagining.

'Frankly,' she said, 'it sounds just as dangerous as what my sister does.'

'I guess it can be. But it's a great way to live. By a lucky accident of nature, all the best surfing spots are in the warmest, most beautiful parts of the world.'

'Like Hawaii?' Katie murmured, spotting the beak-like head of a sea turtle as it suddenly broke the surface of the water in search of air.

'I've ridden the Pipeline – all the big ones, for that matter – Australia, South Africa, wherever. Now I prefer to load up the surfmobile and head off on surfing safari.'

'What's that?'

'I go looking for waves that have never been ridden, in remote corners of the world. I set up camp on a beach or headland, and eat whatever I catch from the sea, and sleep under the stars.'

Katie wrinkled her forehead. 'It sounds idyllic, but I'm not sure how long I'd last away from the comforts of civilisation.'

'You get used to it. It's a simpler, cleaner life.'

He lay back on the tiny strip of sand, and Katie thought she had never seen anyone look so completely relaxed. 'You seem so comfortable with yourself,' she said, intrigued.

'No big secret to it. You have to like yourself and the life you've chosen. If you don't, change it.'

'You make it sound so easy.'

'It is. People just make it complicated so they don't have to face the tough decisions.'

He lay for a while with his eyes shut, dozing in the afternoon sunshine. Sneaking the odd sideways look at him, Katie wondered what it was in the blood that drove people like him and Jemima to travel the world while others were content to remain behind.

When he stirred a little she asked, 'Where are you from?'

'California born and bred. Surfed the big ones at Malibu almost as soon as I could walk. It's the place where modern surfing was born, you know, but it's way too crowded now . . . How about you?'

'I was brought up in a small English village – but now I live in London.'

He looked down at the tan mark where her wedding ring should be. 'With the husband?'

She nodded.

'Happily ever after?'

'I'd rather not talk about that. It's . . . private.'

He touched her arm lightly with his fingers. 'You don't like showing your feelings, do you?'

'It just seems so . . . indiscreet.'

'Then I guess we'd better cool down.' His eyes were twinkling with laughter again as he suddenly grabbed her and pulled her after him into the water. She gave a little shriek as the coldness hit her. Before she had quite adjusted to the shock, Lance scooped up a handful and splashed it in her face. Indignantly she kicked some back, and before she knew it they were involved in a full-scale water fight.

'Enough!' Lance held his hands up in mock surrender.

Katie collapsed back into the water. It was quite pleasant, really, not nearly as cold as it had felt when Lance first dragged her in. She floated contentedly in the shallows, the seagrass tickling her legs, and watched Lance strike out a little further with strong, easy strokes. He must be a swimmer of awesome competence, considering the waves he had faced in the wildest seas of the world.

She didn't know how long she had lazed happily in the sun-warmed water when Lance suddenly called over, 'Time to catch some dinner.' He waded up on to the tiny beach and hefted the cooler bag back to the boat. Katie followed reluctantly, and accepted his hand to help her over the side.

'What sort of dinner are we talking about?' she said.

'Lobster.'

'Then count me out!' Katie shuddered. 'I vowed once I'd never cook those things again.' And she recounted the story of the poor old three-pounder who had struggled so valiantly to escape from her cooking pot in Rock, while Lance laughed fit to burst.

'I'll do the cooking, I swear,' he said. 'And don't worry, I do it the right way round – I kill 'em first.'

They dropped anchor at a patch of brightness on the sea floor which, Lance told her, betrayed the presence of a hunk of coral and a possible lobster hole. He showed Katie how to fit on a snorkelling mask and mouthpiece. 'If you've never done this, it's time you tried,' he said. 'Then you can see my amazing skill with Florida "bugs".'

From a well-organised corner of the boat, he drew on heavy duty dive gloves and tied a mesh game bag round his waist, with a piece of plastic hanging off it on a string. 'To measure the bug,' he said. 'If it's too small, you have to throw it back.'

Katie was amazed to see him select a snorkelling mask like her own. 'Surely you need scuba equipment for this sort of thing?'

He grinned. 'Just a good pair of lungs.'

He hoisted a little 'diver down' flag on the boat, then fixed on his mask and picked up a long metal probe and a net. 'Let's just make sure you've got the hang of this first,' he said.

Katie followed him over the side of the boat and tentatively lowered her masked face below the waterline. At once a whole secret world opened up before her, and she was in its very midst. Soft corals waved spindly fingers, anemones blossomed, little shrimp with large snapping claws crawled over barrel-shaped sponges. She was so enchanted by it all, she quite forgot to wonder whether she would be able to breathe.

Lance watched her for a while, then gave her a thumbs-up sign under the water and kicked off with his flippered feet to investigate the coral outcropping more closely. When he seemed to have found what he was looking for, Katie saw him surface for air.

Moments later he plunged back in, streaking like a creature born to the sea for the hole he had discovered in the coral. With a deft movement he slid in the stick, and a strange clawless lobster emerged on spider-like legs to investigate. Slipping the net in behind it, Lance tapped the lobster's head, and at once it propelled itself backwards with lightning speed straight into the net. Lance slammed it closed while he measured the carapace with the plastic rod. Satisfied, he whipped it into his game bag, and streaked back up to the surface.

Katie emerged too, watching him slide over the side of the

boat and slip the lobster into a cooler bag filled with ice. She gazed at him in wonderment.

'I can't believe you did that in one go.'

'Piece a cake,' Lance grinned. 'When you're dumped by a big wave and you don't even know which way is right side up, first rule of survival is being able to hold your breath long enough to find out.'

As if to prove the point he went back in a further eight times, emerging on five occasions with a squirming lobster to add to the cooler bag. 'Dinner is now on ice,' he said triumphantly. 'My place or yours?'

'I think it had better be yours,' Katie said, unable to resist this opportunity to see how he lived.

Still dressed only in his swimming trunks, Lance prepared them a couple of lobsters each on the terrace of his one-bedroom apartment overlooking the Atlantic. 'Long as I can see the sea, I don't really care where I live,' he told her.

He had killed them painlessly, with Katie refusing to look, and then pulled the tails – the only edible part – assuring her when it was done that the lobsters were quite definitely deceased. Now he cut through the outer shell and butterflied them, sprinkling them with butter, salt and pepper and wrapping them in foil to protect them from the hot coals of the barbecue. A sliced key lime waited to one side.

Katie sipped her wine in a haze of complete physical wellbeing that she had almost never felt before. She was so relaxed in Lance's company, she didn't feel the need for conversation, and he didn't try to fill the pauses with meaningless chatter. She imagined that he had become used to silences in his solitary life beneath the stars. Or did he take companions to those distant horizons where he followed his dream? She felt instinctively that it wasn't the right moment to ask.

After they had gorged themselves on buttery lobster, he took her home on the back of his scooter, her arms tight around his waist, her face pressed to his back. She was so grateful to him for this perfect day he had given her that when he bent to kiss her lips goodnight, it seemed completely natural to kiss him back.

Chapter Thirteen

~

Breakfast at the newly reopened Tropical Hideout now lived up to its description in the carefully rewritten glossy brochure. It was served on a sunny patio paved in recently laid terracotta tiles by a tranquil turquoise pool with matching hot tub. Around the paved area were amphora filled with the bright reds and pinks and mauves of pelargoniums. The tables and chairs were of white wrought iron, and fresh cotton tablecloths in a cornflower blue and white stripe blew in the passing breezes.

The food was piled on the re-thatched and painted tikki bar – exotic tropical fruits, croissants and bagels still warm from the oven, freshly squeezed juices and filtered coffee and pots of thick preserves. Katie had done the breakfast run herself, rising at six to switch on the oven and pop down to the bakery for the selection of fresh breads. Nadine and Conchita had set out the food and would later clear it away, while Alvira and Pearl would start on the rooms of those who had already risen for breakfast. They were a tight-knit and, Katie hoped, well organised team, the only element missing the manager she had not yet been able to find.

So it was Katie who circulated among the guests, introducing them to one another and making them feel as though they were visitors to someone's home rather than entries on a hotel reservations list. She had printed their names – first names only – on a board by the tikki bar to jog sluggish memories. In the Starfish Suite (all units were named after whichever of

Polly's paintings formed the centrepiece) were Micky and Laura, who were planning to take their marriage vows in a small plane over the Gulf of Mexico. Walter and Peggy in the Damselfish Suite were celebrating their silver wedding anniversary. Don had the Red Mangrove Suite all to himself, but not for long, Katie suspected. He had come to hunt for treasure, he said, and from the way his predatory eye roved over the sveltely attractive Laura, he would no doubt be seeking his trophies as much in the bars of Duval Street as on the seabed.

Katie's own unit was now renamed the Green Turtle Suite, and was decorated in soothing creams and purples and greens and corals, with cotton rugs on the polished floors and Polly's wonderful flying turtle in pride of place opposite the windows. Katie longed for the day when she could lure the girls over to see it, and show them the little bedroom she had decorated just for them, with the family of ceramic tortoises on the polished wooden bookshelf.

They would be at Fiona's house in Wiltshire now, roaming free in the fields and woods as she and Jemima had done as children, returning starving hungry to their grandmother's spartan cooking. It would do them no harm just for one week, and she seemed to have been forgiven for not being there, although no word of good luck had come from either Guy or the girls for her quiet reopening of The Tropical Hideout. Lance, however, had sent a huge bunch of flowers with a note that said, 'Don't have too much fun without me', which she had quickly stuffed in her pocket before Nadine could read it and raise her eyes to heaven.

Katie patted the pocket now, where the note still nestled with her keyring and a few loose quarters. Then she noticed Peggy beckoning to her with an arm that jangled with heavy bracelets.

'I sure hope you can tell us where to see the prettiest gardens – apart from yours, of course,' she gushed. 'Walter and I are keen horticulturists, in an amateur sort of way.'

Katie at once advised an in-depth personalised tour of Nancy

Forrester's Secret Garden, where every species imaginable of palm and tropical plant was to be found in abundance, and enthusiasts could also enjoy a picnic lunch in a quiet corner.

'We want to go somewhere we can be on our own,' Laura said, meeting Micky's eye.

Katie smiled to herself. After her trip with Lance, she knew exactly what to recommend. 'I'll give you the name of a company that can take you out in a kayak for two to the backcountry,' she said. 'The trip includes snorkelling and food and wine, and I can promise you won't be disturbed.'

'Sounds perfect,' Micky said without taking his eyes off his bride-to-be.

Don would no doubt want to pay a visit to Mel Fisher's museum to drool over the treasures that eluded all but the luckiest of fortune hunters before he tried his own luck. Katie also had a list in her head of the bars she could suggest at the straight end of Duval Street, where a luckless diver might find liquid solace and sympathetic company.

'You're so knowledgeable about these things,' Peggy cooed. 'Have you lived in Key West long?'

'It certainly feels like it,' Katie said.

It wasn't a question of insecurity, but for some reason Jemima couldn't put her finger on she wanted Guy to see and approve the office premises she was considering in Soho, amidst the collection of narrow streets where market stalls filled with fresh produce and Italian delicatessens and old-fashioned barber shops coexisted alongside the seedier side of city life. At least it was a neighbourhood with character. Jemima felt she could bear living in urban claustrophobia only if it were teeming with its own kind of interesting life.

The office was on street level where she would be able to observe, in idle moments, the ebb and flow outside. A film company had its premises on the floor above, and there was a constant tide of visitors and deliveries. Sometimes a bike messenger would take off his helmet and study the posters she had hung experimentally on the walls, of salmon leaping up the Yukon River, and the rolling sand dunes of El Golea, and giant tortoises on the Galapagos Islands such as Darwin would have seen. Occasionally one of the curious ones would put his head round the door and ask when she would be open for business. Film people, and those who rode motorbikes, were clearly of an adventurous disposition.

On the pavement now she could see the tall and hesitant figure of Guy in his lawyer's suit, studying the street numbers and comparing them to the slip of paper in his hand. She went to go and greet him at the door.

'Thank you for coming,' she said, reaching up to give him a peck on the cheek. 'I'm so longing to know what you think.'

He seemed pleased to have his opinion sought in this way. Taking the responsibility to heart, he paced around the one-room office, studying the white walls covered with posters of remote and inaccessible places, and pacing the empty spaces where she planned to install two identical work stations for her and Tim, equipped with essential computers and telephones.

She almost held her breath, waiting for his verdict. He nodded approvingly. 'It's a busy spot with plenty of passing traffic, you should get your share of walk-ins from the street. For the rest, I presume you're intending to advertise.'

'Of course,' Jemima said. 'In specialist publications, mostly.'

'Then I think you should take it,' Guy said.

'Truly?'

'Yes, truly.'

Jemima looked around her, filled with the warm glow of a job begun if not yet done. 'You know, I'm so surprised by how satisfying I'm finding it all – the business world, of all things. I do nothing except the endless legwork to get the agency up and running, then go back to Daddy's flat . . . my flat . . . to crash out and get some rest. But it's nice to come back at the end of a long day to all the home comforts.'

'You sound just like Katie,' Guy said wistfully, 'the way she used to talk.'

Jemima reached over and gave his hand a comforting squeeze. 'We all need a bit of adventure in our lives too, Guy. Katie was long overdue for hers. The trouble is, she didn't get it out of her system when she was young and had no ties.'

'Nor did I. But I don't feel the need to go gadding off to foreign parts, abandoning my family . . .'

Jemima gave him a speculative look. 'Perhaps you'll break out in some other way.'

'I hope not.'

'Look, let's not talk about gloomy things tonight,' Jemima said briskly. 'I'm in the mood to celebrate. How do you fancy going round the corner for a cheap Italian meal and a bottle of wine?'

Guy thought of the stack of papers in his briefcase requiring his urgent attention and said, 'I'd love to.'

In the reasonably priced trattoria with red-checked table-cloths and wine bottles covered with plaited palm leaves, they toasted Jemima's new life.

'I hate to admit it but I've been wrong about you,' Guy said. 'I never thought you'd stick to anything, and here you are, a company director.'

Jemima grinned. 'Perhaps I've been too hard on you too. You can't be such a stick-in-the-mud or you wouldn't be playing hookey from your work in a Soho restaurant.'

The waiter brought plates of rather over-cooked pasta. Guy said, 'This Tim fellow, is he just a business partner or do you two . . . ?'

'Sleep together?'

'Well, I suppose that's what I was trying to—'

'We had a thing going once, but that's ancient history. He lives with an exotic dancer now.'

Guy carefully would strands of pasta round his fork with the aid of a stainless steel spoon. 'Why do you suppose none of your relationships have lasted very long?'

'Mostly because I didn't want them to. They were good at the time, but then I moved on.'

'Do you think you might feel differently now that you've settled down?'

'I hope I haven't quite done that,' Jemima laughed. 'But sure, I might want to make some changes. Especially when I look at Lucy and Hannah.'

Guy lowered his eyes and traced a little pattern with his fork in the tomato sauce on his place. Jemima thought she had never seen him look so unsure of himself.

'Guy, what is it?'

'I was wondering,' he said hesitantly, 'if you could do me a favour.'

'Of course, if it's in my power.'

Seeming finally to abandon the pasta as wholly inedible, Guy pushed his plate aside and firmly clutched his wine. 'The girls look up to you so much . . . I thought perhaps you could come down with me to your mother's this weekend. It might make them feel a little better if you were there . . . sort of make up for Katie not being.'

'Guy, you poor sweet thing,' Jemima said. 'Don't worry – of course I'll come.'

It was a rainy Sunday morning and ten of Katie's fourteen units were occupied when the pipe supplying water from the street to the entire guesthouse suddenly burst. At once pandemonium broke out as guests realised they couldn't get even a trickle out of their showers or fill up a kettle to indulge in a morning coffee. Nadine took out her tool kit but soon returned, drenched and grumpy, to declare herself defeated.

Katie flipped frantically through the telephone directory. There were two numbers for emergency plumbers, but when she tried to get through to them, she discovered that both had machines on requiring her to leave a message. The minutes ticked by and no one returned her calls.

A knock on the door revealed Peggy in her dressing gown looking flustered and a little indignant. 'It's not just the bath,' she explained. 'I look such a mess – today's the day I always do a full shampoo and set.'

Katie, who doubted she would find a hair salon open on a Sunday morning either, could only assure her that she was trying to get the matter seen to as soon as possible.

As more complaints poured in and the telephone still failed to ring, Katie grabbed an umbrella and headed for Paradise Lodge. The door was opened by Chico in his frilly apron.

'We also had a burst pipe once,' he commiserated. 'The queens went crazy when they couldn't take their showers and the hot tub had no bubbles. We gave them straws and told them to blow their own.'

He led Katie to the office where Harvey sat wading through suppliers' bills and looking tetchy. The rain seemed to have everyone in a blue funk. It was immensely frustrating for Katie to look out of the window and see all that water pouring from the sky, when not a drop of it could solve the problems of her guests.

'Lousy day, isn't it?' Harvey grumbled. 'All my lot have shut themselves away in their rooms.'

'Mine are running round in various states of hysteria,' Katie sighed. She unburdened her tale of woe and Harvey thoughtfully stroked his moustache. 'I once had three appliances break down in one day – an air conditioner, a water heater and a fridge. Welcome to the real world of running a guesthouse.'

'Now don't start on the I-told-you-so's,' Katie begged. 'I don't think I could bear it.'

'Never fear – Uncle Harvey will save your bacon.' He opened an immaculate filing cabinet which reminded Katie of the urgent need to reorganise the mess left by Wade Grenville. Triumphantly Harvey withdrew an invoice and settled down to dial a number.

This time a real human seemed to answer, because Harvey conducted a full conversation which resulted in the welcome information that an emergency plumber would be at The Tropical Hideout in approximately fifteen minutes. Katie jumped up and kissed Harvey on both cheeks.

'You're welcome,' he said. 'Now I reckon we could all do with some cheering up. Let's arrange a trip to the drag show at the La-te-da tonight. And you must invite the delicious Lance.'

Katie hadn't seen much of Lance this past week, with all the chaos of the reopening. She had been meaning to give him a ring, but it wouldn't hurt to have an excuse. 'Won't that put Chico into one of his rages?' she objected half-heartedly.

'Sure, but how else would I keep life interesting?'

As though his words had brought on the Chinese curse, there was an almighty crash from upstairs. Harvey bounded out of the room, followed closely by Katie. They found Chico racing down the stairs, his apron flapping wildly.

'It's those big hunky footballers in number five,' he shrieked. 'Got so carried away, the leg of their bed's gone clean through the floor.'

Harvey was almost tearing strips out of his moustache. 'What is it with those guys? This house is over a hundred years old, can't they treat it with respect?' He looked almost accusingly at Katie. 'And you thought *you* had problems!'

To spare everyone a Sunday lunch cooked by Fiona, and to give the girls a treat that might make them feel they were not being neglected, Guy and Jemima took them to the travelling funfair that had been set up on the village common.

Lucy agreed to go reluctantly, as though doing them all a favour, and turned up her nose at most of the rides as far too tame until she suddenly spotted the divebomber, a nasty-looking red and yellow contraption with metal cars on either end of a long shaft, which hurtled their passengers headlong towards the ground at breakneck speed before spinning round and beginning the ascent again. 'Now *that* looks like fun,' she said, cheering up considerably.

'You can't be serious,' said Guy. Just looking at it made him feel green.

'Don't worry – I didn't imagine for a moment that you or

Hannah would be up to it. But Jemima will come with me – won't you?'

She was already dragging a perfectly willing Jemima towards the ticket booth, and moments later they were being strapped into the metal car with heavy shoulder harnesses.

Guy wasn't sure he could bear to watch. 'Shall we try that?' he asked Hannah, pointing at a rather wonderful-looking Victorian merry-go-round with beautifully carved and painted horses. Hannah nodded enthusiastically.

Surging through the air on his wooden steed, Guy could still hear above the tinny old tune blaring from the speakers the screams of terror from the foolhardy punters strapped into the dreaded divebomber. He glanced across at Hannah, her sandy hair streaming out behind her, her arms wrapped around the painted pole, and felt a sudden rush of gratitude for this easy and contented child.

They all met up again on the ground, Lucy and Jemima staggering a bit like revellers after an all-night party. 'That was *so* cool,' Lucy cried. 'Mummy would never have let me go on it.'

Jemima flicked an enquiring look at Guy. 'I wouldn't want you doing anything your mother doesn't approve of.'

But Lucy was already running towards a rifle range, calling out for some money to try her luck. Guy and Jemima followed with Hannah between them, holding each by one hand.

'Will you show me how to shoot, Aunt Jemima?'

'I bet Daddy's better at it than me,' Jemima said tactfully.

Lucy was too impatient to take instruction, but Guy bent eagerly over Hannah, showing her how to line up the sights on the target, and squeeze the trigger very slowly, and on only her third attempt she hit a bull's eye and threw her sister a look of quiet triumph. The stall man offered Hannah her choice of prizes, and she settled on a teddy with ugly synthetic turquoise fur, which she clutched possessively as they explored the other stalls.

'Oh look,' Jemima cried. 'A Hall of Mirrors – your mother

and I used to love those when we were children.'

'I'm not a child,' Lucy reminded her a little haughtily.

'Of course you're not – but they're still fun.'

Soon she had them all posing in front of a wavy mirror that made them look elongated and odd, like a kind of Addams family, and another that blew them up into rotund marshmallow men, and they were all laughing and pulling the kinds of silly faces usually reserved for holiday snapshots at the seaside.

'I'm starving,' Hannah said suddenly, staring at herself in a mirror that made her look unexpectedly thin.

Lucy refused even to consider the hamburger restaurant on the High Street. 'You could get mad cow disease or anything from a place like that. I've put myself on the vegetarian table at school.'

'Why didn't you tell me?' Guy said irritably.

'I don't have to – it's my body.'

They settled for a place that sold pancakes with a choice of fillings. Lucy ordered the cheese and leek in a loud voice and, when it came, did no more than push it round her plate. Jemima noticed that Guy was beginning to look a little frazzled round the edges.

'Who's for a ride when we get back to Granny's house?' she said brightly.

'My riding boots are falling to bits,' Lucy complained. 'I need some new ones to take back to school.'

'It's a bit late to mention that now,' Guy said indignantly. 'Surely it can wait till your mother gets back.'

'That depends.' Lucy gave him a cocky stare. 'Just when *is* she planning on coming back?'

Guy gaped a little, like a fish out of water, and Jemima said hastily, 'Give me your shoe size and I'll send you some from London.'

'What about our tuck boxes?' said Hannah, who had polished off her creamy chicken pancake with relish. 'What are you going to put in them for us to take back to school? We *can't* have Granny's stale biscuits.'

Guy ran a hand through hair that Jemima only noticed now was thinning slightly on top. 'What does your mother usually give you?' he said with an air of desperation.

'Loads of the most truly delicious things.'

'But what *sort* of things, exactly?'

'I tell you what,' Jemima said, deciding it was time to put Guy out of his misery. 'We'll go down the street and look in the bakery and the supermarket, and if you can't find everything you want there, I'll come down to see you next weekend with extra supplies *and* Lucy's riding boots.'

When Jemima looked across at Guy for approval, there was an expression on his face of the purest gratitude.

Katie was conscious of Lance's eyes on her bare back as she climbed the stairs in her wispy cocktail dress to the Treetop Bar at the top of the La-te-da. Harvey followed more slowly, waiting impatiently for Chico whose tight Chinese silk dress severely restricted his ability to move.

At the big central bar they ordered margaritas – except for Lance, who said he'd stick to beer – and bagged one of the tables with stools from which to watch the act in comfort. Harvey, quickest off the mark, slid on to a stool next to Lance, who pulled one up on his other side for Katie. By the time Chico had tottered over to the table on his stiletto heels, the seating arrangements had already been decided to Harvey's satisfaction.

The place was rapidly filling up with mostly gay couples who stood around the bar cheering for the action to begin. Lance tilted back on his stool and drank his beer straight from the bottle, as relaxed in this environment as on a boat out in the backcountry. He was watching with admiration some very tall and beautiful transvestites in microscopically short skirts. With their rainbow-coloured clothes and long lissome legs, they looked like a flock of exotic birds. Lance shook his head in bemusement. 'Wouldn't trust myself to know the difference on a dark night,' he said to Harvey.

'I look just as good as those bitches,' Chico declared as though daring him to deny it.

'You put 'em all to shame, sweetie-pie,' Harvey assured him soothingly.

Chico took out his compact and checked his Chinese-style make-up with white powder and thick black eyeliner, which Harvey complained had taken him hours to apply and almost made them late. After inspecting himself this way and that in the mirror, he closed the compact again with a satisfied little snap.

'You must drop by our guesthouse one day for a drink on the pool deck,' Harvey said to Lance with a meaningful look. Katie shot a nervous glance at Chico and saw his nostrils begin to flare. But the conversation was stopped in its tracks by a blare of loud music from the speakers as the warm-up act came sashaying on in wig and disco queen skirt, singing an old Donna Summer song. The crowd at the bar erupted into cheers and wolf whistles.

'There sure is a lotta energy in this place,' Lance said, grinning down at Katie with huge enjoyment.

'Want to dance?' Katie found herself saying, as much to get Lance away from Harvey's admiring scrutiny as because she suddenly found she really rather wanted to.

'What happened to the shy English rose?' Lance teased.

'I think I've grown rather tired of her.'

'Don't mind us, we'll amuse ourselves,' Harvey said in a pretended display of the sulks that contained an element of the real thing.

But Katie was beyond caring. She and Lance headed into the thick of the whooping crowd, and, carried along on the wave of excitement, she shimmied and shook with the best of them, glancing up to catch Lance watching her in amused admiration. She grabbed his hand and let him twirl her round and fell against him laughing when the music finally stopped and 'Donna Summer' came round for some appreciation from her fans in the form of dollar bills stuck into her garter belt.

'Well, aren't you the little raver when you let your hair down!' Lance said as he guided her through the crowd back to their table.

'I'm only just warming up.'

'Want to dance with *me* now?' Harvey said hopefully to Lance. 'Chico isn't up to it in that damn dress.'

'How d'you know – you didn't ask,' Chico objected furiously.

'Come on – it's a challenge to walk in that thing, never mind boogey.'

'I'll sit this one out, if you don't mind,' Lance said smoothly. 'Katie's tired me out.'

Harvey looked as though he was going to say something lewd, but thought better of it when he caught sight of Katie's warning frown.

The main act was a Eurasian with extraordinary bone structure and an uncanny ability to impersonate the likes of Cher, Joan Rivers and Judy Garland in a series of lightning-quick costume changes. The crowd went wild for him. Even Harvey and Chico forgot their earlier disagreement as they screamed in unison for an encore.

'Great place,' Lance said to Harvey. 'I'm glad you guys brought us along.'

'You're not gonna leave us yet, are you?'

' 'Fraid so. Promised I'd take the little lady to dinner.'

This was news to Katie, but the kind that was not unwelcome. She stood with indecent haste before Harvey could try to talk them out of it.

Chico didn't look the least bit sorry to see them go.

While Lucy and Hannah were upstairs having a bath and packing their suitcases, Fiona made a pot of her over-brewed tea for Guy and Jemima, who would drive the girls back to school before returning to London. Great aunt Flora had got her hands on one of the packets of jam doughnuts that were supposed to go into the tuck boxes, and was even now greedily probing out the filling with her tongue.

'I think the girls have had a perfectly good time here, all things considered,' Fiona said.

'I'm so grateful to you all for coming to my rescue,' said Guy, meeting Jemima's eye.

She smiled back. 'Nonsense, what else are family for?'

Aunt Flora removed a jammy tongue from her doughnut. 'Lucy is to have my emeralds,' she pronounced. 'It's all settled. In any event, emeralds only come into their own on a true redhead.'

'And what about Hannah?' Jemima said, wondering how her mother could manage to make a simple cup of tea taste so completely vile. 'What did she ask for?'

'Nothing. The girl has no interest in finery, which is probably just as well—'

'Perhaps it's only that she isn't as forward as Lucy,' Jemima suggested.

'Do you think so?' Aunt Flora looked genuinely surprised. 'In that case, perhaps the pearls.'

Guy glanced at his watch. It was simple and unadorned, like his clothing and his speech. Jemima wondered if she had been wrong before to see only his pretensions – a grand house, an expensive boarding school for his children – while ignoring the other basic and solid side of him, the part that would never let his family down.

'Is it time to go yet?' she asked.

'Not quite.' He lowered his eyes to the tabletop before continuing. 'Did either of the girls say anything about their mother not coming home?'

'I explained it to them very clearly,' Fiona said. 'I told them she has work to do in America, and that's the only reason she stayed on.'

'Poppycock!' Great aunt Flora leered suggestively. 'There's a man behind it, mark my words.'

'How dare you!' Guy was almost purple with rage. 'You have absolutely no grounds for such an accusation—'

'Only years of experience in affairs of the heart.'

'Now, aunt Flora, you're rambling again,' Fiona intervened. 'Things were different in your day.'

'Human nature never changes,' aunt Flora said stubbornly.

Guy rose ominously to his feet. At once Jemima jumped up too and took him firmly by the arm. 'We really should go up now and see if the girls are ready,' she said. 'They'll need help carrying down their suitcases.'

Lance took Katie to a small island-style restaurant with tables outside in a courtyard, where they ate spinach salads with grilled shiitake mushrooms and freshly caught fish with tropical fruit salsa, and drank enough wine to make Katie quite light-headed after all the margaritas and the dancing.

They talked only about Key West, avoiding all reference to the lives they led in other places. They spoke of its vivid colours and pungent fragrances, its interesting characters and their easy friendliness towards visitors.

'I like Harvey and Chico,' Lance said. 'Wacko, sure, but fun to be with.'

She smiled, absurdly pleased that he had given them his vote of approval.

When they could linger no longer over their cappuccinos, and the moment of decision had to be faced, Lance said, 'How about coming back to my place?'

She couldn't pretend she hadn't known what he would say, but she couldn't give him the answer he wanted either. 'I can't,' she said simply.

'Why not?'

'Because I'm not free to.'

'What does "not free" mean? Imprisoned . . . or under the control of another?'

'You're just playing with words,' she said. 'You know perfectly well what I'm saying.'

'I only know I never let anyone else tell me what to do.'

'It's not that simple when you have other people to think of besides yourself.'

'OK,' he shrugged. 'Then how about I come and have a drink with you in your garden?'

Katie thought it would probably be quite safe to agree to that. They were bound to have company at The Tropical Hideout, what with all the units being full.

But there were no guests by the pool when she and Lance slipped outside with a bottle of Chardonnay and sat in the wrought iron chairs amidst the lace-like drapery of lights through the trees. The scent of gardenia, not jasmine, was in the air, but even without Lavender's candles, the setting could hardly have been more romantic.

If he touches me, Katie thought, I will just have to say . . .

'You ever wonder how many people are looking at the same moon?' Lance said suddenly.

Katie glanced up and thought that here the moon seemed somehow closer, more radiant, a giant orb hanging so low in the sky that you got the feeling, if you could only jump high enough, you might be able to touch it.

'I mean, when night comes in India, will they see it the way we do?'

'I think it probably looks completely different,' Katie said, 'depending on your point of view.'

'Then maybe some people don't see a moon at all but a great fat cheese with a bite taken out.'

Katie's smile faded from her lips as he bent forward and tucked a strand of hair behind her ear. She tensed expectantly at the touch of his fingers. He was close, so close that the silhouette of his face, blocking out the moon, was framed by a halo of light.

From my point of view, she thought, he is all I see . . .

A gunshot rang out, ear-splittingly close, and Lance and Katie swung round in unison towards Paradise Lodge. For a second neither moved, then another shot erupted from the garden next door.

'Harvey—' Katie whispered.

Then they were both racing round the perimeter fence and into the neigbouring yard. The pool deck was in darkness, but by the light of the moon they saw a figure slumped on the ground. Katie ran to crouch beside it, and at her urgent touch the figure seemed to move, peering through arms closed protectively over its face.

'Harvey?' Katie said.

'Sshh. Stay low. Chico's in one of his moods.'

Katie looked round nervously for Lance. He was cautiously approaching another figure standing in the shadow of a spreading poinciana tree. The figure moved, and Katie saw the glint of moonlight off metal.

'Come on, buddy,' Lance said evenly. 'You've had a few too many. How about you give that to me?'

Katie waited, hardly daring to breathe. Chico stepped out of the shadow, tottering perilously on his heels, clutching the gun possessively to him. 'You stay away from me,' he spat at Lance. 'He's been making eyes at you all night, don't think I didn't notice.'

'Hey, no disrespect, but I prefer girls.'

A shuttered window banged open and a male voice squeaked, 'What's going on out there?'

'Just letting off a few fireworks,' Lance called up. 'The show's over now, go back to sleep.'

'Keep it down, then.' The window banged shut.

Streaks of eyeliner ran down Chico's powdered white cheeks, giving his moonlit face the look of a tragic Pierrot mask. He turned his face away from the prostrate Harvey. 'He's always making a fool of me in public. After you guys left, I found him in the men's toilet with the warm-up act.'

'Sweetie-pie, we were only talking—'

Chico rounded on Harvey, waving the gun wildly so that Katie crouched in breathless fear beside him. 'You were touching him, I saw you.'

'He was showing me his nipple rings.'

'I should have killed you both.'

'Hey, now.' Lance stepped up slowly behind him. 'You're getting yourself all upset over nothing. You should see how your mascara's running.'

Chico put a hand up to his cheek. 'Do I look a mess?'

'You looked gorgeous at the club tonight, but now . . . you need to go fix yourself up. Better still, get some beauty sleep.'

Chico turned to him as to someone who at last understood. 'You're right, all this stress is hell on the face. He doesn't understand what it does to me. I always look like death when I've been crying.'

Lance put a gentle hand on his arm. 'You'll be fine. Just go upstairs with Katie and let her help you to bed . . . Here, I'll keep that for you.'

Lance slid his hand up Chico's arm towards the gun. Katie saw Chico stiffen and for tense seconds prayed that he would not suddenly turn on Lance. But gradually the fight seemed to go out of him and he let Lance take the gun from his hand as easily as if he were a child surrendering an object he knew all along he wasn't allowed to play with.

Beside her Katie heard Harvey expel a sigh of relief. He stood and approached Chico with an ingratiating smile. 'Can I give you a goodnight kiss, sweetie-pie?'

Chico turned his stained cheek and rather disdainfully accepted the touch of Harvey's puckered lips. Then he wobbled over to Katie and leaned heavily on her arm. 'Shall we go up?'

Katie had never been in their bedroom before. There was a great iron bedstead in the middle with an embroidered patchwork quilt. The walls were faux marble and covered with Picasso lithographs. Chico disappeared into the marble bathroom and emerged some time later in a rose-coloured robe with his face scrubbed clean. Even without make-up his high cheekbones and sultry skin had a feminine sort of beauty about them.

'I'm so tired,' he said, shedding the robe and climbing beneath the quilt. 'Would you mind just sitting with me until I nod off?'

'Of course,' Katie said, perching on Harvey's side of the bed.

Chico closed his eyes, so that the long lashes fell heavily against the copper-coloured cheeks. 'I do love him, you know,' he said almost apologetically.

'I know.'

He seemed, almost immediately, to fall asleep, tunnelled down beneath the patchwork quilt that had probably been made by somebody's stern Quaker grandmother and was now drawn for comfort around this slender Cuban man/woman in an alien land less than a hundred miles from the place he should have called home, but had probably never seen.

When Katie went back downstairs, she found Harvey and Lance nursing stiff brandies by the pool and gratefully accepted the glass Harvey offered her. Quite suddenly she found that her hands were shaking.

'What are you going to do about him, Harvey?' she said.

'Hey, it was just a little misunderstanding.'

'You call waving a gun at someone a misunderstanding?' Lance said with disbelief.

'He's just a little emotional. It's his passionate Latin nature.'

'Hey, don't get me wrong, I like the guy,' Lance said. 'But you have to face it, he was pretty scary tonight.'

'I thought he only broke plates when he got angry,' Katie said earnestly. 'Tell the truth, Harvey – has he ever done anything like this before?'

'He sometimes pulls the gun out when he's in a state, but this is the first time he's actually fired it – only into the air, mind you,' Harvey said defensively.

'So you're waiting for him to use you for target practice before you do something about this?' Lance said.

'You're making too much fuss about nothing.' Harvey gave a light-hearted laugh. 'The guy loves me – it's not like he would really hurt me.'

'If I were you, I wouldn't feel safe having him around.'

Harvey put an arm round each of their shoulders. 'Hey, this is my fault – I made him jealous. Besides, it's rather thrilling to be loved so fiercely, don't you think?'

'It's not normal,' Katie insisted.

'No, but then we're not "normal" by other people's standards, are we?'

Katie squeezed the arm around her shoulders. 'Can't you at least persuade him to go and talk to someone?'

'I don't think consulting shrinks is part of the Cuban culture . . . But if it'll make you happy, I guess I could try.'

'And for God's sake lock this thing up where he can't get his hands on it.' Lance slid the gun across the table towards Harvey.

They all stared at the ugly, stub-nosed weapon lying malignantly between them. Then Harvey picked it up and slid it into his pocket. 'Come on, guys, lighten up – I'll take care of it.'

'Promise?' Katie pleaded.

'Promise. Now you two go on home and get some rest . . . and thanks, I really appreciate what you did here.'

They left him sitting in his shadowy back yard, alone with his thoughts and Chico's gun. They stopped on the pavement outside The Tropical Hideout. Lance leaned back against his jeep, circling his arms loosely round Katie's waist.

'I'm so glad you were here tonight,' she said. 'I don't know how I'd have handled it on my own. You were so . . . cool under fire.'

'I was shitting myself,' Lance grinned. 'But I can play a good hand of poker.'

He bent down to kiss her lightly on the cheek. She waited but he didn't ask to come back inside and she didn't suggest it. The spell of the moment had been broken and for now she was safe, and also more than a little sorry.

Chapter Fourteen

~

In the chilly pre-dawn of Monday morning, when she had switched on the oven but couldn't yet do the breakfast run to the bakery, Katie phoned Wolton Abbey to catch the girls before lights out on Sunday evening.

'Oh it's you,' Lucy said languidly as though she had been expecting someone else.

'How did you enjoy half-term?'

'It was fine. We found this funfair and Jemima let me go on the divebomber.'

Katie made a considerable effort to hold her peace.

'We went riding afterwards, and I raced Jemima back to the stable. I was on Hercules and I won by simply lengths.'

'Aren't you clever,' Katie said neutrally.

'Jemima's coming down with Daddy again this weekend,' Lucy chirped. 'They're taking us to the races. I'm going to get Jemima to put on some bets for me.'

Why, Katie wondered, did her elder daughter always try to provoke her? Why did she refuse to ask how her mother was, how the guesthouse was faring? Did she really care for nothing but her own life and her beloved aunt Jemima?

'I'd better speak to Hannah now,' Katie said.

The story from her second daughter wasn't much different. They'd had a perfectly good half-term without their mother, especially after the unexpected arrival of aunt Jemima with their father.

'At least I had someone else to make a fuss of me,' Hannah said. 'Great aunt Flora always pays more attention to Lucy.'

It had been like that for Katie too, when she and Jemima were children and Jemima somehow always got more than her share of the limelight. 'Don't ever forget,' she said to Hannah, 'you have your own special gifts, even if not everyone recognises them.'

Hannah seemed to consider this for a moment. 'You're right – I can shoot with a rifle straighter than Lucy.'

'There you are, then.'

'Daddy taught me, at the funfair. He and Jemima are coming to see us again on Saturday. Aunt Jemima's bringing a new cage for Gulliver because his bars are all loose and I'm afraid he'll escape and get eaten by the school cats.'

'Oh dear,' Katie said. 'Don't you think you should have asked Daddy to buy the cage?'

'Daddy never has time to do things like that.'

But it seemed to Katie that Guy was in fact taking more weekends off work than at any time she could remember.

'Aunt Jemima's also bringing a chocolate fudge cake,' Hannah announced reverently.

Katie thought she might just scream if Jemima's name were mentioned once more in the course of this conversation. 'I'm sorry, darling, I have to go now,' she said. 'I've got to start getting the breakfast ready.'

On her walk up to the bakery, her feet angrily pounding the pavement, Katie told herself not to be so childish. Instead of getting into a jealous huff, she should be grateful to Jemima for stepping into her shoes. But it was only human nature to feel put out when you discovered that you were being missed rather less than you could reasonably have expected.

There were many more names up on the board by the tikki bar, and Katie was kept a great deal busier during breakfast on the terrace, answering all the queries of her guests.

Ron and Sue from Cleveland needed advice on the most

reasonable place to charter a fishing boat. Walter and Peggy, having exhausted the horticultural possibilities of the island, were keen for a guided tour of the cemetery. Marvin from Cincinnati, after pounding the pavements from one end of Duval Street to the other, wanted to know where he could get his shoes resoled. An unfortunate Dutch woman called Hanneke had eaten a bad oyster and was in urgent need of a doctor.

'Lawyer, more like,' said Marvin, thrusting a card into the hand of the woman's startled and long-faced husband.

Katie saw to all their needs and answered all their questions and then borrowed a tiny screwdriver off Nadine to tighten the arm of Peggy's glasses which had been threatening for days to fall off.

'You're a real godsend,' Peggy said. 'Walter and I would be just lost in one of those big hotels where they don't even know your name. We would never manage without you.'

'Thank you,' Katie said. It was only human nature, too, to feel a little warm glow inside when you were genuinely appreciated.

'Phone call for you, Mrs Colman,' Nadine bellowed from the direction of the office.

Katie hastened inside to be met with Polly's breathless tones. 'Oh my, something just awful has happened.'

In a rush Katie remembered the gunshot ringing out next door, and Chico's jealousy over Lance, and her heart beat a wild rhythm. 'Tell me, Polly, quickly.'

'It's Willie. He's fallen down those stairs, just like I always knew he would, and now he's gone and broken his hip, poor old thing.'

Katie's heart was beginning to slow to a steadier rhythm. 'Where is he now?'

'In the hospital. I heard him hollering so I ran straight over and found him lying there, and I called the ambulance right away . . . Oh my, it was so horrible.'

'Are you staying with him?'

'I have to. When he comes round from the operation he's going to be feeling so awful, and I wouldn't want him starting that language of his on the poor nurses.'

A vivid memory came to Katie of Willie standing over her hot tub, calling her a witch. She began to feel very sorry for the nurses indeed.

'Are you sure you can handle him?' she asked, remembering Polly's fear of him.

'Oh yes, I know he doesn't mean all those things he says, especially now he's going to be in so much pain.'

Katie imagined that far from needing her pity, Polly was probably in her element with this opportunity to play Florence Nightingale. 'I suppose at least you didn't have to go looking for his pyjamas – it's all he ever wears.'

'I know, and they're so dirty,' Polly said anxiously. 'I'll have to go buy him some new ones just as soon as he's used to the nurses.'

'I'll come by later and see how he's doing,' Katie promised.

'I knew you would. And if you could just bring some soup for poor Willie – you'll find it in my fridge, you know how awful hospital food is.'

'Anything else?' Katie said wryly.

'Well, the cats are going to need feeding.'

'Don't worry – I've got it all under control.'

'Oh, Katie,' Polly cried. 'I don't know how we ever managed before you came.'

Katie hadn't had time to make any headway on her various missions of mercy when the telephone rang again.

'Katie, is that you?'

It was the voice of a none too sober Guy. Katie glanced at her watch in surprise. It must be past midnight in deepest St John's Wood.

'I've phoned to put a stop to this nonsense once and for all,' Guy almost shouted.

'And what nonsense would that be?' Katie said in a voice

that was ominously quiet.

'I want to know right this minute when you're coming home.'

'I can't tell you that, Guy, because I don't know myself.'

There was a long silence on the other end. Katie listened to the trill of a bird outside her window, and the clink of cutlery as Nadine and Conchita cleared away breakfast. She still had to feed Willie's cats and take the soup to the hospital and check in on Harvey and Chico before she could even start on her own day's chores.

'Is everything else all right, Guy?' she said a little impatiently.

'No, it damn well isn't. I'm telling you I want you on the next plane home.'

Katie took a deep, steadying breath. 'You can't *tell* me what to do. You may not have noticed, but I am a grown woman.'

'You're not acting like one,' he said nastily.

'Really? Don't you think it's rather a case of the pot calling the kettle black?'

There was another silence, followed by a heavy sigh. 'I'm sorry,' Guy said. 'I didn't mean this to degenerate into a quarrel. I just want to know when I can expect you back.'

'Why?'

She waited for him to tell her he missed her, that the children missed her, but he only said, 'Have you any idea how difficult it is, having to cope with the house and the girls and everything on my own?'

Katie looked down at her hands. For some reason she kept forgetting to take her wedding band out of the office safe, where it had nestled in darkness since the day Lance had taken her out on his boat. 'I've been looking after the house and the children on my own for years,' she pointed out.

'But you're used to it.'

'That doesn't mean I never wanted anything else.'

'So we're not enough for you any more, is that it?'

Katie could feel waves of offended hurt coming at her down the line.

'Look, Guy,' she said wearily, 'there are things going on here that you don't know about.'

'And there are things going on with your own family that *you* don't know about.'

Katie sighed. 'I try to talk to the girls as often as I can, but sometimes it's difficult to know what they're really thinking, Lucy especially – you know what she's like.'

'Yes, well your being away doesn't improve matters,' Guy said sourly.

'Oh Guy, she was going through a difficult patch long before that . . . Besides, you know I can't leave here till I've hired a new manager.'

'Why is it taking so long?'

'It has to be the right person. But I'm bound to find someone soon.'

He gave a little snort. 'I expect you'll keep me informed, then,' he said in the tone of one who knows when he is being fobbed off.

That evening Katie sat out by the pool in the soothing darkness, trying to wind down with a glass of wine after her hectic day.

A twig snapped behind her and she jumped. Stop being so edgy, she told herself, it's probably one of Willie Vance's cats. But something much larger seemed to be moving through the shrubbery towards her. When the figure stepped into the moonlight she gave a little gasp.

Lance looked at her huge round eyes and an expression of remorse came over his face. 'Sorry, didn't mean to scare you – just wanted to check how you're doing.'

'My nerves are rather frayed,' Katie confessed.

'Poor baby.' He came up beside her and stroked the hair back from her forehead. The motion of his fingers was soothing against her scalp, and she found herself arching her neck like a cat.

'How are your friends next door?' Lance said.

'Better, I think. Harvey took Chico to the doctor for some tranquillisers. They're doing the trick, he says – Chico's very calm and apologetic about his behaviour last night. Harvey is too – he's promised to turn over a new leaf and stop flirting with other men. And the gun's been locked away.'

'Harvey should get rid of it.'

'I know, but I've done all I can for one day.'

'Poor baby,' Lance said again, still stroking her head. 'What you need is someone to take care of *you*.'

His hands moved down to her shoulders, and he tut-tutted as he felt the tension nodules with his fingers. He began to knead them with little circular motions, and Katie closed her eyes and leaned against him and let his fingers soothe away the anxieties and the pain. A gentle languor began to steal over her.

'What would really do the trick,' Lance said, 'is a relaxing lie in the hot tub.'

He took his hands away and she opened her eyes to see him peeling off his shorts and T-shirt and underpants until he stood before her naked and glorious and totally unselfconscious. 'Come on,' he said.

She thought of going inside for her polka dot bikini. But she had told him she was tired of being the shy English rose. To hell with it, she thought, lifting her top up over her head.

When she was down to only Lavender's necklace, Lance touched it and said, 'What's this?'

'Just a good luck charm.' Katie reached back to undo the clasp. Lavender had warned her once never to wear it if she was planning on . . . Not that she was planning anything, she told herself firmly, but it might be better to remove it just in case.

They both lay back against the jets of water, allowing them to massage their shoulders, only their legs touching. Then Lance began to rub his slowly up and down the length of hers, and she felt a tingle up her spine that had nothing to do with the bubbling water. Lance inched closer till his arm was behind her head and the entire length of his body pressed against her side.

'What intrigues me about you,' he said, 'is the way you're on the brink of discovering all these new things about yourself. I want to be part of what makes it happen.'

For a moment she couldn't trust herself to speak. Then she said, 'My sister always told me people only travel to other places to find out what's inside themselves.'

'That's just part of it. Sometimes you need another person to unlock all those buried feelings.'

When he kissed her, parting her lips with his tongue, she felt he was trying to probe right down to the heart of her, as a diver knows to go deep for the most valuable treasure. When he parted her legs she felt as though she was opening herself up to him, allowing him to peel back her defences layer by layer until he reached the very core of her. She felt quite dizzy with the intensity of it.

Lance pulled back and looked down laughingly into her eyes. 'I think we'd better go inside before we shock the pants off one of your guests.'

The morning light filtered through the pretty curtains Polly had chosen on her trip to Miami with Lance, in the days of Katie's angry, confused inability to admit how much she wanted to be with him herself. Katie jumped up and pulled them open so that the sunlight streamed on to the cotton sheets and she could stretch out lazily in its warm glow.

The impression of Lance's head was still on the pillow beside her, the memory of his body still imprinted on her flesh. It filled her with such an exhilarating joy that she was almost afraid to move from this place where it had all happened, where she had at last let go of all the inhibitions that had bound her to a safe and uneventful life, and cried out with sheer gratitude.

'You have the essence of a truly loving person,' Lance had said afterwards, speaking as though he were Lavender with her belief in alchemy and mysteries. And Katie felt that all the love she knew she had been storing up inside her – because nobody else seemed to want it – could now be lavished on him.

'You've cheated on your husband,' she told herself sternly, trying to quell the absurd happiness flowing through her veins like wine. But no matter what efforts she made, the guilt would not come, nor could she rid herself of the luxurious contentment that had stolen over her, mind and body.

She would snatch just a few more moments in this glorious bed before she rose to face the world, she decided. It was later than her usual waking time, but fortunately Nadine had insisted on coming in to start breakfast this morning, picking up the bread on her way. She would have switched on the oven by now, and chopped the fruit, and laid it all out on the tikki bar with the help of Conchita. Everything must run with the smoothness of clockwork today, Nadine had decreed, because of the guest they were expecting. While Katie might feel that nothing was important except her glorious liberation of the night before, her staff were behaving as though they were expecting a visit from the queen – which in a sense they were. Mrs Jessie Wilhelmina Grenville had let it be known that she wished to come and inspect the premises of the newly renovated Tropical Hideout.

'This is a real honour, ma'am,' Nadine said when Katie finally made it down to breakfast, fearing the smile on her face must give her away to all who saw it. 'Mrs Grenville hardly leaves her house to go any place these days.'

Gone were Nadine's biker shorts and cut-off T-shirt, replaced by the sole dress she owned, the white one she had worn on the day Katie had taken her to lunch at the Casa Marina. Her curtain of straight black hair had been freshly washed. 'Ain't no running water in the old Conch house where I live,' she said, 'only cold out back. I was hollering in that shower at six this morning fit to raise the dead.'

Nadine had also been bullying the maids into polishing banisters and furniture and floors till you could see your own reflection in them. There were fresh flowers from the garden in every room. More fuss had been made over this visit than the opening itself. Katie began to feel infected by the general sense of anticipation.

Because Mrs Grenville had no use for a car any more, it was a taxi that pulled up outside The Tropical Hideout at exactly noon. Nadine, watching through the window, alerted Katie, who went outside at once to meet her important guest. Nadine, Conchita, Alvira and Pearl lined up behind her like a reception committee for a foreign dignitary.

Mrs Grenville emerged from the car, aided by the faithful Dolores. As soon as she had pulled herself upright, her beady, bird-like eyes focused with fierce concentration on the pale apricot façade of the building meticulously restored by the contractor she herself had recommended. The others seemed to hold their collective breath, waiting for her verdict.

Finally she nodded her head in satisfaction. 'Joe Roth's done a fine job,' she said. 'So have you, Mrs Colman.'

'Thank you,' Katie said, wondering why she felt such unspeakable relief.

She led the way inside, Mrs Grenville following slowly, leaning heavily on Dolores' arm. She made her stately progress around the downstairs rooms, stopping to admire whatever caught her sharp eye. She was particularly struck by Polly's luminous paintings.

'They bring so much light into a room,' she said. 'Perhaps I should think about buying some myself.'

Sometimes Katie thought The Tropical Hideout functioned almost as a gallery for Polly's work. Most of the guests remarked on the paintings, many asking where they could buy one of their own. Polly was always amazed and delighted, but she would be particularly thrilled to add Mrs Grenville to her list of clients.

When she had thoroughly inspected the reception rooms and the adjacent Damselfish Suite recently vacated by the grateful Walter and Peggy, Mrs Grenville graciously declined to view any rooms on the other floors. 'The stairs would present too great a challenge to these old bones,' she said firmly. But she agreed to take a pre-lunch gin and tonic with Katie in a shady part of the garden.

'It really is quite charming here,' she said to Katie as she sat beneath the jacaranda. 'No wonder you don't want to give up the running of it to some stranger.'

Katie flushed a little. 'I'm so sorry about turning down all those people you sent—'

'You don't have to apologise. When you feel the timing is right for you, then let me know. Until then, I won't bother you with any more applicants.'

Katie began to wonder if she would ever feel ready to leave the scene of the previous night's delights. A little silence fell between them, in which they listened to the hum of insects and the soothing ripple of water from the hot tub where it had all begun.

'You know, it's supposed to be only people born here who are called Conchs,' Mrs Grenville said at last. 'But we have so many visitors who fall in love with our island and end up staying on, we've had to make a new category. Now the old-timers are called saltwater Conchs and anyone who's been here more than seven years is called a freshwater Conch. I think they probably outnumber us by now.'

'I've met a few,' Katie said, thinking of Harvey and Brad and Donna and Polly.

'Well, I guess no one can help falling in love.'

Katie looked at her sharply, wondering if the canny old lady had sensed her secret. But Mrs Grenville, after swallowing a healthy mouthful of gin and tonic, briskly changed the subject. 'Now tell me about old Willie Vance from next door. How's he coming along?'

'The doctors say he's going to be fine. They've put some pins in the broken bone, but of course it's painful.'

'I can just imagine how the old codger's acting up,' Mrs Grenville cackled.

'Well, you know they like to get patients moving as soon as possible, but every time the nurses try, he yells abuse at them for inflicting grievous bodily harm on him.'

'That sounds like Willie.' Mrs Grenville shifted in her chair. 'I'm afraid I'm going to call it a day, Mrs Colman. Too much excitement tires me out. Could you kindly call a cab for me?'

As Dolores helped Mrs Grenville out to the waiting taxi, another one pulled up behind it, and a large figure swathed in lavender silk heaved itself out of the back. Mrs Grenville stopped and waited until the figure approached. They stood on the sidewalk facing each other, the tiny, bird-like woman in black and the vast vision in purple.

'Lady Lavender, it's a pleasure to meet you at last,' Mrs Grenville said.

'The honour be mine, all mine,' Lavender said, clasping her frail hand fervently.

The two ladies, one from a mansion on Caroline Street and the other from a shotgun shack in Bahama Village, gave each other a little bow of mutual respect.

When Mrs Grenville's taxi had turned the corner at the end of the block, Lavender said abruptly to Katie, 'You be sending me a message to come see you?'

'I didn't send any message,' Katie said in some confusion, not sure whether Lavender even possessed a telephone.

Lavender gave her an impatient look. 'There be ways and ways of lettin' a body know when they services be needed. Now, you gonna talk to me or what?'

Katie glanced around nervously. 'We'd better go inside, then.'

She led Lavender to her office, transformed now like the rest of The Tropical Hideout. But the underwater theme that dominated elsewhere had here been modified to more earthy tones – brick-reds and taupes and golds and natural woods – with a huge leopard-print sofa against one wall. This was where Lavender chose to deposit herself.

Under her scrutiny, Katie lowered her eyes to her desk. She didn't want her seeing into those innermost places in her soul where she hugged her secret to her like a jealously guarded treasure.

Lavender snorted. 'Didn't I tell you plain as day not to go havin' no gentlemen callers?'

'Sometimes people have to make up their own minds,' Katie said defensively.

'What you be wanting me fo' then, less it be to give you guidance?'

Katie considered reminding her that she hadn't actually asked her to come at all, but thought better of it when she caught a glimpse of Lavender's stony face.

'I guess you be saying to yo'self, why don't she mind her own business? I do that, you be coming back to me down the line sayin' Lavender, I got all these problems, why didn't you warn me 'fore it got too late? Better you spit it out now, girl, 'fore it be growin' into something mean an' ugly.'

Katie walked over to the window and looked out at the trees that seemed to form a protective shield around her, like her father's encircling arms when she was a child. Whatever doubts I may feel, she thought, they are not about Lance, or the feelings he has aroused in me.

She turned back to Lavender and said firmly, 'If there *is* anything I need advice about, I suppose it's where I'm going to find a manager to run this place properly for me.'

Lavender's eyebrows snapped together in a fearsome frown. 'You be tellin' yo'self them stories but don't be tellin' me, 'cause I ain't no babe in diapers, no sirree.'

'But I mean it,' Katie said indignantly.

'Mebbe you think you mean it, but that ain't the same thing. What you really want to know, girl, is what gonna be your *own* future. Now I can tell you all that stuff I be feeding them tourists down in Mallory Square. Is that what you want?'

Katie sighed. 'I don't know what I want.'

'Or I can tell you straight what you knew in yo' own heart

first day you set foot on this here soil. There ain't gonna be no manager.'

Katie sat quietly looking down at her hands, tanned a golden brown by the unfamiliar blessing of constant sunshine so that her ring mark had long since disappeared. In her mind the mists were beginning to part, the curtains Lavender spoke of drawing back to give her a glimpse of the future.

'You ain't going nowhere, child,' Lavender said. 'You be stayin' right here where you belong. You ain't never goin' home 'cause this *is* home for you now. Is that clear?'

Katie nodded slowly. It had become, in a simple flash of revelation, as clear as a truth that has long been known but never, until this moment, acknowledged.

Later Katie sat staring at the telephone, as though by looking at it long enough she might discover a way of making it do the dreaded deed for her. She had shut herself away in her office for most of the day, trying to think of the words she would use to break the news to Guy, and finally coming to the unwelcome conclusion that there were no words adequate to the occasion.

Sixteen years they had been married, sixteen long and sometimes good years. But over that time hope had gradually become resignation and two people who had pledged to share their lives had inexorably become strangers. And now that Katie had glimpsed another kind of life, trembling with possibilities, she found the old one wasn't enough for her any more.

If only she could make Guy see that he had, in fact, ceased to need her too in any vital, fundamental way. He thought he did because of the inconvenience of fixing his own meals and running the girls' errands and figuring out how the washing machine worked. But any good housekeeper could accomplish as much, and it wasn't as if he couldn't afford one.

She eyed the telephone again with something close to panic. Putting off the moment was only increasing her dread.

Purposefully she picked up the receiver and dialled the familiar London number.

He answered far too quickly, on only the second ring, and caught unprepared she said in a rush, 'I've phoned to tell you I'm not coming home.'

'About time,' Guy said. 'Good.'

'Guy, I said I'm *not* coming back.'

'What do you mean?' he said irritably. 'I don't understand—'

Katie took a deep breath. 'I've decided I want to live in Key West. I'm happy here, I have a life which is much more satisfying than anything I've known in London for a very long time.'

There was a stunned silence. Then Guy said in a tight voice, 'Is there someone else?'

Katie had not expected the question and her heart pounded with sudden guilt. 'Why do you ask?' she said evasively.

'Your great aunt Flora said you would only have stayed away this long if there was a man involved, and I foolishly sprang to your defence.'

'Well, she's wrong. I *have* fallen in love, I suppose, but with a place – with Key West and the life here and the sort of person I've become.'

'It sounds like nothing but self-indulgence to me,' Guy said bitterly.

'But it's not, it's a bid for self-fulfilment, which isn't the same thing at all. I think that's why Daddy wanted me to have The Tropical Hideout.'

'Nonsense,' Guy said, his voice rising. 'He can't have meant you to abandon your husband and children.'

'Oh Guy, I'm not abandoning the girls—'

'Really? How do you think they're going to feel when they hear this news?'

Katie didn't think she could bear to ask herself that, and yet she couldn't feel that the blame was entirely hers. 'You have no idea, Guy, how abandoned *I* felt when you made me send them away to boarding school. Before that they were the centre of my world and I of theirs, I think. But afterwards it was never the same. They didn't really need me any more, at least not the way they used to. To all intents and purposes they don't really live with us any more, they only visit for holidays. The way I look at it, they can visit me just as easily in Key West.'

There was another angry silence. Then Guy said, more menacingly this time, 'Don't count on it, Katie. I'm not at all sure they'll want to, not once they realise their mother's walked out on them.' There was a click as he replaced the receiver, leaving Katie to silence and her own dark thoughts.

Chapter Fifteen

~

Lance reassured her in bed. They never seemed to get out of bed these days, cocooned in their own world by the salmon-pink mosquito net suspended over the delicate iron pillars of the four-poster. Once Katie had imagined that she would share this bed with Guy, on holiday escapes with the girls from the dreary London weather. Now she could not imagine being in it with anyone but Lance.

'I think Guy's going to explain this to the girls in a way that's going to turn them against me,' she said.

'Why would he want to do anything to hurt them?'

'He seems to think that sending them *here* would hurt them – that I've gone crazy and can't be trusted, that I'd let them mix with the wrong sort of people.'

'What kinda people are those?'

Katie rolled her eyes. 'If you knew Guy, you wouldn't have to ask.'

'Whatever he thinks, your kids are still your kids,' Lance said firmly. 'The mother-child relationship is the strongest bond in the world. You'll find a way of making them understand.'

'How often do you call your mother in California?'

He gave a rueful shrug. 'OK, so I'm not the best communicator in the world.'

'Lucy doesn't phone me either, not unless she wants something. Hannah's a bit better... but sometimes I wonder if they've already got used to living without me.'

'Impossible,' Lance said, nuzzling the back of her neck where the hair was damp and tangled from their love-making.

'I don't dare call them with my side of the story,' Katie said, wriggling from his grasp. 'There are certain things you simply can't say on a telephone. Besides, Lucy would never give me the chance, she'd be flying off the handle in no time. She's so touchy with me at the best of times.'

'Bet she still loves you, though.'

'I suppose so, but she can be so aloof.'

'It's good for kids to develop a bit of independence.'

'But I like being needed.' She giggled. 'I love the way you look at me as if you'll burst if you can't have me.'

He pulled her against him with mock fierceness. 'I'm going to have you now.'

Later, lying against the curve of his shoulder, she said, 'I don't want you to think I made this decision because of you.'

'Thanks a bunch—'

'No, I mean it. There's the age difference for one thing.'

'You've got one foot in the grave, I'll soon be shot of you.'

She swatted his arm. 'And then there's the way you live, travelling the world, never settling in one place.'

'I could stay right here in this bed, no sweat.'

'I just want you to know I don't want to tie you down.'

'Can I tie you down, then?'

He held her wrists imprisoned in one hand while he stroked her thigh with the other, and she struggled half-heartedly. He looked down into her shining eyes. 'I live for today, sure, I admit that, and at this moment we feel very good together. Why try to guess the future?'

But everyone wants to know what fate has in store, Katie thought, as a sort of insurance policy against possible suffering. That was why Lavender did such brisk business down in Mallory Square.

When he was asleep in her bed, she eased herself gently from the circle of his arms and went to find her light cotton robe, which usually hung unused on the back of the bathroom door. It would have felt too strange, too unlike her former self, to sit naked beneath the green turtle writing a letter to her daughters.

She glanced briefly at the pretty pale apricot guesthouse stationery she'd had designed to match the colour of the façade. But she didn't dare hand-write this letter until she had got the phrasing just right. There would be too much crossing out, too many attempts to rephrase the inexpressible, explain the inexplicable.

She went to sit by the open window where her laptop, with its convenient delete button, lay open and waiting. She inhaled deeply the scents of warm earth and new rain and fecund growth, then she switched on the power and watched the screen blink to life.

Dear Lucy and Hannah,

I want, more than anything, for you both to understand that I have always loved you from the bottom of my heart and always will. What has happened to me here in Key West hasn't changed that one bit. The only thing that has changed is the way I feel about my own life, the part I live when you're not there.

Daddy is a very good man and a wonderful father, but sometimes people grow apart and that's what's happened to us. But we're still your parents, and we'll always be there for you.

The difference now is that Daddy will be there for you in London and I in Key West. It really is the most wonderful place, and I hope more than anything that you will want to visit me here in your holidays so that you can learn to know it and love it as I do. I have a little apartment for us in my guesthouse, and the prettiest room with twin beds that I've decorated especially for you.

I know this is going to be a shock for you at first, but I truly believe it will be better for all of us in the long run. Daddy and I want you to be happy and I'm sure you want the same for us. I can't be happy in London any more.

The Easter holidays are coming up soon, and I hope you might feel up to visiting me then, if Daddy says it's all right.

In the meantime you are always in my thoughts, and I am only really a phone call away any time you want to talk.

All my love, Mummy.'

Katie made herself read the final version several times. Each time she winced with uncertainty. Was it too patronising for Lucy, too much for Hannah to comprehend? Perhaps she should write to them separately, or would that be twice as upsetting?

In the end she copied it out by hand on to the apricot writing paper without making any further changes. Whatever she said was bound to be woefully inadequate. She would just have to hope for the best.

The door of Katie's office swung open and a huge arrangement of flowers, all familiar from her garden, advanced towards her above a pair of bare, muscular legs. Only when the flowers were deposited with a thump on her desk did Nadine's face emerge from behind them.

Katie eyed the arrangement with astonishment. It must have taken several hours of patient labour. 'Thank you, Nadine. What's the occasion?'

Her housekeeper seemed unusually tongue-tied. 'Begging your pardon, ma'am, I wouldn't want to go putting my foot in it, saying something that ain't proper about your situation at home—'

'I see . . . I can't discuss that, of course, but I appreciate your concern.'

'Thing is,' Nadine went on, 'me and the staff just wanted you to know we're real glad you're staying on. Wouldn't have been the same round here without you.'

'Thank you, Nadine. You've no idea how much that means to me.'

Nadine nodded awkwardly. 'Excuse me then, ma'am, I got a shower attachment needs fixing.' She hitched up her toolbag and made good her escape.

She was no sooner out of the door than it was flung open again. Good gracious, Katie thought, has everyone forgotten how to knock?

This time it was a huge canvas that bore down on her. There was no mistaking its creator, nor the slim, pale legs beneath it.

'What can I do for you, Polly?' Katie said.

Polly lowered the canvas to the floor and leaned on it for a moment with an expression of relief, before resting it against the wall. Katie looked at the finely etched lines of a red-brown Key West deer standing knee-deep in water, nibbling the leaves of a mangrove tree.

'Do you like it?' Polly said eagerly.

'I love it, but I'm not sure I have space to buy any more of your paintings.'

'Oh my, no, I'm not trying to sell it to you,' Polly said in a fluster of embarrassment. 'It's a gift.'

'That's very sweet, but why?'

'To say a proper welcome to Key West – and I'm so glad you're staying.'

Tears suddenly pricked Katie's eyes, and she had to turn away for a moment.

'We all feel that way,' Polly said, 'even Willie.'

Katie turned back with a smile on her face. '*Now* you're exaggerating.'

'Not a bit. He's got a heart of gold, you know, under all that bluster. Some of the nurses are getting quite fond of him.'

An even bigger exaggeration, Katie suspected, but she let it pass.

'You won't have a problem staying, will you . . . being as how you're British and all?'

'It seems not,' Katie said. 'Fortunately I have enough capital invested in this country – thanks to my father – and I employ enough American citizens to qualify for a special type of immigrant visa, or so I'm told by the powers that be. Now it's just a question of filling in hundreds of horrible forms.'

Polly gave a broad smile of relief. Katie looked at the delicate deer propped beside her. 'Where do you think I should hang it?' she said.

'I thought perhaps in your kids' room, so they'd have something pretty to look at when they visit.'

'Oh Polly,' Katie said, almost dissolving into tears again, 'I'm not sure yet they'll ever want to come.'

Polly's eyes were round with sympathy. 'But surely—'

'There she is,' cried a voice from the doorway.

'*Querida*, we're just so thrilled with your news,' trilled another.

Harvey and Chico burst in with no more thought of knocking than anyone before them. 'We've brought champagne to celebrate,' Harvey declared, waving a vintage bottle at her.

'Shall I fetch glasses from the kitchen?' Chico said, a-quiver with excitement.

'But it's only eleven in the morning,' Katie protested weakly.

'A mere detail,' Harvey shrugged as Chico headed for the kitchen, returning with Nadine in tow and five long-stemmed champagne flutes.

Harvey made a great display of twisting out the cork with the deftness of a seasoned vintner and only the subtlest of pops, and then busied himself filling everyone's glass to the brim.

He raised his flute to Katie. 'To the newest resident of Key West and everybody's favourite. Welcome home!'

To everybody's relief Fiona had dispensed with the tea and brought out the brandy and the Bristol Cream Sherry in tacit acknowledgement of the crisis nature of their meeting.

'Well,' she said, looking round at the assembled company and repeating her words to Katie of only a few weeks before, 'this is a fine kettle of fish, I must say.'

Guy's shirt was unbuttoned at the collar, his tie hung at half mast, and there were even the beginnings of a shadow on his chin and upper lip. Jemima, looking at a sight so unfamiliar, wondered what was happening to them all to bring about these changes.

She patted Guy's hand, to prevent him running it yet again through his hair. 'I can't believe Katie's actually serious about not coming back,' she said reassuringly.

'She seems deadly serious . . . And she denies completely that it's because of a man.'

'Hmph!' great aunt Flora snorted.

'She says she's happy in Key West,' Guy said wretchedly, 'which, of course, implies that she *isn't* happy living with me.'

'I don't see why not,' Fiona said indignantly. 'She's had all the support she could want from you and the rest of her family. It's not as though we've done anything to drive her away—'

'I've tried to be a good husband and provider,' Guy said defensively. 'I don't think Katie has anything to reproach me with, considering the lifestyle I've given her and the girls.'

'No one's blaming you, Guy,' Jemima said, and he looked both surprised and relieved, as though in the past that was exactly what he would have expected her to do – and what she probably might have done, she acknowledged to herself. But that was before everything started changing . . .

'Where are the nuts?' great aunt Flora demanded. 'There should be cashews and some of those hickory smoked almond things, to soak up the alcohol.'

'Don't drink so much, then, you know you're not supposed to,' Fiona scolded.

'It's just so perverse of her,' Jemima said. 'Katie's always wanted a family and a settled life. *I'm* the one who's more at home in odd corners of the globe.'

'Expect she's gone native.' Great aunt Flora gave a sad shake of her red wig. 'Happened to some of our best men, faced with the seduction of the tropics. Damn shame, really.'

'But *I've* been to dozens of exotic places, far more than Katie has, and *I* never went native,' Jemima cried.

'It's a question of character,' great aunt Flora pronounced. 'Some resist, some fall.'

'But what can it possibly be about this place that's more attractive to her than being amongst her own kind, her family?' Fiona said incredulously.

Guy held up a hand, as though it were all too painful. Jemima noticed the dark shadows under his eyes. No one, she thought, has ever looked like that when I've upped and left. The trouble with Katie is, she doesn't appreciate what she's got.

'Are you all right, Guy?' Fiona said solicitously.

He nodded weakly. 'But I'm worried about the girls.'

'What have you told them?'

'The truth, of course – that their mother isn't coming back and we must try to make the best of things without her.'

'And how did they take it?'

'As you'd expect,' Guy said testily.

Jemima poured him another hefty slug of brandy. When she reached over to give his arm a squeeze of solidarity, great aunt Flora seized her chance and nicked the bottle.

'I can't help thinking,' Fiona said, 'that Katie must have been harder hit by her father's death than any of us realised at the time.'

'But it's been awful for all of us,' Jemima objected. 'Why is *she* the only one who's acting up?'

'I think your mother's hit on something there,' Guy said, seizing gratefully on the suggestion as though it might somehow let him off the hook. 'I *do* think she hasn't been quite in her right mind since Robin passed away. The things she's done have been so . . . unlike her usual self.'

'I hope you're not suggesting some form of insanity,' Fiona said warily.

'That was Tom Eliot's game – that poet fellow,' great aunt Flora said. 'Saw a very good film on it just the other day. He locked his poor wife up in some wretched institution till the day she died – and paid for it with her own money, the cad.'

'Now, aunt Flora, no one's going to lock Katie up.'

'Too smart for you, is she?' Aunt Flora cackled gleefully. 'Left the country in the nick of time? Good for her!'

Lance rested his head contentedly against the side of the Boston whaler as it bobbed at anchor off the coast. Katie lay heavily against his shoulder. Mallory Square with its ant-like revellers was far behind them, too far for the noise of the sunset celebration to carry across the water and intrude on their tranquillity. A few mangrove islands shimmered up ahead in the fading light. The sea was like strands of multi-coloured pearls changing moment by moment as the sun made its steady progress towards the western horizon.

Lance drank deeply from his beer, then wiped his mouth with the back of his hand. 'Now *this* is how to watch a sunset,' he said with lazy satisfaction.

Katie thought how truly lucky she was to be able to experience unique moments like this, but even so the anxiety kept gnawing at the edges of her consciousness with mindless and rodent-like persistence.

There had been a letter from England that morning, but not the one she had prayed for, not written by the girls. There had been no indication yet whether they understood or forgave.

'Did you know the folks round here have a sunset rating chart?' Lance said. 'You can't say you've *seen* a Key West sunset till you score the required points.'

'How does it work?' Katie said, making a determined effort to banish all other thoughts.

'Well now, let's see . . . you get an automatic five just for being here to see it, 'cause that means you're a survivor.'

Or a fool, Katie thought to herself, with a flash of panic for all she had left behind.

'After that it gets trickier, you actually have to do a bit of work. For one, you have to catch the exact moments when the bottom and then the top rim touch the horizon.'

Katie looked over to where the sun trembled like a fiery

mirage in the western sky. 'There's still time,' she said.

'Yeah, but it'll be over before you know it.'

Like that sweet dependent baby stage of childhood, Katie thought, with fat little arms clutching round your knees to steady uncertain legs. And then, before you've had time to get used to it, they're skipping and running and not even stopping to look back.

'You'd better keep your wits about you,' Lance warned. 'There's a point for seeing the pre-glow round about now – that's the sun's reflection across the water before it takes the final bow. Later, when it's gone, there's the after-glow when all the colours go sort of pastel.'

Katie leaned back in the circle of his arms and tried to focus on the spectacle of changing light and colour. It was so breathtakingly beautiful, it shouldn't be hard just to lose herself in the glory of it . . . and yet phrases from Guy's letter kept popping into her memory, like corks bobbing to the surface of a pond. 'You must understand that, if you're serious about not coming home, you will get no further financial help from me . . .' That wasn't quite as bad as the part that said, 'Don't expect to hear from the girls any time soon, they have taken your news very badly indeed.' And then, humiliatingly, 'I have spoken at length to all your family who are unanimous in their support of me and their disapproval of what you are doing.'

'There, did you see it?' Lance demanded, making her jump with guilt.

'What?'

'Hopeless!' Lance shook his head in mock disapproval. 'The bottom rim of the sun just touched the horizon. Minus one point, Mrs Colman.'

She wished he wouldn't call her that, it didn't seem to fit any more. 'Oh dear, sorry,' she said.

'I bet you were always having to write lines in school: "I must concentrate during science lessons." '

'Actually, I was a bit of a swot. Jemima was the one who was always getting into trouble.'

Lance grinned. 'How the times are a-changing.' He took her head between his hands and gently turned it towards the correct point on the horizon. 'Now, you'll still be in with a chance if you see a boat or a bird pass in front of the sun as it's setting.'

Katie wrinkled her brow in determined concentration, but luck was not with her. 'Hah,' she said suddenly, 'the top's touching the horizon – that's worth another point, isn't it?'

'Not bad, seven out of ten so far ... but keep looking, at this exact moment you could still score an automatic ten and win the car plus a holiday for two to your dream destination.'

'I think I'm already there,' Katie laughed.

'Don't split hairs. Now tell me, did you see a sort of green flash as the sun disappeared?'

Katie hesitated. 'I can't truthfully say I did.'

'Then you have not won the car, Mrs Colman—'

'Miss Fraser,' she said tartly.

'—but you do go away with a small seagoing vessel complete with hunky captain.'

'Even if you say so yourself!' Katie said reprovingly. 'And what's this green flash thing that would have scooped me the jackpot?'

'Gee, and there I was thinking *I* was the jackpot.' Lance switched to a dry academic's tone. 'It is the effect of the refraction of sunlight as it passes through the thick layers of atmosphere near the horizon.'

'Did you see it, then, genius?'

Lance looked up at the puffy pink clouds hanging like little fat cherubs in the sky above them. 'Impossible on a day like this. Rare at the best of times ... and then only in completely cloudless conditions.'

The canvas of sea and sky was now painted in milky blues and mauves and pinks and violets. 'I can definitely see the afterglow,' Katie said smugly. 'That makes eight.'

Lance patted her head, as though she were a puppy showing progress in obedience classes. 'Good girl – *now* you're concentrating. Maybe I've cured you of that bad ol' habit of worrying at last.'

Instantly his words brought the frown back to Katie's face. 'I can't help it, my worries are real. For one, I'm going to have to start being very careful about money.'

Lance smiled indulgently. 'You own a great property in the middle of the historic district. You're not exactly out on the street yet.'

'But it positively eats up capital, and I've spent all my own already. From now on The Tropical Hideout has to be self-financing *and* pay my living expenses.'

'Don't sweat, it will. You're booked solid, aren't you?'

'For now, but who knows down the line?'

'Still worrying about tomorrow, huh? I haven't made much progress curing you of that.'

She struggled out of his arms, giving him a severe look. 'It's *normal* to worry about certain things – like how to make ends meet on your own, with no help, when you've never had to before.'

'I love you when you're mad,' he said, kissing the tip of her nose.

'There you go again, refusing to take me seriously. I've just walked away from a totally secure life – a husband, a house, a guaranteed salary – for a future that's filled with uncertainties.'

'But that's all any of us have,' Lance said more gently. 'Nothing in life is guaranteed – the rest is just an illusion.'

'It's a very comforting illusion,' Katie said wistfully.

He put his arms round her again, and this time she didn't push him away. 'You're entitled to a share of the money you accumulated during your marriage.'

'Guy doesn't think so, and I don't feel justified in fighting him,' she said, watching her breath ruffle the little bronze hairs of Lance's chest. 'The house is our biggest asset and I couldn't ask Guy to sell that – it's the girls' home, and right now they don't need any more upheaval.'

Lance gave her a little squeeze. 'Then just let it go. You've shown you don't need your husband's money – look at the way you've fought to hold on to The Tropical Hideout and turn it into something special. You're smart and you're a survivor – you can make it on your own.'

'Sometimes I think you're right, and then, in bad moments, all the doubts come flooding back.'

'If all else fails, you can always join me on the surfing trail,' Lance teased, 'and discover the joys of the simple life – a deserted beach, no roof over your head to block out the stars.'

Katie looked up. The dome of the sky was beginning to turn indigo blue, the stars appearing like lanterns lit up one by one. The gentle motion of the boat on the waves was comforting, like the rocking of a cradle. A feeling of peace began to steal over her, a sense that there are moments so perfect, so completely right, that all doubt is suspended while the magic lasts.

'Isn't it beautiful?' Lance said. 'Don't you feel privileged, at this moment, just to be alive?'

Katie nodded wordlessly. It was also an affirmation of all the reasons why she wanted to stay.

I'm going to phone the girls, Katie told the green turtle on her sitting-room wall. It stared at her balefully with the eye that faced her way. There's no point, it seemed to be saying, Lucy will only get angry and hang up the phone. And Hannah's too young to understand, even if you could put it all into words, which you can't.

Katie marched into another room to escape the turtle's gaze – the room she always thought of as belonging to the girls. The letter didn't do the trick, she said to the family of ceramic tortoises, the girls haven't contacted me – I must do *something*.

No point rushing them, they seemed to reply, you have to give them time to come to terms with it.

Katie strode back into the sitting room. Keeping her back firmly turned on the turtle, she dialled the number of Wolton Abbey. 'Lucy Colman, please,' she said to a passing girl who happened to answer the call box in the residence.

It seemed an interminable wait until she heard her elder daughter's voice, almost as though she were in the same room, saying, 'Hi, who is it?'

Katie took a deep breath. 'It's Mummy, darling, how are you?'

There was another silence which felt even longer than the first. Then Lucy said almost rudely, 'What do you want?'

'Nothing, except to know that you and Hannah are all right.'

'What do *you* care? You're not a part of our lives any more.'

'Don't say that,' Katie begged. 'I'm still your mother, that hasn't changed.'

'Everything's changed,' Lucy said in a small, flat voice.

Katie glanced round cautiously at the turtle. It gave her a glassy stare, implying she would have to handle this on her own.

'Lucy,' she said, 'you may think I'm being selfish, but that's not why I'm doing this. If I choose a life that makes me happy, then I'll have more to give to you and Hannah.'

'Oh please, Mummy, don't give me that,' Lucy snorted. 'If you really cared about us then you'd—'

What? Katie wondered. Return to St John's Wood? The thought of going back to her lonely life in the dark, over-furnished house made her feel quite cold inside.

'You should damn well leave us alone to get on with our lives without you,' Lucy cried.

Katie took a steadying breath. She loved this wild and wilful daughter, but perhaps she hadn't always been firm enough with her when it counted. 'Lucy, however hurt you are, you shouldn't speak to me like that,' she said in an even tone.

'I hate you,' Lucy shouted. 'You've been horrid to poor Daddy, you've broken his heart, and you're only pretending to be worried about us. Well, don't bother – I never want to see you again and nor does Hannah.'

'I know you probably feel that way now,' Katie said as

calmly as before. 'But perhaps when you've had time to think things over, you'll decide to give me a chance to show you I love you as much as ever. I so much want you and Hannah to come to Key West at Easter.'

'Forget it,' Lucy said coldly. 'I'm spending Easter with Granny and Daddy and Jemima – my real family.'

Abruptly the phone went dead. Katie sat there holding the lifeless receiver and feeling utterly wretched. The green turtle eyed her reproachfully, as if to say I told you so.

Lance was determined that Katie wasn't going to stay at home every night and mope. 'We're going out to dinner,' he said, 'even if I have to pick you up and carry you.'

'I'm not in the mood.'

'You have to sit this one out,' he said. 'Your kids will come round in the end, you'll see.'

'Not if they only hear Guy's side of the story.'

After Lucy had hung up on her, Katie had telephoned Guy to try to get his support.

'The girls can't be allowed to take sides,' she had said. 'Children need both their parents.'

But he only said disapprovingly, 'Then why aren't you here with them, like any normal mother?'

'What's normal, Guy?'

'There's no point discussing that with you in your current frame of mind.'

When, Katie wondered, had he become so pompous? Had it crept up on him gradually with the passing years, or was Jemima right when she said he was born a stuffed shirt?

'I have a right to see my children – as much right as you do,' she said angrily. 'I want them to come and visit me here in the Easter holidays.'

'There's just one problem,' Guy said smugly. '*They* don't want to visit *you*.'

'And I suppose you're doing absolutely nothing to convince them that they should?'

'I'm not going to send them to you against their will when your behaviour has been so bizarre. I'm not even sure you're in a fit mental state to look after them properly.'

Katie clenched the phone till the knuckles showed white through her skin. 'What an arrogant and typically male response, Guy. Now you're accusing me of being crazy just because I no longer want to make a life with you.'

It was an unwise thing to have said, given the reason for her call. He had coldly terminated the conversation without promising anything about the girls.

In a dark frame of mind, Katie made a trip down to Bahama Village to see Lavender. There was a queue outside the door to her little shotgun shack. Old men leaned on sticks, bare-footed children chased chickens in the dusty road, women stood around in colourful groups and gossiped. By a sort of unspoken accord, they all stood aside to let Katie pass.

'I want to know if my children are ever going to visit me here,' she demanded of Lavender in the room with the shrines to the saints and the spirits, where she received the followers who sought her spiritual help in dealing with the problems of their everyday lives.

'You telling me you want yo' *Ifa* read?'

'What's that?'

'I be asking the spirits to reveal yo' destiny.'

I don't think I'm quite ready for that,' Katie said warily. 'All I want is *your* advice.'

Lavender wagged a finger. 'You stick to yo' guns, girl, your whole family be comin' after you, an' no mistake.'

Katie smiled wryly. 'You're quite wrong. Guy would sooner drop dead than set foot in Key West, and my mother never leaves Wiltshire—'

'I ain't naming names. I juss said don't be gittin' yo'self all stirred up when the saints be having plans of they own.'

Katie looked at the great plaster statue of the Virgin, surrounded by the garish faces of painted saints. 'My own children won't speak to me,' she said miserably, remembering the pain in Harvey's voice when he had told her the same thing.

Lavender fingered the chain on the table in front of her, its use, for Katie, still shrouded in mystery. 'Something goan happen to shake things up. That be the way of it.'

'But shake them up how? And what am I supposed to do till then?'

Lavender gave her a stern look. 'How many times I got to tell you, child? You sit tight and doan do nothing till you hear them voices in yo' head.'

There was no getting any more out of her for now. Remembering the patient line of people waiting outside, Katie reluctantly took her leave.

Lance told her to look on the bright side. 'She told you your children are coming, didn't she?'

'But she didn't say when. For all I know she could mean in ten years' time, and I'll walk right past them in the street without recognising them.'

'OK,' Lance said, 'so you're not gonna let anyone cheer you up. But while we're waiting for you to hear those voices in your head, can we *please* go out for dinner?'

Katie allowed herself to be tempted by the promise of fresh seafood from BO's Fish Wagon. 'And let's ask along that friend of yours, Polly,' Lance suggested.

'Why?' Katie said suspiciously.

' 'Cause I have an old schoolfriend staying, name of Jack. Always wanted to be a writer, so he's come down here to do the tour of Papa Hemingway's town.'

The evening turned out to be just what the doctor ordered. They ate delicious shrimp straight from the sea at the outdoor tables of BO's eccentric little restaurant with its strange decor and noisy crowd. Jack and Polly vied with each other in the modesty stakes.

'So what's this book you're writing?' Polly asked him.

'I wouldn't go so far as to call it a book, at this point it's just a few chapters.'

'Do you have a publisher yet?'

'Oh no, I wouldn't dream of showing it to anyone until I've done at least a couple more drafts.'

'Polly's a great artist,' Lance said. 'If you show her yours, she'll probably show you hers.'

They both looked furiously embarrassed. 'Don't feel obliged, they're nothing special,' Polly said quickly.

'Come on,' Katie said, taking pity on them, 'let's show Jack the town.'

They had their first drink in Captain Tony's Saloon, its walls covered with a bizarre mixture of business cards and various items of underwear. Jack was very impressed to learn that Captain Tony had been a friend of the great Hemingway himself. Next they stopped at Sloppy Joe's, another of Papa's favourite watering holes that traded heavily on the connection, with photographs of the writer wherever you turned. Katie supposed there couldn't have been the same live bands and whooping revellers in Papa's day. The atmosphere was so infectious, Jack even summoned up the courage to ask Polly to dance.

By the time they reached Jimmy Buffet's famous Margaritaville, none of them were walking very straight. It was three in the morning and Duval Street was still humming. Katie left her frozen margarita at the table with Jack and Polly, locked in earnest conversation, and let Lance rock her round the dance floor till the magic of the town was flowing through her veins once more.

Guy had been summoned to see the headmistress of Wolton Abbey – Miss Hardinge with an 'e' as Lucy called her – as a matter of some urgency. Christ, he though immediately, what's Lucy been up to now?

It was all very inconvenient. He'd had to get his secretary to move some long-standing appointments with clients he didn't like to inconvenience in this way. Frankly, it wasn't good for business. Damn Katie, he thought, she should be handling this.

Come to think of it, he wasn't sure whether she'd ever been summoned by the headmistress in the past. If so she hadn't mentioned it – but there were a lot of details about the girls' school life that he'd never had time to discuss with her. And now he was having to deal with it all himself.

He parked his car on the gravel drive in front of the gracious old main building and presented himself at reception for directions to the headmistress's office. He'd only ever been there once, it must be over four years ago, when he and Katie had first been considering the school for Lucy. He found himself wondering rather nervously if she had been caught smoking in the dormitories – or worse, in possession of some illegal narcotic. Perhaps he would be told to take her away from the school at once – and then how on earth would he cope?

Miss Hardinge was friendly but reserved and offered him tea, when he would really have preferred something a bit stronger, like whisky.

'I believe your wife is still away in America,' she said, which Guy did not regard as a very promising opening.

'That's right.'

'I'm sorry to trouble you in her absence, but we have to take it quite seriously when a girl refuses to eat.'

This wasn't quite as bad as Guy had feared – at least not an offence punishable by expulsion. He began to relax a little. 'Lucy has never had a very big appetite,' he pointed out.

'I'm not talking about Lucy, Mr Colman. It's Hannah's eating I'm worried about.'

'*Hannah*!' This was rather more difficult to take on board. Hannah was the sort of child who had always, even as a baby, eaten all her food with what Guy could only describe as a sort of religious fervour.

'If it's any consolation, I'm sure we've caught the problem at an early enough stage to do something about it,' Miss Hardinge said soothingly.

Guy wasn't at all sure what that something might be. 'What do you suggest?'

Miss Hardinge sat very straight in her chair, her hands folded in her lap, her whole posture a lesson in correctness. 'I'll come to that,' she said. 'First I'd like to discuss another problem.'

Oh dear, Guy thought weakly, I'm not sure I can deal with any more.

'Lucy has done rather poorly in her end-of-term exams. She's one of our brightest pupils, yet she scored some of the lowest marks. Obviously all is not well with her either.'

Guy wanted to tell Miss Hardinge that it wasn't his fault, it was their mother bolting off to Florida that had done the damage, but he wasn't up to making such a confession to a virtual stranger.

'I don't mean to pry into your personal business, but in circumstances such as these I feel I should speak my mind.' Miss Hardinge gave him an enquiring look.

'Please, go ahead,' Guy said meekly.

'It would seem your wife has been in America rather longer than Lucy and Hannah expected. Obviously they must be missing her.'

'The problem is,' Guy said heavily, 'she's decided not to come back.'

'I see – I'm sorry.' Miss Hardinge cleared her throat. 'Does she have any plans to see her daughters?'

'She's asked me to send them to her in Florida for their Easter holidays, but I'm not sure it would be right for them—'

'Mr Colman,' Miss Hardinge interrupted, 'it is my firm opinion that your children need to see their mother, whatever the difficulties involved. If I were you, I would make the necessary arrangements as soon as possible.'

Chapter Sixteen

~

The girls' room was a fantasy in shell pinks and creams and aquamarines. The pillows had been plumped into fat cream mounds and the mosquito nets tied back with enormous pink bows by Alvira and Pearl, who had polished and scrubbed till floors shone and mirrors gleamed. On the wall the little red deer pricked its ears expectantly, watched placidly by the family of ceramic tortoises on the bookshelf. Katie had filled it with horror stories for Hannah and horse manuals for Lucy. On their beds two brand new bikinis were laid out with masks and flippers. Lance had promised to teach them how to snorkel.

'You can't keep on living with me while they're here,' Katie had warned him. 'They would never handle it if they thought I was having sex with a man. They probably think I never did it with their father either – except for the necessary two times, of course.'

Lance groaned and crossed his legs. 'You'd better make this up to me when they're gone.'

She went to check that he had remembered to remove all obviously male items from her bedroom and bathroom, where sharp young eyes would be sure to find them. She found him stuffing a pair of Y-fronts into an already bulging overnight bag, his long shaggy hair tied back in a ponytail, his chest bare above his denim shorts. Touched by how good-naturedly he was accepting his temporary dismissal from her life, she went over and put her arms around him.

'Sorry about this,' she said. 'We'll still see each other while they're here – I'm not going to disown you or anything – but I'll have to introduce you as a friend.'

'What if they don't buy it?'

Katie looked alarmed. 'Heaven knows, Lucy can be so difficult—'

'So what're you trying to tell me? She's the Teenager from Hell?'

Katie laughed. 'She tries to be, and often I've let her get away with it, which isn't too good for her or for me.'

'I don't know what to say. I can't handle girls – they're too scary.' He rolled his eyes.

Katie took a guilty peek at her watch. Lance had snatched it from her once and dangled it out of the window, but then he had finally given in and admitted she would always be ruled by the clock. Now, as if taking his cue, he bent to pick up his bag.

Suddenly Katie felt childishly desolate that he was going to leave her. She clung to him so fiercely that he almost dropped the bag again.

'Hey, hang on there,' he said, looking down into her face that was full of conflicting emotions. 'Are you sure you don't want me to drive you to the airport?'

'That would look rather suspicious, wouldn't it?'

He ruffled her hair and then gently disentangled himself. 'Whatever you say, Mummy. Now you'd better hit the road. And one little parting piece of advice—'

'Yes?'

'Don't let them see how worried you are.'

The girls came slowly, hesitantly, through the doors from the arrivals hall, looking round at their strange surroundings in a way that made them seem vulnerable and much younger. For a moment Katie just stared at them without moving. They were so pale compared to Florida children, and Hannah was much thinner than the last time Katie had seen her. But I'll soon change all that, Katie thought eagerly as the life flowed back into her limbs and she rushed forward to her children.

Hannah flew into her mother's arms, as she used to when fetched from boarding school, and Katie hugged her tightly. She felt smaller, more fragile than the last time Katie had held her like this. She opened her other arm to Lucy, who was standing awkwardly to one side, and to Katie's surprise she sprang forward and clung to her mother fiercely in a way she hadn't done for years. Katie held on to both her children for all she was worth.

When she finally released them, Lucy quickly adopted her usual air of cool indifference. 'This airport is gross – not nearly as nice as Heathrow,' she said scornfully.

It wouldn't do, Katie knew, to let on that she had noticed Lucy's moment of vulnerability. 'I know,' she said, 'but things get better the further south you go – you'll see.'

They hauled the suitcases to the car park, and Katie opened the gleaming boot of the red sports car which she had bought off the rental company for a good rate, while Lucy circled round it with eyebrows raised.

'Bit flashy for someone your age, isn't it?' she said.

Katie laughed. 'I'm not forty yet, so you can't accuse me of having a mid-life crisis.'

'What are you having, then?'

'A wonderful time.' Katie gave them both another brief hug as she unlocked the doors for them. Lucy claimed the front seat as her right, being the elder, and Hannah clambered with docile acceptance into the back.

Katie remembered the drive so well from her own arrival all those months ago, but now she was seeing it all again as though for the first time through the eyes of her daughters – the great glimmering expanses of ocean to either side, the mangrove islands alive with colourful birds, the seemingly endless stretch of the Seven Mile Bridge. At times she let them drink it all in in silence, at others she told them the history of interesting landmarks like the ruin of the great railway line built by Henry Flagler. Glancing now and then towards the passenger side, she saw Lucy in a languid pose, seemingly unmoved by the extraordinary beauty around her.

'Give them time', Lance had said, and at least now she had that time to win them over.

They followed Highway 1 into Old Town, and superstitiously Katie took them all the way to Mile Zero, as though if she retraced her own steps her daughters would learn to love this island as she did.

'Wow,' Hannah said as she looked at the little green and white painted sign, 'is this the end of the world?'

'Don't be so daft,' Lucy scoffed, 'you know perfectly well the earth is a sphere, it doesn't have an end as such.'

'But it *is* the end of America,' Katie said. 'Isn't that something?'

Lucy seemed quite determined to be less impressed than Hannah by just about everything. But as they entered Duval Street, she was suddenly straining forward with eyes darting this way and that, trying to take in all the shops and bars and restaurants and hoards of young college kids on spring vacation, surging down the pavements in search of a good time.

'What is this place?' she said.

'It's the sort of hub of the town's social life.'

'Can we come up here some night and check it out?'

'Of course we can.'

'Coo-ool. Is this where you hang out?'

'Sometimes.'

Lucy looked at her mother with a sort of fascinated disbelief that also held an element of new respect. Trying to hide her smile, Katie turned into Fleming Street.

By the time they reached the guesthouse the girls were longing to stretch their legs, and ran about here and there with a spurt of energy, investigating every new delight and wonder.

'Wow, look at all these incredible trees and flowers,' Hannah cried.

'Big deal, they're just dumb plants.'

'There's a swimming pool too.'

'Oh major good news – a jacuzzi.'

They wanted to get into their swimming costumes at once. Katie insisted they must first meet Nadine, who grinned broadly and pumped their hands.

'Your ma's been just itching for you to come. Now you're here, you treat her right, do you hear me? She's a fine lady.'

Nadine hefted the bags upstairs and they followed meekly behind.

The sight of their new home from home brought on a new rush of enthusiasm. 'Cool, it looks over the swimming pool,' Lucy said.

Hannah was in raptures over their bedroom. 'I love it, it's so pretty . . . Oh, look at the cute tortoises.'

'I don't have to *share* with her, do I?' Lucy said in exaggerated horror.

'I'm afraid you do,' Katie confirmed, 'unless you want to come in the double bed with me.'

Lucy looked no more enamoured of that suggestion. 'I'll just have to put up with her snoring, I suppose.'

'I do *not* snore,' Hannah protested indignantly.

'Do too – your room-mates told me.'

'Do *not*.'

'How about something nice and cold to drink?' Katie intervened. 'I don't suppose you're used to the heat yet.'

'I *love* the heat,' Lucy said. She was enchanted, too, by her new red and black bikini, which she decided looked sexy on her, far better than Hannah's red and white one which she said made her look like a Christmas cracker. 'You'll frighten off all the boys for miles around.'

'Shut up,' Hannah said, her face turning a matching red. 'I don't like boys anyway.'

Listening to their familiar bickering, Katie looked up at the green turtle and gave it a conspiratorial wink.

Lucy lounged luxuriously in the 'hot tub', as her mother had told her it was called here, beneath the tree with the blazing purple flowers whose name she didn't know. The foliage around her was so lush, she could almost imagine herself in the midst of some steamy jungle. It was all so amazingly different from the life, the surroundings, the colours she was used to. She didn't know what to think of it yet, but of one thing she was quite certain: she wasn't going to let her mother make up her mind for her.

A sleek head broke the surface of the swimming pool, and an arm waved over at her. It was Nadine's son Sam, who seemed capable of holding his breath under water for longer than should be humanly possible, and would disappear from her view for whole minutes at a time. Sam knew how to scuba dive and water-ski and handle a sailboat, accomplishments that left Lucy secretly filled with awe. She had to remind herself that if she'd grown up in a fantastic climate like this, on a tropical island paradise with sea all around, she would probably have been a water baby too.

But Sam was quite cool, she had to admit, even though he was only a year older than she was. He had long straight black hair like Nadine's which he wore tied back in a ponytail. No schoolboy she'd met in England had ever looked quite like Sam. His sister Jolene wasn't nearly as good-looking, she had frizzy brown hair and a bit of a weight problem. 'Takes after her father,' Nadine told them with cheerful resignation.

Jolene and Hannah were bored with swimming and had gone upstairs to play video games. No one else was around. Nadine and Katie were working inside (her mother had offered to show Lucy one day how she ran the guesthouse, and she'd agreed without sounding too keen). It was the middle of the day, and most of the guests were out sightseeing or having a siesta in their rooms. So Lucy and Sam had the pool to themselves, which suited her just fine.

Not that she was interested in boys since Tom Blackstone had gone off with Sophie Jackson and broken her heart. Sophie was prepared to 'do it', Tom said. If Lucy would just grow up a bit, then maybe things could be different . . . But Lucy didn't feel ready yet to grow up in that particular way, and Tom had moved on to more fertile hunting grounds.

There was a little splash as Sam slid into the hot tub beside her and leaned back with a grin. 'So what do you think of your mother's place so far?'

'It's OK, I suppose,' Lucy said indifferently. Back in England, she hadn't been able to imagine what The Tropical Hideout was like, or how her mother could possibly care about it more than she did about her own children. She still felt angry and resentful when she thought about it in that light, but at least now she'd had a chance to see what all the fuss was about. Sure, it was a really pretty place, and it did have a sort of comfortable atmosphere, more relaxed and fun than their house in London. In fact, she couldn't picture her father in these surroundings at all.

'My ma loves working here,' Sam said. 'She's always going on about how great your mother is.'

That was another thing Lucy couldn't get used to. Everyone here kept telling her and Hannah how lucky they were to have such a 'fantastic' mother. It was weird, at home no one ever made that sort of fuss of her. First there was the man with the moustache who'd come to tea that morning with his strange friend dressed like a woman. Lucy had tried not to stare, but she wasn't sure she'd pulled it off. They'd brought round the most delicious thing called a Key Lime Pie. Hannah had gobbled up heaps of it, their mother smiling in a sort of satisfied way that got on Lucy's nerves, but even she hadn't been able to stop herself eating a whole slice. And all the time the man with the moustache had told them stories about what a dump The Tropical Hideout had been before their mother got her hands on it, and how she'd masterminded this brilliant transformation. The one in the dress obviously liked Katie too, but at least he also talked about other things. In fact he'd been quite flattering about Lucy, telling her what beautiful bone structure she had and offering to do her make-up for her one day. That might come in quite handy when she checked out Duval Street, like Mummy had promised.

They'd been joined soon afterwards by yet another new friend of her mother's – it was weird how many friends she had here compared to at home. This one was an artist called Polly. She said Lucy and Hannah could come across to her studio any time and mess around with her paints. Lucy thought it might be quite cool to try creating something in a real artist's studio.

She hadn't been quite so pleased, though, when this guy with long hair arrived and introduced himself as Lance. He had a funny way of looking at her mother that was somehow worse than the others going on about how wonderful she was. And her mother acted all strange around him too, laughing more than usual even when he said things that weren't particularly funny. The whole thing got her hackles up in a way she couldn't explain, and even though Lance tried to be nice to her and ask her questions about herself, she replied as briefly as she could without being rude enough to get into trouble.

Watching her mother closely, Lucy realised she was looking a whole lot younger these days. It was like all the laughing had smoothed the worry lines from her face. Lucy couldn't remember a time when she had seemed so happy, and she knew she should have been glad for her – but it made her angry and confused to think she might be feeling that way because she had walked out on her children and their father. How dare she be happy if that was the reason? What Lucy just couldn't understand was why she sometimes smiled back, or found herself skipping down the stairs as though a weight had been lifted from her that seemed to have descended with her teens and been there ever since.

'You've gone all quiet,' Sam said. 'It's all this warm water making you sleepy. Come with me for a dip in the pool.'

'I'm not sure I feel like it,' Lucy said languidly.

'Tell you what – if you fetch your mask and flippers, I'll teach you how to snorkel.'

Lucy agreed nonchalantly, like she was doing him a big favour. Snorkelling was one of the things she longed to do most in her life.

The plan was for Lance to take Katie and the girls for a dinner on Duval Street on Easter Saturday night. It was a plan made long in advance, since the town was so full that restaurant tables had to be booked in good time. But Katie wasn't entirely sure it would work out.

She had seen the hostile looks which Lucy and even Hannah had cast at Lance the first time they met him. They had known at once, through sheer filial instinct, that this man was more to her than the other friends who had dropped by to meet them. Katie hated to see them quivering with suspicion, yet she felt that by absenting himself from her bed Lance was making as much of a sacrifice as could reasonably be expected of him. She couldn't turn her back on him altogether, and if she could just reassure her daughters that he had stolen no part of the love she felt for them, then all might yet be well.

'Can't Sam and I go down to Duval Street on our own and listen to some live music?' Lucy had objected when told that Lance would be fetching them in his surfmobile.

Thinking of the hordes of drunken college kids on the rampage, Katie said firmly, 'It wouldn't be safe. Besides, Hannah also wants to see a bit of the night life.'

'It's not fair – I'm always being stopped from doing what I want because of Hannah.'

Lucy only cheered up when Chico came round in a chiffon cocktail dress to do her make-up. They shut themselves away in her room, from which even Hannah was banned, and when she emerged in full war paint, looking more like the star of a drag show then a fresh young teenager, Katie gritted her teeth and said nothing.

Lance pretended to be quite bowled over. 'Wow,' he said, staggering back, 'you look so sophisticated.'

Lucy flashed him a look of disdain. 'Yeah, why shouldn't I – I'm nearly fifteen, not some little kid.'

Katie opened her mouth to intervene, but Lance flashed her a warning look. 'I'll remember,' he said mildly.

Lance drove down Duval Street as though negotiating an obstacle course as he tried to avoid collisions with high-spirited students on scooters.

'What a nightmare,' Katie said.

'Only if you're *old*,' Lucy muttered in the back.

They stopped at the quiet little restaurant where Lance had brought Katie after their outing to the La-te-da. It was fuller tonight, of course, but the prices attracted a more sophisticated crowd than the drunken revellers outside.

'Couldn't you have picked somewhere a bit more fun?' Lucy said sulkily.

Lance didn't rise to the bait. 'There's a Hard Rock Café down the road – but we'd have had to stand in line.'

Hannah looked rather wistful. Lucy said, 'I don't mean a *hamburger* place. I wouldn't be caught dead eating red meat.'

Guy had told Katie about Lucy's new eating habits, in the same conversation when he had confessed that Hannah had stopped eating altogether and he thought perhaps they should both visit her in Key West after all. Katie had been wracked with a guilt that was only now beginning to dissipate as she watched Hannah's appetite come back with a vengeance and even Lucy eat more than was her custom, particularly when she thought no one was watching her.

'There's plenty of fish on the menu,' Katie said.

'That isn't my particular favourite,' Hannah pointed out.

'This is fresh from the sea – not at all like English boarding school fish,' Katie promised.

When the wine came Lance poured Lucy a small glass

without asking, and for just a moment she looked as though she didn't loathe the sight of him.

'What about you, Hannah?' he said.

'No thanks, it tastes disgusting.'

But there were no complaints about the pan-fried yellowtail snapper with passion fruit or the seared tuna with tomato-basil vinaigrette or the spicy Jamaican barbecued prawns or the herb-encrusted chicken on penne pasta.

'Yummy,' Hannah said, just like her old self.

'Aren't you sorry now for all those college kids eating their boring old burgers?' Lance grinned.

'Why are there so many of them?'

'It's their spring break and they're here looking for a good time, which means sleeping six to a room and crashing into everything on their scooters and trying to pay for it all on their parents' credit cards.'

'Sounds like a lot more fun than we're having,' Lucy muttered as she wolfed down her food.

'Everyone here *wants* them to have fun, even when they're behaving badly. The town sets up special courts where retired judges sit from about six in the morning to deal with the kids who've been caught drinking with a fake ID and stuff like that. They're sentenced to something easy like picking up litter on the beach, and their lives don't get messed up by having criminal records.'

'I thought about taking students in The Tropical Hideout, but I decided the other guests wouldn't be able to handle it – especially with having to put up with you two little monsters,' Katie said, ruffling her daughters' hair affectionately.

'Don't do that – you'll mess it up,' Lucy said crossly, pulling away.

Hannah looked up at the star-studded sky. 'It feels so funny to be here instead of Rock,' she said. 'I wonder if Daddy's having a nice time with Granny and aunt Jemima.'

For a moment Katie stared at her, almost open-mouthed, then she quickly dropped her eyes to her lap.

'What's wrong, Mummy?' Lucy said defensively. 'Daddy has to have company too, you know, now that you're not there.'

'I know he does,' Katie said evenly. But he hadn't told her that company would be her own mother and sister. Was it only last summer that Katie had gone to his chambers and practically begged him to allow Jemima to stay with them in the very place he had now invited her of his own accord?

'Anyone fancy a dance?' Lance said, glancing with a frown of concern at Katie.

'No thanks,' said Lucy. 'This music's like from the Dark Ages.'

'That's the way we oldies like it,' Lance said, offering his hand to Katie.

Lucy watched the gesture with thinly veiled hostility. 'You're not as old as my mother,' she said, 'even if you *are* trying to make out with her.'

Lance allowed his hand to fall. There was a small embarrassed silence, then Katie looked directly at her elder daughter. 'I think you should apologise.'

'Are you saying he's not – ?'

'I'm saying you've been rude and ungracious all evening, and it doesn't do you credit when all we're trying to do is give you a good time. I think you should apologise.'

Lucy dropped her eyes and a faint colour suffused her cheeks. 'OK, then, I'm sorry,' she mumbled.

'Good, because you've made me ashamed of you when I would rather be proud.'

The waiter came to clear away their pudding plates and for a while no one spoke. Then Lance said, 'Lucy's right, it's way too quiet here. Let's go and find where the real music is.'

Lucy shot him a tentative look of gratitude.

On Sunday Guy and Jemima and Fiona and great aunt Flora took themselves off to the little church in St Enerdoc, which was illuminated by banks of real candles and was always impossibly full for the Easter service. In the little cemetery outside tourists trampled over other historic graves in search of John Betjeman, who lay oblivious to all the fuss beside his old friend Granny Bone.

Guy had been coming here year after year with his wife, ever since their children were no more than toddlers. Now, for the first time, they were all thousands of miles away from him in a place he had never seen, and he had been forced to come with what remained of his wife's family and subject himself to the scrutiny of those who knew she had left him and didn't know why – which, he supposed, was hardly surprising since he didn't really know himself.

'Are you getting divorced?' Lucy had demanded bluntly when he had broken the news to her. Guy had said there was no question of divorce at this stage. They would just have to take things one step at a time.

In the doorway of the church they shook the vicar's hand, and to Guy's relief he mumbled something impersonal about the time of year and the promise of sunshine, though there was hardly a break in the threatening clouds overhead. Still, it wasn't worth starting up a conversation over the weather that might lead to other things.

He drove everyone back to their rented cottage and the preparations for Sunday lunch. Henry and Sylvia Blackstone were going to join them. Jemima had left a leg of lamb in the oven, and promised to deal with the rest after church. By her own admission Jemima was nowhere near as good a cook as Katie, being still something of a novice, but her efforts weren't as unappetising as Fiona's either, and Guy could have kissed her for coming to his rescue. He had driven her down to the familiar little village himself to buy the mint jelly, and the new potatoes and green beans from the market stall, which he carried for her in their little paper bags.

Guy wasn't sure he could have faced Henry and Sylvia without Katie's family ranked around him like a sort of protective bodyguard. He hadn't grown accustomed yet to being an object of the Blackstones' pity – in fact, he found it both embarrassing and unnerving. With Katie's family there to restrain them, perhaps they might not even mention the touchy topic of his wife's decision not to come home.

'Heavens,' Henry said as soon as he was seated at the table, 'who would have thought that quiet, predictable little Katie would just up and leave and never come back? Any idea what made her do it?'

Jemima shot him a warning look, which he blithely ignored. Fiona said stiffly, 'She hasn't been quite herself since her father passed away.'

'Guy darling,' Sylvia trilled, 'is there anything we can do?'

Guy avoided Sylvia's eye and bit into his lamb. It was only slightly overcooked, not a bad effort at all, really. 'Thanks for the offer, but I think it's best to leave things as they are for now.'

'I knew a bolter once,' great aunt Flora said. 'Daphne Plunkett . . . left her husband with six children to bring up, and only four indoor servants.'

'But surely Katie will change her mind when she sees the girls?' Sylvia said.

Guy shook his head. 'I don't think I can count on it.'

'Poor Guy. Would it help if I phoned her and tried to reason with her?'

Guy suspected that was the last thing that would help, but he was saved from having to say so by another interjection from aunt Flora.

'Daphne Plunkett came back, of course, when she'd gambled away all her inheritance. But by then her husband had developed a penchant for the young music master. And the children didn't recognise their mother since they'd hardly ever seen her anyway, even when she lived with them.'

'Perhaps,' Henry said to Guy, 'you shouldn't apply for your silk just yet – put things on hold for a while till your personal life settles down a bit.'

The words hit Guy like a bitter blow to all his hopes and dreams. How many years had he worked and sacrificed a host of pleasures for the honour of being one of the youngest silks in the land? And now it would all come to nothing, because of the selfishness of a wife whose behaviour was quite beyond his control. He found himself suddenly very angry with Katie indeed.

'And what's your news, Jemima?' Henry said, at last changing the touchy subject.

'We were so devastated when you couldn't finish that polar race,' Sylvia gushed. 'We were just certain you would have won.'

'I suppose we'll never know,' Jemima said without rancour.

'So what is the next extraordinary challenge?' Henry enquired.

'Nothing, really,' Jemima admitted. 'I've become rather boringly settled, I'm afraid.'

'I don't believe it,' Sylvia cried. 'What do you mean?'

'She's started her own travel business,' Guy said proudly. 'Doing very nicely for herself, too.'

'A woman couldn't start a business in my day,' aunt Flora sighed. 'Daphne Plunkett ended her days in the gutter.'

'Really,' Fiona objected, 'I think we've heard quite enough about this person.'

'It seems such a shame, Jemima, that you should give up your exciting life for something so . . . ordinary,' Sylvia said rather crossly. 'After all, you were such an inspiration for what women can achieve.'

'Perhaps now I just want to achieve something different,' Jemima said serenely.

'Judging from your sister's behaviour, that would seem to run in the family,' Henry smirked.

Mallory Square was alive today with a different kind of celebration. Apart from the usual street performers, there was a great spectacle taking place out on the water, as the US Coast Guard engaged in a fierce water fight against the local Conchs.

It was no safer on land, where other missiles hurtled through the air in the form of conch fritters and hamburger buns and a whole range of other edible weaponry.

'Duck!' Lance yelled as a rocket-shaped hot dog honed in on Hannah with deadly accuracy, so that despite his warning it struck her on the back of the head and disgorged its cargo of ketchup into her sandy hair.

'Great food fight,' Lucy said. 'Even better than the ones we have at school.'

They had come in a group – Lance, Katie, Lucy, Hannah, Sam and Jolene – to watch the Conch Republic Independence Celebration. 'Is this really called the Conch Republic?' Hannah had said with a frown of confusion.

'As far as the locals are concerned,' Lance said with a grin. 'You see, back in '82 the US Border Patrol set up roadblocks between Key West and the mainland to screen for drugs and illegal aliens – damn near ruined the tourist trade – so a group of angry local citizens seceded from the union and declared war on the United States, then surrendered immediately and applied for foreign aid. Of course they didn't get it, but there were no more roadblocks. And they've been flying the Conch Republic flag ever since. It's their way of saying they don't like too many rules and regulations, or too much interference from the mainland.'

As if to illustrate the point, a large jammy doughnut smacked Sam straight between the eyes. Lucy shrieked with laughter, and Sam blushed crimson. She had been flirting with him outrageously, Katie had observed (showing remarkable powers of recovery from the episode with Tom Blackstone), and the poor boy was quite dazzled by her. Now she took him aside and whispered conspiratorially until the colour faded from his cheeks and he broke into a grin.

'So we're all supposed to celebrate this independence thing, right?' Lucy asked, turning back to Lance.

'That's the idea.'

At once Sam produced a huge bag of fries from behind his back, and he and Lucy started hurling them at Lance, pelting him mercilessly about the head. Catching on quickly, Hannah and Jolene grabbed handfuls of their popcorn and rained it down on him from the other side. Looking on nervously, Katie saw Lucy's face contort with concentration, as though she was finally getting a chance to release all the pent-up anger she felt against Lance for his place in her mother's affections. Katie raised her hand with the sinking sense of someone trying to stop an avalanche – then to her astonishment she saw them all, including Lucy, burst into howls of laughter.

'Got you!' Hannah cried.

'You got me good,' Lance said ruefully, shaking the popcorn out of his hair.

'You should have seen your face,' Lucy whooped.

Lance grabbed her and pretended to strangle her, and they ended up in a sort of half-embrace.

The incident seemed to have broken what remained of the ice. There had already been a thawing in Lucy's attitude, following the confrontation in the restaurant which had never again been mentioned. The next time they saw Lance, he took them in his Boston whaler to the backcountry with a picnic hamper Katie had packed herself with the makings of a delicious feast. Lance patiently showed each of the girls how to breathe through their snorkelling gear, which Lucy had already mastered in the swimming pool with Sam, so he taught her next how to hold her breath and dive, then clear the breathing tube afterwards. Soon she was streaking in and out of the water, revelling in the sheer physical exhilaration, while Hannah paddled round on the surface examining the under-water life with an almost scientific curiosity. She kept emerging to ask Lance the names of this fish or that species of coral, committing them earnestly to memory. Katie resolved to buy her a book so she look everything up later and remind herself, back in grey England, of this colourful other world.

There had been a nasty moment, watching Lance help Lucy over the side of the boat while she clung to his powerful forearms, when Katie had been struck with the sudden realisation that he was almost exactly halfway in age between her daughter and herself. It would be no more surprising, then, if he were dating Lucy instead. If anything, society seemed less disapproving of a big age gap if the woman were the younger of the two. Only Lucy wasn't yet a woman, she reminded herself rather crossly.

Now that they were all proficient at snorkelling in shallow water, Lance had promised to take them out to the coral reef on the *Indigo Jane*, where even greater underwater delights awaited them. 'It's the third largest reef system in the world,' he told them. 'You can see anything from stingrays and nurse sharks to barracuda and a whole host of other fish, not to mention the corals and sponges.'

Hannah's eyes had lit up at the prospect of more material to study. Lucy had said with impatient excitement, 'I can't wait to tell aunt Jemima.'

Katie had smiled, feeling no resentment this time at the mention of Jemima's name, because for once Lucy would be telling her aunt about an adventure she had shared with her mother.

Now she looked over to the corner of the square where Lavender always set up her stall. 'Come,' she said to her children, 'there's someone I want you to meet.'

Lavender was looking particularly splendid today, in a grape-coloured gown sparkling with beads, her starburst headpiece aflame in the dying rays of the sun.

'I like your crown,' Hannah said reverently. 'Are you a queen or just a lady?'

Lavender cackled. 'I be both, child. Hasn't yo' mama told you 'bout the powers of the Lady Lavender, queen of fortunes?'

Lucy looked up curiously at the sign that promised a glimpse into the future. 'My great aunt Flora says I'm going to be a famous beauty like her, but my aunt Jemima thinks I'll be a well-known explorer because that's what she is. What do *you* think?'

Lavender gave her a stern look. 'I be thinking other folks

didn't ought to go filling up little girls' heads with big ideas makes 'em vainer than a peacock.'

Lucy gave a stubborn toss of her red curls. 'I *am* going to be famous for something – you'll see.'

'We all be following our own dream. But don't go wishing for nuthing you don't understand, 'case yo' wish come true an' bite you in the tail.'

For once in her life Lucy was at a loss for words. Hannah, impatient at being always pushed from the limelight, suddenly announced in a solemn voice, 'I think I want to be a marine biologist.'

'Is that a fact?' Lavender caught Katie's eye. 'Then you be coming to the right place, child, juss like yo' mama.'

The great thing about Jemima, Guy thought, was that she could match you drink for drink like a man, but give you advice on your problems that could only come from a woman.

'I don't understand why Katie's doing this to me,' he said mournfully, having reached the stage when the whisky was making him maudlin.

'Perhaps she's not doing it *to* you,' Jemima pointed out, 'but rather *for* herself.'

'The bloody damage is the same. Everything I've worked for is in ruins. I won't be made a silk if there's a bloody scandal attached to my name.'

Jemima banged her glass down on the coffee table, making Guy wince. They were alone in the rural-style sitting room of the Cornish cottage, Fiona and great aunt Flora having long since gone off to bed. 'Who are these reactionary old dinosaurs who decide what makes a scandal?' she demanded.

Guy eyed her warily. 'You know... the powers that be, judges and top civil servants—'

'But if one in two marriages fails, as we are told, then surely half of them are in the same boat?'

'I doubt it,' Guy said, his eyes misting over. 'Divorce is a dirty word in those circles.'

Jemima waved an unsteady finger at him. 'You know your trouble, Guy, you always worry too much about what other people think. They sound like a bunch of stiff old bores. You're better than the lot of them – just remember that. If they don't want you, it's their loss, not yours.'

Her words were like a breath of fresh air through the musty corridors of power up which he had been trying to crawl for so long. Suddenly Guy began to see that there might be a different kind of light at the end of the tunnel, a new truth illuminated for him by Jemima.

'Hear, hear!' he said, clinking his glass against hers. She was wearing a big fisherman's jersey over tight leggings, and she looked to him, at that moment, unutterably adorable.

'Now stop feeling sorry for yourself,' she commanded. 'When you're not drowning in self-pity, you're actually quite an attractive man, you know.'

It was true, Jemima realised with a sudden shock, it wasn't just the whisky talking. For all those years she hadn't been able to see past the sanctimonious front which Guy put up. She had regarded him only as her sister's priggish husband, never once seeing the man beneath the façade. But now that all his defences were down, she found herself noticing with surprise that his features had a pleasing symmetry to them, and the pale blue eyes, which she had always thought of as insipid, were really rather striking. So that when he suddenly buried his face in her fisherman's jersey, she found herself stroking his hair and holding him tight and murmuring over and over, 'It's all right, Guy, I'm here. I'm not going to leave you, I promise.'

Chapter Seventeen

~

Lucy sat on the huge leopard-print sofa in the guesthouse office and looked around at the private world her mother had created. The colours were so warm and vibrant, it was like being inside one of great aunt Flora's glowing jewels. Funny, back in England Lucy would never have guessed that Katie would choose such exotic surroundings, she had always thought of her as a traditionalist. But a *leopard-print* sofa, for heaven's sake! And a jaunty little red sports car... It just showed you never really knew anyone, not even your own mother.

Katie had been showing her for most of the morning what the business of running The Tropical Hideout involved, while Nadine kept an eye on Hannah and Jolene. You might as well learn the ropes, her mother had said, because one day this place will belong to you and Hannah. Lucy had looked at it all in a new light after that. It was quite awesome to think of herself as the joint owner of something so... seriously solid.

So she paid attention when Katie showed her how she checked the Internet at least three times a day for enquiries, and mailed out brochures to potential guests and confirmation letters to people who'd already made bookings, and did the accounts and paid all the bills. It was quite responsible and important stuff, when you considered how much money was changing hands. Weird how her mother had started her new working life so far from home, while Jemima had returned to the safety of familiar ground.

'I think it's really cool what you're doing, Mummy,' Lucy said suddenly from her retreat on the sofa.

Katie looked up from her books with an expression that was both pleased and surprised.

'I didn't understand, back in England. I thought you were just tired of us.'

'Oh, Lucy.' Katie at once left her papers and came to sit beside her daughter, taking both her hands and squeezing them firmly.

Lucy lowered her eyes. 'Just tell me the truth – is it more fun doing this than bringing up children?'

Her mother put her hand out and gently raised up Lucy's chin so she was looking her full in the eyes again. 'It's just different. You can't imagine how rewarding it is to guide a child on its first steps to adulthood. But at a certain point you have to face the fact that the child has learned most of what you can teach and doesn't need you any more, at least not in the same way. That's when it's good to have something for yourself as well.'

Lucy could see that, but the anger wasn't quite gone, not yet. 'It's just that I always thought your job was being a mother. I know you worked in the library, but somehow that didn't count. It didn't take you away from us like this has.'

She could see Katie struggling to find the words to reassure her, and after all the swirling confusion and resentment of the past months, she realised she was finally ready to accept that reassurance. She waited expectantly, and finally her mother said, 'Nothing will ever take me away from you. I'm still here for you, only I'm here in a different place.'

Lucy nodded. 'I think I understand now. Perhaps it's even been good for me. I suppose I sort of took you for granted before, because you were always there. I know sometimes I wasn't very nice to you.'

'Not always, no, but you were only suffering from normal

teenage growing pains which can be pretty painful for everyone else as well. It's all part of the process.'

'I never took it out on Jemima, though,' Lucy said in a voice laden with guilt.

'People seldom do if they see someone so rarely it's a treat rather than a habit.'

'Now *you'll* be the treat, but it can't be just now and then, that wouldn't be enough. I want to spend all my holidays here – it's such a neat place.'

Her mother reached out and touched her red curls, which were piled on top of her head because she had gone for a swim straight after breakfast, with Sam. 'Darling,' Katie said, 'that would be wonderful, but—'

'When we went to Rock all the time, I used to think I could only be cool if I was in with the right crowd – people like Tom Blackstone. But now I've been here and met Sam and some of your nice friends, I realise you don't have to be one kind of person, you can make your own choices.'

'Oh Lucy,' Katie said joyfully, 'I was so hoping you'd discover that. But you shouldn't turn your back on your old life either. You have to spend some time with Daddy too.'

Lucy frowned. There was something she'd been worrying about, not knowing who to confide in, but now it seemed her mother might be the right person after all. 'Daddy's always with Jemima lately,' she said experimentally. 'It's dead peculiar.'

'Peculiar how?'

Her mother didn't sound too upset. Lucy screwed up her courage. 'They're so friendly all of a sudden. It just doesn't feel right – they weren't exactly bosom buddies before.'

Katie was silent for a moment, and Lucy was afraid she might have gone too far. But then her mother said in a voice that was gentler than she'd expected, 'Daddy's never been alone before. We've been married since he was twenty-two, you know. I expect he's just lonely.'

'But you aren't divorced, are you?'

'No.'

'So it's not like he's free to—'

'I'm sure it's nothing like that,' Katie interrupted firmly. 'I want you to be good to Daddy . . . and to Hannah.'

Seeing the worry come into her mother's face, Lucy realised it was her turn to give the reassurance. 'Don't worry,' she said, 'Hannah's OK now that we've come here to see you. But I'll keep an eye on her – make sure she eats and everything.'

'And your exams?'

'That was just a temporary glitch. I'll do fine from now on, promise.'

'Good.' Katie winked at her. 'You need a whole range of skills to run a successful business, you know.'

Lucy cocked her head to one side. It was interesting, knowing that from now on that would be one of her options. She hadn't been feeling quite so sure about her future since the Lady Lavender had made her think twice about what it was she really wanted. Perhaps she had been wrong up until now. Perhaps she was really destined to follow in her mother's footsteps.

There were tears and smiles and many hugs and kisses exchanged in the departure lounge of Miami Airport when the moment came – as always, far sooner than was welcome – for the girls to leave.

'Look after the lovely tortoises,' Hannah said, as though the little ceramic family needed feeding and mucking out like Gulliver her guinea pig, who had been left in Fiona's care.

'And everything in The Tropical Hideout,' Lucy added with the smile of a co-conspirator, making Katie feel that this piece of independence which Robin had given her must now be guarded for future generations as well.

'I will,' she said. 'And both of you take care of your father.'

She had not intended these to be her final words to them, but now that they had been spoken they seemed the most fitting.

When she had stood waving for far longer than was sensible

– long after they had passed through the jaws of passport control from which no one ever returns – Katie walked briskly back to her car and turned it determinedly in the direction of Key West.

There was pain in her heart, of course, at the difficult parting, but none of the desolation that had filled her when returning from the girls' boarding school in Wiltshire to the silent house in St John's Wood. Now, at her journey's end, there would be a houseful of guests and all the bustle and business and sense of purpose that came from being needed. She smiled as she headed on to the narrow highway that was now becoming as familiar as an old friend, and pressed her foot down a little harder on the accelerator, impatient to be home.

When she finally parked the car on Fleming Street, The Tropical Hideout seemed to glow with welcome, bathed in the warm light of a late afternoon sun. She gave it a fond smile, but her feet carried her on to Paradise Lodge where she knew Harvey would be waiting with the coffee and the Key Lime Pie.

He fussed around her, plumping up cushions and generally treating her like an invalid. 'Now you just sit there and tell Uncle Harvey exactly how you're feeling – unless it's all guilty for not going back with those wonderful kids, 'cause there's no need for that any more. They're smarter than you think – they understand exactly why you want to be here.'

Katie leaned back against the fat cushions and smiled. 'I think they finally do. I had a real mother/daughter talk with Lucy – our first for ages.'

'We just *loved* your girls. Chico said it made him realise how much he longs to be a mother himself. He would've been real good to my kids, if they'd just given us a chance.'

'I'm so sorry about your children,' Katie said gently. 'Are you quite sure there isn't a way . . . ?'

'You can't live a lie, even for your kids, however much you love them. That's what *you* found out when you came here.

I'm happier being myself even if they won't accept it.'

'But it's so sad not to be accepted by your own family.'

'Chico is my family now – and you for that matter.' He squeezed her hand affectionately. 'So it's not like you only have your husband to rely on. Is he still refusing to send you money?'

'I don't need his money,' Katie said defensively.

' 'Course you don't, but that doesn't mean the old brute shouldn't offer. It makes me so mad the way women get treated – the minute there's trouble, men try to manipulate them into doing what they want by pulling the purse strings.'

'And you're not like that, I suppose?'

'I most certainly am not. But then I guess I'm not a real man either.'

Katie smiled. 'I bet Chico wouldn't agree. Where is he, by the way?'

'Taking a little afternoon nap. The tranquillisers sometimes make him sleepy. So I guess we won't have any coffee unless I fix it myself.'

Katie followed Harvey to the kitchen, suspecting he would need some guidance in the use of the filter machine, things domestic not being his usual department. He put out the cups on the big pine table, and some brand new plates that Katie remembered seeing on offer at the Winn Dixie for bargain basement prices.

'We haven't had any breakages for weeks,' Harvey said proudly, following the direction of her gaze. 'So I can serve you on a real plate this time. We're getting to be just like a regular family round here, all Mom and Key Lime Pie.'

'Is Chico really all right now?' Katie said, pouring milk into the new china jug.

'He's great, just fine.'

Katie raised a questioning eyebrow.

'I mean it, I swear. The quack's got him so pumped full of pills, his temper's sweeter than Shirley Temple's. We haven't had a cross word in weeks – it's like honeymoon time round here.'

'And the gun?'

'Safely locked away.'

'Good. Now look, Harvey, when the water's all gone through it means the coffee's ready for drinking – and all at the press of a button, really.'

'Jeez,' Harvey said, stroking his moustache. 'And there I was thinking I'd never get by without Chico.'

Katie patted his hand. 'Getting by is easier than you think – with a little help from your friends.'

As soon as Katie crossed the threshold of The Tropical Hideout, she was swept up into the series of minor crises that were an almost everyday occurrence.

'My air conditioner's broken down – and in this *heat*,' complained Mrs van Allen, a plump and wealthy widow, fanning her sweat-spotted face indignantly with a brochure.

'I tried to fix it, ma'am – no luck,' Nadine said with a shrug.

'Don't worry, Mrs van Allen, I'll have a technician over immediately.'

'Thank you, dear, I knew I could count on you.' She swept off into the garden, all smiles again, to await the promised technician's arrival in the shade of the jacaranda tree.

Before she could take one more step, Katie was accosted by another guest, an athletic looking boy in his early twenties. 'Hey, Mrs Colman, is there a restaurant in town with a big screen where I can watch the game tonight?'

'There are several, Harry, but I can give you discount vouchers on the drinks for the one a couple of blocks down.'

'Thanks.' He gave her a lopsided grin. 'I was planning on knocking back a coupla beers.'

Katie went to the office to phone the air conditioning people and dig out the vouchers. There wouldn't be too many quiet moments to brood about the children during what remained of the working day. And later, when the sunset cruise came in, there would be Lance.

* * *

The moment Lance walked through the door, he dumped his overnight bag stuffed with all the things he had taken away to accommodate her daughters, and dragged Katie straight off to bed, where he made love to her twice without even pausing for breath. 'That's better,' he sighed, collapsing at her side.

'Why do you make me feel so good?' she said, her cheek against the bare skin of his chest.

' 'Cause I taught you how to be bad and not guilty.'

She gave him a little shove. 'Don't say such awful things or I'll throw you out of my bed.'

'But it's good to be a little bit bad.'

'You like playing with words, don't you?'

He propped himself up on one elbow and looked down at her lying contentedly beside him. 'I'm serious. If you don't let off a little steam now and then, the whole machinery blows. As a matter of fact, I probably saved you in the nick of time.'

'Thanks a lot!'

'You should know what happens to women in Thailand.' He collapsed back beside her and stared up at the ceiling through the draped mosquito nets that formed a protective seal around them.

'What do you know about women in Thailand?' Katie demanded, just a hint of jealousy creeping into her voice.

'I heard the stories when I was surfing over that way a couple years back. Now *they* are very repressed little ladies. You know all that stuff they're expected to do for their husbands – bow and cook their meals and bow again and satisfy them in bed and bow again . . . then they have to curl up at the foot of the bed like a dog and sleep there.'

'Well, of all the brass nerve—'

'They do it for years and years like perfectly programmed little robots, and then one day one of them just snaps, out of the blue, and you know what she does then?'

'What?'

'She cuts it off.'

'Cuts what . . . oh, that!'

'Yes,' said Lance, involuntarily crossing his legs.

They both lay there, staring up at the ceiling. 'Are you trying to say,' Katie asked, her voice shaking with suppressed laughter, 'that you've saved Guy from a fate worse than death?'

Lance pushed himself up and winked at her. 'I'm starving – I'll go make us some sandwiches.'

At once she began to get up too. 'I'll show you where—'

'Oh no,' he said, pushing her back on to the pillows. 'Little woman must stay right there to await big man's pleasure when he returns.'

He was gone for no more than five minutes, and came back with prawn and avocado sandwiches sliced into neat triangles and a bottle of chilled white wine.

'I hope you're going to bow before you serve that to me,' Katie said, 'otherwise I might just—'

Lance grovelled before her and she haughtily selected a little triangle from the proffered plate and bit into it, chewing reflectively for a while before saying, 'Not bad, you may stay on as my slave.'

'Oh thank you, my queen.'

'We're going to get crumbs in the bed, you know.'

'I will eat them from between your thighs.'

They munched in silence for a while, Katie carefully holding her sandwich over her plate. She found her thoughts involuntarily returning to Guy, though not quite in the way Lance had suggested. Lucy's words had found their mark.

'I've been rather worried about things at home,' she confessed, 'especially Guy.'

'He doesn't seem too worried about you.'

'He wouldn't admit it even if he was. He's got his pride, you know. Imagine what it's like for him – people knowing his wife's run off and whispering behind his back.'

'What's the problem – is he pining for you?'

She picked a crumb from the bed with her fingernails and dropped it on to her plate.

'Rather the opposite, it would seem. Lucy thinks he's

becoming too . . . intimate . . . with my sister Jemima.'

Lance gave a low whistle. 'That's gonna cause a few fireworks.'

'It's not that I think I'm in a position to point fingers or tell him what to do,' Katie said, continuing in a methodical – almost obsessive – way to pick up crumbs from the bedclothes. 'But I'm afraid if a relationship develops between the two of them, it will hurt and confuse the children far more than if he found someone who wasn't quite so close to them . . . and me.'

'Sure will. It's never a good idea to keep that sort of thing in the family.'

'But I'm the last person who can say anything, I'd feel such a hypocrite . . . For all I know one of the girls might have said something to Guy about you and me.'

Lance closed a hand over hers, stopping it in its frantic search for more breadcrumbs. 'You're separated,' he said. 'Having a boyfriend is allowed.'

'But a boyfriend half my age?'

'Don't exaggerate,' he scolded, kissing her nose. 'Besides, don't all married women in their thirties and forties fantasise about taking a younger lover? The only difference with you is you actually did it.'

She leaned against his chest, drawing comfort from the simple fact of his physical presence. 'Lance—'

'Yeah?'

'We never mention the word "love".'

'Why talk about it? Isn't doing it enough?'

He turned her face towards him and covered her mouth with kisses so that she found herself unable to reply, 'No, I don't think it is.'

Jemima sat very still in her half-darkened office in Soho, in the typist's chair that the salesman had said would be so supportive of her back, and let the quiet wash over her. Tim had left some time ago, headed for a regimental dinner, he said, and the tide of people along the pavement outside had dwindled to a trickle, and the motorbike messengers had stopped clumping up and down the stairs to deliver packages to the film company above. There was still some noise from up there – footsteps across Jemima's ceiling and occasionally a choice swearword uttered at full volume. Jemima wondered what little crises were being dealt with by her upstairs neighbours and whether they could in any way be compared with hers.

As a woman of action, she had never been prone to much inner reflection. Generally she preferred getting things done. When there are miles of frozen ice to cross, with life-threatening hazards on every side, it is what you *do* that counts. Only what she did before had never affected other people's emotions – or at least, not in the way it might this time.

She looked up at the simply framed poster of the giant tortoises on the Galapagos Islands which she had hung on the wall even before the desks and chairs were delivered. If Darwin had never gone there on his epic voyage, what knowledge might have been lost to the world? How many more years would mankind have had to wait for the theories of evolution and natural selection? Jemima could never describe what she had learned on her travels, the knowledge of the otherness of places most people had never seen which she had absorbed and stored away in those places of her soul that needed to understand the diversity of things. But now she was beginning to wonder whether she had concentrated on the external world to the exclusion of gaining any real insight into herself.

'I am not a jealous person,' she said aloud to the blank computer screen which a short while before had reflected back to her a whole list of new bookings for her expanding business. 'I don't want what Katie has – only what she doesn't want any more.'

Jemima had played no part, she reminded herself firmly, in her sister's decision to go to Key West and then to stay there, abandoning all claim to the life she had led before. There was a time when Jemima had wondered if Katie was the jealous one, trying to compensate in one grand gesture for all the adventures Jemima had experienced over the years. But Lucy said that wasn't true, her mother had chosen this other life because it was what *she* wanted. It had nothing to do with anyone else, Lucy had almost shouted so that Jemima had felt obliged to say something soothing to calm her down.

Perhaps, then, it would be Lucy who stood in the way of the thing Jemima now wanted, more than she could have imagined possible. The problem would not come from Katie, who had renounced all her claims, but from the quarter Jemima had least expected. She was so used to Lucy taking her side against her mother that now she wasn't sure how to deal with her niece's sudden protectiveness towards both her parents, and the waves of hostility she felt emanating from her every time Jemima got too close to Guy.

But I'm actually *good* for him, she thought with a little rush of self-justifying anger. In her company Guy was beginning at last to relax, to talk of booking theatre tickets or taking a picnic to Glyndebourne, to regard it as less of a crime if he didn't spend every evening chained to his desk. The worry lines around his eyes were more often crinkled in laughter when he was with her. Guy, cracking jokes! He'd never done any such thing, to her knowledge, when Katie was around. If their marriage had failed, if Katie didn't want him any more, why shouldn't he seize this chance to find happiness with someone else?

Impatiently Jemima pushed aside a pile of airline tickets with neatly printed itineraries attached to them with staples. She had advertised to scuba diving clubs a trip to the cenotes of the Yukatan, the longest underwater cave system in the world, and been oversubscribed with enquiries. It helped so much, potential clients would tell her, when the person they did business with had been there and could make a personal recommendation. Jemima remembered how much she had needed to get away from her mother's cloying attentions after her accident in the Southern Ocean, and how overwhelmed she had been by the spectacle beneath crystal clear waters that were sacred reservoirs to the ancient Mayan civilisation. Even people who had dived in the Red Sea and on the Great Barrier Reef were awed by the Yukatan caves.

Lucy had told her all about the wonderful snorkelling trips with her mother in Key West, but she had been a lot less forthcoming about who her mother's new friends were. Was there some man in Katie's life? Jemima felt a little stab of hurt that this was the first secret Lucy had refused to confide to her. Surely the special closeness that had always been between them was not, so suddenly, to become a thing of the past?

But Jemima knew the reason. It was that other closeness, the new one that had grown up between her and Guy, and which Lucy now perceived as a threat to the way her world had been structured before. Children hated change, especially when it involved their parents. Children might seem adaptable but at bottom they were fundamentally conservative.

Was it this knowledge that had made Guy hold back in Cornwall, when he had laid his head on her shoulder and she had put her arms around him and it had almost led to other things? But why shouldn't he be allowed to make his own choices, as Katie had made hers without regard for him? Guy had his needs too – and so, for that matter, did Jemima. And what she had begun to need was something more solid than the casual comings and goings of her past relationships. What she wanted was a man who would be there tomorrow and even beyond. Yes, there were complications and people could get hurt. But it was Katie who had left the gap Jemima was so tempted to fill. Whatever events were still to come, it was Katie who had set them all in motion.

The seafood risotto was made with only the softest varieties of fresh fish, nothing too chewy like muscles or squid. Katie wasn't sure how many teeth Willie Vance had left to deal with that sort of thing. When it had simmered gently till it was cooked right though, she put it in a plastic bowl with a sealed lid and balanced on top the Key Lime Pie that Chico had contributed. Then she carried them with exaggerated care down the path between her house and the one next door and up the rickety stairs that had apparently been Willie's downfall. Katie still wasn't entirely convinced that he hadn't merely tripped over one of his own cats.

Polly opened the door to her. 'Mind yourself, we don't want any more injuries,' she said with an anxious frown, rescuing the pie dish from the top of the bowl. 'Oh my, aren't you kind bringing poor Willie all these wonderful things.'

Katie stepped into the gloom of the old Conch house that looked as though it hadn't seen a fresh coat of paint for the last hundred years. This was the first time she had visited Willie since he had come out of the hospital, and consequently her first look inside his home. But Polly seemed to know her way round, leading her straight to the kitchen and storing Katie's offerings in the ancient little fridge.

There was almost no furniture in any of the rooms. The kitchen had only a small pine table with a single chair. In the sitting room a shabby sofa faced the outdated TV set, and the rest of the floor was strewn with cushions covered in cat fur and, in some cases, actual cats. Looking around Katie felt mildly embarrassed, as though she had been given an unauthorised glimpse into the private loneliness of Willie Vance.

'This way,' Polly said, leading Katie into another small room with a single iron bedstead by the wall and the rather shrunken form of Willie lying in it, propped up on his pillows.

He eyed Katie mistrustfully over the top of the sheet. 'Come to laugh at me in my misery, have yer?'

'Now, Willie,' Polly objected, 'you know she's done no such thing.'

'After my cats then, is she, while I'm still too weak to stop her?'

Polly put her hands on her hips. 'That isn't very nice. Katie's brought you a meal fit for a king and the best you can do is act like a mean old grouch. Now you apologise, Willie Vance.'

To Katie's amazement, Willie looked totally cowed. 'Sorry,' he mumbled into the sheet. But Polly kept on looking at him till he added reluctantly, 'Mighty good of yer to take all the trouble.'

'That's better,' Polly said. 'Now I'll just go and warm up some of that lovely risotto while Katie keeps you company. And you be nice to her, hear?'

She went through to the kitchen where they could hear the banging of Willie's single pot against the stove.

'You know what that girl is?' Willie said.

Katie eyed him warily, remembering his outburst at the hot tub.

'She's an angel, that's what,' he said reverently.

Katie raised an eyebrow. 'I can remember a time not so long ago when you didn't see it that way.'

Willie waved dismissively, as though brushing the past aside. 'That was afore my troubles. And when they came, I didn't expect no one to go bothering themselves about crazy old Willie Vance, not the way *she* has.'

'Polly has a heart of gold,' Katie agreed.

'She's solid gold right through. No one else came running, oh no, not that no-good wife I wasted all those years on afore she walked out on me, nor those good-for-nothing brats she raised who don't think of no one 'cept themselves. Since my hip got broke, it's just been me and Miss Polly, though she be no kin of mine.'

As soon as Polly returned with a steaming plate of risotto, Willie put on his glowering face again. She sat on a chair by his bed. 'Now doesn't that smell good?'

He wrinkled his nose suspiciously. She held out a forkful to him but he turned his head away. 'I'll feed myself, if it's all the same. I ain't paralysed yet.'

'You're right, I'm sorry,' Polly said with perfectly good humour, passing him the plate.

While he slurped up his food, Polly said to Katie with a

wink, 'Willie's agreed at last to have his cats fixed – isn't that right, Willie?'

He muttered something grumpy and incoherent into his plate.

'And then we'll have to try and find other homes for some of them – won't we, Willie?'

He carried on eating as though he hadn't even heard.

Looking round at the spartan and neglected room, Polly said, 'Then it might even be worth doing something to fix this place up.'

Katie imagined Polly's busy fingers scrubbing away at Willie's surfaces and floors, and her luminous paintings hanging on his walls.

'I hope,' she said under her breath, 'you're going to start charging him by the hour.'

Lavender took up a whole bench to herself at the wooden picnic table in the back yard of The Blue Heaven, her favourite restaurant in the heart of Bahama Village, where she sat with Katie beneath shady palms with roosters scratching in the soil at their feet, waiting for a tasty morsel to fall from a careless fork.

'Now *this* be what I calls breakfuss!' Lavender said, tucking with relish into a plate of shrimp and grits. Katie took a guilty bite of her pancakes with maple syrup. A line she had once read in a woman's magazine kept replaying itself unhelpfully in her head: 'A minute on the lips and a lifetime on the hips.' Perhaps, she thought, she would take a walk down to Lance's apartment after brunch to try and work off the damage.

'This is such an extraordinary place,' she said to Lavender, looking round at the weird decor which was like a cross between primitive African and a throwback to the hippie era. One corner was set aside for a rooster cemetery, the sign boasting that even some of Papa Hemingway's pet cocks lay beneath the soil. On the other side was a sort of ramshackle open-air shower cubicle with gaping holes in its grass-weave walls. '$1 for a shower,' the notice said, '$2 to watch.'

Lavender pointed up to the first-floor art gallery full of strange hippie artefacts. 'Used to be a bordello,' she said. Katie thought that nothing would surprise her. Even Lavender did not look the least unusual in these surroundings.

'The spirits be telling me things 'bout you,' Lavender said, mopping up the last of her shrimp and grits with a huge wedge of bread. 'They be visiting me in my dreams.'

'Why would they do that?' Katie said warily, fingering her necklace as though for protection from bad news of any kind.

'So you be ready for the changes.'

'But I don't want any more changes,' Katie protested, 'at least not for a while. What I want now is time to consolidate.'

Lavender fixed her with a steady look. 'The world don't stand still, child, whether you wants it to or not.'

'But my girls are only just getting used to the changes that have already happened.'

'Don't you be worrying 'bout them chillun no more. They be fine. You gotta keep watch over the ress so as you don't miss what's happening right in front of yo' eyes.'

A waitress wafted over to their table with a large jug full of freshly brewed coffee. She wore a long flowing robe and bells threaded between her toes.

'What I sees coming,' Lavender said, 'is more of them travels 'cross the water.'

'Not for me, surely?'

'The spirits don't say. Could be you, could be someone close.'

Katie dropped a large lump of raw cane sugar into her coffee mug. In for a penny, in for a pound. 'As long as it doesn't mean more trouble,' she said.

'Trouble be coming in all shapes and sizes. Old Satan himself can put on a pretty face if he has a mind to, but that don't mean he changed his spots.'

'What are you trying to tell me?' Katie said a touch impatiently, stirring in the sugar so hard that her spoon banged against the sides of her mug.

Lavender threw a piece of Katie's uneaten pancake to the ground, and at once a rush of feathers descended as the roosters squabbled over it. 'You guard what's yours, girl, and you let go what ain't. The trick of it be knowing which is which.'

The door to Lance's apartment wasn't locked. There was no point, he said, since he had no interest in accumulating the sort of possessions the average thief would consider worth stealing.

There was no sign of him in the half-furnished sitting room, but Katie followed the sound of music from a tape deck out on to the terrace and found him kneeling on the ground with his back to her. She felt a childish temptation to sneak up on him from behind and make him jump. He would never hear her over the pounding of the Bruce Springsteen number on his tape deck. But then something about his poised concentration made her curious, and instead she circled round quietly to his side to see what he was up to.

On the ground in front of Lance was a teal-blue surfboard with luminous orange trim, pointed at one end and rather shorter than she had expected for someone of his height and build. But she knew so little about such things, she realised as she watched him rubbing the board reverently with sandpaper, almost as though stroking a lover.

It was several minutes before he became aware of her eyes on him. He looked up and his face broke into a grin. 'She's called a thruster,' he said. 'Isn't she a beauty?'

'Yes,' Katie said, not wanting to point out that she had no means of judging.

'This part is the blank,' Lance told her, running his hands along the foam body in a manner that was almost erotic. 'And the strip of balsa wood in the middle's called the stringer, it's put there for extra strength. And this, of course, is the fin.' He turned the board over to reveal a bright orange tail underneath.

'What are you doing to it?' Katie asked.

'Just mending a few dings, making sure she's in perfect shape for—'

His words hung in the air, and a slow realisation began to creep to the surface of Katie's consciousness, like a sinister thing that has long lain forgotten at the bottom of a murky pond.

'There aren't any waves in Key West,' she said expressionlessly.

'I know.' He bent his head, busying himself with the task of carefully cutting out a piece of glass fibre in the shape of the hole he was repairing.

'Of course, I should have remembered,' she said with surprising calm. 'May's the end of high season – it's time for you to move on.'

He looked up quickly. 'I haven't made any plans. I wasn't going to just up and leave without talking to you first.'

Katie sat down heavily on the terracotta tiles of the terrace and felt their warmth rise up through the thin fabric of her skirt, which she gathered protectively round her knees. 'But what would you be doing right about now if you hadn't met me?'

'Hitting the surfing trail,' Lance confessed. 'Looking for the wave I haven't ridden before.'

'Is the challenge so important?'

'Sure – and the rush when you survive the danger and the old adrenalin pumps through your body. There's no feeling on earth quite like it.'

'I see.' And she did, at least better than she had before, when Jemima had been putting her life at risk in what had then seemed to Katie such a senseless fashion. But since that time Katie had taken a few risks of her own. Since then she had learned that if you didn't take a chance now and then, you began to feel that you weren't really alive at all.

'Where were you thinking you might go this time?' she said.

'South America. I've surfed Rio, of course, but there must be wilder places further south—'

Katie lowered her head and stared unseeingly at the sun-warmed tiles. Lance at last put down the surfboard and came to sit beside her. 'I could stay on, you know. The cruise boats run all year round, it's not like I'd be out of a job . . . And there's the sport lobster season in July – that should be a gas.'

'There's always something happening in Key West,' Katie said softly. 'But there aren't any waves.'

He reached out to touch her hair, turning her face towards him. His eyes suddenly lit up with excitement. 'You could come with me,' he said. 'That's it – we could head off together in the surfmobile.'

'Come on, Lance, I couldn't possibly—'

'Sure you could. Just throw a few possessions in the back – you wouldn't need much. We'd find our very own deserted beach and I could surf and you could swim and lie in the sun. Then I'd catch dinner straight from the sea and you'd cook it over a fire, and we'd make love right there on the sand, beneath the stars.'

He caught her to him and kissed her on the mouth with such fervour that she was swept up in the sheer enthusiasm of it, the dream of the glorious life they could lead if they had the whole world all to themselves, and no one to answer to except each other.

Chapter Eighteen

~

Guy pressed a glass of white wine into Jemima's hand. 'Sorry,' he said, 'it's a bit warm. That's always one of the complaints at these gatherings, I'm afraid.'

Jemima took an experimental sip and wrinkled her nose. 'I suppose they save all the decent stuff for the gentlemen-only dinners.'

'It's not as bad as that any more.'

'Isn't it?' Jemima looked up at the towering neo-Gothic façade of the library that overshadowed the North Gardens of Lincoln's Inn, where a charity cocktail party was in progress on the lawn. Then she let her eyes drift over the little groups of people knotted in conversation, throwing back heads now and then and laughing with the horsey bray of the home counties set. The women all wore flat sensible shoes and unremarkable frocks and some even sheltered beneath the brims of unflattering hats. The men were sober-suited and for the most part quite indistinguishable from one other. Jemima hoped she could avoid too many introductions, since she was quite certain she would never be able to recall which name went with which forgettable face.

'Heavens,' she said to Guy. 'What Katie's been putting up with all these years!'

Guy felt a little rattled by her remark. He had never really seen things in that light. Katie hadn't seemed to mind when she turned up year after year at these cocktail parties, always managing to look just right – not as drab as some of the other women but not different enough to draw attention to herself either. Which could hardly be said for Jemima. Guy looked admiringly at the cerise pink silk wraparound dress she wore, shot through with a sort of gold thread, and the matching high-heeled strappy gold sandals on her feet – outrageously impractical in such a place. She looked like some exotically plumaged foreign species of bird amidst all the other common garden sparrows on the lawn. Had he really once disapproved of her style of dressing, considering it a deliberate slap in the face of understated English taste? Had he really been that pompous?

'You look beautiful,' he said to Jemima.

'Thanks.' She lightly touched the tie that was only loosely knotted at his neck. 'You don't look too bad yourself.'

'Ha, what have we here?' wheezed a voice at Guy's shoulder. He turned to see ancient Judge Harris peering myopically and lecherously in Jemima's direction. Reluctantly Guy made the required introduction while Jemima gave a brief comic roll of her eyes so that he had to struggle to keep the laughter out of his voice.

'You're a fine young filly,' Judge Harris declared, inspecting her like so much horseflesh.

'Oh no, I assure you, I'm getting quite long in the tooth.'

'Nonsense – there's a few furlongs in you yet.'

Before Guy could rescue her there was a tug at his elbow, and Henry Blackstone was steering him away across the lawn.

'Really, Guy,' he said in an undertone, 'do you think it was wise to bring *her* here?'

'I don't see why on earth not.'

'Listen, old chap, no one can blame you for going after a bit on the side, not after what your wife's done, but—'

'Jemima's not a bit on the side,' Guy said hotly, his voice rising so that Henry looked round in alarm. 'She's my wife's sister.'

Henry dug him in the ribs. 'Revenge is sweet, eh? Look, I'm

not judging you, but flaunting her round here, under the noses of all the top brass – don't you think it's rather drawing attention to all those little marital problems you'd rather keep under wraps?'

'Henry,' Guy said simply, 'I'm not sure I care any more what anyone else thinks.'

'Now, Guy, you know you can't afford to take that attitude . . . Besides, just look at her.'

They both turned their eyes to where Jemima stood, tall and remarkable, wrapped in her cloud of pink and gold. Guy thought his heart might burst with pride.

'She doesn't exactly . . . fit in here,' Henry said.

'No, she doesn't,' Guy agreed. 'And I'm beginning to think that I don't either . . . Excuse me, Henry.'

Guy walked purposefully across the lawn, leaving Henry in mid-objection, and seized Jemima's arm, extricating her in a single move from the unwelcome attentions of Judge Harris.

'Are you enjoying yourself?' he said.

'My heels keep sinking into the lawn. Any moment now I'll be stuck here for ever.'

'Heaven forbid! I suggest we leave immediately.'

He held her arm firmly as he steered her across the lawn, and he had the impression of a sea of faces parting to let them pass, and miraculously allowing their escape before closing up seamlessly behind them again.

The word from Alvira and Pearl was that Mrs Grenville was feeling poorly. She had caught a chill and it had gone to her chest, the doctor said. Anything in the chest could be tricky at her time of life, and the doctor was keeping a close eye on the situation.

So Katie drove down to Caroline Street with a bowl of soup on the passenger seat. The other half of the batch had gone to Willie – or rather to Polly, who would warm it up for him in between feeding his cats and laundering his sheets and painting his walls. He was paying her ten dollars an hour, she told

Katie – he'd insisted on it himself, she hadn't even had to ask.

When she reached the gracious old mansion, Dolores showed Katie into the bedroom since her mistress wasn't well enough to dress for visitors. Mrs Grenville was sitting up straight in her high wooden bed against starched pillowcases to receive her guest.

She smiled at Katie with only a hint of the weariness she must be feeling. 'I guess I'm about ready for that old plot down in the cemetery.'

Katie felt it would be unforgivable to patronise her with denials. 'If you truly feel ready, then perhaps your time has come.'

Despite her laboured breathing, Mrs Grenville almost laughed. 'You think we get to choose the moment of our going, do you?'

'Not always,' Katie said painfully, thinking of Robin. 'But sometimes, when we're given the time to prepare—'

'I've made my peace, if that's what you mean.' She watched how Katie's eye was drawn to the ruby ring and bracelet which she had discarded on the heavy teak chest of drawers beside the bed. 'I'm ready to let go of my earthly blessings. All the finery means nothing in the end, it's what you did with it that counts. I hope I've served my community to the best of my ability, I hope I helped those less fortunate than me. I certainly never turned anyone away.'

Katie remembered the old lady's kindness to her, a complete stranger, and how her generous intervention had given her a new start in this strange town. She took Mrs Grenville's hand. 'The Lady Lavender once said you're a righteous woman chosen by the saints as a channel to do their work.'

'Did she really?' Mrs Grenville gave a gratified smile. 'Well, now, that's praise indeed, coming from *her*.'

She leaned back against her pillows and closed her eyes. There was an aura of peace around her that Katie remembered well from those last weeks with her father in Cumberland Terrace. She rose as though to leave.

'Stay where you are,' Mrs Grenville said, her eyes still closed. 'We haven't spoken about *you* yet.'

'Me?'

'It's your life that counts now,' Mrs Grenville said, a smile playing about her lips. 'I'm taking my last curtain call, but you, I suspect, are only pausing for the intermission. So tell me, how is your play going to turn out, my dear?'

'I only wish I knew,' Katie said frankly.

'Life today is so full of choices, sometimes you only know later, when you look at the results, whether you've made the right ones. You have two fine children, I hear.'

'I think they're pretty wonderful.'

'And the reputation of The Tropical Hideout is growing in leaps and bounds.'

'I hope so,' said Katie. 'I do my best.'

'None of us can do more.' The old lady paused, her breath coming in ragged gasps. Katie wanted to ask her if she shouldn't rest, but she could sense she hadn't finished yet.

When her breathing had steadied a little, Mrs Grenville said, 'You'll make a fine freshwater Conch, Mrs Colman, when you've been here the required seven years. And Key West should be privileged to count you as one of her own.'

'Thank you,' Katie whispered, bowing over the frail hand so that Mrs Grenville wouldn't see the tears that were falling thickly down her face.

A merciless sun beat down from a cloudless sky. Katie wriggled as a little line of sweat trickled down between her shoulder blades beneath the thin cotton fabric of her dress. If this was June, she thought, then what on earth would August bring?

She shifted a little, positioning herself right in the middle of the small patch of shade cast by the thatched umbrella, and took a cooling gulp from her bottle of beer. Then, just as she was beginning to despair of him, she saw the tall, rangy figure of Lance, head and shoulders above the rest of the crowd as he threaded his way towards her.

'What's up?' he said, flopping down on to the chair beside her. 'Or is this just an excuse for a romantic rendezvous?'

He wiped a towelling wristband over his sweat-soaked forehead. The *Indigo Jane* had just come in from a snorkelling trip to the reef. He would be taking another batch of tourists out later for the sunset cruise. He had been doing the same run to the same places day after day, with almost no variation, for the past six months. It wasn't his style, as Katie well knew. And lately he'd been doing it only for her.

'Lance,' she said as he knocked back some soda, 'I think it's time you headed south with that surfboard of yours.'

He put down the soda and gave her a searching look. He'd been so restless lately, pacing up and down whenever he was confined indoors, unable to sit still for more than a few minutes at a time. Even his love-making had an edge of impatience to it that hadn't been there before.

'Does that mean you're coming with me?' he said.

Katie looked away, her eyes travelling round the familiar features of the Schooner Wharf Bar where she and Lance had so often come to drink in the evenings, after the *Indigo Jane* came in. It was here Katie had found him on the long-ago day when it all began. So it was fitting that they should be here again now, for this.

'I'm not coming, Lance' she said bluntly. 'I'm staying here in Key West.'

He was silent for a while, then he said, 'Mind if I ask why?'

'Because I've come about as far as I can go. I've reached Mile Zero, the end of the road. I know the whole world doesn't stop here, but I think it does for me. This is where I have my business and my friends, and the only home I can still offer my girls when they come for holidays. So this is where I have to stay.'

Lance shook his head. 'But there's so much world out there still to see, so many other ways to live you haven't tried. It seems a real shame to stop now you've started.'

'Maybe one day I *will* get to see those other places. But I still need a base, somewhere I can call home. This whole thing was never about running off to see the world, it was about finding somewhere I belong.'

An elongated brown and white dog with impossibly short legs came sniffing round the legs of their chairs. Finding no carelessly dropped titbits, he wandered off in mournful disgust.

Lance said, 'I don't think I belong in any one place.'

Katie smiled sadly. 'Nor to any one person. That's why you have to go, even though I can't.'

He bent forward and kissed her on the forehead. 'We were good together, though, weren't we?'

'Yes.'

'I'm the prince who woke you from your slumber. You won't forget me in a hurry, Katie Colman.'

'I'll never forget you.'

A voice bellowed across the water from the *Indigo Jane*. 'Hey Lance, I need you over here.'

He glanced briefly in that direction, then back at Katie. 'I gotta go.'

'I know.'

She watched him ease his powerful frame through the crowd in that graceful, unhurried way he had, at no one's command but his own, until he ducked down on to the deck of the *Indigo Jane* and was lost from her view.

From all the litters that used to have the run of Willie Vance's property, only two kittens remained, curled in lazy fluffy balls on a cushion with a freshly laundered cover. Of the many miracles Polly had achieved in Willie's house, the greatest by far, Katie thought, was finding new homes for the scores of kittens and even some of the older cats, and taking the required precautions with the remaining toms to ensure the whole process need never be repeated.

'How on earth did you manage it?' Katie demanded.

'People have been so kind,' Polly said with that wide-eyed innocent look of hers. 'I explain to all Willie's visitors how difficult it is to give so many cats the care they need, and most of them are good enough to take some off my hands.'

Katie looked at Polly with amazement. She knew it took a certain touch to convince people to take on that kind of responsibility. Only someone with Polly's unfailingly sweet nature could have shamed so many people into doing it. Not to mention drawing them to visit in those numbers. It was unlikely the attraction was the crabby invalid, who had undoubtedly never had so much company in his life before – at least not the two-legged kind. Katie knew quite well who the real draw was, though Polly seemed modestly unaware of it herself.

And while they were there, Polly somehow persuaded her artist friends to help her paint the walls with wonderfully coloured murals to cheer the old man up. Her girlfriends inexplicably found themselves bathing cats while they chatted to her. An aspiring novelist had taken to reading *Gulliver's Travels* out loud to Willie, which always had the desirable effect of sending him off to sleep. Cyrus from the bakery arrived every day with a new selection of cakes, so that Polly always had something to offer the stream of guests for tea. Willie himself had a voraciously sweet tooth, and could get through a startling quantity of confectionery without any help from his well-wishers.

When Katie had looked in on him earlier, he'd grumbled, 'Not another visitor! Never seen so much commotion in all my life,' trying his best to look cross instead of pleased.

'He's been so good to me,' Polly said to her afterwards.

'Honestly, Polly, even you must see it's the other way round.'

'But you've no idea how generous he is. He's even letting me use one of his big rooms upstairs as a studio so I can get on with my painting. It makes such a difference, having so much space.'

'I hope he's still paying you for all the other work you're doing for him.'

'Oh yes, and he's told me to spend whatever I think is right doing up the house. Turns out he has quite a few savings tucked away. He just never bothered to use them 'cause no one ever came to see him, poor old thing, and he figured it wasn't worth splashing out on only himself and the cats.'

Katie heard the hum of the new washing machine in the kitchen as it went into its spin cycle. It must have been working on overdrive because all the curtains and cushion covers were freshly laundered.

'Anyway, enough about me and Willie – I want to know how *you* are,' Polly said, her face softening with concern. 'How are you coping without Lance?'

'Oh, much better,' Katie said lightly. 'I only think of him about twelve times a day now.'

Polly looked almost comically dismayed. 'Katie, I'm so sorry.'

'Don't take it to heart,' Katie said. 'I'm fine, really. I'm glad Lance and I had that time together, even if it had to end.'

He had come to say his final goodbyes with his few possessions packed into the back of the surfmobile, and his precious surfboard stored away in the specially designed attachment on top.

'You'll probably see me next season,' he said. 'I could be back working the cruise boats as soon as I run out of cash.'

And Katie had gone along with it, pretending this wasn't a final parting though she knew very well that it was – that he tended to stop off wherever he was at the time to find work, and even if he did come back, both their lives would have moved on and they would never be able simply to pick up where they had left off.

But she didn't give voice to what they were both thinking. 'Say hello to the world for me,' was all she did say before he climbed into the surfmobile and drove it off down Fleming Street for the last time.

That night she could hardly sleep, like her first night in The Tropical Hideout when she had been haunted by visions of her father. She lay staring up at the huge mosquito net that had protected her and Lance in their own private world, and now seemed more like a cage trapping her in her loneliness. But the next night, though still fitfully aware of the gap on his side of the bed, she managed to snatch a few hours of rest before the dawn light battled its way in through the curtains. And after a week she found she had almost grown accustomed to the lack of a warm breathing body beside her, though it would always be night times when she missed him most.

But her days were filled with her guests and her chores and the contentment of living the life she had chosen among people who would have noticed her absence if she had done as Lance suggested and ridden off with him into a totally new and unknown future. And perhaps, in all truthfulness, he hadn't really wanted her to. Now the powerful romance of the idea would never be crushed by the mundane realities of a difficult existence. Now they would never have to think up inadequate excuses to end a relationship that had simply run its course.

'I'm just getting on with my life and trying to be thankful for what I still have,' Katie said to Polly. 'If you don't count your blessings, you could turn round one day and find you don't have any left.'

'You're so brave. I wish I had half your courage.'

Katie smiled. 'I'm not brave enough to walk out of here with two kittens unless Willie says it's all right. I daren't have him confronting me in the hot tub again, accusing me of stealing them.'

'He should be grateful,' Polly said. 'And he is, I promise, only he's sort of got out of practice when it comes to saying these things.'

'You're doing a great job of reminding him.'

Katie picked up the two little balls of fur. When she had spoken to the girls on the telephone, Lucy had claimed the ginger one – probably to match her hair, knowing her tendency to vanity – and Hannah had been quite happy to call the tortoiseshell one her own. Katie was under instructions to name them Tiggy and Winkle.

'I hope they won't be too much trouble,' Polly said doubtfully.

But Katie was looking forward to having two little furry intruders to dispel the solitude in her apartment. 'I'll just go and say goodbye to Willie,' she said.

Despite her misgivings, Willie didn't mention the kittens she carried possessively, one under each arm. Instead he rolled his eyes in the direction of the sitting room where Katie had left Polly stitching a torn cushion cover.

'You know what that woman is?' he demanded.

'You told me – an angel.'

Willie's eyes misted with tears. 'She's the daughter I never had.'

When the phone rang late at night in Katie's apartment, she had the sudden wild notion that it might be Lance, though he must by now be miles from anything as civilised as a telephone. Nevertheless she ran for it far too quickly to notice the puddle left by Winkle on the wooden floor, only becoming unpleasantly aware of it when she stepped right in the middle.

'Damn!' she said into the receiver. 'Who is it?'

A rather pinched voice said, 'There's really no need for that language, Kathryn,' adding unnecessarily, 'It's your mother.'

Katie suppressed an urge to say something even stronger. 'Sorry – bit of a potty training crisis here.'

'Ah – the new kittens.'

'Exactly.'

'Hannah speaks of nothing else.'

Katie smiled to herself. 'She'll see them in the summer. I hope they haven't grown too much by then.'

'Perhaps *I'll* see them rather sooner – then I can give her a full report.'

Katie fell into silent confusion.

'I thought perhaps I might come and visit you in Key West,' Fiona announced like a bolt from the blue. 'In a week or so – if it's not inconvenient.'

Caught completely unprepared, Katie looked around at her bright apartment, a setting in which she had never pictured her mother. 'But you don't even like going up to London,' she pointed out.

'It's not the place I wish to visit but my daughter,' Fiona said sharply. 'I would've thought that was reason enough for coming.'

Katie wondered what her father would say to such a turn of events – Fiona leaving her horses and great aunt Flora. There would be travels across the water, Lavender had said, but Katie had assumed it applied only to Lance – and for a few mad moments, maybe to herself.

'Well?' her mother said in an offended tone.

'Of course I'd love you to come,' Katie said quickly. 'I'm thrilled about it, honestly . . . But what will you do about great aunt Flora?'

'I'll hire a nurse for a couple of weeks. I've got to have my own time too, you know, now and again.'

'I couldn't agree more.'

'And I'll pay the girl from the stables down the road to come in and see to the horses. If anything goes wrong, Jemima can always drive down from London.'

'So she isn't planning on visiting me too?'

There was a little silence at the other end of the phone. Then Fiona said, ' I don't think that's on the cards right now.'

At least that wouldn't create a problem with space, Katie thought, knowing how her mother would dislike sharing the girls' bedroom with anyone else, even Jemima. And all the other rooms were booked, what with sport lobster season and the Hemingway Festival coming up.

'Good,' Fiona said. 'I'll let you know my dates when I've bought my air ticket.'

Katie put the receiver down and stared at it for long moments. 'Yo' whole family be coming after you, an' no mistake,' Lavender had told her months ago, but she hadn't believed it for a moment. She began to wonder now what else

Lavender might know through those mysterious forces that gave her guidance, which she hadn't yet revealed.

This time Katie quietly waited her turn in the line of people who seemed to be a constant fixture on Lavender's front porch.

Seeing the way she twisted her fingers in her lap, a young black woman in a vividly coloured shawl leaned over and asked Katie, 'Is this your first time having your *Ifa* read?'

'Yes,' Katie said, realising that was in fact what she had come here to do.

The woman patted her shoulder. 'Don't worry. The Lady Lavender has the gift. She told me even before the symptoms came on that I was getting a stomach ulcer. The doctor gave me some medicine, but it was the Lady Lavender's herbs that really did the trick – and the sacrifice to Oshun.'

'Sacrifice?' Katie said in a tremulous voice.

The door opened and at once the woman jumped up. 'It's my turn. Good luck.' And she disappeared into the gloom with one last flash of her bright shawl.

Katie had many more minutes to wait, wondering what she was doing here, while the line ahead of her grew shorter and the line behind ever longer, before the door suddenly opened again and it was her turn to go in.

She stepped into Lavender's familiar front room which now seemed suddenly alien and shrouded in mystery. The same plaster statue of the Virgin, the same strange African emblems stood with banks of fresh flowers and food offerings before them, but now they seemed to take on a powerful and sinister life. Even Lavender herself, sitting at a small table to one side, had an aura about her that seemed to transform her into something quite different from the woman who had become Katie's friend.

'You be coming for real this time?' Lavender said, sensing the change in her. 'You be wanting to know what the *Ifa* say 'bout yo' future?'

'I think so.'

'Why now?'

'I don't know . . . I suppose I just can't see for myself where my life is going. Lance has left, I'm alone again . . . and now my mother has announced out of the blue that she's coming to stay, and I've got this uneasy feeling she wouldn't be doing it without a reason.'

Lavender gave her a narrow look. 'Ain't no use asking 'less you be doing what the *Ifa* say.'

'I'll try, as long as it doesn't involve any funny rituals I wouldn't be comfortable with.'

'Hmmph!' Lavender hesitated a moment, then she took a square of paper and wrote Katie's name at the top. In her other hand she held the thin chain broken at intervals by small tortoiseshell disks that had long been a source of fascination for Katie.

'What exactly is that thing?' she now felt bold enough to ask.

'The *ekwele* – the tool I be using to tell you yo' destiny.' Lavender pinched it in the middle, then laid it down on the table so that the curved pieces of shell fell in a pattern with either their concave or convex sides up. Then she began to write a series of symbols on the paper in pairs of vertical lines or circles. So deep was her concentration that Katie thought better of asking her what she was doing now.

Finally she stopped writing and took a shell, a stone and a piece of bone from the table drawer. 'When I be telling you to take one, you puts it in yo' hand and you hides it so as I can't see which.' Lavender demonstrated with a closed fist. Katie nodded.

The process was repeated eight times, with Lavender throwing the chain each time and then asking Katie to show her what was in either her left or right hand. Again she wrote down a series of symbols on the piece of paper.

Katie could contain her curiosity no longer. 'Why are you doing that?' she asked.

Lavender tossed her another impatient look.

'I'd really like to know,' Katie said, 'and I think I have the right. After all, this is *my* life we're talking about.'

'There be reason in that,' Lavender conceded, relenting enough to explain that the first time she threw the chain she was looking for Katie's *letra* – a combination of sixteen possible essential life situations. The exercise with the shell, stone and bone then enabled her to ask the oracle more detailed questions about the *letra*, and it would reply with a 'good' or 'bad' answer, or a 'yes' or 'no'.

'Like heads and tails,' Katie said.

Lavender frowned. 'I be all done with the questions now. You want to know the answers or not?'

'Yes please,' Katie said meekly.

Lavender studied the inscrutable symbols on the piece of paper. 'There be trouble coming from someone close to you.'

Katie pictured Fiona on her way to see her. But it was ridiculous imagining that her own mother would bring her harm. She began to think quite crossly that this *Ifa* wasn't all it was cracked up to be.

Lavender was watching her closely, as though reading her thoughts. 'The *letra* be warning me of danger close to you. There be loss waiting, but after the loss there also be gain. From the pain be coming riches.'

She could understand that, Katie thought, in relation to her past – the death of her father that had brought such sorrow but also given her the means for a whole new life. 'Are you sure you're talking about my future?' she said.

Lavender nodded firmly.

'Has it got something to do with my mother's visit?'

'The *Ifa* doan be telling me that.'

Katie felt a little prickle up her spine. 'So what do I do?' she said warily.

'You muss take the herbs I be giving you, to guard you 'gainst those be wishing you harm. You muss honour the spirit of your father and pray to Oshun, spirit of the river, who be guiding you.'

'I'm not sure I could pray to a spirit—'

'Her Catholic face be the blessed Virgin of Caridad, who be watching over souls at sea. I be giving you her image before you leave. You muss put five yellow candles and five sweet pastries before her, 'cause she loves sweet words and foods. Then after five days you muss take the cakes to fresh flowing water and offer them to her there, so she look kindly on you and help you win back the one you love.'

'And who is that?' Katie said, thrown into momentary confusion by the change of subject.

Lavender shook her head. 'You don't know that, child, you don't know nothing.'

To save Katie the long drive to Miami airport and back, Fiona had elected to fly all the way to Key West, changing to one of the small planes that serviced the route. Katie watched her crossing the tarmac in her crisp cotton dress with her back ramrod straight and her hair brushed into its neat auburn-grey bun, and thought she could never be mistaken for one of the American tourists slouching along in shapeless T-shirts and flat sandals and baseball caps with the peaks turned to the back.

In the arrivals hall they embraced briefly and awkwardly before Katie hurried off to look for a trolley while Fiona stood watch over the baggage carousel. She cast the odd politely curious glance at the woman beside her whose vast thighs were squeezed into cycling shorts that forced her stomach to cascade over the too-tight waistband like a waterfall of pale flesh. The woman was struggling to remove a large battered suitcase from a pile-up on the carousel, while her husband chased after three fat and disobedient children.

'Hank,' the woman yelled as the suitcase escaped her grasp and spun off on another circuit, 'enough with the kids already. Get your butt over here and give me a hand.'

Fiona raised an eyebrow and said to Katie, 'Who was it who said the English and Americans are two nations divided by a common language?'

'I don't remember.'

'Nor do I.' She gave a little shrug. 'Your father would have known.'

Her words filled Katie with the sudden bleakness of realising they could never ask him such things again, and she had to turn away for a moment.

When they reached The Tropical Hideout, Fiona inspected everything with the same objective interest with which she had regarded her American travelling companions, as though it were all quite fascinating but nothing to do with her.

'I hadn't imagined you would go in for such . . . colourful decor,' she said to Katie.

'Bright colours work better in the sort of strong sunlight we get here.'

Fiona fanned herself with a white cotton handkerchief. 'Yes, I suppose they do . . . I was rather concerned, in England, about what it was you were pouring your father's capital into, but it looks as though you've made a solid investment – as long as you're getting a good return?'

'I'm averaging an eighty per cent occupancy rate,' Katie said proudly.

'That sounds promising, but does it make you a living?'

'I've been self-supporting since I arrived here. Guy certainly hasn't sent me any money.'

'Hasn't he?' Fiona's lips tightened. 'Well, good for you.'

Katie wondered whether it was concern for her finances that had brought her mother here. In any event, she was rather relishing the unfamiliar sense of having emerged from their discussion with the upper hand.

Fiona proved to be the model guest. She provided no distraction at all in Katie's working day, setting off each morning armed with her guidebook to see all the places of historical interest, such as Audubon House and Truman's Little White House and the home where Hemingway lived. 'Fascinating,' she said of the office loft where the writer had penned most of his great works. In the afternoons she rested in a shady deckchair with a copy of *To Have and Have Not*, which she said was giving her an additional flavour of the island. But an hour or two's inactivity was usually quite enough, after which she would pursue Tiggy and Winkle with a camera so she could take the photographs back for Lucy and Hannah. Any little accidents resulted in a firm visit to the sand box, so that it wasn't long before Katie had no more concerns about stepping out of bed straight into a warm puddle.

In the evenings Katie and her mother ate meals in the better restaurants, for which Fiona always insisted on paying. If they didn't feel like going out, Katie cooked fresh fish or pasta and salad and they ate in the apartment overlooking the garden, while speaking of neutral topics and never once touching on why Fiona had felt compelled to come, beyond a natural curiosity to discover what her daughter's life was like in this strange place she had chosen to call home.

Towards the end of the first week, something occurred to cause a change in the routine of Fiona's afternoons.

'I met your neighbour in the street today,' she told Katie.

'Which one?' Katie said, her heart sinking at what Fiona would have made of Chico in one of his more outrageous frocks.

'The one who sent over the Key Lime Pie before I arrived. Such a nice young man. I can't think why you haven't introduced us before.'

'Do you mean Chico?' Katie faltered.

Fiona gave her a hard stare. 'I am not a prejudiced person, Kathryn, whatever you may think. I know these gay people are friends of yours, and Lucy and Hannah seemed to like them. I can't imagine why you thought I wouldn't too.'

'I'm sorry,' Katie said weakly.

'Anyway, I praised his pie and he promised to teach me how to make one.'

Katie looked at her mother in dismay.

'I know – none of you think I can cook, and you're right,' Fiona said. 'But Chico says it's never too late to learn.'

'*Where* are you going to learn?' Katie said pointedly.

'In his kitchen, of course.'

Katie had been rather afraid of that. 'You do realise Paradise Lodge has an optional dress policy?'

'Heavens, Kathryn, what sort of prude do you take me for?' Fiona said indignantly. 'I've had two children, you know – there isn't much I haven't seen.'

From then on Fiona disappeared to Paradise Lodge every afternoon at four, leaving Katie to get on with her chores, and returned at six with some exotic dish for supper like crab cakes with rum-mango sauce or pan-seared pork chops with shiitake mushrooms, so mouthwateringly delicious that Katie could scarcely believe her mother had had a hand in them.

Fiona blushed quite pink when Katie paid her extravagant compliments on her progress. 'No need for us to go out for any more expensive meals,' she said smugly. 'And no need for you to slave over a hot stove after a long day in the office.'

Before long Chico began to appear in the mornings too, and he and Fiona would disappear off to the markets to shop for the finest ingredients, their skin protected from the sun beneath stylish straw hats. Katie would watch with amazement as they headed off down the street with their baskets, chattering and laughing like sisters, their heads as close together as the wide brims of their hats would allow.

'What on earth do they find to talk about?' Katie asked Harvey on a snooping visit to Paradise Lodge while one of the cookery sessions was in progress.

'You don't think they'd tell *me*, do you?'

'Is my mother really doing any of the cooking, or is she just claiming half the credit?'

'Mind what you say,' Harvey warned in mock alarm. 'Chico won't hear a word against her. He says she's the perfect pupil – he instructs and she obeys.'

'Now that really *is* a miracle.'

'You're telling me. Not a single plate broken since the cookery lessons began. Chico is in his element with your mother here. You may think he's doing her a favour, but in fact it's the other way round. I only wish she'd stay for ever.'

But when Katie suggested they should join the others in the kitchen for a drink, Harvey looked more wary. 'I'm not sure the maestro would like that. Best not to interrupt the flow of all those cooking juices, eh?'

It was only on the last night of Fiona's visit that she finally came out and told Katie what she had presumably travelled so many hundreds of miles to say.

They had invited Harvey and Chico over to share the sautéed sea scallops served on a bed of poached spinach with a mustard cream sauce that had been prepared as a grand finale by the master chef and his pupil.

'Superb,' Harvey said, beaming at them both. Chico made a mock curtsey. Tonight he was wearing a particularly dramatic scarlet off-the-shoulder dress.

'I shall have to start throwing dinner parties in Wiltshire,' Fiona said. 'All my new skills will be wasted on just me and aunt Flora.'

'What about the dogs?' Katie said mischievously, and was surprised when her mother roared with laughter.

'Pah, the English – they'll never appreciate you like we do,' Chico said fervently.

'Perhaps you're forgetting that Kathryn and I are English,' Fiona pointed out mildly.

'Nonsense, I refuse to believe it – you're far too adorable,' Chico cried, and Fiona looked as coy as a schoolgirl.

When their guests had reluctantly left, extracting promises from Fiona that she would visit Key West again as soon as possible, Katie and Fiona cleared away plates to the little kitchen. Fiona always insisted on doing the washing up by hand, saying it was sheer extravagance to use the dishwasher when it was really no bother.

'I thought perhaps we should have a little chat,' she said when she had deposited her load by the sink.

'Now?' Katie said, looking up from scraping the mustard sauce off a plate.

'Why not?' Fiona threw what remained of the French loaf into the waste disposal. 'These things are so useful, aren't they?'

She filled the sink with soapy water before continuing. 'I used to think you'd taken leave of your senses when you told us all you weren't coming home. But it's never a simple matter of right or wrong, is it? Life is more complicated than that.'

Katie rubbed at a stubborn spot of spinach that wouldn't come off the plate.

'Guy's worried that you're being influenced by all sorts of unsuitable people. But there's nothing wrong with your friends. Harvey and Chico are delightful . . . and sweet little Polly across the way . . . I haven't met your fortune teller, but I can only assume she's a perfectly decent sort.'

'She's a very good woman,' Katie said, picking up the tea towel to dry the dishes her mother was washing at such a frantic rate, and wondering what Fiona would have made of Katie's shrine to the Virgin of Caridad and the spirit Oshun, with its five yellow candles and five sweet pastries, which she had cast into flowing water as instructed only days before Fiona's arrival.

Fiona banged a plate on to the dish rack with a force that made the rest of them rattle. 'Has she warned you about the trouble you're facing at home?'

'That depends what trouble you mean,' Katie said, watching warily as her mother attacked another plate.

Fiona stopped washing for a moment, and then, without warning, she said, 'I imagine you've had some other man in your life?'

Katie stared down at the bright pink towel, uncomfortably aware that she did not want to meet her mother's eye.

'Aunt Flora says there's always a man involved in these cases, and I'm inclined to think she's right. Is it over now?'

'Yes.'

'Oh, let's leave these wretched dishes," Fiona said suddenly, 'and have a glass of wine.'

Sitting by the open windows, she inhaled deeply the scent of gardenia. 'Your father and I were very worried when you decided to marry Guy so young.'

'Really?' Katie shook her head in disbelief. 'You didn't say anything at the time.'

'You seemed so sure of what you wanted, we didn't feel it was our place. After all, we had nothing against Guy ... But sixteen years is a long time to have led such a settled life when you're still a young woman, really. I suppose something like this was bound to happen.'

'If you mean the other man, his name was Lance and he made me realise what's been missing from my marriage for a very long time.'

Fiona leaned forward intently. 'But was it there in the first place?'

'I don't know.' Katie tried to cast her mind back to those early heady days when Guy had been the man she wanted more than any other. 'I suppose it must have been.'

'Then there must be some hope of reviving it.'

'I haven't really thought—'

'Then you'd better start thinking,' Fiona said grimly, 'because soon you won't get the chance – not if Jemima has her way.'

Katie gave her mother a wary look, not sure she could be suggesting something even slightly critical of Jemima.

'I know what you're thinking,' Fiona said. 'You expect me always to take Jemima's side, and perhaps I deserve that. I haven't been as even-handed with you girls as I should have been. But I assure you, when it comes to watching Jemima trying to take over your husband, I wholeheartedly disapprove of her behaviour, whatever you've done to allow it.'

Katie reached out a hand and took a steadying sip of wine. 'Perhaps you'd better tell me exactly what's been going on.'

'I'm not sure anything's actually *happened* yet. But if you don't go back and claim your husband then believe me, Jemima will. And I don't have to tell you she's used to getting what she wants.'

Long after Fiona had gone to bed, Katie sat nursing another glass of wine in the perfumed breezes from the garden and mulling over what her mother had said. Her words had stirred up old feelings which Katie had thought were long dead, memories of a time when Guy had been the centre of her world, their love for each other never in question. 'He belongs to *me*, not Jemima,' said a little inner voice which Katie recognised quite well as jealousy. But why, after all this time of enjoying her freedom, was she suddenly feeling jealous over Guy?

Someone wishes you harm, Lavender had said . . . there will be loss and gain . . . you must make an offering to win back the one you love. But Katie still couldn't truthfully say that the words referred to Guy. Nor, in all fairness, could she try to hold on to him just to prevent Jemima from having him. You must guard what's yours and let go what isn't, Lavender had said, but until Katie finally worked out which was which, she felt it would be quite wrong to do anything at all.

Chapter Nineteen

~

Katie tried to remember afterwards how long she had been away, dropping her mother off at Key West airport for her flights back to Miami and London. It couldn't have been that long – no more than an hour, at most. How could such a terrible, life-changing thing have happened in the one short hour her back had been turned?

She kept asking herself, in the days that followed – if she had been there would it have made any difference? Would she have been able to change the course of events? They weren't the sorts of questions to which there could ever be answers, but that didn't stop them recurring endlessly in her head.

She and Fiona had said their goodbyes to Harvey and Chico on the pavement outside Paradise Lodge. There had been extravagant hugs and praises for Fiona, and some for Katie too, just for good measure. Was there something she should have read into those frantic embraces, some mute appeal she had missed?

The ambulance was parked directly outside Paradise Lodge when she returned, its flashing lights turning to garish red the canopy of leaves above. People stood in little knots around the police cordon, speaking in hushed voices. Some she recognised as guests from Paradise Lodge, wearing scant clothing that had clearly been thrown on in haste and leaning against one another for support.

Katie's own legs suddenly went very weak and she wasn't

sure she would be able to get out of the car. She simply sat there, staring stupidly at a police officer trying to clear curious onlookers out of the road, until a small figure detached itself from the crowd and ran over to her car.

'Oh Katie,' said a voice which she knew belonged to Polly though she couldn't bring herself to look at her. 'Oh Katie, this is so bad—'

Katie stared straight ahead through the windscreen. 'Is Harvey . . . ?'

'Both of them, Katie. They're both dead.'

Still she sat there, motionless, while Polly wept silently beside her.

A thickset young police officer headed purposefully towards her. 'Excuse me, ma'am, could you back up your car? We're trying to get another ambulance in here.'

Like an obedient robot Katie switched on the ignition. As the engine idled she said to the officer, 'Could you please tell me what happened?'

He leaned against the side of the car, relaxed and friendly. 'Seems like the Cuban one shot his boyfriend, then turned the gun on himself.'

Katie closed her eyes. 'Does anyone know why?'

'Some kinda jealous rage . . . caught him with another guy . . . you know how these people are.'

Katie's eyes flew open and she gave the smiling officer a frozen stare. 'Yes, I did know them – very well. Did you?'

At once he removed his arm from her car and straightened up. 'No offence meant, ma'am. Now would you mind moving your car?'

Katie put it carefully into reverse and made room for the second ambulance whose siren could now be heard screaming down the quiet and leafy spaces of Fleming Street. Then she beckoned Polly inside The Tropical Hideout and closed the door against the sight of stretcher-bearers and body bags and gaping crowds, and they fell into each other's arms and wept.

* * *

The funeral procession passed slowly down the paths of the cemetery, laid out in neat parallel rows like the streets of a well-planned city. Tourists languid from the heat turned to watch with undisguised curiosity when they saw the unusual coffin, painted by Polly in bright colours as requested by Harvey in his will, with designs that depicted the extraordinary beauty of the island he had come to call home. The tourists began to snap off cameras, hoping to capture what they supposed was a quaint local custom to show the folks back home.

Katie kept her eyes raised to the saluting soldier on top of the monument to the sinking of the USS *Maine*, which started the Spanish-American war. It was a fitting reminder, on this day when they would be laying to rest two men, one from each community, whose lives had also been so tragically cut short.

The pallbearers carrying Harvey's colourful coffin were all prominent members of the Key West gay community – a city councillor, a well-known playwright, representatives from the Business Guild and the Metropolitan Community Church. Their heads were respectfully covered as they headed for B'Nai Zion, the Jewish section of the cemetery. Chico would not be accompanying them there. He had left no will expressing his wishes, and his family had claimed his body for a sombre Catholic and family tradition which he had long since rejected for a wholly other way of life. So he would not lie by Harvey's side for all eternity, as would undoubtedly have been his wish.

The mourners crowded round the freshly dug hole in the coral rock. Excavations were never too deep for fear of hitting the sea water lurking beneath, and graves were always covered with cement to prevent the coffins coming to the surface if water levels rose. Only the previous night Katie had woken from a nightmare in which Harvey's open coffin swirled away in a terrible flood while she vainly tried to swim after it.

There were no family members amidst the friends and colleagues and the simply curious who stood around the grave.

Katie had no way of knowing if anyone had even tried to contact Harvey's ex-wife and children. She only realised now, when it was too late to ask, that Harvey had never even told her which city they lived in. Nor had he mentioned other family – parents, siblings, cousins – except to say that nobody approved of his lifestyle.

She watched numbly as the coffin was lowered into its shallow hole. Suddenly she realised that the distinctly unconventional rabbi had stopped intoning the conventional prayers and was looking directly at her, holding out a spade.

She stared at it, comprehension slowly dawning. 'You and Chico are my family now,' Harvey had once said to her, but there was no Chico any more. Katie was the only one left who could perform the traditional family and usually male duty of throwing the first spadeful of earth on to the coffin.

Head held high, she took the spade from the rabbi and scooped up some soil from the pile by the grave, flinging it down into the hole. It hit the wood with a sickening thud.

She looked around at the gay friends who had been Harvey's other family, and passed the spade over to the first pallbearer. Each of them in turn followed her example. Each time Katie winced at the sound of earth hitting coffin, covering forever the friend she would never see again.

'Sweet dreams,' she said softly when she could no longer see even a hint of colour beneath the layer of soil.

People were already beginning to shuffle off, some heading for the Catholic section where Chico was to be buried shortly afterwards. There was a strange feeling in the air, something unavoidably shameful about the whole proceedings, evident in the lack of eye contact between mourners, and the way no one spoke about the manner in which the two men had died.

At the gate from B'Nai Zion, the city councillor shook Katie's hand. 'I'll be heading on back to town.'

'You're not staying to pay your respects to Chico?'

He gave a small apologetic shrug. 'Wouldn't want to embarrass the family.'

Looking round, Katie realised that most of the gay mourners, even friends of Harvey and Chico, had simply melted away. She wished more than ever that Polly had come with her, but Willie was having a bad day and she hadn't been able to leave him.

So Katie headed off alone through the city of the dead. Lavender said the dead walk among us, but today Katie couldn't feel their presence. Here lay William Curry, Florida's first millionaire. There an obelisk pointed to the sky, reminding the world of Jose Marti and his Cuban martyrs. It was all just memories now, words on stone. 'Dr Robin Fraser, heart surgeon, husband and father—'

Yet here, in the Cuban section, the other world began to make itself felt. There were stones placed on graves in deliberate patterns, signifying who knew what mysterious communications with the afterlife. It was here also, so the rumours went, that the followers of *santeria* came to chant and speak to the ancestors and sacrifice to the spirits or *orishas,* the chickens that were to be found in such abundance in Bahama Village. Nobody in Key West liked to come down to the cemetery after dark on a night like Hallowe'en.

Chico's people seemed to be rooted in a more conventional Catholic tradition. The coffin was of unpainted mahogany. The men wore sober suits and mournful moustaches and a quietly prosperous air. Katie remembered Harvey telling her that they ran their own stores and small businesses and kept out of island politics. The women grouped together in their dark dresses, their thick black hair covered with shawls. The younger ones must have been Chico's sisters, the ones whose dresses he had borrowed as a child, experimenting with his fragile identity.

What was he wearing now inside the closed coffin? Undoubtedly the family would have rejected as wholly unsuitable the gowns he had so loved. As the priest recited his prayers of redemption through faith, Katie offered up her own thanks that the mourners could not see Chico scrubbed bare of the make-up that had been his protective mask against the world, and forced into some purpose-bought and ludicrously masculine suit intended to disguise what he truly was.

Perhaps it took bad news of this magnitude, Fiona thought, to make a person see what had to be done.

First she drove across to Wolton Abbey to tell the girls. They would be breaking up soon for the summer holidays, spending the first couple of weeks with their father in London and Rock, before flying out to Key West to be with their mother. They would have to know what had happened before then – the sooner the better, in Fiona's opinion, to give them the time they needed to get used to it.

So she explained to them, as calmly and factually as possible, that Mummy's friends – the ones who lived next door in Paradise Lodge – were dead. They asked a lot of questions, of course, and Fiona, who didn't believe in patronising children, answered them all quite truthfully. The girls were a little shocked and sad, but all in all they took it rather well. They hadn't become particularly close to Harvey and Chico on the one visit they had made so far to Key West.

Fiona, on the other hand, had. She kept bursting into tears in the most unsuitable places, remembering one of a dozen intimate moments in the fragrant kitchen of Paradise Lodge where Chico had shared with her the secrets of preparing food with dedication and love. Or the times when Harvey had extravagantly praised their efforts, looking at Chico with such obvious devotion. They were charming and funny and wonderful people, and they had been good to her daughter when she was far from home and sorely in need of true friends. Fiona would always be grateful to them for that.

Katie had sounded so utterly forlorn and lost when she had broken the news to Fiona on the telephone. It would be some time, Fiona knew, before her daughter would feel up to dealing with any of the other problems that threatened her life. So it was Fiona who made the telephone call to Jemima, inviting her to dinner.

'Heavens, Mummy, this is delicious – where did you get it?'
Jemima said after her first mouthful of the sautéed scallops on
spinach which had been the last meal Fiona had prepared with
Chico and which she had wanted to make again now as a sort
of tribute to his memory.

'I cooked it myself, as it happens.'

'You're pulling my leg.'

'She's not, you know,' great aunt Flora said morosely. 'It's
been the same every night since she came back from America
– always something fancy on the table.' Great aunt Flora had
been sorely missing her usual piece of dry meat with two
overboiled veg.

'If you don't want any I'll help you upstairs,' Fiona said
firmly. 'You overdid the cakes at tea time, that's your trouble.
Besides, you're looking tired.'

Great aunt Flora at once began to imagine an assortment of
illnesses she might be suffering from, and said she thought she
had better go to bed at once.

'Isn't it dreadful, this business with Katie's friends?' Jemima
said as soon as she was alone with her mother.

Aunt Flora had said it was tragic, like what happened to
poor Oscar Wilde. Then she had reminded Fiona crossly that
she didn't like people to talk in front of her about death.

'Guy's in quite a state about it,' Jemima added.

'And why, pray, should *Guy* be in a state?' Fiona inquired
coldly.

'You know, thinking Katie was friends with such unstable
people, and what might have happened to her if she'd been
there at the time.'

'Sometimes,' Fiona snorted, 'Guy can be a real ass.'

'Mummy!'

Fiona resisted the urge to get up and start clearing away the
plates, as she usually did when agitated. Instead she reached
for her drink. 'What would Guy know about people he's never
met? It's not as though he's had the initiative to go and visit
his wife in Key West and see for himself.'

371

'That isn't fair,' Jemima objected, two spots of colour appearing in her cheeks. 'You're forgetting *she* was the one who walked out on *him*.'

'And does he think he behaved so perfectly that he played no part in that? Doesn't he accept any responsibility for the breakdown of his marriage?'

'I don't know,' Jemima said awkwardly. 'We haven't really talked about it.'

'What *do* you and Guy talk about, then?'

Jemima gave Fiona an indignant look. 'Honestly, Mummy, I don't know what's got into you. You can hardly expect me to—'

'What I expect from you is a little more loyalty towards your own flesh and blood. Katie is your *sister*, in case you've conveniently forgotten. And Guy is your sister's husband.'

'But she doesn't want him any more.'

'That's for her to sort out with him,' Fiona said firmly. 'It's really none of your business, Jemima.'

Jemima was so shocked at the tone her mother was taking with her – the pampered favourite – that her mouth quite literally fell open in a gape of astonishment.

But Fiona hadn't finished. 'If it's a man you want, find one of your own. And if it's just another challenge, I suggest you attempt something a little more noble than stealing your sister's husband.'

'You can't talk to me like that,' Jemima cried. 'I'm not a child – you can't tell me what to do.'

'No, I never could,' Fiona said sadly. 'What I'm hoping is that you'll have the common decency to make the right decision yourself.'

Harvey's attorney was a handsome gay man called Roger who wore a lot of discreet gold jewellery and could afford to live in a house in the historic district, which he had lovingly restored and decorated in a style not dissimilar to Paradise Lodge.

'Thanks for stopping by,' he said to Katie in the office which he ran from home.

'No problem,' she said. And in truth, she hadn't been doing much of anything when he'd phoned. She'd been leaving rather a lot of the running of things at The Tropical Hideout to Nadine these last few days.

Roger twisted the gold and garnet ring on his little finger. 'Damn shame about Harvey, isn't it? I mean, we knew Chico was the jealous type, but how could we have imagined . . . ?'

Katie wondered whether by 'we' he meant himself and the partner he no doubt shared this house with, or whether he felt he was authorised to speak for the whole gay community.

'Anyway,' Roger said, becoming suddenly businesslike, 'he left a letter he wanted you to read in the event that he and Chico . . . passed away simultaneously.'

He held out a pastel blue envelope with the logo of Paradise Lodge, and Katie took it gingerly from his manicured hand.

'He asked if I would let you read it alone,' Roger said, 'so if you'd like to sit out on my porch with a jug of lemonade . . . ?'

Katie obediently followed him out to a porch that overlooked a landscaped back yard with the obligatory hot tub and pool, and ornamental borders filled with stiff star-shaped poinsettias. Katie thought irrelevantly how she had always hated the rigidness of that particular flower.

Beside a green wicker chair with fat pink cushions, a jug of lemonade stood waiting. Roger disappeared discreetly back inside, and Katie sat down feeling an enormous sense of gratitude to Harvey for insisting his last words to her should be in private, without the intrusive presence of his attorney.

She poured out a glass of lemonade and took a long, steadying drink. Then she unfolded the pages covered in Harvey's beautifully neat hand.

My dearest Katie
I'm so sorry to have left you so suddenly at a time when you
must feel you need all your friends around you. But you

really mustn't blame yourself for not doing more to save me and Chico. Believe me, nothing you could have done would have made any difference.

You see, sometimes he wasn't himself, and then he didn't know what he was doing. But I wouldn't have abandoned him, no matter what anyone said. I let him stay knowing the risks to us both, because I loved him and was happier with him than I could possibly have been without him. You see, he helped me to discover who I truly was. So don't feel sorry for me. With Chico I had the life I wanted, even if it didn't last as long as I might have wished. It was worth it just the same.

Now I want you to have the life you want. So I've given you a parting gift, from me and Chico. I want you to have Paradise Lodge. That way you'll be able to deal with your husband on equal terms. You'll be truly independent of him or anyone else for that matter, and you can make the choices that are right for you.

I know you've had sentimental notions about me being reconciled with my family, but believe me it would never have worked. I left my ex-wife and kids half my money before I ever came to Key West. I'm sure they're doing just fine. Please don't try to find them because you feel Paradise Lodge should belong to them. They wouldn't want it. Besides, if you're reading this letter then the worst has happened and I'd rather they didn't know. I've put them through enough already.

Remember you were my family in the end, so it's right that Paradise Lodge should be yours. I won't mind if you decide to sell it – it would be pretty heavy going to expect you to run it yourself. All I ask is that you make sure it continues as a gay guesthouse. Key West is where I found acceptance and self-respect as a gay man, and I'd like others to be able to do the same.

Remember Chico and I both loved you and those of your family we were lucky enough to meet. Thank you for the

gift of your friendship. Be happy and follow your dream.
   With all my love
   Your friend Harvey

Katie wasn't sure how much time had passed before she felt up
to going inside and tapping hesitantly on Roger's office door.

He took a quick concerned look at her face and asked if she
would like something a little stronger than lemonade. She
shook her head.

'I assume the letter told you that Paradise Lodge is now
yours?'

'Yes,' Katie said, her voice coming out as a whisper.

'It's all legally binding. He left his affairs in meticulous order,
you know.'

He would have, Katie thought, knowing – though he denied
it even to her, his friend – that the end might come at any
time.

'I'll give you all the necessary paperwork, then, shall I?'
Roger said, riffling through a file.

Paradise Lodge had been closed since the tragedy, its guests
farmed out to other places with vacant rooms. Katie had taken
in a few of them herself. Now she realised, with a sinking
sense of responsibility, that it would be up to her to decide
when it should reopen, and who was to run it now that Harvey
and Chico were gone.

After the scandal of the double killings, it was almost a relief
for the people of Key West when Mrs Jessie Wilhelmina
Grenville passed away quietly in her sleep and the city could
come out *en masse* to honour one of its own.

Katie found herself once again walking the orderly paths of
the cemetery. I mustn't make a habit of this, she thought with
gallows humour as she passed between densely packed tomb-
stones. What was it T. S. Eliot had said about death taking so
many? You couldn't come here without realising just how
many it must be.

The cemetery was so overcrowded now that graves were often recycled, it was said up to five times. The new trend was to build in stacks above the surface, New Orleans-style. But none of that applied to the Grenvilles. Even in death, Key West knew how to show the proper respect to its most illustrious citizens.

The great twin headstones of Senator John Grenville and his wife Jessie stood side by side bedecked in flowers. The coffin had already been lowered into the most recent grave in the presence of family only, and the fresh layer of cement poured over it, before the rest of the town was invited to pay its respects.

Katie waited her turn in the long line to find a place amongst the many other floral tributes for the gardenias she had picked fresh from her garden. The fragrance which rose from the basket was as heady as the scent of incense.

There was a light tap on her shoulder. When she turned round, she found herself face to face with the last person she wanted to see.

'I hear you got your hands on Paradise Lodge as well,' Wade Grenville said almost bitterly.

'That's right,' Katie said neutrally, not wanting to cause a scene at the graveside of the woman to whom she owed so much.

Even his best suit had sweat stains under the arms. He mopped his brow with a crumpled handkerchief. 'Aren't you the lucky one?'

'I wouldn't exactly put it like that.'

'I guess I better stay on your good side, now you're taking over half the island,' Wade said with a leer that might have been intended to charm her but only succeeded in filling her with disgust.

'I'm sorry about your aunt, she was a great lady,' Katie said with as much grace as she could muster, before turning her back on him to find that she was almost at the front of the line.

She laid her gardenias out on the fresh cement, then she looked up at the headstone that had been waiting for its occupant ever since the Senator passed away and his widow prebooked her place beside him. The date of death had finally been filled in. For the first time Katie saw the inscription that had been chosen by the deceased herself, because she couldn't trust her family not to make a maudlin mess of it.

'Reports of my death have been greatly exaggerated,' Katie read. The corners of her mouth twitched up in a smile. So the old lady was having the last laugh. This inscription would no doubt become as famous as that other one always quoted in the guidebooks and sought out by the tourists which said, 'I told you I was sick'.

Fortified by the stoicism of the late Mrs Grenville, Katie left the cemetery hoping it would be her last visit for a long time.

It was Angie's week for getting a tan in the bars of the Costa del Sol, and Guy found himself for the first time holding the fort with no help whatsoever in a house overrun by Lucy and Hannah and a seemingly constant stream of their friends.

He stood in the kitchen painstakingly reading the labels on an awesomely huge pile of dirty washing which had been dumped out of their school suitcases at his insistence. Now, however, he wasn't at all sure what to do next.

'That's handwash only,' Lucy said, snatching from his grasp a dress that was so short it would have been a great deal more suitable worn as a top.

'In that case, you can do the honours,' Guy said firmly.

Lucy looked horrified. 'But I don't know how.'

'Nor do I. But you'll find it has a label with instructions.'

Lucy grudgingly turned the dress inside out and held up the tiny label to the light. 'Boy, it's at times like this that I really miss Mummy.'

'She'd be charmed, I'm sure,' Guy said as he hesitantly picked up a handful of his daughters' school knickers and, holding them at arm's length, bundled them into the machine.

'Do *you* miss Mummy?' Lucy demanded suddenly.

Guy stopped in the middle of loading in a pile of dirty socks. It was the very question he had been avoiding asking himself since this whole ghastly mess started. Blast Lucy and her imperviousness to other people's feelings.

'Well?' Lucy insisted.

'Of course I miss her,' Guy said irritably.

'Then you should tell her.'

'I don't think it's your business, young lady,' Guy spluttered, 'to instruct me how—'

'You should also write something nice to her about those two friends of hers dying like that,' Lucy went on unrepentantly. 'Imagine how upset she must be feeling.'

The trouble was, Guy thought, he couldn't really imagine it. His wife had developed this whole new life he knew nothing about among people he had never met, though Lucy and Hannah had, and even Fiona, who wouldn't hear a word against Katie's strange neighbours who had met with such a sticky end. Guy had pointed out that he'd felt uneasy about them from the start, but Fiona had said that was stuff and nonsense. She had seemed quite different from her usual self since her return from Key West – another one seduced by the apparent magic of the wretched place. Jemima had told him she was quite mystified by the change in her mother.

Guy took out the washing machine manual and tried to figure out which of the bewildering array of buttons he should press. It had to be perfectly simple, surely, for someone of his intellect. But he'd forgotten to read all the information on the labels and now he wasn't sure whether he should select the spin or non-spin option. Too bad, he was damned if he was going to pull everything out of the machine and start again.

'Spin option,' he muttered to himself, stabbing at the button. 'Forty degrees centigrade, non-colourfast cotton, heavy soil—'

'Shouldn't it be gentle action?' Lucy said, fixing herself a peanut butter sandwich.

'How on earth should I know?' Guy said crossly.

Lucy sniffed. 'As long as you don't ruin our things.'

'If that's how you feel, perhaps you'd like to figure out this bloody thing yourself.'

'Temper, temper,' Lucy tisked, continuing to spread peanut butter on bread.

Guy decided to take the plunge. He pulled out the knob to start the machine, and turned his back on it as though abdicating all responsibility for the outcome.

'Where's Hannah?' he said.

'Upstairs with her nose stuck in some book . . . Daddy, can I have my navel pierced?'

Guy's eyebrows flew up in horror. 'Absolutely not.'

'I just knew you'd say that, you're such an old square.' Lucy gave him a petulant look. 'How about my ears, then?'

'I don't know . . . why don't you ask your mother?'

'Because she's not here, in case you hadn't noticed.'

'I meant on the phone—'

'Why should I have to phone America for a simple decision about my earlobes? Honestly, Daddy, you're hopeless. Don't you think it's time you started taking some responsibility for us yourself?'

'I just did,' Guy said, looking meaningfully at the ominously growling washing machine.

'I'm serious. When it comes to anything to do with Hannah and me, you've always left everything up to Mummy. What's it going to take to make you do your bit? You're running out of time, you know – I turn sixteen next year.'

Guy looked at her in blank astonishment. Sixteen! It wasn't possible. He could still remember, as though it were just last week, how he'd gone to visit the maternity ward and looked down into her little scrunched-up face with the red hair sprouting from the top of her head. He'd missed the birth itself, of course – an urgent court date. And now it seemed that wasn't all he'd missed. Had he really allowed the girls' childhood to pass him by, as Lucy accused, an outsider in his own family, leaving all the decisions to their mother?

'OK, then,' he said resolutely, 'you can pierce the ears as long as you leave the navel alone.'

'Thanks,' Lucy said, her eyes lighting up. 'Three times on each lobe?'

'Don't push your luck.'

'Twice, then?'

Guy could feel himself wavering. 'Is that what all the other girls do?'

Sensing victory, Lucy swooped down and gave him a smacking kiss. 'See – that wasn't so hard. You'll be great at this once you've had a bit of practice.' She raced to the door on her way to impart the amazing news to Hannah. But when she reached the threshold, she suddenly stopped.

'Daddy, just one more thing—'

'What?' Guy said warily.

'I'm really looking forward to going away with you to Rock. But if you invite Jemima to come with us, I'll absolutely kill you.'

There was only one person Katie made a deliberate effort to visit in the aftermath of all the deaths.

'The *Ifa* was certainly right about the loss,' she said to Lavender, looking bitterly at the chain with tortoise shell disks.

Lavender touched it defensively. 'I been doing the *Ifa* for twenty years, mebbe more. I never known it be wrong.'

'But what's the point,' Katie burst out, 'if I couldn't use the knowledge to stop what happened? It was Harvey who was in danger, not me. Why didn't the *Ifa* tell you that?'

'It doan be telling me 'less those who need protecshun come ask for it theyselves,' Lavender said, looking over at the offerings of food and flowers placed before the emblems of the *orishas* by those who wished to placate them to prevent some disaster from befalling them.

'But if I'd known, I would have made the offerings on his behalf,' Katie said angrily. 'Only I didn't, because he kept denying Chico was a risk even though he knew very well that he was. I was his *friend*, why wouldn't he let me help him?'

'A body gotta *want* help afore he goes looking for it, child. It gotta be his own choice.'

'But surely he didn't want to die?'

Lavender sighed. 'We never be knowing the truth of it now. But I 'spect he chose love over life 'cause he didn't want the one without the other.'

'I keep wondering if I could have saved them both,' Katie said, the guilt still weighing on her mind like a burden she couldn't shed.

'A body's gotta *want* to be saved too. Ain't you been listening?'

But Katie didn't want to listen, she wanted to protest her loss. 'What was the good, then, of making *me* drink those horrible medicines and throw those cakes in the river?'

Lavender gave an impatient frown. 'I told you, child, those herbs be keeping *you* safe from those be wishing you harm, and far as I sees they be doing they job. And the offerings be to win back the one you love.'

'I loved Harvey and Chico,' Katie said in a hollow voice.

'You know my meaning.'

Katie slumped her shoulders in defeat. She seemed to have exhausted the endless 'whys', like a dog pointlessly chasing its own tail without getting anywhere. 'The *Ifa* was right about something else too,' she said expressionlessly. 'There was gain of a kind from the loss. Harvey left Paradise Lodge to me.'

Lavender gave a low whistle. 'You be one rich woman now, child. What you goan do with it?'

'I don't know. I feel like I'm back to square one, like when Daddy left me The Tropical Hideout and I didn't know what to do with that either. And the worst of it is, the one I always turned to for advice before was Harvey.'

'You'll figure it out fo' yo'self,' Lavender said more gently than usual. 'You be yo' own woman now.'

Katie knew that Lavender was right, that she didn't need

anyone else's advice any more and might not even have taken it if it had been offered. But it was at times like this that she missed not having someone else in her life to share the load, someone with whom she could talk things through in an effort to reach her own conclusions, a partner to travel the long road with her.

'The strangest part of all,' she confessed to Lavender, 'is that I find I'm not really missing Lance any more. The one I really want to confide in is Guy.'

'You be thinking of going back to him?'

'I don't know.'

Lavender pointed an admonishing finger so that the shells rattled on their chain. 'It's time you be knowing yo' own heart, girl. If the heart be willing, the feet follow after.'

Chapter Twenty

~

It was amazing how truly unbearable London could be on a hot August day, when the air seemed to sit heavy and immovable over the city. Jemima stood by the open balcony doors of her flat in Cumberland Terrace in the hope of catching even a slight breeze, but to little avail. That was the trouble with living in a city where no one had enough faith in the possibility of warm weather to install air conditioning. Which was exactly why Guy would soon be escaping to the Cornish seaside.

At the sound of the buzzer from the street, she eagerly crossed the sitting room to let him in. But as soon as she saw his face, she knew something was wrong. Normally, if he came round from the office in a sombre mood, she would at once begin to tease him out of it. But there was something about Guy today, a sort of tense defensiveness, that warned Jemima to tread softly.

He headed for the chair he always used to sit in when he came to visit Robin. He was such a creature of habit, really. She hadn't been able to cure him entirely of that.

'Would you like a drink?' she said and he accepted a little too eagerly, like a man waiting at the confessional who finds to his relief that he can put off a little longer the unburdening of his guilty secret.

She fetched a bottle of her father's best twenty-year-old Scotch. Robin had always liked the finer things in life. There was a time, in her exploring days, when Jemima would have considered anything more than melted snow water a deliciously wicked indulgence, but now even she was beginning to rely on her little comforts.

When he had taken his first sip of the liquid gold, Guy gave her an appreciative grin and she almost began to breathe freely again.

She raised her glass to his in a toast. 'To the summer holidays and all the lovely lucrative business they're bringing me.'

At once Guy's expression darkened again, as though her words had reminded him of the true purpose of his visit.

'Jemima,' he said tentatively, 'remember we talked about how you might come with me and the girls to Rock . . . ?'

He couldn't quite meet her eye. Suddenly she felt she had to say something before he did.

'I don't know how to tell you this, Guy, but I'm going to have to let you down. It's awful of me, I know, but it's really quite impossible for me to get away in August. I'm just too busy at work.'

Guy couldn't quite hide his relief. Jemima made a determined effort to keep the apologetic smile on her face.

'That's a shame,' he said, and he sounded as though a part of him really meant it. 'Still, business must come first.'

'Anyway, it'll be good for you to spend some time alone with Lucy and Hannah. You never have before – you'll be amazed how much closer you'll become.'

Guy gave her a real smile this time, one that reached right up to his eyes. 'Thank you,' he said simply. 'You've been a good friend to me when I needed a shoulder to cry on. I just hope it hasn't been too much of a strain on you.'

'I'm a big girl,' Jemima said brightly. 'And anyway, we'll always be friends.'

He reached out and touched her arm with such tenderness, for a moment she was afraid all her new-found resolve might crumble.

'One more for the road?' she said, jumping up so that his hand fell away from her arm.

'I daren't. I've left Lucy in charge – God knows what I'll be going home to.'

When he had left, Jemima looked around the flat where she would now be staying alone all through the summer holidays. It could be worse, she told herself, at least she'd be miserable in comfort. Robin had done her proud, leaving her his beautiful home. By giving her this base he had put an end to her wanderings and changed her life just as surely as he had altered the course of Katie's when he set her off in the direction of Key West. Now Jemima had to figure out what to do with this fixed place in the world she had taken over from her father.

Perhaps, after all, what she had really relished about the life of the traveller was not just the constant moving on but the ability to make her own decisions, the sense of being in control of her own destiny. Now, with her own business and a place to call home, she had control of a different kind, and it didn't seem necessary any more to push herself to the old limits. Had Robin foreseen this result from the parting gift he had given her? Had he really known her that well?

She looked around at Robin's good solid furniture and traditional prints, which she hadn't thought to change before because possessions had never seemed to her a necessary expression of personality. But now she suddenly felt that she had been living in borrowed finery for too long. Get your own life, her mother had implied on that last extraordinary visit to Wiltshire, and tonight she had made a difficult and painful start. Maybe a few changes in this flat, *her* flat, would be the next logical step.

And afterwards there was the prospect of visiting Katie in Key West – a place she had never had any desire to see until it had worked this strange transformation on even those members of her family she had previously regarded as quite set in their ways. It was high time she saw her sister again, Jemima decided. It was time she found out for herself who the new Katie really was.

* * *

It took some time before Katie could face walking through the quiet spaces of Paradise Lodge, knowing she would not bump into Harvey or Chico just around the next corner. Her footsteps seemed to echo on the wooden floorboards through the empty guesthouse which she had kept closed since the tragedy, out of respect, not caring about the lost revenue.

'Nice stuff,' said the pale-skinned, dark-haired man from up north to whom she was giving the guided tour, as he fingered one of the richly coloured kelims hanging on the wall. 'Will you be selling with contents included?'

'Definitely,' Katie said. The last thing she could bear to do was surround herself with poignant reminders of her friends.

'Good quality workmanship too,' the man said, getting down on his knees to inspect the polished floorboards. 'Was it done by a local firm?'

'I don't know,' Katie admitted. 'Before my time.'

His name was Quentin Woods and he came from Boston. He wanted to drop out of the corporate rat race, he said, do something with a little less pressure. Katie didn't think it was her place to warn him about the guesthouse business and the three appliances a day that inevitably broke down. He would find out in his own good time.

He hadn't asked her how she came to be the owner of a gay guesthouse. But she could tell there was something else he was longing to know. She waited, and finally he plucked up the courage to say, 'So where did it actually happen . . . the shooting, I mean?'

She might have known it would be the macabre that held the most fascination for him. 'In the private quarters upstairs,' she said flatly. 'Do you want to see?'

He had the grace to look embarrassed. 'If it's not too . . .'

Katie led the way upstairs. If Quentin Woods was expecting blood and gore he was in for a disappointment. Nadine had come over herself with Alvira and Pearl to supervise the removal of all traces of the tragedy. She would have settled for nothing less.

Quentin prowled round the bedroom with the faux marble-painted walls. Finding nothing to satisfy his ghoulish curiosity, he began to inspect the Picasso lithographs. 'You selling these too?'

'Everything,' Katie confirmed.

He gave a little nod of satisfaction.

Katie was relieved when he transferred his attentions to the marble bathroom, and she could turn her back on the bed with its memories of Chico curled up, sad and vulnerable, beneath the patchwork quilt.

She stood by the window and looked out over the garden. The turquoise pool seemed to have lost some of its sparkle, though she still paid a firm to come in and clean it every week. But no matter how well she maintained it, the whole place had a forlorn and abandoned air without the bustle and laughter of happier days. She hoped that this Quentin Woods would buy it soon and fill it up again and chase away old ghosts.

'There's just one condition,' she said to him as they sat afterwards in Harvey's immaculately tidy office to discuss terms.

'What's that?' he said warily.

'You have to undertake that you will continue to run Paradise Lodge as an all-male gay guesthouse.'

He seemed to find that hugely funny. 'Honey, that's no sweat,' he laughed. 'In case you hadn't noticed, I'm as bent as a three-dollar bill.'

'I'm afraid I'd have to insist that it was formally written into the contract,' Katie said.

'Like I told you, no problem.'

'And I'd like to ask, if you decide to sell it later on, that you'd consider doing the same.'

The look he gave her now was openly curious. 'Why is this so important to you?'

'I'm honouring the wishes of a friend,' Katie said softly.

* * *

Guy had managed to stake a claim to a little patch of beach at Polzeath where he had put up his umbrella over a small oblong of towel and erected his chair like a barrier of defence against the zealous ball games of a young family settled in immediately beside him.

Lucy and Hannah had dragged him here, protesting weakly, because it was the best surfing beach in the area and therefore bound to attract the sort of boys who liked showing off on surfboards in front of girls. One strapping lad was even now trying to explain some basic manoeuvres to Lucy, who seemed to spend a great deal more time on her back in the water than upright on his board. Judging from their shrieks of laughter, neither of them seemed to mind much.

Guy relaxed back on his towel. Instead of pulling out the new biography of Hitler which he had brought along especially, he found himself drifting off into a half-slumber, disrupted every so often by the thud of a ball against his beach chair and a childish whoop of victory. He tried to remember whether the girls had liked playing beachball games when they were small. Katie would know.

There were a lot of things about the girls that Katie knew and he didn't, but perhaps, this holiday, he had made a start on redressing the balance. Jemima had told him he should be alone with his children, that it would bring them closer. He wondered now why he hadn't worked that out for himself.

'Daddy, can I have some money to buy chips?' Hannah's voice called out from behind him.

He turned to squint up at his younger daughter. Just like Lucy, she was growing up before his very eyes, her figure beginning to look frighteningly mature in the bikini her mother had bought for her in Key West. At least he had woken up in time to be there for what remained of her childhood.

'What about all those sandwiches I made for lunch?' Guy reminded her with a martyred air.

'But they do the *best* chips here, can't you smell them?'

Guy could indeed and he was less enamoured of the

experience than his daughter. But knowing it would be point-less to argue, he scrabbled round in the beach bag for some change.

The sandwiches would probably go to waste now, since Hannah would spoil her appetite and Lucy showed no inclination to come out of the surf. Guy tried not to feel resentful that he had woken up half an hour earlier than he would have liked to prepare this picnic that no one was going to eat. No doubt it was all part and parcel of the unpaid, unappreciated job of being chief cook and bottle washer, the role his wife had played for years without complaint. Only now that he had reluctantly taken over the job did he realise just how much effort it required, and how little gratitude you got for it.

There had been moments during this holiday in the Cornish stone cottage they always rented when Guy had found himself thinking he didn't blame Katie after all for running off to Key West and refusing to come back. Especially when contemplating unmade beds and unswept floors and unwashed towels and feeling quite overwhelmed by the sheer physical effort required to do something about them all. It had made him face for the first time the questions he had been pushing to the back of his mind, questions about how much he himself was to blame for his wife's defection. In Rock, even in London, Katie had made life easy and pleasant for everyone except herself, and no one had given her the credit for it, least of all Guy himself. Perhaps it was only in Key West that she had discovered people who truly appreciated her worth.

'You're a damn fool, Guy Colman,' he said out loud, and the mother of the rowdy children – a pink-faced woman with wildly permed hair tied up off her shoulders in a matching pink bow – leaned over the beach chair barrier and said, 'Pardon?'

He looked at her with genuine curiosity. 'Does your husband appreciate you?' he said. 'Does he realise what it takes to look after all those children?'

She smiled uncertainly, not sure what kind of an odd one

she was dealing with. 'Forget it, love,' she said. 'None of 'em ever do.'

'Pity,' Guy murmured as she ran off to pick up her howling toddler who had tripped over a baseball bat and was lying face down in the sand.

If he could have his time over again, Guy thought, what would he not do differently. It had to be possible to run a successful law practice and still find the time to tell your wife, just occasionally, that she was looking particularly pretty tonight, or perhaps she should let *him* cook the dinner for *her* for a change. When had it last occurred to him to take Katie to the theatre? He'd never got round to it because it was always there – just one of the other things he'd taken for granted.

In the vacuum left by Katie's departure, he had found the time to wine and dine her sister and confide in her his outrage at the way he had been treated. His practice hadn't collapsed, his clients hadn't deserted him in droves simply because he spent the odd few hours in a restaurant over a bottle of wine. Jemima had reminded him not to take life so seriously, she had taught him to have fun again, and he would always be grateful to her for that. But now he found that he didn't need to be with Jemima to put those lessons into practice. On this holiday he had laughed more with his daughters than at any time he could remember since the long-ago days when he used to chase them round the garden of their Hampstead maisonette with a hosepipe.

They had rented a boat for the fortnight so he could teach them to water-ski, which gave them all hour upon hour of amusement. At other times he drove the boat up and down the coast to find beaches with interesting rock pools where Hannah could investigate the strange marine life she had developed such a passion for in Key West. What Guy had not once done, however, was play golf at St Enerdoc's with Henry Blackstone. He was surprised at how little he missed it.

There was a loud scream from the surf and Guy, like all the other parents, at once put his head up like a periscope checking for trouble. But it was only Lucy and her new admirer throwing handfuls of water at each other. Poor boy, he thought, another one to lose his heart after just one flutter of Lucy's eyelashes. But Guy didn't worry the way he used to about what Lucy would get up to as soon as his back was turned. She was developing quite a sense of responsibility these days, taking care of herself and Hannah and even Guy in a dozen little ways, as though trying to fill her mother's shoes.

But no one could fill Katie's shoes, Guy realised with a heavy heart – not him, not Lucy, not even Jemima.

'You're a stupid bloody fool,' he said again out loud, and the mother with the frizzy hair shifted her children away a little, out of arm's reach of the strange man next to them who kept talking to himself, just to be on the safe side.

Now that his hip was mending nicely, Willie was starting to get about a bit, a situation which gave Polly – pleased though she was with his progress – a whole new set of worries.

'What am I going to do about those stairs?' she wailed to Katie. 'I'll have to get someone in to fix them right away – I can't have him doing himself a damage again.'

Katie reminded her of Joe Roth, the building contractor sent to her by the late Mrs Grenville, who had done such a wonderful job of restoring The Tropical Hideout.

'Oh my, you're a genius,' Polly said. 'I'll call him right away. And once he's doing the stairs, he may as well fix up the whole of the outside, it's such an eyesore.'

'Are you sure Willie can afford it?' Katie said, remembering Joe Roth's rather large bill.

'He sure can. I told him he should be ashamed of himself, letting this poor old house go to rack and ruin when he's got all that cash just sitting in the bank.'

So Joe came round to survey the damage. While Polly took him off on a circuit of the house, pointing out her many concerns, Katie went in to check up on Willie.

He was sitting on a new three-seater sofa in front of a colour television set, watching a game show with almost childish enthusiasm. Instead of the striped cotton pyjamas which were the only attire Katie had ever seen him in before, he wore a checked shirt and a pair of cotton trousers which looked as though they had only just had the labels cut out of them.

'Mind if I join you?' Katie said, perching in a chair which miraculously wasn't already occupied by a cat. Come to think of it, she had seen no more than half a dozen cats on the premises since she arrived.

Willie waved at her to make herself at home. Chuck Rogers from Culver City was going for the car, and Willie had eyes for nothing else. But a rude noise from the buzzer indicated that Chuck had got the answer wrong, and would have to settle for a microwave oven. 'Damn moron,' Willie snorted, switching off the television in disgust.

'You're looking much better,' Katie remarked.

'No surprise in that. I got the best care a man could ask fer.' Willie waved at the footstool in front of him and the pot of coffee and selection of fresh cakes that stood on a table just within reach. 'Help yerself.'

While Katie played mother, Willie said, 'I hear you got yerself another guesthouse.'

'Not for much longer. I'm in the process of selling Paradise Lodge.'

Willie chuckled. 'Bet that'll do wonders for yer bank balance.'

Katie smiled in bemusement. She still hadn't quite got used to the idea that she was now a woman of substantial independent means.

'That friend of yers, the gay one,' Willie said. 'He had family, didn't he – kids, the whole works?'

'They didn't want anything to do with him.' Katie looked awkward. 'Do you think the money should really go to them?'

'Hell no!' Willie exploded. 'Where were *they* when he needed 'em?'

A house cat jumped into Katie's lap, a handsome tabby that

made a gratifyingly loud purring noise when she stroked its well-groomed coat, while all the time marvelling at Willie's sudden rush of solidarity with Harvey's sentiments.

'I got family too, yer know – miserable lot just like yer friend's. Do you see any of 'em coming by asking how I'm keeping in my old age?'

'No,' Katie admitted, while the tabby settled nonchalantly into her lap for a snooze.

'When my time comes, I don't want 'em swarming down here like vultures, trying to get their claws on my cash. I told Miss Polly she's to chase 'em away like the scavengers they are.'

Somehow Katie couldn't picture Polly in that role, but looking at Willie's agitated face she decided against mentioning it.

'It's only Miss Polly done anything fer me. But what she don't know,' he said, tapping his nose conspiratorially, 'is what I done fer her.' He waited, hoping, perhaps, that Katie would ask, and when she didn't he said rather crossly, 'I'll tell yer if yer promise not to breathe a word.'

'I promise.'

'That friend of yers who passed away, he got me thinking – why shouldn't I do like he did? I got the right to leave my hard-earned cash to whoever I please. So I called in my lawyer to write me a new will. It all goes to Miss Polly now – the house, the money, the works – except fer one thing.'

'What's that?' Katie said, feeling it was expected.

'I put aside a sum in trust fer the lawyers, so as they can fight off any no-good member of my family who has the nerve to show their face round here, contesting the will. Miss Polly'll have the finest help money can buy.'

That was probably just as well, Katie thought, given that Polly was not at her best in a confrontation.

Willie suddenly grabbed Katie's arm. 'I want yer to make sure she gets what's coming to her,' he said fiercely. 'Don't let that soft heart of hers get the better of her – make sure she fights fer what's rightfully hers.'

'I will,' Katie said, patting his skinny arm much as she had previously stroked the cat.

'That's good,' Willie said, withdrawing his hand and nodding with satisfaction. 'That'll teach my flesh and blood yer gotta work fer what you get in this life.' He chuckled gleefully. 'I only wish I could be around to see their faces.'

There were voices from the doorway, and Polly came back in with Joe Roth. Willie put his finger to his lips in a gesture of warning.

'You all right there, Willie?' Polly said.

'I ain't complaining.'

'And you, Katie?'

Katie thought she felt much the better for this visit. It was somehow very comforting to know that one day Polly too would be a woman of means, settled in cosily next door, reaping her reward for her goodness alone. It was reassuring to discover that the meek could indeed inherit the earth.

Lately Katie had taken to walking the streets of Key West when she had a half-hour to spare, trying to absorb the sights and sounds and smells that had made her fall in love with it in the first place – the tangle of tropical foliage hanging heavy in the humid air, the jangling of bicycle bells, the smell of baked earth and pungent almost over-ripe flowers, the silhouette of a cat perched on a garden wall, the feeling of heat coming up from the pavement through her shoes and warming the soles of her feet.

But though she was still stirred by these things, memories of different scenes and places had begun to insert themselves treacherously into the corners of her mind. She found herself sometimes filled with an almost unbearable longing for the smell of fresh earth and crisp, clean air after the rain has fallen, or the sight of a field of buttercups stretching away to gentle woods, or the throaty diesel roar of a London taxi cab.

But more than that, she kept remembering moments from the early days with Guy – the serious talks they would have about the life they were going to build together, the passion they both shared for books and long exhausting country walks, the way they used to finish each other's sentences as though instinctively knowing what the other had been about to say.

Stop this, she told herself sternly, you can't have everything. It's no good wanting people and things on demand like a spoilt child. For all the blessings you have in life, there is always the sacrifice of others which are no longer possible.

But perhaps the truth was that every time you moved on from a place where you had lived and made some mark, you left a little bit of yourself behind. Perhaps we are all fragmented into many parts that inhabit all the landscapes we have known.

If so, was it not equally possible that we lose something of ourselves to all the people we have loved? Was that why she had suddenly begun to miss Guy and her mother and her sister, not to mention the girls, and to wonder what she was doing in this place so far from the people with whom she shared the common bonds of blood and marriage? She hadn't noticed the pull so much when she was surrounded by friends, but it must have been there all along, like the tug of the moon on the tides – an underlying fact of the universe that held true whether you were aware of it or not.

Now it was simply more apparent to her because some of the friends were gone, and the empty spaces left by their loss were inevitably filled by yearnings of a different kind, for those who still remained but were far away. But did she really want to leave all she had built in Key West and go back to her old life? Or was it just that she longed to have her family here with her? They had given her little indication lately of their own wishes. Fiona and Lucy and Hannah seemed as much in love with Key West as she was herself and might prefer her to remain where she was so they would have an excuse to visit. As for Guy and Jemima, if she went back now they would probably simply feel she was in the way.

Life in London had moved on while she was busy doing other things. Even if she wanted to return – and she was by no means sure she did – she couldn't even think of doing so unless she was absolutely sure of her welcome.

In the midst of all her doubts, Katie received in the space of a single day a whole batch of letters from England. Here, perhaps, were some of the answers she was seeking. She sat on the sofa beneath Polly's green turtle to read through them one by one, and weigh up what her future held.

There was a wonderful note of sympathy from her mother, full of wise words. 'I know how hard it must be for you, when you are still grieving for your father, to believe you will ever get over so much loss,' Fiona wrote. 'But you will because there are other people who love you – we, your family – and that is what, in the end, will heal your pain.'

One of the other things Fiona made quite plain was that there had been a change for the better on the home front. 'The problem I warned you about with Guy and Jemima seems to have blown over,' she wrote, 'so at least you can rest easy on that score.'

But she said nothing at all about wanting Katie to come home. Nor did Jemima, though her letter was just as warming in its way. 'Somehow, ever since we grew up, we seem to have gone off in opposite directions. And then, just when I thought I was venturing back on to your turf, you set off for completely new pastures. Maybe it's time we met up again at the still point of the turning world. For reasons that seem to me quite illogical but nonetheless true, that point seems to be Key West. Mummy and Lucy say you've changed since you've been there – both of them seem to think for the better. I'm not sure I knew you very well even before, but I'd like to get to know you now. Do you think, after the girls have gone, I might come to visit?'

It wasn't quite an apology, but it was certainly an attempt of sorts at reconciliation. Perhaps, after all, Fiona was right – the spirits had done their work and there would be no more threat from Jemima. But neither had there been any suggestion from her that Katie should think of coming home.

The girls, who would be seeing her soon anyway, had sent just a few lines scrawled on a postcard which nonetheless conveyed perfectly that they were longing to be back in Key West, and to see their kittens, and that Lucy had a crush on a new boy – which would break Sam's heart if he ever found out, Nadine said he was just counting the days till she arrived – and that both of them were having a whale of a time with their father, who seemed to be coping perfectly well with the demands of looking after them on his own. Katie didn't know whether to feel relieved or unwanted.

But it was the letter addressed to her in Guy's handwriting – only the second she had received in all her time in Key West – that filled her with the greatest trepidation. She had left it till last, remembering how wounded she had been by the first one. Now that the moment had come, she tore open the envelope with reluctant and trembling fingers, looking up at the green turtle for moral support.

The first word that sprang out at her from the page was 'angry'. On second thoughts, she was going to need support of a slightly more tangible kind. Leaving the letter unread on the sofa, she went through to the bright little kitchen to open one of the bottles of wine she had bought on her last trip to the Lost Weekend liquor store.

With some liquid fortification inside her, she attempted to read the first line again. 'I have been too angry to write before, but now I begin to question whether I had the right to be angry with anyone except myself,' Guy wrote.

'Well, now, that wasn't too bad,' Katie said to the green turtle. 'Perhaps I can take a little more of this.'

'I let you down because I took you for granted,' she read. 'I know it's too late to say how sorry I am, but it's the truth. I hope you find more happiness in your new life than I was able to give you.'

She paused again, her thoughts in turmoil. An *apology* –

now that was something. But what about the last line? Was that also a rejection?

'Your mother has told me all about your friends Harvey and Chico and how good they were to you. They seem to have made a better job of it than I did. They've even ensured that you've been left financially secure which, to my shame, is more than I have done. I'm so sorry about what happened to them. If I've said anything boorishly prejudiced about them in the past, I'm sorry about that too.'

The apologies were coming thick and fast. Katie read the two paragraphs over again, just to be sure. But there could be no doubting either the sincerity or the meaning of Guy's words.

Her eyes skipped to the last paragraph, her stomach tightened with hope. 'When you've come to terms with everything that's happened, I'm sure you'll be wanting to make some final decisions about your life. If you want a divorce I won't stand in your way. I don't believe I have the right to cause you any more unhappiness. I will also, of course, offer a fair settlement.'

Divorce ... settlement! Katie swallowed. The very words had such a ring of finality to them. Was this the only option Guy had considered?

He had signed off with only formal regards. There was no postscript, nothing to suggest the thought of reconciliation had even crossed his mind.

Katie cast the letter down on the sofa. It wasn't as though she had ever really expected him to give up his successful law practice in London for a guesthouse in Key West. It wasn't as if she was prepared to give up her new life and just take up the old where she had left off. She wasn't even sure she wanted to mend her marriage to Guy. But she did think the least he could have done, if he was as sorry as he said, was mention the possibility.

'Damn him,' she said out loud, glaring up at the turtle and wondering why her eyes were so filled with tears that he was no more than a fuzzy green blur.

* * *

'Hurricane coming!' Lavender cried, entering The Tropical Hideout like an advance whirlwind.

She threw herself down on the sofa and fanned her shiny black face with a lavender scarf. Katie quickly poured her a glass of water. 'Did you get that from the *Ifa*?' she said.

Lavender gave her a pained look. 'I be hearing it on the TV, juss like all the other folks in town. Where you been hiding your head, child?'

Katie grabbed the remote control and snapped on the weather channel. There were threatening-looking squiggles all over the map of the southeastern United States. The anchorwoman spoke in an agitated voice.

'When is it expected to hit?' Katie said, quite unable to take in the babble of words.

'That bad old wind be blowing up off the coast of Africa, it be getting angrier every mile it cross the oshun. It be reaching us mebbe in thirty-six hours. By then it be real mean.' Lavender sniffed the air, as though she could almost smell it coming.

Katie made a quick mental calculation. Evacuation procedures to the mainland would take at least twenty-six hours, with residents and visitors sitting bumper to bumper on the one narrow road out to safety and praying they would not be caught there like sitting ducks.

'I have to get my guests out of here,' she said.

Lavender gave her a narrow look. 'You be getting out with them?'

'Are you?'

'Ain't no way that bad old wind gonna catch me out on one of them bridges with the sea rising up like a wall of death. I be staying right where I am.'

'Then why would I go?'

Lavender shook a finger at her. 'I know what's coming, child, I seen them storms before. It ain't no spectator sport, that's for sho'. Them trees be ripped up by the roots, them houses be torn right off they foundations. If it gets real bad, there be folks gonna die, ain't no mistake.'

Katie was already on her way to the door. 'I'll think about what I'm going to do when I've made sure all my guests are on their way.'

The next hours were a scramble of mad activity as panic broke out and guests stampeded Katie's office demanding a seat out on the first available plane. The trouble was there were hardly any seats left, as Katie had discovered in her first few phone calls. She made what reservations she could, giving priority to the elderly and the children, and then begged and blackmailed those guests who had cars to take with them however many others they could fit in.

Soon the hallway was filled with suitcases packed so hastily that shirts and towels poked randomly from poorly closed seams. Nadine was a total marvel, running up and down stairs to carry bags for those who couldn't manage their own and hefting even the heaviest of them into the trunks of bursting cars. All up and down Key West the streets were already jammed with people trying to make their escape. With the authority of a police officer Nadine stepped out into the traffic time and again and held up a hand, so that other frightened motorists meekly stopped for this woman with the fierce tattoos and the even fiercer face, to allow the guests of The Tropical Hideout to pull away from the kerb.

Within a matter of hours the guesthouse had been emptied of all its occupants save Katie, Nadine and Lavender, who sat stubbornly in Katie's office waiting for her decision.

'There's no point looking at me like that, I still have things to do,' Katie said rather crossly as an e-mail flashed up on the screen of her computer and she tapped the keys to retrieve it.

'Then you better be hoping they ain't the last things you be doing in this world,' Lavender said darkly.

Ignoring her, Katie scanned the urgent message from Wiltshire sent by her mother. Fiona had been surfing the net when she came across the hurricane warning. She urged Katie to leave Key West as soon as possible and come back to England and safety. She had spoken to Guy and Jemima too, and they were all agreed it was the only sensible thing for her to do.

So, Katie thought, the invitation she had been waiting for had finally been issued. It had taken the threat of a killer storm for her family to say they wanted her to come home.

'Begging your pardon, ma'am,' Nadine interrupted, 'but there's the windows to see to.'

'I know – I'm coming to help you now,' Katie said, avoiding Lavender's fearsome frown. 'But first I'm just going to check that Tiggy and Winkle are safely inside.'

It was a mammoth task to board up every window and door of both The Tropical Hideout and Paradise Lodge. Katie knew just as well as Lavender that there would be little hope of getting it done in time to leave within the safety margin. But there was no question of abandoning her guesthouse to those deadly winds, nor Harvey's for that matter – though technically what remained of it would soon belong to Quentin Woods.

Next door Polly was scurrying round securing Willie's house – the house that if it survived this storm would one day be hers, though she didn't know it. They gave her shouts of encouragement, promising to come over and help as soon as their job was done. There was an amazing sense of solidarity among the women as they scaled ladders and hammered up boards and collected stray cats, making Katie feel suddenly more content than she had for weeks.

When all three houses were as safe as their efforts could make them, Katie and Nadine went back inside and found Lavender still occupying the office. She swayed on the leopard-print sofa, chanting below her breath as though in the midst of some fervent prayer.

'I want you to go back to your place and fetch some things,' Katie said. 'You'll be much safer here during the storm.'

'No can do,' Lavender said stubbornly. 'I got mighty powerful business with the saints.'

But Katie was in no mood for arguments. 'I'm sure the saints will understand if you do your business somewhere that's less likely to get blown away . . . And Nadine, you must bring Sam and Jolene and stay over too.'

These old houses had been built by ships' carpenters to withstand even the highest winds, Harvey had told her. They were held together by wooden pegs so that they would bend in a gale and not blow over. The Tropical Hideout had outlasted many a hurricane and it would survive this one too, she was willing to take a bet on it.

She picked up the keys of the red sports car.

'You going now?' Lavender said.

There might still be just enough time to make it down the Overseas Highway over the perilously narrow bridges to the safety of a flight back home. Lavender and Nadine watched her with questioning eyes.

'I'm going to the grocery store to buy in more provisions,' she said.

'There ain't no time, child.'

But Katie was no longer listening. If Jemima could face danger without fear, then so could she. She wasn't afraid any more of taking a calculated risk, and the knowledge filled her with an exhilarating sense of freedom.

'I'm a resident, not a visitor,' Katie said firmly. 'I'm staying right where I am.'

Chapter Twenty-One

~

In the little downstairs office that housed her computer, Fiona was once again hunched over the screen, searching the vast and confusing global communications network for news of whether one of her daughters was alive or dead.

Who would have thought, all those months ago when Jemima was risking her neck in the Antarctic, that it would be Katie, the sane and sensible one, who was now courting mortal danger? Who would have dreamed it would be Jemima sitting safely here beside her, anxiously scanning the screen for news of her sister?

Perhaps now Jemima had some understanding of what it was like for those left behind at home, waiting and worrying. Perhaps she had finally learned to think of the feelings of others, as Fiona had been hoping ever since Jemima had abandoned her pursuit of Guy. If the final realisation was at last coming home to her, it was Robin they all had to thank for it.

At the time Fiona had wondered if he had been in his right mind when he drew up that final will. But she knew better now. Her husband had understood exactly what was lacking in his daughters' lives, and his last act had been of a far-reaching wisdom that Fiona was only now beginning to appreciate. She had also found herself lately talking to him out loud about ordinary everyday things, as though he were still sitting in the worn old chair by the fire that had been his favourite for an after-dinner snooze. No one else ever sat in that chair. Fiona wouldn't allow it.

Oh, she knew her girls – Katie especially – had sometimes been critical of the way she conducted her marriage, wondering why she and Robin spent so much time apart, imagining it must be a lack of affection on her part. But sometimes it was giving each other a little space that kept people together. Robin had understood. Katie perhaps was beginning to find out.

And now, because of what Robin had done for her – though it could hardly have been his intention – Katie was in the path of a hurricane with a fearful power to destroy. And she had stubbornly refused to leave the guesthouse her father had given her. 'Watch over her, Robin,' Fiona silently prayed. 'Keep our daughter safe.'

She thought of Guy out there on the road, driving up from Cornwall with the girls. They had cut their holiday short as soon as they heard news of the impending disaster. It would be even worse for him, Fiona thought, not daring to turn on the radio for fear the children might hear the worst.

'Oh my God, look,' Jemima cried, making Fiona start with fear. And there it was on the screen, the first news from the island since the hurricane was presumed to have hit. All communications with Key West had been wiped out. There was no telling if anyone there had survived the onslaught of Hurricane Zoe, as the killer storm had come to be known.

The passage of Hurricane Zoe had left behind an awesome trail of destruction, as though a wanton power had played havoc with the order of things. Huge trees lay across roads, their roots naked and exposed, their petals spilled like blood. Cars were overturned on to their roofs, less sturdily constructed buildings torn apart and scattered like so much driftwood.

But at the last possible moment Zoe had veered off to the south, so that the worst of the winds did not rip through the city as everyone had feared. What finally hit Key West was not a full-blown hurricane but a severe tropical storm, which cut the power and telephone lines so that the dazed survivors had no means of letting the outside world know of the miracle of their escape.

The Tropical Hideout had passed the gruelling test with flying colours, justifying all Katie's faith. Some sheets of galvanised steel had been torn off the roof, but apart from that the grand old lady had remained defiantly intact, even when the winds howling outside were at their worst and Lavender had to shout her incantations for fear the spirits would not hear above the storm.

When at last it had quieted to only a gentle, rhythmic rainfall, Katie and Nadine and Lavender cautiously ventured out into the wind-tossed garden. They called across to Polly who came scurrying over to clasp them all in an embrace overflowing with relief. Lavender looked up at the skies, now streaked with patches of light, then she began to sway in a slow circle, singing and chanting, her back bent and her feet tapping out a complex and delicate rhythm. Katie lifted her face to the heavens and felt the water flow over it like a cleansing, a blessing. Then she too began to sway – and Nadine, and Polly – and soon they were all laughing and dancing in the rain for the sheer joy of their deliverance.

Paradise Lodge had survived too, and Willie's place – almost the entire historic district. Damage to the box-like modern houses in New Town where Nadine lived was more severe, and Katie told her that she and the children were welcome to stay in The Tropical Hideout for as long as it took to restore their home. It would be some time, anyway, before the tourists would return.

Lavender's shotgun house had also taken a battering, but no sooner had the storm abated than the people of Bahama Village donated their services and materials – even before they fixed their own homes – to repair what they regarded as their shrine to the old religion which had saved their town.

Hour after hour Katie waited edgily for emergency electricity to be restored. Her computer screen stared at her blankly, useless without the power that fed it. The telephones remained obstinately dead. She pictured her family waiting anxiously for news in Wiltshire, and felt quite sick with the frustration of not being able to provide it.

'There be only one way,' Lavender told her. 'When the first plane come in, you sends yo' message out. Trust me, child, they be flying over them government do-gooders soon as they can get 'em in.'

So Katie wrote letters of reassurance and watched the skies and planned how she would beg or bribe some sympathetic crew member to carry out the news of her safety. When she finally heard the drone of engines overhead, she jumped straight into the red sports car – only slightly dented from where a flying garbage can had hit one door – and manoeuvred her way through the partially cleared streets, swerving round obstacles at full speed so that she pulled up in front of the airport in record time.

The plane had already taxied to a halt on the tarmac and was disgorging its load of officials in suits and bearded volunteers from the relief agencies who had been sent to help the beleaguered citizens of Key West. Katie scanned their ranks, looking anxiously for the uniform of a crew member, praying they would not simply turn the plane round and take off again before she had a chance to make her pleas.

Her eye was caught by a man in a distinctively cut English raincoat who strode purposefully across the tarmac, outstripping all the others. There was something about him that reminded her sharply, poignantly of Guy. He had the same tall, narrow build and fair sandy hair, though he wore it longer. Guy would never have allowed his hair to curl up on the collar of his shirt.

And then he was through the doors of the arrivals hall and with a shock that jolted through her veins she realised that it truly was her husband.

At almost the same moment he saw her, suspended in dazed recognition, and stopped dead in his tracks. They both stood on the spot, separated by an empty expanse of tiled floor, just staring at each other. The expression on Guy's face was one of the purest relief.

How he had got here in such record time from Cornwall was a miracle she couldn't explain. What he had said to the relevant authorities to barge his way on to the first plane in was beyond her powers to speculate.

But here he was, and suddenly that was all that mattered. Katie's heart beat out a wild tattoo of joy. It wasn't as though she had ever really expected him to give up his successful law practice in London for a guesthouse in Key West. It wasn't as though she was prepared to abandon the dream that had brought and then kept her here. But if they put aside the conventions, the usual rules of how married couples were supposed to live, as her parents had before her, perhaps they could find a way of sharing their lives between both places. Maybe they could have the best of both worlds. As Lavender would have said, if the heart be willing, the feet follow after.

She crossed the distance that separated them, and found that it was really no distance at all.